Laura had never realized how *long* five minutes could be.

She scowled at the vial, as if intimidation could speed up whatever mysterious chemical reactions were taking place inside it.

Heat lightning flashed outside the bathroom window, hinting of the storm to come. Normally, summer storms in Arizona's high country never bothered Laura.

But tonight was different. Tonight she felt as if the electricity had gotten into her blood, making her edgy. She looked at her watch again. Only one more minute.

The indicator's damning red plus sign confirmed what she'd suspected all along. It hadn't been stress or the flu.

She was pregnant.

With her lover's child. Not her husband's.

Hours later Laura awoke from a troubled sleep. Though heavy eyed, she recognized the familiar face. A sound like an early Fourth of July firecracker shattered the nighttime stillness. Pressing her hand against the searing heat at her breast, seeing the crimson blood, Laura realized she'd been shot. She opened her lips to ask why, but a second gunshot broke the dead of night.

Also by JoAnn Ross

A WOMAN'S HEART
LEGACY OF LIES
NO REGRETS
BAIT AND SWITCH
SOUTHERN COMFORTS
TEMPTING FATE
STORMY COURTSHIP
DUSK FIRE

JoAnn Ross

Confessions

ISBN 1-55166-752-5

CONFESSIONS

Visit us at www.mirabooks.com

Printed in U.S.A.

To Jay

ACKNOWLEDGMENTS

With special thanks to my editor,
the incomparable Malle Vallik, my partner in crime.

And heartfelt gratitude to Detective Joe Paglino
and Mauro Corvasce—two of the good guys—
who taught me everything I know about homicide
investigation and will hopefully forgive any liberties
I've taken in the name of creative license.

Chapter One

Laura Swann Fletcher had never realized how long five minutes could be. Especially when you were holding your breath.

She scowled at the vial atop the cultured marble countertop, as if intimidation could speed up whatever mysterious chemical reactions were taking place inside it.

Heat lightning flashed outside the bathroom window, hinting of the storm to come. A distant taste of rain rode on the sultry air. Normally, summer storms in Arizona's high country never bothered Laura.

But tonight was different. Tonight she felt as if the electricity had gotten into her blood, making her edgy.

"Dammit, hurry up," she begged. As if she didn't have enough to deal with. "Please, hurry up."

She took a deep breath that should have calmed, but didn't. "It's only stress," she insisted, as if saying the words could make them true.

Perhaps she should have taken Fredericka Palmer up on that offer of Valium. Only last week her longtime best friend had professed concern about her. *If only Freddi knew the whole story.*

"Dammit, get hold of yourself." Laura hardly recognized the high, nervous voice. She pressed her palms against her rib cage and, taking several more deep breaths, willed herself to relax.

But her mind continued to churn restlessly, tossing up the myriad problems that had been plaguing her. Problems without end. Dilemmas without solutions.

Nerves humming, Laura decided to see if one all-important call she'd been waiting for had come while she'd been out buying the home pregnancy kit.

The answering machine was downstairs, in the den. The red light was blinking, signaling four calls. She pushed the Rewind button. Then, Play.

Unbearably restless, she prowled the plank floor.

Beep. "Laura. It's your father." His recorded voice was as gruff as always, but she thought perhaps it was only her imagination. His next words confirmed that it wasn't. "I heard a story today that damn well better not be true. If you're there, pick up."

There was a slight pause as he waited for her to do as instructed. As she always had. "Hell." Another frustrated pause. "When I get back from Santa Fe, you and I are going to have a talk. Because you've got a lot of explaining to do, girl."

So, he'd found out. Even as Laura reminded herself that she'd been going to tell him herself, painful memories, buried but never forgotten, snaked through her.

She looked down at her watch.

Two more minutes.

She continued to pace.

Beep. "Laura, it's Alan. Thunderstorms kept us on the ground at National, now we're stuck on the runway at O'Hare. We're going to be late getting into Phoenix, then with the ninety-minute drive to Whiskey River, it'll probably be past midnight before I get home. Don't bother waiting up.''

It was not the first time her husband had been delayed while on a trip with Heather Martin, his ambitious and sexy chief of staff. Laura doubted it would be the last. The difference was, this time she honestly didn't care.

Alan Fletcher was a rising political star, the brightest, most promising light in the Republican political firmament. Having won reelection to the U.S. Senate by a landslide, he was being touted as the party's best hope to regain the White House.

Laura had never enjoyed living in Washington. She hated the artifice, the parties that were nothing but power plays, the emphasis on political prestige rather than character. The role of senate wife had been difficult enough. The idea of becoming First Lady gave her hives.

Beep. ''Hi, Laura. It's Mariah. Kill the fatted calf, the prodigal daughter is coming home! Do I have a lot to tell you! Guess it'll have to wait until I show up on your doorstep, which should be around midnight, which I know is an ungodly hour, but I'm dying to share my news with my big sister. Love ya.''

Damn. Laura dragged a trembling hand through her auburn hair. Trust Mariah to choose this weekend to return to Whiskey River. Nothing like throwing a lit match into an already volatile situation.

Then again, Laura considered, if anyone could appreciate what she was about to do, it would be the woman who, like their glamorous mother, had been banished from the Swann family.

She looked at her watch again.

Only one more minute.

Beep. ''Hi.'' The deep, intimate voice sent a familiar heat surging through Laura.

''I just wanted to make sure you're okay. Hell, the truth

is, I'm worried about you, babe. I still wish you hadn't insisted on doing this alone.

"Christ, Laurie—" she could picture him dragging his hands through his thick black hair "—I don't remember you being so stubborn twenty years ago. If you had… Oh, hell. Forget I said that. One day at a time, right?"

"One day at a time," Laura whispered.

It was the same thing she'd been saying for months. The problem was, she knew Clint Garvey would not wait any longer. The last few times they'd managed to be together, they'd wasted valuable time—time they could have spent making love—arguing.

Finally, last weekend, Clint had issued an ultimatum. She knew, with every fiber of her being, that if she didn't keep her promise to leave her husband, she would lose the only man she'd ever loved.

She sighed as she looked down at her watch again.

Finally!

The indicator's damning red Plus sign confirmed what she'd suspected all along. It hadn't been stress that had caused her to feel so tired lately. And it hadn't been flu that had brought about the occasional bouts of morning queasiness.

She was pregnant.

With her lover's child.

Timing, Laura considered weakly, was indeed everything.

With her back against the wall, both literally and figuratively, she slid down to the tile floor, wrapped her arms around her bent legs and rested her forehead on her knees.

What on earth was she going to do? A fleeting dread shot through Laura. Her first thought was that Clint would think she'd been lying when she'd assured him that she could not get pregnant. But how could she have known otherwise? After having spent years trying to conceive?

When pollsters had informed her husband that a pregnant wife was worth from eight to fifteen points in the opinion polls, Alan had begun dragging her to infertility clinics all over the country. None of the increasingly esoteric, uncomfortable and horribly embarrassing treatments had worked.

Finally, last year, after her thirty-sixth birthday, Laura had given up the quest for a child. Alan, needless to say, had not been pleased. It was, after all, a great deal easier to campaign on a family values platform with a smiling wife and darling children by your side.

Alan. Laura groaned. Her husband was going to be absolutely furious. What if he attempted to pay her back for her infidelity by refusing to grant her a divorce? Worse yet, what if he decided to claim this child for his own?

"I won't let that happen!"

Laura reminded herself that her husband's most consistent personality trait was that everything Alan Fletcher said, everything he did, including marrying her, was geared solely toward enhancing his career. If he attempted such a ploy, she'd hold her own press conference and tell the entire world the truth.

Ronald Reagan had proven that a divorced man could get elected president. But would voters choose a candidate involved in a messy paternity battle? Laura didn't think so.

"It's going to be all right," she assured herself. And her baby. "Granted, this complicates things. But Alan will see that a quick, quiet divorce is in his own best interests."

Latching on to that optimistic thought, she pressed her hands against her still-flat stomach in an unconscious gesture of maternal protection.

Her churning mind gradually calmed as she began to

view her unborn child—hers and Clint's child—as a reward for all the pain they'd suffered.

There would still be problems. Problems with her autocratic father, with Alan, with the press. And there was no way this baby could ease her current troubles regarding the ranch.

But as she ran a bath in the ancient, lion-footed copper tub, for the first time in a very long while, Laura felt capable of sorting everything out. A heady, forgotten confidence flowed warmly through her veins. Dual feelings of joy and wonder bubbled up from some hidden wellspring deep inside her.

Sometimes miracles really did happen.

Laura was soaking in the perfumed water when the storm that had been threatening earlier arrived. The sharp staccato of rain sounded on the roof. Thunder rumbled. A bolt of lightning forked just outside the window.

Suddenly, a sound like a Klaxon blare echoed through the house.

"Dammit." An irritating flaw in the security system was that the sensors on the windows couldn't tell the difference between a storm rattling the glass or an intruder breaking in.

She rose from the water, wrapped a towel around herself and ran back downstairs, leaving a trail of wet footprints. After deactivating the blaring alarm, she placed a call to the sheriff's office—which was automatically alerted each time the alarm went off—assuring the dispatcher it was a false alarm.

"Stupid thing," she muttered, clutching the towel to her breasts as she glared at the computer control panel. Alan had been promising to change the system for months. After tonight, Laura vowed, she was just going to tear the damn thing out.

At the age of thirty-seven, Laura was determined to

reclaim control of her life. Along with the house and the 20 thousand acres of prime Arizona ranch land her grandmother Ida Prescott had bequeathed her.

After years of unhappiness, she'd returned home to Whiskey River. Where she belonged. And where she had every intention of spending the rest of her life with the man who, for eight blissful hours, in what seemed another lifetime, had been her husband.

Laura returned back upstairs, traded her towel for a long seafoam silk nightgown, then climbed into the cedar log bed.

Knowing she'd never be able to fall asleep, she sat bolt upright and twisted her hands together atop the Sunshine and Shadows quilt she and Clint had unearthed in a quaint Shenandoah Valley antique shop during a clandestine, love-filled weekend. The same weekend their child had been conceived.

The storm stalled overhead, wrapping the house in its grip. Rain pounded against the windows. Thunder boomed like cannon fire; psychedelic flashes of lightning streaked across the sky. Wind wailed outside the bedroom window like a savage spirit.

It was going to be, Laura thought, a very long night.

Although she'd not considered it possible, Laura eventually fell asleep. She dreamed of Christmas, could actually smell the pungent scent of the pine tree taking up most of the living room. Beneath the tree were gaily wrapped presents. Enough toys to fill F.A.O. Scharwz spilled over the floor.

A fire blazed in the fireplace; fat white flakes drifted down like snowy feathers outside the window, creating a scene straight out of Currier and Ives.

Laura saw herself sitting on the couch in front of the fireplace, Clint sitting beside her. A little boy with her husband's jet hair and solemn blue eyes sat on her lap, listening intently as his father read aloud from Dylan Thomas's *A Child's Christmas in Wales.*

It was an idyllic scene, born of Laura's most private yearnings. One she was loathe to leave. Which was why, when the sound of the bedroom door opening filtered into her consciousness, she fought waking up.

The bedroom lamp, operated by a wall switch beside the door flashed on. Still struggling to hold on to her dream, which was rapidly disappearing like morning mist over the tops of the tall ponderosa pines outside the ranch house, she mumbled an inarticulate complaint.

The dream faded from view. Laura reluctantly roused, blinking against the blinding light.

Her sleepy mind recognized the familiar face. As her lips curved in a groggy, puzzled smile, a sound like an early Fourth of July firecracker shattered the nighttime stillness.

Startled, and unaware she'd been shot, Laura pressed her hand against the searing heat at her breast. Crimson blood flowed over her naked flesh, staining her fingertips.

Still uncomprehending, she stared up at her attacker, tried to ask *Why?* but discovered she'd gone mute. A mist covered her eyes.

Silvery rain snakes streaked down the bedroom window. Her wounded heart continued to beat.

Pumping out precious blood.

Laura's last conscious thought was regret that she hadn't told Clint about their baby.

And then, as a second sharp retort filtered through the fog clouding her mind, Laura Swann Fletcher surrendered to the darkness.

Chapter Two

"Well, this is another fine mess you've gotten yourself into," Mariah Swann muttered.

Her fingers gripped the steering wheel of her new fire-engine red Jeep Grand Cherokee. A drenching downpour streamed across the windshield, as the ineffectual *swish swish* of the wipers added accompaniment to Travis Tritt singing on the CD player about the perils of falling in love with an unfaithful woman.

The storm, which had stuck like glue overhead all the way from her Malibu beach house had her two hours behind schedule. The digital clock on the dashboard said two o'clock. In the morning. She still had another twenty miles to go before she reached Whiskey River. And then there was that death-defying drive up to her sister's ranch.

"You've been gone ten years, dummy," she scolded herself for her impatience. "What's another two hours, more or less?"

It shouldn't matter. But it did. Because recently she'd been thinking about Laura. A lot.

The time had come for making amends. For healing old

wounds. And who better to begin with than the woman who, once, had been Mariah's best friend?

Her thoughts in a turmoil as she relived the tempestuous day she'd left Whiskey River, Mariah almost didn't see the white barricade blocking the roadway. She slammed the brake pedal to the floor, grateful for the antilock brakes that kept her from sliding through the barricade into the swirling, churning waters.

The rain had caused the river to flood its banks. Attempting a crossing, especially in the dark, would not only be foolhardy, but possibly deadly.

"Damn!"

Mariah glared out at the raging river, at the rain streaming down the windshield, at the stormy sky and considered her options. She could sit here, wait until dawn, and check out exactly how deep the water was running. Or she could turn around, head back the way she'd come, get a motel room in Camp Verde and wait the storm out.

Choosing caution for once, she managed, just barely, to make a U-turn. Fifteen minutes and thirty-five dollars later, she was sitting on a too soft mattress in the Pinewood Motel, telephone receiver in hand trying to get through to her sister, so she could advise Laura not to wait up.

Mariah frowned at the busy tone. "Who could she be talking to at nearly three in the morning?" She tried once more. Again, the line rang busy.

"Maybe she took the phone off the hook." Mariah wondered if Laura was avoiding her. It wouldn't be all that surprising, considering their rocky past. But during the past two years when they'd begun speaking again, she'd hoped that she and her sister had put those days behind them.

Perhaps the storm had knocked down the lines.

"Shit."

Patience had never been Mariah Swann's long suit. It wasn't now. She dug through her purse, searching out the cigarettes she'd bought in Kingman, swearing, as always, they'd be her last. She located the already crumpled pack, shook a cigarette loose and picked up the matches from the tin ashtray on the bedside table. The matchbook cover suggested she was only a free test away from a career as a commercial artist.

As she lit the cigarette, drawing the acrid smoke into her lungs, she could almost hear Laura lecturing her, the same way she had the first time Mariah had gotten caught smoking in the girls' bathroom at school.

Their mother, unable to stand the remoteness of ranch life, had fled Whiskey River—and her domineering husband. The same day Margaret McKenna Swann packed her Louis Vuitton suitcases and returned to Hollywood, Matthew Swann had filed for divorce.

Angry, unable to understand their mother's defection, and chafing under her father's iron hand, Mariah became the rebellious Swann daughter. Which left Laura, by default, the role of the solid, responsible daughter.

Only lately had Mariah begun to understand how having so much responsibility dumped on Laura's shoulders at such a young age must have cost her older sister. Not that Laura had ever complained.

Except the time she'd shocked everyone by eloping with Clint Garvey. The ill-fated marriage had lasted less than a day.

After their father brought her home Laura never mentioned Clint again. A few years later, she married the man her father had chosen for her, and if the glowing articles Mariah read in all the magazines were any indication, her sister was happy.

But sometimes, when the camera lens was focused on the senator while Laura stood loyally in the background, a photographer would capture a candid, unpracticed expression on her face. An expression so filled with sadness that Mariah wanted to cry.

"I'll make it up to you, Laurie." Guilt and regret snaked through her. "I promise."

Unable to sit still, Mariah began to pace and smoke. Waiting for morning.

Trace Callahan was dog tired. Throughout the night he'd driven the back roads, setting up barricades in the pouring rain, trying to keep idiot vacationers and drunk residents of Mogollon County from driving their four-wheelers into the raging Whiskey River.

When he'd first applied for the job of sheriff, he couldn't help thinking of the old days when cowboys got drunk and smashed up Whiskey River's saloons. These days, kids got drunk and smashed up their daddies' pick-ups.

He hung his dripping poncho on the rack by the front door and tossed his hat onto a nearby table. Rotating his aching shoulder, which went stiff when it rained, he went into the kitchen, ignoring the trail of muddy footprints he left in his wake.

He opened the refrigerator and had just pulled out the beer he'd been thinking about for the last hour, when the phone rang. The caller I.D. screen announced the call was from his office.

"I told you I was going off duty, Cora Mae," he barked into the mouthpiece. "This had better be important."

"It is if you consider a possible one-eighty-seven in progress important, Sheriff," Cora Mae Jackson shot back.

A wave of adrenaline rushed through his body. Fatigue was immediately forgotten. "A one-eighty-seven?"

A murder? In Whiskey River? Impossible. There hadn't

been a murder in the Arizona mountain town since 1957, when Jared Lawson got drunk at a family Thanksgiving dinner and shot his mother-in-law to death over a white meat-dark meat argument.

"A one-eighty-seven," the night dispatcher repeated. "At senator Fletcher's ranch."

Trace could feel his body relaxing again. He hunched his stiff shoulder, holding the receiver against his neck as he unscrewed the beer cap.

"You mean a possible burglary." There'd been at least a half dozen false alarms at the ranch. Trace wished Fletcher would either get the damn system fixed, or tear it out.

"After thirty-five years I should know my codes, Sheriff," Cora Mae sniffed. "I meant a murder. The senator just called in on 911. He's been shot. He thinks his wife was shot, too."

Trace's pulse rate soared. "Is the gunman still in the house?"

"The senator said he heard them run out. He thinks there were two of them."

Trace slammed the bottle down onto the counter. Foam ran over his hand. "Why didn't you say so in the first place?"

"I believe I did, Sheriff."

"Dispatch the county medical unit," Trace instructed. "And get hold of J.D."

"J.D. was here when the call came in. He's on his way to the ranch now."

"Radio him and let him know I'm on the way. Oh, and tell him not to touch anything."

"Ten-four," she said. Trace would have had to have been deaf to miss the smug satisfaction in the dispatcher's voice.

As he marched back out into the stormy night, Trace

remembered a time when he'd genuinely loved being a cop. When he'd been filled with an overwhelming need to help.

He'd especially enjoyed being a homicide detective—the murder police. The top of the rung, the cream of the crop. The goddamn best. He'd gotten off on the crime scenes, the countless cups of coffee, the chain smoking, the pursuit, the face-to-face confrontation with a killer. And that inimitable sound of handcuffs clicking around the wrists of the bad guys had never failed to give him an adolescent rush.

He woke up each morning juiced, ready to hit the streets and save the world. But that had been in what now seemed like another lifetime.

Unfortunately, justice had proven to be not only blindfolded, but deaf and dumb as well and Detective Sergeant Trace Callahan had learned the hard way that one man couldn't save the world from itself.

Now all he wanted was a chance to build himself a quiet, uneventful life where he didn't have to worry about some coked-up drug dealer pumping bullets into him. As he climbed into the black-and-white Suburban, Trace considered that he thought he'd found exactly that when he signed his contract six months ago.

Cursing whatever lowlifes had so rudely intruded on his peaceful existence, he gunned the engine and headed, emergency lights flashing, toward the Fletcher ranch.

Whiskey River was sleeping as Trace drove through the darkened streets. Even in the slanting rain, the town had a certain charm about it, a quaintness that had little in common with the dirty business of murder.

Whiskey River, Arizona, was home to 350 full-time residents and at least triple that many during the summer, when vacationers came streaming north to escape the desert heat. If it looked familiar to first-time visitors, it should. Whiskey River had served as a movie set on more than one occasion.

Gene Autry, John Wayne and Clint Eastwood had all ridden horseback down Main Street. So had Doc Holliday and Wyatt Earp, but the make-believe cowboys had bigger displays in the local historical museum.

Originally settled more than fifteen hundred years ago by prehistoric people classified by archaeologists as the Mogollon Culture, the area had subsequently been home to Apaches, soldiers, prospectors, loggers and ranchers. While Tombstone residents were making headlines by shooting at each other, Whiskey River became known for its taverns and brothels.

Once upon a time, settlers had run into town for protection from marauding Indians. These days citizens tried to liven things up again by holding rodeos at the fairgrounds.

Five miles outside of town, Trace turned onto a narrow graded road that snaked its way in a breath-stealing ascension up the rocky escarpment of the Mogollon Rim.

He arrived at the ranch right behind the ambulance.

His deputy's black-and-white was parked in front of the house. The bubble gum lights atop the cruiser were sending out flashing blue strobes. The driver's door was open. As he passed the patrol car, Trace cursed and yanked the keys from the ignition. A recent graduate of University of Arizona, with a bachelor's degree in criminal justice, J.D. Brown was intelligent, enthusiastic and showed a willingness to learn. He was also green as new grass and prone to the same mistakes made by rookies in jurisdictions everywhere.

The deputy was waiting at the door. "The senator's in the den, just to the right of the front door," he told the medical team. "He's been shot in the side."

"Is he conscious?" the female paramedic asked.

"In and out."

"What about the wife?"

The deputy frowned. "She's upstairs. But take care of the senator. It's too late for her."

"You sure?" Trace asked.

"She was ten-seven when I got here," J.D. insisted.

Ten-seven. The police code for Out of Service. Crude, but applicable, Trace decided.

"I spent summers working in the emergency room at Louis R. Pyle Memorial," the younger officer, the son of a nurse, reminded Trace. "I sure as hell know a lost cause when I see it."

Trace accompanied the trio into the book-lined den where he found a man clad in a pair of paisley silk boxer shorts sprawled on his back on the floor by the doorway. He was in his midforties, with the kind of firm, lean body that came from working out. His deep tan and sun-streaked hair suggested afternoons spent on a Georgetown tennis court. A small amount of blood was draining from what appeared to be a single wound in his side. He'd obviously been lying on the couch when he was shot. Blood spatters stained the fawn-colored leather.

Beside the couch was a table. Atop the table was an empty glass, an open briefcase and a telephone. The phone was off the hook. The desk drawers had been rifled through; papers were strewn across the floor. A black carry-on suitcase was beside the couch, unopened.

"Senator?" The female medic wrapped a blood pressure cuff around the man's upper arm. The other paramedic slammed an oxygen mask over his face. "It's okay. You're going to be okay. We're here to help."

"My wife," Alan Fletcher gasped, his words muffled by the plastic mask. "Help...Laura."

Trace squatted down, bringing himself eye to eye with

the injured man. "Can you tell me what happened, Senator?"

"I heard a s-s-shot." He stuttered painfully. "Then another. At first I thought it was a dream, you know. By the time I realized they were r-r-real shots, one of the burglars, the one rifling my desk, s-s-shot me."

"You were downstairs at the time of the shooting?" Trace knew that from the blood spatters, but he wanted to hear the senator's explanation.

"I got in late." He drew in a deep, shuddering breath. Even with the oxygen assist, the effort of talking seemed to be giving him great pain. "Damn f-f-flight delays. I didn't want to wake Laura up, so I just crashed on the couch."

"When was that?"

"About midnight."

"Was the security system on when you arrived?"

"No. And I didn't set it." He groaned again. "Storms always set the damn thing off. I've been promising Laura... Oh, God." He began to sob. "I had my secretary call the company yesterday. They couldn't come out until after the fourth."

He bit his lip and appeared to be struggling for calm. "If only I'd called sooner, this wouldn't have happened."

That might be true, but Trace wasn't into Monday morning quarterbacking. "Did you happen to get a look at the guy who shot you?"

"Not really. He was wearing a mask."

"A ski mask?"

"Uh-uh..." He closed his eyes. "It was brown. And sh-sh-sheer. Like he'd pulled a nylon stocking over his face." He sucked in another breath. "Oh, God, it hurts," he moaned.

"You're doing great, Senator," the paramedic advised. "Just try to stay calm. Everything's going to be all right."

"I heard the g-g-gunmen run out the door. I t-t-tried to get to Laura after I called 911. I was crawling across the floor. Then I guess I passed out...."

Tears welled up in his light blue eyes and ran down his cheeks in long wet ribbons. "Oh, C-C-Christ. How could this happen?"

No one in the room answered. While the paramedics continued to work on the senator, Trace left the den, gesturing for his deputy to follow.

"Turn on my overhead lights," he said, handing J.D. the keys to the Suburban the Mogollon County supervisors had included in his deal as an enticement to sign.

It wasn't every day a big-city crime buster was willing to come to work in the boondocks and they'd wanted to ensure he wouldn't change his mind once he learned that jaywalking and the occasional drunk and disorderly was about as bad as it got in Whiskey River.

What they hadn't realized was that Trace would have taken the job without the new truck.

"Check around the outside. See if you can find a point of entry. Also, with all the rain, there should be footprints."

"Yessir." J.D. snatched the keys with an enthusiasm that reminded Trace of himself in what seemed another lifetime.

Taking his .38 Detective Special from its hip holster, Trace climbed the stairs, all his senses on alert. The odds of the shooter still being in the house were slim to none. But Trace had the scars to prove that a cop couldn't be too careful.

He studied the crime scene from the doorway of the master bedroom, his gaze sweeping over the warm pine flooring, the white walls adorned with expensively framed western art. The bed had been handcrafted from cedar logs. The headboard, along with the wall behind it, was marred by a sweeping, red-pink arc.

A quilt had slid halfway off the mattress. In the center of the bed a woman lay faceup, her arms outstretched, as if reaching for something, or someone, no longer there. Her palms were open, her fingers slightly curled. Her green eyes were fixed in an expression of vague surprise Trace had seen before. The drawers of the two nightstands on either side of the bed were open. As were those of the bureau. The contents of the drawers had been tossed haphazardly onto the floor.

Atop the dresser were various perfume bottles, a silver-backed mirror and a crystal-framed wedding picture. The smiling faces of Laura and Alan Fletcher looked out of the frame at the grisly scene. The glittering contents of a mahogany jewelry box had been dumped out, scattered across the gleaming pine planks.

Stepping over the damp towel lying on the floor by the dresser, Trace approached the bed.

Even as he noted absently that Laura Fletcher was still beautiful, even in death, he began to emotionally distance himself. It was not a deliberate decision. Rather, it was as if a self-protective switch had clicked on inside his brain. He'd developed the ability to detach himself early in his career.

In his sixteen years on the Dallas police force, he had been witness to the most basic of human evil—the taking of another life. When faced with the nude body of a female, who only hours earlier had, perhaps, been laughing and loving, a cop could not waste time pondering theological questions about man's inhumanity to man.

What he had to concentrate on was whether that bloody hole in her breast was an entrance wound or an exit wound. He had to judge the distance and caliber of the weapon that had made that circular wound in her left temple.

And, as he lifted her wrist, clasping the flesh that was already growing icy now that the life had drained out of it, rather than notice that her fingers were long and slender, he took note of the blood on the fingertips of her left hand—which gave evidence that she'd been aware of being attacked—and wondered why it was that the senator's dead wife wasn't wearing a wedding ring.

J.D. had been right. There was nothing they could do for Laura Fletcher now. Except find her killer.

He took a notebook from his pocket and quickly sketched the position of the body, the bed, the rest of the crime scene. Then he went back downstairs and repeated the process in the den.

The paramedics had stabilized the senator and had him lying on a gurney, ready to wheel him out to the waiting ambulance.

"You taking him to Payson Hospital?"

"That's the plan," the paramedic answered. "His wound isn't critical enough for air evac."

"I'll follow you."

"What about Laura?" Alan Fletcher groaned. "Is she—"

"Don't worry about her right now," the paramedic broke in, exchanging a look with Trace. The senator's color wasn't good and the way he kept going in and out of consciousness suggested that he could go into shock. This wasn't the time to tell the man his wife was dead. "Just worry about yourself, Senator."

Trace followed them out. "Find anything?" he asked his deputy.

"No sign of false entry. But you're right about the footprints. Got a real good set coming from the driveway. Tire tracks, too."

"Good." Trace nodded. "I'm going to call DPS and have them send over their crime lab guys."

J.D.'s eyes widened at the idea of involving the state Department of Public Safety. "You're bringing outsiders in?"

"I don't have much choice," Trace pointed out. "The average high school chem class probably has more equipment than we do. This is going to be a high-profile case. I want to make sure there aren't any mistakes made."

"Ben isn't going to like this," J.D. warned.

Ben Loftin. A lifelong resident of Whiskey River, cousin to the mayor, a fifteen-year deputy and the man who'd expected to be promoted to sheriff. From his first day on the job, Trace had suspected Loftin was also one of those redneck bullies who gave cops—especially those in small towns—a bad name.

"Ben Loftin isn't sheriff," Trace reminded his deputy gruffly. "I'm going into Payson with the senator. I want you to lock this place up tight and don't let anyone in until the medical examiner and the crime lab guys get here."

"Even Ben?"

"Especially Loftin," Trace stressed. "From what I've seen of the guy, his investigative skills would make Barney Fife look like Columbo."

J.D. began to laugh, then choked it off when one look at his boss's rigid face told him the comparison hadn't been meant as a joke. "I've got the tape in the trunk of the black-and-white," he said. "I'll cordon off the perimeter."

Once again the deputy's eagerness reminded Trace of himself and made him feel about as old as dirt. The near-fatal shooting that had taken his partner's life had left Trace with scars—both physical and mental—that he figured he'd carry for the rest of his life.

"You do that. I'll check in after I neutron the Senator."

J.D.'s eyes widened. "You're going to test the senator for gunpowder residue?"

"He was at the scene of a murder."

"But he was shot."

"So was his wife. His dead wife," Trace said patiently.

"But he's a senator."

"And we're cops. With a job to do. Which includes checking out all possible suspects."

"Christ, the shit's really going to hit the fan when this gets out," the young man muttered.

"Don't look now, J.D.," Trace drawled, jerking his head in the direction of the ranch house. "But it already has."

Chapter Three

Trace arrived at the hospital on Ponderosa Street just as the technician he'd requested from the Department of Public Safety was pulling into the parking lot.

They were forced to wait while the physician on call conducted a cursory examination of the wounded senator. After the exam, X rays were taken. Throughout it all, Alan Fletcher remained conscious and coherent.

"The wound isn't life threatening," the doctor advised Trace, "but I need to remove the bullet and stitch up any damage to internal organs." He frowned. "Small caliber bullets have an unfortunate tendency to bounce around like pinballs once they're inside the body."

"Sounds as if you've spent some time on the front lines."

"I worked ER for eight years at Oakland's Highland Hospital." The doctor shook his head. "I figured I put all that behind me when I moved here."

"Join the club," Trace said dryly.

"Getting back to the senator, there's no way to tell how much damage was done until we open him up. And we'll need to clean the wound to prevent peritonitis."

"I know the drill, Doc." Trace glanced over to where the senator was lying on the gurney. A pretty blond nurse in a white pantsuit was holding his hand and assuring him that he'd be all right. "But since the guy's not critical, I'll need to test for residue before you take him into surgery."

The doctor, too, knew the drill. "Of course."

Alan Fletcher didn't. "You want to test me?" he asked unbelievingly. "Why?"

"It's nothing to take personally, Senator," Trace said, accustomed to such protestations. "It's strictly policy."

"It's policy to harass shooting victims?"

"It's policy to test everyone involved in a crime. Once we eliminate you as a suspect, Senator, we can get on to the business of apprehending the perpetrators." Trace had switched to the tone he used in the old days whenever it became necessary to appease police department brass.

"Well, since you put it that way..." Beads of sweat glistened on the senator's forehead and above his top lip. "Go ahead." Alan Fletcher invited magnanimously. He held out his hands. "Do whatever you have to do."

"Thank you, Senator," Trace said politely. He watched as the DPS technician opened the kit and used a cotton swab to wipe a weak solution of nitric acid over the senator's hands, concentrating heavily on the palm and the webbing between the thumb and first finger. Fletcher's gold wedding band gleamed in the fluorescent overhead light.

After she was done, the technician peeled the protective seal from a piece of paper, pressed it against those same parts of his hands, then sealed the samples in an evidence jar.

"Thank you, Senator," Trace said again, once the test was finished and he'd gotten the wounded man's signature on a consent to search form. This case was too high profile not to be played strictly by the book. "Have you remembered anything else about the man who attacked you? Height, weight, clothing?"

Fletcher shook his head, then winced as if the gesture were painful. "Sorry."

"Don't worry about it. Perhaps after your surgery, when you're feeling stronger, things might come back."

"Do you think so?" The senator looked hopeful and sounded doubtful.

"Sure. It happens all the time," Trace said, not quite truthfully. More often than not time only faded memory. He closed the notebook and returned it to his shirt pocket. "I'll keep in touch." The statement, spoken with a deliberate lack of inflection could have been a promise. Or a threat.

As he watched Alan Fletcher being wheeled off to surgery, Trace considered the fact that during the more than thirty minutes Senator Fletcher had been in the emergency room, he hadn't again asked about his wife.

Trace recalled his own experience after the shooting that had ended his homicide career and almost his life. He remembered lying on a gurney, furious that the trauma team wasn't working on Danny. His concern for his partner had been so strong he hadn't even experienced pain from his own near-fatal wounds until much later.

Daniel Murphy had been his partner for five years. During that time they'd become closer than most brothers. But though they'd known almost everything there was to know about one another, their bond had still not been as intimate as a man and wife.

Trace had been divorced for ten years. But even during that last year of marriage, when his home had felt like an armed camp, if Ellen had been injured in any way—let alone shot in the head by masked intruders—a SWAT team wouldn't have been able to stop him from being with her.

"Different strokes," he murmured as he walked over to the nurses' station. Trace also could not discount the possibility that the senator's lack of curiosity regarding his wife's condition was because he was guilty.

Worried that the shooting may have been some cockeyed attempted political assassination plot, he telephoned Ben Loftin at home, instructing him to get to the hospital and stand guard outside the senator's door.

When he returned to the ranch, Trace saw that J.D. had followed his instructions, securing the crime area with yellow plastic police tape. The Evidence Technical Unit had arrived on the scene.

As primary investigator, Trace was in charge of supervising the meticulous search of the premises. Sticking to the old adage that a victim could only be killed once, but a crime scene could be murdered in countless ways, he kept the pace slow and methodical. He'd witnessed too many occasions when speed had resulted in the destruction of vital evidence.

Without a detailed description of the armed intruders, he put out an APB on anyone seen driving in the vicinity of the ranch that night. The mayors of the nearby communities of Pine, Payson and Strawberry had offered to send additional police to join in the search of Rim backroads and the sheriff from neighboring Coconino County had volunteered additional manpower.

The much appreciated cooperation allowed Trace to remain at the house with the ETU crew. He watched the photographer snap away on a 35 mm, then shoot a videotape record of the scene.

Eager to help, J.D. had donned a pair of surgical gloves and was on his hands and knees, combing the bedroom carpet for fibers.

"We need to contact Matthew Swann before he hears the news on the radio," Trace said.

"Cora Mae called Swann's ranch right after the 911 call came in," J.D. revealed. "The housekeeper says he's in Santa Fe. Some livestock convention or something."

"Does she have the name of the hotel?"

"She did. She also called it. But the desk clerk said Swann got into some kind of argument with the night manager over room service hours so he checked out.... Bingo!"

The deputy happily plucked a blue thread from the carpet, dropped it into a plastic bag and carefully labeled it. Trace observed the action with mild amusement thinking how you never forgot your first homicide. Trace hoped like hell this would be J.D.'s last one for a very long time.

"The clerk didn't know what hotel he moved to. But Cora Mae's on the case," J.D. assured him as he resumed his methodical carpet combing. "She'll track him down."

Of that, Trace had no doubt. The woman had a tongue like a razor blade, cursed like a lumberjack at spring thaw and guarded her precious records as if they were the Holy Grail.

But she was remarkably efficient. She also made the best cup of coffee west of the Pecos and could bluff at poker with the best of them.

Thinking he might be dealing with a sexual assault as well as a murder, Trace began going through the lingerie strewn over the floor, checking the frothy bits of silk and satin and lace a piece at a time to see if by chance any of the skimpy pairs of panties had been stripped off the victim.

"Jesus!" He picked up a garment so sheer he could see his hand through the diaphanous silk.

J.D. glanced up and couldn't quite repress his grin. "It's a teddy. I bought Jilly a red one for Valentine's day. At

Victoria's Secret. She liked it a lot.'' His grin widened. ''I liked it even better.''

''I'll bet.'' Trace wondered why, if the senator's wife was such a fan of sexy lingerie, she went to bed nude. Perhaps, he considered, thinking of what Fletcher had said about not wanting to wake his wife up, she didn't bother dressing seductively when she knew she was going to be sleeping alone.

Ellen had always come to bed wearing his ratty old oversize police academy T-shirts. It crossed Trace's mind that if she'd favored underwear like this, they might still be married.

Then again, probably not. Sex had never been their problem. At least, not in the beginning. By the time they finally called it quits, neither of them had felt like rolling around in the sheets.

Trace held up an ivory teddy. The early morning light streaming through the bedroom window rendered it nearly transparent.

''You actually walked right into a store, in a public mall, where anyone could see you and bought something like this?''

Shit, he'd been married nine months before he worked up the nerve to buy tampons at the 7-Eleven. For the second time today, Trace found himself feeling like an over-the-hill dinosaur.

''Actually,'' J.D. admitted, ''I ordered it from a catalog.''

Deciding that he'd love to get a look at J.D.'s catalog, Trace moved the teddies aside and found the letters, tied with a blue satin ribbon.

Love letters, he figured. So the lady had been a romantic. He could have guessed that from the fancy underwear and the romance novel on the nightstand. What Trace did find interesting was that the bold black script on the outside of the envelopes didn't begin to resemble the precise cursive found on the pages of Alan Fletcher's appointment book.

Holding one of the letters gingerly by the edges, Trace turned it over. It was signed simply *Love always, C.*

The postmark on one of the envelopes was stamped right here in Whiskey River a little over a week ago, which added an interesting twist to the murder. Although Trace never spent much time dwelling on why a crime was committed—humans were willing to kill for often ridiculously mundane reasons—sex often proved as strong a motive as greed.

Sometimes stronger.

"Where the hell is the M.E.?" he demanded impatiently. He'd placed the call to the county medical examiner over an hour ago.

"Someone looking for me?" a tobacco-roughened voice asked from the doorway.

"It's about time you got here."

"Don't know what the hurry is," Dr. Stanley Potter drawled around a fat cigar. "Looks like this little lady isn't going anywhere." He chuckled at his own bad joke.

It took an effort, but Trace reminded himself that back in Cook County, before he'd gone into semiretirement, Potter had performed more than fifteen hundred autopsies and observed thousands more. He'd also appeared as an expert witness in innumerable cases around the country, proving himself a valuable member of the prosecution team.

"Just call the death so we can get her out of here."

The physician dutifully recorded the victim's lack of pulse. "She's dead, all right." Next he took her temperature. "Ninety-four degrees."

"Which would set the murder between two and three a.m.," Trace calculated. The exact figures varied with environmental differences, but the rule of thumb was about one and a half degrees Fahrenheit temperature loss per hour.

"Close enough for government work," the M.E. agreed. He turned over her hand. Her nails were unpainted. "No skin or signs of a struggle."

"That could mean she was surprised," J.D., who'd risen to his feet to watch the examination, offered.

"It could also mean she knew her killer," Trace said.

After the doctor finished his initial examination, Trace stood by as the body was wrapped in a white sheet, slid into a thick bag, placed on a stretcher, and carried downstairs, where she was strapped onto a gurney in the M.E.'s wagon.

When the gunmetal gray van pulled away from the scene, Trace allowed himself a momentary feeling of frustration at a life cut too brutally and tragically short.

Then, shaking off the brief regret, he turned, intending to go back into the house, when he heard a voice calling his name.

"Sheriff Callahan!"

Trace glared at the man hurrying toward him, past the yellow tape barricade. Rudy Chavez was the sole reporter for the *Rim Rock Weekly Record.* The young reporter reminded Trace of Jimmy Olson. With just enough Bob Woodward thrown in to make him one helluva pest. Reporters were not Trace Callahan's favorite people. He considered them akin to vultures, only lower down on the evolutionary scale.

"I caught the call on my police scanner." Rudy whipped out a long narrow notebook and a transparent plastic pen. "Is it true? Was the senator shot?"

Knowing that there was no way he could avoid the publicity on this case, Trace said, "I'll be holding a press conference in my office at noon. You'll get a statement then."

"But that's six hours away."

"You can tell time, too," Trace said with mock admiration. "Congratulations." He caught sight of his deputy out of the corner of his eye. "J.D., escort Mr. Chavez to his car."

The reporter visibly bristled. "You can't run me off the property!"

"Watch me," Trace advised easily. But there was steel underlying his tone.

"Come on, Rudy," coaxed J.D., who'd worked with his boss long enough to recognize when not to argue. "You know you can't interfere with a crime scene."

"So there was a murder?"

"I didn't say that." A red flush rose from the starched khaki collar of the deputy's uniform. "Dammit, Rudy," he muttered, practically dragging the reporter back to the Subaru Justy parked behind the phalanx of police vehicles. "You're going to get us both in a world of hurt."

"I'm just trying to do my job."

"And I'm just doing mine," J.D snapped. This was the most exciting day of his career—hell, his entire life so far—and he damn well didn't want to waste a minute of it arguing.

"Haven't you ever heard of freedom of the press? I just need one quote," Rudy persisted.

"If you don't get out of here, I'm going to run you in for interfering in a criminal investigation." The young cop's tone sounded like a copy of Trace's earlier one.

Rudy looked inclined to argue. His dark brown gaze went from J.D. to Trace, who was watching the exchange with an unblinking gaze, back to J.D. again.

Apparently knowing when he was licked, he turned to leave just as another truck turned into the driveway.

"I'll be damned," the reporter breathed as he recognized the driver. "Talk about timing!" His belief in journalistic good fortune restored, Rudy Chavez headed in the direction of the muddy red Jeep.

J.D. watched as the driver's door opened, revealing a pair of long legs clad in tight black jeans and red cowboy boots. The legs were followed by a female body which, while slender, had curves in all the right places. Her sun-streaked blond hair fell in loose soft waves to her shoulders. Her eyes were hidden behind a pair of oversize sunglasses.

As she marched toward them in a brisk, ground-eating stride, J.D. recalled how, in his boyhood, though many residents of Whiskey River had clucked their tongues over Mariah Swann's outrageous behavior, he'd suffered a secret crush on the high-spirited girl who'd been his babysitter before she had run off to Hollywood like her mother.

During his hormone-driven adolescent days he'd raced home from school to watch her steamy love scenes on "All Our Tomorrows" and fantasized acting out those scenes with the woman who'd become locally known as the "Vixen of Whiskey River."

"Who's that?"

Trace's deep voice, coming from just behind him, made J.D. jump. For such a big man, it was downright nerve-racking the way the sheriff could sneak up behind a guy without making a sound.

"That," he answered, as a few of Mariah's more infamous escapades came to mind, "is trouble. With a capital *T*."

Mariah was stunned by the swarm of activity surrounding the ranch house. At the sight of that unmistakable yellow plastic tape, she cursed. Just last month her beach house had been broken into.

She jumped down from the driver's seat and headed

toward the two men standing in the driveway. One was of average height, with the slim-hipped build of the cowboys Mariah had grown up with. He was wearing a Smokey the Bear hat pulled down low over his forehead like a Marine drill instructor and the khaki uniform of the sheriff's department. A silver star was pinned to his starched uniform blouse.

The other man was large enough to play offensive line for the Raiders. Even without the wedge-heeled cowboy boots Mariah would guess his height to be about six-four. Clad in a green-and-black plaid flannel shirt and jeans, he reminded her of Paul Bunyan. He radiated a palpable authority.

She directed her question to the larger man. "What's going on here?"

"Good morning," Trace said in his best Joe Friday, just-the-facts-ma'am voice. He raised two fingers to his black Stetson. "May I ask who you are?"

Although his greeting was unfailingly polite, Mariah knew instinctively that this was a man who could give her authoritative father a run for his money. His firm, unshaven square jaw suggested an equally unyielding nature. She noticed he hadn't answered her question.

Refusing to be intimidated, she stopped close enough to him that the toes of their boots were nearly touching, and realized her mistake when she had to tilt her head back to look a long, long way up into his face.

"I'm Mariah Swann. Who are you?"

"Sheriff Trace Callahan." Trace held out his hand.

"Sheriff?" A blond brow climbed her forehead as she absently extended her own hand in response. His palm was rough, calluses on top of calluses. "What happened to Walter Amos?"

"Amos retired six months ago." Her skin was as soft as it was fragrant. "Last I heard he was spending his time telling lies about birdies and eagles on the golf course in Sun City. This is Deputy Brown."

Mariah was momentarily sidetracked by the introduction. "J.D?" Pushing the sunglasses to the top of her head, she gave the younger man a longer, second look. "Is that really you?"

Trace watched in amazement as his deputy blushed scarlet. "It's me," he mumbled.

"Why, you're all grown up."

Unlike so many of her Hollywood peers, Mariah had never paid any heed to birthdays. Especially these days, since she had given up acting and turned to writing. Now her livelihood depended not on her look but on her talent to craft a gripping television drama.

But seeing this boy she'd baby-sat all those years ago, dressed in the uniform of a deputy sheriff made her realize exactly how much time had gone by since she'd left Whiskey River in Laura's powder blue Mustang convertible.

"I just graduated from U. of A.," J.D. said, sounding as if he'd stuck a handful of marbles into his mouth. "In criminal justice."

"Criminal justice." Mariah mulled that one over, amazed that this was the same bratty little kid who, at age five, had seemed destined to grow up to be a world-class juvenile delinquent. "Your parents must be proud."

J.D. mumbled something inarticulate that could have been agreement.

Christ, Trace thought, next J.D. would be rubbing the toe of his boot in the dirt like some tongue-tied sixth grader. Mariah folded her arms over her scarlet shirt. "So, which of you officers is going to tell me what the hell is going on here?"

"I'm afraid there's been a shooting," Trace said.

"A shooting?" It was as if he'd suddenly switched to Greek. Or Swahili. Mariah couldn't comprehend his words. She turned and stared at the house as if hoping to find the explanation written on the double front doors. "Not a burglary?"

"It's Laura," J.D. blurted out.

"Laura?" Mariah blinked and looked at Trace. "My sister shot someone?"

The idea was incomprehensible. Laura was the gentlest person Mariah had ever known. Why, she'd never been willing to so much as step on a spider.

"I'm afraid your sister's the one who was shot." Trace kept his voice low and steady and watched her carefully.

This was a dream, Mariah decided. In a minute she'd wake up, find herself in the tacky motel, with its amateur seascape on the wall and the portable television bolted to the dresser.

She blinked again. Then she shook her head. *Wake up, dammit,* a frightened voice in her mind shouted.

Trace saw the confusion in her slanted turquoise eyes give way to fear. "I'm sorry to have to tell you this, Ms. Swann." This time he took off his hat. "But your sister's dead."

"Dead," she repeated blankly.

Trace didn't think she'd grasped his meaning yet. He knew shock had a way of numbing such staggering blows. She glanced back at her Jeep, then beyond, down the serpentine road she'd just driven. Trace could practically see the wheels turning inside her head and knew she was thinking of the gray van she'd obviously passed on the way to the ranch.

"Oh, my God." A ragged, involuntary keening sound escaped her lips. Then she swayed.

Catching her by the upper arms, Trace lowered her to one of the flat-topped red boulders lining the driveway. He squatted in front of her.

"Get rid of Chavez," he instructed a stricken J.D. when

he saw the reporter, who'd stayed to watch the drama, headed their way. "Then go back in the house and help the lab guys."

"Yessir." J.D. gave Mariah one last worried look, squared his shoulders and headed toward Rudy Chavez with a swagger that would have done John Wayne proud.

"Put your head between your knees," Trace advised Mariah gruffly. He pressed his palm against the top of her head, urging it down. "That should help."

She shook off his touch. "Help?" Her laugh was short and bitter. Her eyes were dull with the sheen of shock. "Help who? Laura?"

The question didn't demand a response, but Trace answered her anyway. "I'm afraid it's too late for your sister."

"Too late." She squeezed her hands together until her knuckles turned white and pressed them against her eyes. "It was the damn river."

"The river?"

"It was flooding. Someone had put up a stupid barricade and I was afraid to try crossing it in the dark." Her hands limply dropped to her sides. She lowered her forehead to her knees, not to keep from fainting, but because the pain shooting through her was so intense. "I spent the rest of the night in Camp Verde."

A slow breath shuddered through her. She lifted her head again. "When was she killed?"

Trace knew where she was headed. He also knew second-guessing fate was asking for trouble. "We don't know exactly," he hedged. "Not yet."

"Surely you have a ballpark estimate."

"The coroner's currently putting the time of death between two and three."

"This morning."

"Yes."

"Dammit." Trace recognized the expression in her bleak gaze. It was one he was personally familiar with. *Guilt.* "If I'd only gotten here on time, she'd still be alive."

Something made him want to take both her soft hands in his and hold on tight until he could convince her that such thoughts were self-destructive. That they could eat away at your insides like battery acid. Cursing softly, he sat down beside her.

"You can't know that," he said, attempting to soothe the accusations running rampant in her head. He knew, all too well, exactly what those voices sounded like.

"I told her I'd be here by midnight. If I had—"

"The intruders might have killed you, too."

"Intruders?" She looked at him in surprise.

"Right now it appears your sister woke up during a robbery."

"A robbery." She bit her lip, taking it in. "Then Alan wasn't the one who killed her?"

"Why would you think the senator shot your sister?" he asked with a studied lack of inflection. *Just the facts ma'am.*

"Because Alan Fletcher is a son of a bitch who only married my sister for her money and her political connections."

Her color had returned. Her eyes cleared. Scarlet flags waved in her cheeks. Trace watched her spine stiffen and knew she wasn't going to faint.

"If that's true, you'd think he'd want to keep her alive."

"Not really," Mariah argued. As she reached into her bag for her cigarettes, the mists began lifting from her mind. She was beginning to be able to think again.

On some distant level she knew there would still be pain to deal with. A horrendous amount of pain and remorse and regret. But at the moment, she found it easier to concentrate on the crime as if it were a new script she was writing.

"Since I doubt if Laura asked Alan to sign a prenuptial, he'd be first in line to inherit her money, not to mention a sizable trust fund. And this ranch.

"As for political support, our father handpicked the ambitious bastard to be his son-in-law." She shook out a cigarette and went digging for the art test matches in the depths of the bag. "The only thing that would make the mighty Matthew Swann retract his political support would be if he discovered a Communist Party membership card lurking in Alan's wallet.

"Of course, now that the Evil Empire is no longer a threat, he might even turn a blind eye to that." She jammed the cigarette between her lips and was appalled to discover that her hands were trembling too badly to light it.

Her scorn, Trace noted, appeared to be evenly divided between her brother-in-law and her father. She was angry and bitter and didn't bother to hide it.

As he took the matches and lit the cigarette, Trace also realized she hadn't yet asked about the senator.

"Your brother-in-law was shot, too," he told her.

"Is he dead?"

"No. He's in surgery, but the doctor says he's not in any danger."

"Too bad." She drew in the smoke and shook her head. "Hell. This will probably earn him another fifty thousand votes come election time.

"Has anyone notified my father?" Now that she thought about it, Mariah was surprised that he wasn't here trying to control this scene and everyone in it.

"My dispatcher has been trying to reach him. Apparently he's in New Mexico. No one seems to know how to get hold of your mother."

"That's probably because she left town when I was five."

"I'm sorry."

Mariah shrugged and exhaled a thin blue cloud. Her throat was raw from a night of cigarettes. She really was going to have to stop one of these days. "There's no need to apologize."

She looked back at the house, her gaze drifting to the upstairs window as if hoping to see her sister standing there.

Trace remembered how, when he'd finally gotten sprung from the hospital, he'd taken a cab to the police garage and sat in the driver's seat of the unmarked cruiser, imagining Danny riding shotgun beside him.

At the time, he'd felt foolish and hoped like hell none of the other detectives would discover him there. They hadn't, and oddly, for that brief time, he'd actually felt a little better. Not good. But better.

"My mother lives in Bel Air. I see her quite often." Since it was obvious he didn't know, Mariah decided she may as well be the one to tell him. "She's Margaret McKenna."

Mariah gave him credit for keeping the surprise from showing. Instead, his eyes narrowed and moved slowly over her face in a judicious appraisal.

Margaret McKenna had been an old-style, Hollywood bombshell. Her haughty, Ice Queen performances had radiated with the type of carnality often imitated but rarely equaled. Kathleen Turner had come close in *Body Heat,* Trace decided. Madonna? Sharon Stone? Forget it.

Her voice had been the kind of sultry, whiskey baritone that could make all of a man's nerves stand on end. And when those huge one-of-a-kind emerald eyes bore down on you from the oversize movie screen, it was as if she were aiming down the barrel of a gun. As a bonus, she'd been a helluva good actress, too.

"Now that you mention it, I can see the resemblance," Trace decided finally. It was in the unflinching directness of the eyes, the remarkable cheekbones, the pointed, argumentative chin. But mostly it was attitude.

"Actually, Laura looks more like our mother."

He didn't miss her use of the present tense. Death took getting used to. Murder took even longer.

Belatedly realizing what she'd said, Mariah sighed and stabbed the cigarette out on the rock. "This sucks."

"Yes. It does." He stopped being a concerned listener and went back to being a cop. "Look, I don't know when we're going to be able to track down your father and with the senator in surgery—"

"You need someone to identify my sister's body," Mariah guessed flatly.

"The sooner we get an ID, the sooner we can compile more evidence to help us apprehend her killer."

Mariah realized that he was talking about an autopsy. Her lips pulled into a tight line. Her gaze drifted, once again, to the bedroom window.

He stood up and put the Stetson back on, adjusting the black felt brim so that a shadow fell over his face. "I'll drive you into town."

Mariah was not fond of men who issued orders. But at the moment, she didn't feel up to driving back down that steep winding road, either.

"Let's go." She stood up and although he wouldn't have thought it possible, given how tight those jeans were, managed to jam her hands into her back pockets. The gesture pulled the crimson shirt tight against her high, firm breasts.

They walked side by side to the Suburban. He opened

the door and with a palm to her elbow, helped her up into the passenger seat.

"I'll be right back. I want to tell J.D. where he can reach me and arrange to have your Jeep driven into town."

"The keys are in the ignition."

Mariah watched him enter the house that had smelled like gingerbread cookies, lemon oil and Pine Sol back in the days when it had belonged to her grandmother.

Experience had taught Mariah to trust her intuition about people, and that sixth sense was telling her that Trace Callahan was both intelligent and competent. Her sister was in good hands.

Laura.

Mariah felt the tears stinging at the back of her lids and resolutely blinked them away. There would be time for tears later. Right now she had work to do.

She lit another cigarette and began to compile a mental list.

First she had to identify Laura's body. Then she had to call her mother and inform the woman she'd always known as Maggie—never Mama, or heaven forbid, Mom—that her firstborn daughter was dead.

She'd have to face her father's unrelenting disapproval for the first time in more than a decade. She had to try to offer condolences to her wounded son-of-a-bitch brother-in-law without gagging.

And then, somehow, she was going to have to dig down deep enough to find the inner strength to get through the funeral.

In addition to all that, although he didn't know it yet, Mariah had every intention of helping Whiskey River's new sheriff apprehend her sister's murderer.

Then, and only then, when the heartless monsters who'd shot Laura dead, cruelly cutting short a very special life, were behind bars, would she allow herself to cry.

Chapter Four

The medical examiner's office was in the basement of the town's eighty-year-old redbrick courthouse. Since the ancient elevator tended to be iffy, Trace decided to skip it.

As Mariah accompanied him down first the narrow flight of stairs and then the long, poorly lit hallway, she couldn't quite shake the feeling that none of it was real, that she was plotting out a script.

Beautiful wife of charismatic senator is killed in an isolated ranch house during a thunderstorm, she set up the scenario. With the help of the murdered woman's sister, an award-winning television writer, the crime is solved, the politician husband is arrested and justice wins in the end.

No, Mariah considered. That plot left the wife still dead. She erased the mental slate in her mind and began again.

Beautiful wife of charismatic senator is *shot and wounded* during a thunderstorm. While she lies in a coma, dogged small-town sheriff and glamorous television writer, estranged from her family for years, set out to prove the husband guilty.

The smoking gun is found. The senator gets a pair of silver bracelets and a ride in the back of a patrol car to jail, where he breaks down and confesses.

His wife wakes up in the hospital, seemingly no worse for her harrowing experience and requests a cup of herbal tea and a divorce.

The sisters embrace. The music swells.

"Whatever would I have done without you?" the older sister asks tearfully.

The younger one shrugs. She is not only glamorous and famous, but modest as well. "Hey," she says, "that's what sisters are for."

So, in sixty minutes, minus commercials and a network newsbreak, justice is served, a family is reunited, and the story ends on a happy, upbeat note.

It was a nice scenario, Mariah considered with an inward sigh. Too bad things didn't work that way in real life.

Unfortunately, there was one thing that was exactly like it appeared on television. And that was the morgue.

Trace flipped the switch beside the door. The rows of fluorescent tubes flickered to life, casting a bright, but complexion-draining light over the scene. Cool air was blowing from the vent above the loading dock door of the windowless room. "The doc's probably out getting breakfast."

"I'm amazed he could eat."

Trace's only response was a shrug. Taking a new cop out for a Denny's Grand Slam after he'd watched his first autopsy had long been viewed as a rite of passage.

A metal table stood in the center of the linoleum floor. Beside the table was a scale, like that used in supermarkets to weigh apples and oranges. Although a camera was fixed to the ceiling overhead, allowing photographs of record to be taken, the room lacked the overhead microphone that would allow the forensic pathologist to record his findings for later transcription. Instead, metal clipboards hung from hooks on the bilious green wall.

Between the clipboards and the old-fashioned black wall phone was a cork bulletin board covered with official memorandum, some of which, Mariah noted absently, were years old. Against the opposite wall, rather than the tidy steel compartments she routinely wrote into her scripts, was a walk-in freezer.

Trace gave her a judicious look. ''Are you sure you're up to this?''

''I'm sure.''

Watching her wrap her arms around herself, Trace suspected that it was not the cold she'd find inside the freezer Mariah Swann was trying to ward off, but the iciness that had taken hold of her heart.

She took a deep breath. ''Let's get it over with.''

Mariah had witnessed death before. She had even, on one memorable occasion, in the name of research, sat in on an autopsy. She had to leave the room to throw up when the pathologist popped the top of the skull with a tool that resembled a crowbar, but so had the detective assigned to the case.

This time, however, she had a personal connection to the sheet-draped body stretched out on the wheeled gurney. This was no anonymous skid row slashing victim; this was her sister.

Trace drew back the cloth covering Laura Fletcher's face. He watched the myriad emotions flicker across Mariah's face: first shock, then startled recognition, followed an instant later by pain. Then, ultimately, love.

When she reached out to smooth away a few strands of auburn hair from her sister's cheek, he made a move to stop her from contaminating the evidence, then decided, what the hell.

"That's where she was shot?" she asked, observing the smudged wound at the left temple. Though she was almost as pale as her sister and her trembling hands betrayed her tumultuous emotions, Mariah's voice remained steady.

"There and in the chest."

"I want to see."

"I'm not sure—"

She raised her chin. "I said, I want to see what was done to my sister, Sheriff."

Their stares locked and held. Fuck it, Trace decided. He didn't feel up to arguing the point.

Hoping she wasn't going to faint on him again, he yanked back the sheet.

At the sight of Laura's nude body, Mariah flinched and unconsciously put a hand to her own breast as if she suddenly felt the impact of the gunshot herself.

Trace watched her thoughtful gaze move back and forth, from one wound to the other. The lady, he decided, was no cream puff.

"There's carbon stippling," she murmured, pointing out the unmistakable tattoo of powder soot imbedded in a ring around the head wound.

"Yeah. Interesting you should recognize that."

She heard the question in his voice. "In case J.D. didn't have time to fill you in, I'm a television scriptwriter. I specialize in crime shows." She tossed off the names of a few of the more successful ones and a made-for-television movie.

"I've caught a couple of those. The ones I saw were pretty accurate," he allowed.

"Thank you. I pride myself on my research." She looked up at him. The earlier anguish in her eyes had been replaced by an anger much chillier than the artificially cooled air in the freezer. "You know what this proves, don't you?"

He crossed his arms. "Why don't you tell me?"

"It proves I'm right. Alan shot Laura."

"I'm not sure I get your drift."

"I don't need a degree in forensic medicine to tell that my sister was shot from intermediate range."

"I'd say twelve to sixteen inches," Trace agreed.

"You said on the drive over here that you found her in the bedroom. In bed. Without any clothes on."

"Yeah." He was still bothered about that part. Why lay out all that dough for fancy nightgowns if you weren't going to wear them? "So?"

"So who else would Laura have allowed to get that close to her under those circumstances?"

"Why don't you tell me? I didn't know your sister."

"There are only two people most women will allow to see them stark naked. Their husbands and their gynecologists."

"What about lovers?"

"Husbands, lovers, same thing."

"Sometimes not."

Mariah shot him a sharp look. "What the hell does that mean?"

"It means that a woman's husband and her lover are not necessarily always the same person."

"Are you accusing my sister of having an affair?"

He thought of the ribbon-bound letters and shrugged. "At this point I'm not ready to accuse anyone of anything."

"She was not having an affair."

"Whatever you say. Are you finished looking?"

Her mind reeling with what the sheriff had just implied, Mariah dragged her gaze back to Laura's body, looking at it so intently Trace thought she might be memorizing her sister's features. She was.

"Yes." She bit her lip as he drew the sheet back over the lifeless form.

Her emotions in a turmoil, Mariah latched on to the one thing she could handle right now. It was up to Mariah to make certain Laura's killer did not get away.

"It was Alan," she insisted.

"Maybe." He shrugged. "Maybe not."

Frustrated, Mariah tried another tact. "Did you find the weapon in the house?"

"Sorry. But I'm not at liberty to discuss the investigation."

"Not even with the victim's next of kin?"

"No offense intended, Ms. Swann, but technically the senator's the next of kin."

Mariah's response to that was an earthy, pungent curse.

Trace turned off the lights. They were walking back down the dingy hallway when Mariah suddenly said, "Could you tell me where the rest rooms are?"

Her face had turned the color of the puke green walls. "Right around the corner. First door to the left."

She was gone before he could finish his instructions.

After throwing up, Mariah splashed her face with cold water, then swirled more water that carried the scent and flavor of chlorine around in her mouth. She dug through her purse and located a lint-covered peppermint Life Saver, which she popped into her mouth. Then, taking a deep breath, she rejoined Trace, who was waiting exactly where she'd left him.

"You okay?" His gaze briefly swept over her too pale face.

"Fine. Thanks," Mariah lied.

Although the basement was a great deal warmer than the autopsy room, she still felt chilled all the way to the bone. She felt, Mariah thought bleakly, as cold as Laura.

His sharp eyes caught the slight shiver she tried to conceal. "My office is upstairs. How about I buy you a cup of coffee? Or tea," he amended, thinking about her dash to the toilet.

The way her nerves were jangling, the one thing Mariah didn't need was any caffeine. But she'd try anything to warm up. "Tea always makes me feel like a kid with flu. But I could use some coffee, thank you."

His office, tucked away in a corner on the third floor, was shabby, but neat. Two chairs, covered in an uninspiring mud-hued Herculon dating back to the earth tones of the 1970s, sat in front of a weathered pine desk.

A law enforcement recruiting poster featured a scrubbed and polished young man in a starched khaki uniform standing beside a patrol car.

A second poster advertised the Silent Witness program, while another more colorful one featured McGruff, the crime dog, dressed like Sherlock Holmes and advising citizens to Take A Bite Out Of Crime. Taped to the beige wall beside the poster were crayon drawings from a class of third graders, thanking the sheriff for a tour of the jail.

On the opposite wall were FBI posters of most wanted felons who looked as if they'd come straight from central casting: a long-haired, tattooed biker, a wild-eyed Charles Manson lookalike and a sullen woman with a frizzy blond perm and four-inch long black roots who looked like a poster girl for sexually transmitted diseases.

"Nice photo collection," she murmured. "And so much more original than the usual candid vacation snapshots of the wife and kids."

"I don't have a wife. Or kids." He gave the wanted posters a cursory study. "And sometimes, as clichéd as it might seem, the bad guys really do look like criminals."

"But not all the time," she noted significantly.

"No." Trace frowned as he thought of the mild-mannered sixth grade science teacher and Boy Scout leader who'd strangled, then methodically dismembered five hookers before he and Danny had finally caught up with him. "Not all the time."

He gestured toward one of the chairs. "Have a seat. Nobody's made coffee this morning, so I'll have to get some from the machine down the hall. How do you take it?"

"With cream. Two sugars."

He reached into a top drawer, grabbed a handful of change and left the office.

Drained, Mariah sank down onto the seat he'd indicated. The wood-framed window offered an appealing view of the town square across the street.

She watched as a young man threw a Frisbee to a remarkably talented springer spaniel who, from what she could tell, never missed. She envied both man and dog. They were playing on the fragrant green grass in the bright morning sunshine, oblivious to the horrors of the world around them.

Had it only been yesterday that she'd been the same way? Until this morning, murder had always been an intriguing challenge. Fortunately, enough people shared her fascination with violent, unpredictable crime to have made her a very wealthy woman.

Although she made her living thinking up innovative ways to kill people in the crime dramas she was best known for, her stories had always been born in the fertile ground of her imagination. She would painstakingly create her characters, weaving in enough sympathetic traits to win the audience's empathy, then murder the victims in ways that occasionally inspired letter-writing campaigns to the networks and advertisers from religious and moral watchdog groups.

The complaints never disturbed her. In Mariah's world,

any publicity you didn't have to pay for was good publicity.

And when the script was completed, she moved on to the next story, the next murder, never giving those deceased characters another thought. They weren't real, after all.

But, dammit, Laura was.

Mariah lit another cigarette to get the smell of the autopsy room out of her nostrils.

"It'll probably taste like toxic waste," Trace warned when he returned to the office. "And the cream is that nondairy stuff. But it's hot." He put a brown-and-white cardboard cup down in front of Mariah, then went around the desk, pulled an ashtray from one of the drawers and handed it to her.

"Thanks." She took a sip of the coffee, found it as bad as he'd predicted, but drank it anyway, willing the warmth to replace the ice in her bloodstream. "May I ask you a question?"

The leather chair behind the desk creaked as he leaned back in it. "Shoot."

"Are you religious?"

"Not particularly." Trace grimaced as he took a taste of his own black coffee. But like her, did not put it down. Unlike her, he needed the caffeine.

"Do you believe in God?"

He stared off into the middle distance as he considered that. His eyes were the color of steel, set deep in his unshaven, hollow-cheeked face. "I suppose I believe in what AA would call a higher power. Why?"

"I didn't think I did. Not anymore, anyway." She drew in on the cigarette, thinking that the fiery hell she'd been taught to fear during her catechism days was too good for the man who'd murdered Laura. "But I realized, down in that room, that I'm not nearly the agnostic I thought I was."

She took another drink as she tried to put what she was feeling into words. "It's not that I want to believe Laura's in some mythical wooded glen like all those near-death experiences people describe, visiting with all our dearly departed relatives, listening to some heavenly choir," she stressed. "It's just that what's down in that room—her body—isn't her."

She shook her head in mute frustration. "Does that make any sense?"

Trace put his cup on the desk and locked his hands behind his head as he remembered an instance, during his days as a rookie cop, when he'd gotten into a similar theological discussion with a sergeant who, whenever he looked at all those bodies in the morgue, saw nothing but dead meat.

At the time Trace had disagreed. He still did.

"You look at the faces," he said quietly. "And they're empty."

"Exactly. Everything that made Laura who she was, everything that made her special is gone," she stressed. "So where did it go? It couldn't just disappear into thin air."

"All souls go to heaven?" Trace asked.

Thinking that he was being condescending, she bristled. "Why not?"

She'd expected a smirk. Instead he smiled and she was surprised to note that it held considerable charm. "Sounds good to me."

Mariah was in no mood to be charmed by some small-town, black Irish cop. Even if his firmly cut lips did remind her of a Celtic poet.

"Callahan," she murmured, "wasn't that Dirty Harry's last name?"

He didn't directly answer her question. "You know," he mused out loud, "sometimes I think I should have become a chiropractor."

"A chiropractor?"

"Or a dentist. Going through life as a cop with the name of Callahan isn't always easy." This time the smile reached his weary eyes, turning them a gleaming pewter.

Even as Mariah found herself momentarily intrigued by their warmth, she shook off the feeling. "So, when are you going to question Alan?"

"As soon as he's out of surgery."

"Too bad you can't do it while he's still under the sodium Pentothal."

"Are you insinuating that the senator is a liar?"

"He's a politician, isn't he? It comes with the territory." Her gaze turned serious. "You realize, of course, that this is going to turn out to be a media circus."

"The thought had occurred to me."

"Are you also aware that Alan Fletcher has a great many powerful friends? Not only here in Arizona, but in the rest of the country as well?"

"You don't get to be chairman of the Armed Services Committee without some powerful friends."

His easy drawl irritated her. Her gaze met his and held. "I just thought I should warn you."

"Consider me warned." His gray eyes darkened, but his tone remained mild. Only a well-honed ear could have detected the steel in it.

Mariah swallowed the rest of the thick brown brew and stood up. "Well, thanks for the coffee, Sheriff. I'd better check into the lodge. I've got a lot to do."

"Before you go, I need to ask you a couple of questions. About your sister."

She sat back down. "All right."

"Were you close?"

"When we were kids, we were as close as two people can be."

"And later?"

Mariah sighed. "Not as close as I would have liked."

She'd never forget the knock-down-drag-out fight between them on her last night in Arizona. Laura had only been attempting to soothe the always turbulent waters between father and daughter when Matthew Swann had discovered her intention to become an actress, like her mother.

But at the time, Mariah had viewed Laura as a traitor. Embarrassed, angry and young, Mariah had struck out with her most powerful weapon—words. She'd flung hurtful accusations like bullets, claiming Laura had abandoned her the same way she'd abandoned Clint Garvey on their wedding night.

Knowing that her sister had never gotten over the painful events of that disastrous night, Mariah had gone so far as to suggest that Laura would never marry any man because of her unhealthy relationship with her own father.

The word *incest* was never spoken, but the unpalatable suggestion had hovered over the room like a deadly cloud.

When an apoplectic Matthew had demanded Mariah apologize, she'd refused. It was the last time she was to see her sister for a very long time.

Then, two years ago, during a trip to California, Laura had surprised her by showing up on the set of a made-for-television movie. Their first meeting had been cautious. Their stilted conversation had reminded Mariah of two boxers, circling the ring, feeling each other out in the early rounds.

Gradually, emotional walls began to go down. Enough so that Mariah believed that while they'd probably never regain the relationship they'd once shared, perhaps, if they both continued to try, they'd be able to create something equally satisfying.

She began turning the empty cup around in her hands as she considered bleakly how she'd thought they would have time to patch things up.

"Did she happen to discuss her marriage with you?"

"Only in passing."

"Did you get the impression her marriage was a happy one?"

"How could it be? Considering who her husband was."

"That sounds a lot like conjecture."

Mariah swore. "All right, I'll admit to being prejudiced. But that doesn't mean the man isn't a rat. And although Laura never got into specifics, whenever the conversation would drift Alan's way, I received the definite impression that she was far from happy. Which wasn't that surprising, considering all the rumors about his infidelity."

"Rumors aren't necessarily fact."

"True. But believe me, Sheriff, in Alan's case, they were more than true. In fact, the worm even hit on me once. During one of his political fund-raising trips to California."

She scowled. "He actually had the gall to invite me up to his hotel suite. Allegedly to discuss my relationship with Laura, but since his hand was on my knee at the time, I had the impression that his wife wasn't uppermost in his mind."

The senator was either incredibly nervy. Or stupid. "You didn't take him up on his offer." It was not a question.

"I assured him that if he ever touched me again, he'd learn exactly how a bull feels when a cowboy with a pair of nutcutters turns him into a steer."

Trace inwardly flinched. "Did you tell your sister about the incident?"

"Of course not. I figured she had to know what kind of man she'd married. Why should I make her feel worse?"

"Did she ever mention another man?"

There it was again. That not very subtle accusation. She lifted her chin and met his veiled gaze straight on. "My sister would not sleep around."

"You're sure of that."

"Absolutely."

"Would you happen to know if she had a friend whose name began with the initial *C?*"

C? Clint Garvey immediately came to mind. Deciding that Laura's brief, disastrous elopement was none of this man's business, Mariah said, "No."

From the way she'd begun tearing that cup into little pieces, Trace knew she was lying. He'd bet the Suburban, along with a year's pay on it.

"Your sister and her husband have been married a long time not to have children."

She arched a brow. "I believe that's what they call a leading question, Sheriff."

"I suppose it is," Trace said agreeably.

"Not that I can see what bearing it would possibly have on this case, Laura always wanted a large family. But things didn't work out."

Trace decided against mentioning the home pregnancy test the evidence unit had found in the bathroom wastebasket. "One more question."

Something new had crept into his voice. Something that had her instantly on alert. "All right."

"Your earlier comment about all the senator's powerful friends—" he braced his elbows on the scarred wooden arms of the chair, linked his fingers together and eyed her over the tent of his hands "—were you concerned about my competence to investigate this case?

"Or were you worried that when push came to shove, I'd turn out to be just one of those stereotypical, corruptible rube cops you write into your television programs?"

Mariah had the grace to flush. A band of tension tightened at the back of her neck. But she held her ground.

"I'm not sure."

The answer wasn't the one Trace would have preferred to hear. But he couldn't help respecting her honesty. He pushed himself out of the chair. "When you decide, let me know."

"I'll do that." Mariah stood up as well and tossed the tattered pieces of cardboard into the metal wastepaper basket. "Are you finished questioning me?"

"For now. I'll drive you to the lodge. When J.D. arrives with your Jeep, I'll have him drop it off there."

"I'd appreciate that."

Silence settled over them on the short drive. Suddenly exhausted and emotionally drained, she leaned her head against the passenger window.

When he pulled up in front of the lodge office, she unfastened her seat belt and opened the door. "Thanks for the ride."

"No problem." She was already on the curb. "Oh, one more thing, Ms. Swann."

Mariah glanced back over her shoulder and found herself staring into a rigid, determined face that was a dead ringer for Dirty Harry. His heavily lidded eyes were hard gray stones, his poet's mouth was pulled into a grim line.

"Yes?" Her voice was neither as strong or self-assured as she would have liked.

"You don't have to worry about me bowing to political pressure." Deep hash marks like goal posts slashed their way between his dark brows. "Because if the senator does turn out to be the one who killed your sister, I will personally nail his balls to the jailhouse door."

"I'm glad to hear that." Mariah refused to flinch at the crude cop language she suspected he'd deliberately chosen to shock her. "And when you do," she shot back, "I want to be the one swinging the hammer."

With a toss of her head, she turned on her heel and marched away.

Trace returned to the Fletcher ranch, where the evidence team was methodically continuing their investigation.

The crew would never be given a *Good Housekeeping* award for neatness. Papers and other items were strewn throughout the house, fingerprint powder clung to furniture and doorframes.

He climbed the stairs to the bedroom, careful not to touch the bannister. The room, which had been messy earlier, now looked as if a hurricane had blown through it.

He bent down, picked up the towel he'd noticed on the floor the first time he'd been in the room, and lifted it to his nose. An exotic oriental scent rose from the still damp terry cloth.

"Shalimar perfume," a female voice offered behind him. Trace turned around and saw Jessica Ingersoll, Mogollon County Attorney standing in the doorway. She looked cool, crisp and professional in a white linen suit.

"There were bottles of bath oil and cologne in the bathroom," she informed him. "Along with some talc. It appears to have been the late lady's signature scent."

He bagged the towel. Then, using the edge of his hands, he carefully unscrewed the top of a turquoise jar atop the dresser. The scent of the fragrant pink cream matched that on the towel.

"Does that mean it's the only one she wore?"

"Very good, Callahan," she said with a nod. Her hair, the tawny hue of autumn leaves, had been pulled back with a gold filigree clasp at the nape of her long, slender neck. More gold gleamed warmly at her earlobes and wrists.

A Philadelphia-born graduate of University of Pennsylvania and Harvard Law, Jessica Ingersoll was thirty years old and as smart as a whip. She was also a tigress in bed. Their affair had begun his first week in town. It had been as hot as it had been brief and when it was over they'd remained friends.

She glanced around the room with disdain. "Christ. It's a good thing Fletcher's going to be able to afford an army of maids when he gets out of the hospital. This place is a pigsty."

"It wasn't all that neat before the ETU guys got here."

"So they tell me. So, what do you think we're looking at? A B&E gone bad?"

"Perhaps." He squatted down and began going through Laura Fletcher's underwear again, lifting each piece to his nose. "Perhaps not."

"Gracious, Callahan," she drawled on the unmistakable Main Line accent that always reminded him of Katharine Hepburn in *Philadelphia Story,* "if I'd known you were so kinky, I wouldn't have let you get away."

"Give me a break. I'm looking for the nightgown the victim wore to bed."

She arched a brow. "I was told she was nude."

"She was when we found her. But I've got a hunch.... Jackpot." He held the seafoam gown out to her.

"Nice," she murmured, running her fingers over the sheer lace insert. "But not my size. In case you've forgotten, sweetheart, hidden beneath my staid, Philadelphia lawyer suits are breasts Miss Universe would kill for."

"And she's modest, too," he muttered, feeling that familiar tightening in his groin. "Would you quit trying to turn me on for old time's sake and just smell the damn thing?"

"Kinky," Jessica repeated, even as she did as instructed. "Shalimar," she murmured. She rewarded him with another smile. "I knew you had a clever head on those wide, manly shoulders."

He stuffed the silk nightgown into an evidence bag. "The question is, why did she take it off?"

"Why, Callahan," the attorney said with mock shock, "surely it hasn't been that long since you've bedded a woman. Why the hell do you think she took it off?"

Although he wasn't about to admit it, it had been a long time since he'd gotten laid. Too long, if the way just looking at Mariah Swann's jean-clad ass sashaying across the parking lot had made him hot was any indication.

Remembering the raunchy sex he and Jessica had shared, he considered that perhaps there might be some advantages to this case, after all. While what he and the winsome prosecutor had was admittedly a long way from love, there'd also been a lot more involved than casual fucking.

What it had been, Trace decided, was affectionate lust.

"My guess would be that she wasn't alone all night."

"And I'd guess that you're right." She shook her head with regret as she took in the bloodstained mattress. "You know, as good as sex can be, it sure as hell isn't worth dying for."

"Amen." He pulled a ballpoint pen from his pocket and tagged the evidence.

Smiling, she patted his cheek. "But if any man could make the choice a close one, Sheriff, it'd definitely be you."

The contrast between her cool looks and uninhibited attitude had been one of the things that had attracted Trace to Jessica Ingersoll in the first place. "Thanks. I think."

"Any time." Her voice was throaty and every bit as seductive as the rest of her. "And I mean that literally."

For the first time since Cora Mae had called him with the one-eighty-seven code, Trace found something to laugh about, just as she'd intended. Relaxing slightly, he shared what he'd learned so far.

"I think I might have an idea who your writer is," she said when he got to the letters. "You may want to go talk to Clint Garvey."

The name rang a bell. Trace knew Garvey to be the Fletchers' nearest neighbor.

"The woman who does my hair used to have a thing going with Garvey," Jessica elaborated. "Last time I was in, a couple of weeks ago, she was waving the scissors around like she wished she could be hacking away at something else besides my hair, if you know what I mean."

"I think I have the picture. So she was mad at Garvey?"

"Livid. But actually, now that I think about it, she seemed angrier at your victim. Kept muttering about the lady already having one man and how she had no right taking someone else's."

"Want to give me her name?"

"Not really. Since she's the only decent hairdresser I've managed to find in this part of the state and if she ends up in the state pen for murder I'm going to be really pissed." She scowled. "It's Patti. With an *i.* Patti Greene. She runs The Shear Delight on Pinewood Drive."

Trace wrote the name in his notebook.

"There's something else," she said. "Patti said something about telling Matthew Swann about his daughter's affair."

"Not the husband?"

"If she had that in mind, she didn't mention it. Apparently Swann broke the couple up once before. Patti was hoping he'd have the clout to do it again."

Trace thought about the message left on the phone recorder and decided that he had a pretty good idea exactly what Swann had been so angry about. He also thought about the fact that Cora Mae still hadn't managed to track the rancher down in Santa Fe.

"You know," Jessica said thoughtfully, "this is going to generate a lot of heat. We'd better start the paperwork for obtaining a search warrant."

Trace had already decided to do just that. "Worried the senator might withdraw permission?"

"Cases like this, the killer is usually a family member." She told Trace nothing he didn't already know. "If Fletcher is involved, and he gets spooked, he could do just that."

"Wouldn't want to step on any murderer's constitutional rights," Trace agreed dryly.

She laughed. "Spoken like a true cop. That's the difference between you and me, Callahan. All you have to do is put on your blue body stocking with the big red *S* sewn on the front of it, outrun a few locomotives while dodging speeding bullets and apprehend the bad guys.

"While I, on the other hand, have to make certain they make it through the convoluted maze of our judicial system without escaping through some legal loophole."

He thought of Laura Swann lying all alone in the morgue and vowed that would not happen.

"I think I'll stop by the Garvey place on the way back to town," Trace said. "And I'm calling a press conference for noon. Doc Potter should be done with the autopsy by then and we'll know more."

"You realize there's a good chance most of the national media won't be able to make it here by then?"

"One can only hope."

"You're incorrigible, Callahan." She shook her head

and gave him a saucy grin. "That's probably why I like you. Along with the fact that you're not bad in bed."

There were a lot of reasons Trace liked her. And for more than terrific sex.

"I assume you want to be there?"

"You ever known a politician who wouldn't jump stark naked through flaming hoops at a chance for national publicity? I'll be there."

Jessica Ingersoll might be a politician, Trace thought. But she was also, as they would have said in the Dallas PD locker room, "a stand-up guy."

"Stop by my office about eleven-thirty," he suggested. "The doc should be done by then."

She stepped over the lingerie and walked over to the bed. "It's a date."

"Well, I've got an autopsy to attend. And some paperwork to get started on. Later."

"Later." She was frowning at the bloodstained headboard and didn't bother to look up at him.

Trace was unlocking the Suburban when a voice called out to him. "Hey, Callahan!"

He looked up and saw Jessica leaning out the bedroom window. "Yeah?"

"You are going to shower and shave and change your clothes before the press conference, aren't you?"

"Sure," he said, not wanting to admit he'd been too busy to give any thought to the matter.

"Good. Because you look like roadkill." She wiggled her perfect patrician nose. "And no offense, Sheriff, but you kinda smell like one, too."

He waved off her accusation, but as he drove back to town, he lifted his arm and sniffed.

As usual, she was right.

Chapter Five

The Lakeside Lodge had begun its existence as the family home of a millionaire lumber baron. Built at the turn of the century, the stately mansion could have inspired, in its day, a year's worth of sermons on conspicuous consumption. It had also been a startling contrast to the sawmills and saloons of the lusty, booming community of Whiskey River.

The mansion had changed hands several times, eventually falling into disrepair. Five years ago it had been lovingly restored by its current owners, who'd decorated it with an eclectic, but attractive mix of antique and western furniture, and established it as a landmark lodge and conference center.

As a girl, Mariah, along with the rest of Whiskey River's kids, had prowled the decaying, boarded-up mansion, scaring themselves silly telling ghost stories they swore were true.

Now, while she admired the transformation, the golden oak columns and paneling of the lobby—which had been the original entry hall—represented yet another sign of change in a hometown she'd always believed to have been frozen in time.

Although the desk clerk informed Mariah there were no rooms—the lodge was booked months in advance for the holiday, the young man sniffed—all she had to do was mention the Swann name and *presto,* a suite just happened to open up.

"You're right down the hall from Ms. Martin," the clerk volunteered as he handed Mariah the coded card.

"Ms. Martin?"

"The senator's aide. She checked in late last night."

"Was she alone?"

"Actually—" he leaned over the counter "—the senator was with her when she arrived. He also went upstairs with her." He'd lowered his voice, but Mariah couldn't miss the implication in his tone. The man liked to gossip. Terrific.

"Tell me, Kevin," she said, reading his name tag and smiling conspiratorially as she leaned toward him, "would you happen to know how long the senator was upstairs with Ms. Martin?"

"Well." He raked a hand through his hair and looked around, as if to ensure the manager wasn't hovering anywhere nearby to observe his indiscretion. "Although I'm not one to spread gossip...."

After having successfully pumped the desk clerk, Mariah was headed across the plant-filled lobby when she heard a voice call out her name. She turned and saw a vaguely familiar face headed toward her.

"I thought that was you," the woman exclaimed with a warm, welcoming smile. She embraced Mariah with an enthusiastic air kiss on both cheeks. "Lord, it's been absolutely ages!"

"Ages," Mariah agreed. She managed a wan smile. "How are you, Freddi? You're certainly looking well."

That was an understatement. Fredericka Palmer definitely did not look like a woman who'd spent her entire life in a small mountain town. Her jet hair curved stylishly beneath her chin in a sleek smooth line as shiny as a raven's wings. Mariah could not see a single strand out of place.

Her makeup, like her hair, was flawless. Her turquoise silk blouse, short black leather skirt and buttery soft Italian high heels suggested Neiman Marcus chic.

"Aren't you sweet." Fredericka's smile was as bright as the diamonds adorning her earlobes. "Of course I'm just a small-town Realtor. I'll never be a glamorous television star like you were." She visibly preened as her dark eyes took a quick, judicial tour of Mariah's own disheveled state. "But all a girl can do is try her best, right?"

"Right." Mariah was reminded of the days when Fredericka Palmer had been elected homecoming queen. She hadn't changed in all these intervening years. All that was missing, Mariah considered, was the rhinestone tiara.

For not the first time, Mariah wondered what it was that Fredericka and Laura could have in common to have allowed them to stay friends since kindergarten days. It must simply be a case of opposites attracting.

As for being a small-town Realtor, Mariah knew from Laura that Fredericka had made a fortune subdividing ranch and timber land into recreational developments. Laura had also told her that in addition to the family ranch, the thrice divorced and recently widowed Freddi owned a sprawling home situated on the ninth hole of a prestigious Scottsdale golf course, a beach house in La Jolla and a penthouse apartment on Chicago's Gold Coast.

"Are you staying here?" Fredericka asked.

"For now."

"I'd have thought you might stay at the ranch." Her

voice went up on the end of the comment, turning it into a question.

Mariah shrugged. "The senator and I tend to get on each other's nerves."

"You know," Fredericka lowered her voice as she leaned toward Mariah, "you could have bowled me over with a feather when you called my office out of the blue that way the other day."

After the events of the past few hours, Mariah had completely forgotten about that phone call. "I'm afraid I'm going to have to postpone our meeting."

"Oh?" An ebony brow climbed a forehead free of worry lines or wrinkles. "Postpone? Or cancel?"

"I don't know." At the time, the impulse to return to Whiskey River had seemed like a good idea. Now, with Laura gone, Mariah realized that there was no longer anything—or anyone—to come home to.

Laura.

Pain clawed at Mariah's heart. She debated breaking the news to Freddi, then decided she wasn't up to answering the inevitable questions. "I'll call you," she hedged.

"I'll be looking forward to your call." Freddi's eyes narrowed as if a thought had suddenly occurred to her. "Did you tell Laura you were returning to Whiskey River?"

The question caused another of those painful little heart clenches. "Yes." It was not exactly a lie. She had, after all, left the message on the recorder. "Why?"

"I spoke with her recently and she didn't mention you. So, naturally I didn't mention our appointment. Since you said you wanted to keep it confidential."

"That was very considerate of you," Mariah allowed.

"Well, I certainly wouldn't want to cause any more trouble between you and your sister. After all that's happened in the past."

Mariah murmured something vague that could have been taken as agreement.

Fredericka glanced down at her trendy black Movado museum watch. "Well, as much as I'd love to stay and chat, I have to dash. The Cow Belles are sponsoring the Fourth of July barbecue, as always, and there's still tons of last minute detail work to do.

"For instance, the bunting for the grandstand," she elaborated on a huff of frustrated breath. "You'd think finding red, white, and blue crepe paper, especially this time of year would be easy, wouldn't you?"

Mariah found it uncomfortably surrealistic to be talking about crepe paper bunting while her sister's body was lying in a locker across town. "Well, now that you mention it—"

"But it isn't simple." Fredericka shook her head, sending her hair flying in a glossy dark arc. "Not at all. There's navy blue and royal blue, not to mention cobalt. And, Lord, I don't even want to get into the reds."

She expelled another dramatic breath through her pursed vermillion lips, then brightened. "Oh, well. I'm sure you have more important things to do than to listen to me going on about my petty problems."

"Actually—"

Mariah was cut off by another brief air kiss to the cheek. "I'm off to my meeting. Give my love to Laura and tell her that if she's not returning to Washington immediately after Alan's rally, I insist we get together for lunch next week.

"To tell you the truth," Freddi divulged, "I've been a little worried about your sister. Whenever she's come back to town these past months, she's seemed a bit distracted."

When Mariah didn't immediately answer, Fredericka shrugged her silk clad shoulders and said, "But knowing Laura, I'm sure whatever is bothering her will work out.

She's always been disgustingly capable. I swear, if she wasn't my very dearest friend I'd be pea green with envy."

The grandfather clock across the room tolled the hour on a musical peal of Westminster chimes.

"I really must run." Freddi waggled her manicured fingers and said, "'Bye, Mariah, dear. I'll look forward to your call."

Mariah felt her shoulders sag as she watched the chic Realtor dash back across the lobby, headed in the direction of the meeting rooms.

"You should have told her," she said out loud.

Reminding herself that Freddi had always been Laura's friend, not hers, Mariah took the old-fashioned gilt cage elevator to her suite on the third floor.

She had to call her mother. Mariah definitely didn't want Maggie to learn the tragic news from some reporter. But first she had something even more important to do.

As soon as she entered the spacious room loaded with what appeared to be genuine antique furnishings, she placed a call to the sheriff's office, gave her name and was frustrated to learn he wasn't there.

"Do you know when he'll be back?"

"Well, he's got a press conference scheduled at noon. So I guess he'll be back by then." The voice sounded young. And vaguely bored. Mariah heard the unmistakable snap of bubble gum.

"It's urgent that I speak with him."

"I can try to radio him and have him call you," the dispatcher said obligingly.

Mariah bit back her frustration and raked her hand through her hair. "I suppose that'll have to do."

"When I do track Trace down, want me to give him a message?"

Mariah's mind was still reeling from her earlier conversation with the desk clerk. "Tell him I have evidence that will prove who killed my sister."

Jessica had definitely called this one right. Trace leaned both hands against the porcelain rim of the bathroom sink, grimly studied his reflection in the mirror and decided that the hollow-eyed face looking back at him was not a pretty sight.

He looked like the head doorman at the Whiskey River drunk tank. He ran his tongue over his fuzzy teeth. Coffee and not enough sleep had left him feeling as if the Persian Gulf war had been fought inside his mouth.

After brushing, he gargled with cinnamon-flavored mouthwash. While waiting for the water to warm in the shower, he stripped, leaving his clothes in a heap on the floor.

When clouds of steam began fogging the glass door, he stepped into the stall, soaped down, shaved, then leaned his head against the brown-and-cream tiled wall. He thought back on the autopsy which had left him with more questions than answers and fell asleep. Standing up.

A sudden jolt of icy water woke him. Trace cursed, twisted the faucets shut, then shook himself off like a dog who'd just had a hose turned on him. Making a few half-hearted swipes at his wet body with a towel, he went into the bedroom and surveyed his closet.

The uniform he'd been given the first day on the job was still in its plastic dry cleaner's bag. Trace had never worn it, knowing that the khaki symbol of authority J.D. so obviously relished would make him feel like he was six years old again, playing cops and robbers on south Dallas's mean streets.

Back in his old neighborhood, there'd admittedly been a lot more kids who'd wanted to be the robbers. Trace decided things hadn't changed all that much. The only difference was that these days, instead of cap pistols, kids were packing real guns.

The blue suit he used to wear to testify in court hung in a similar plastic bag beside the uniform. Though it looked presentable on TV, it was definitely overkill for Whiskey River.

Opting for the middle ground, jeans and a sport coat, he'd just finished dressing when the phone rang. "Callahan."

"Hasn't your office gotten hold of you yet?"

Trace dragged a hand down his face. All he needed was an amateur sleuth trying to solve his crime. "Yes, Ms. Swann."

"You haven't called back."

"I've been a little busy. I spent the last two hours attending an autopsy." He did not mention stopping by the Garvey ranch and learning from a hired hand that the rancher had ridden off into the hills around dawn.

"What time did Alan say he arrived home?"

"Why?"

"Because Heather Martin checked into the Lakeside Lodge at ten o'clock last night." Her tone was smug.

He rubbed his hands over his face again. "Okay. I'll bite." His words were muffled by his palms. "Who's Heather Martin?"

"His so-called chief of staff. Although *mistress* is probably a better job description. Room service sent up a bottle of Chivas and two glasses at ten-oh-five. Alan was seen leaving the lodge at midnight. So what time did he tell you he got to the ranch?"

"I can't answer that. Not while—"

"There's an ongoing investigation," she finished up for him. "Shit. I've probably written that line myself a hundred times."

"Then you should know it by heart."

"Are you always this sarcastic, Sheriff? Or do I just bring out the worst in you?"

He silently admitted he wasn't going to win the Mr. Congeniality award. But the clock was ticking down and he still had to get to the hospital in Payson and interview Fletcher again before the press conference. And then there was the scorned beautician with the scissors.

"Neither. Is there a third choice?"

Her curse was short and imaginative. He wondered if she could get away with using it in her TV shows.

"Look, I'll bet my last Emmy that Alan's sleeping with his assistant. That gives you the motive."

"Motive's for trial lawyers, crime novelists and you Hollywood writers. To tell you the truth, Ms. Swann, in real life cops don't spend a helluva lot of time looking for motive."

"You don't?"

Trace could tell he'd momentarily sidetracked her. "Sometimes the motive behind a crime can be interesting. Sometimes it's even helpful. But it's usually beside the point.

"For future reference, forget the *why*. Worry about finding out the *how* and nine times out of ten it'll give you the *who*."

From the silence on the other end of the line, Trace suspected she was thinking that over. He was right.

"That's very interesting." Another little silence. He strapped on his watch and decided if he didn't wind this up soon, he was never going to make his appointment with Jessica.

"I'm glad you think so. Now, if you don't mind—"

"So, what I have to do is figure out *how* Alan killed Laura."

"What you have to do is be a good girl and let me do my job," he corrected.

"In the first place, I'm no longer a girl, Sheriff. And in the second place, even when I was, I was never, ever good. Ask anyone in Whiskey River." Despite the seriousness of the circumstances, he thought he detected a bit of wry humor in her tone. "I'll get back to you."

"I'll be waiting with bated breath." He wasn't usually rude, although he could admittedly be so when it suited him. Fatigue had made him speak his mind and now that he had, Trace was considering whether or not he should apologize when her next statement stopped his thoughts dead in their tracks.

"You're a sarcastic son of a bitch, Callahan. But since my sources in Dallas tell me you were one of the best—in your day—I'll forgive you."

"You had me checked out?" Surprise and irritation made him ignore the crack about *in his day.*

"Of course. I told you, I pride myself on my research. I'll be watching your press conference on the tube." She hung up.

As he drove to Payson for a little heart-to-heart with the senator, Trace considered that Mariah Swann was turning out to be a royal pain in the ass.

At the same time, in his mind's eye he could see her struggling to be brave when she'd viewed her sister's body. He remembered the infinite tenderness with which she'd brushed away her sister's hair from her face. He thought about how she'd thrown up afterward.

And now he had the discomfiting feeling that she had no intention of leaving this investigation—or him alone—until she'd achieved justice for Laura.

That she was stubborn was obvious. She was also intelligent. And, although he'd tried like hell not to notice, she was also more than a little sexually appealing. There had been a couple of suspended moments, back in his office, when he'd felt the age-old stir inside him—man for woman.

When his mutinous mind conjured up, without difficulty, her springtime scent, her expressive turquoise eyes, her full ripe lips, Trace cursed. He couldn't discern all the emotions working through him, but he knew damn well that they weren't comfortable.

J.D. had been right. Mariah Swann was definitely trouble.

After breezing through the brief surgery, Alan Fletcher had been wheeled into a private room. Ben Loftin had arrived, as ordered, crowding his considerable bulk into a molded vinyl chair outside the senator's hospital room door. He was eating a Granny Smith apple while pondering the gynecological mysteries in this month's issue of *Playboy.*

"How's the patient doing?" Trace asked.

"Bright-eyed and bushy-tailed." As Loftin turned the magazine sideways and nodded his approval of the centerfold, Trace wasn't certain whether he was referring to Fletcher or the voluptuous blonde clad in red hooker high heels and a fire helmet.

"Did the doctor say what he was shot with?"

"Yeah," the deputy managed around a huge bite of apple. Most of his breakfast appeared to have spilled onto his tie and rumpled shirtfront. "It was a .25."

"The autopsy showed the wife was shot twice with a .38." Which, Trace supposed, added credence to the senator's allegation that there were two men in the house.

Loftin's adam's apple bobbed as he swallowed. "Too bad for the lady the guy with the peashooter wasn't the one who went upstairs."

"Isn't it?" Trace agreed dryly.

He entered the hospital room and found Fletcher sitting up in bed with an IV attached to his right arm. An attractive brunette Trace guessed to be in her late twenties was sitting in a chair beside the bed. She was wearing a V-necked white silk blouse, a short navy skirt and navy and white spectator pumps.

Her hand was currently enclosed in the senator's. He didn't need a scorecard to figure out that this was the chief of staff with a liking for expensive Scotch.

Trace doffed his hat. "Good morning, Senator."

"Good morning." The senator flashed the standard politician's smile—quick, seemingly sincere and disarming as hell. He reminded Trace of Redford, back in his Sundance Kid days, before the unrelenting western sun had turned the actor's face to spotted boot leather.

"Oh. You're the sheriff." The smile faded as quickly as it had appeared.

Trace nodded. "You've got a good memory."

"Occupational necessity. I never forget a face. Or a name." This time the smile, which Trace realized was automatic, died half born. "How is Laura? I've asked the nurses, but they refuse to tell me a thing."

Trace glanced over at the woman. "Excuse me, but—"

"Anything you have to say to me, you can say in front of Heather," Alan said.

The woman stood and extended her hand. "Heather Martin," she said. Her light brown eyes were friendly and intelligent. "I'm the senator's chief of staff."

"Trace Callahan." He shook the hand the senator had been holding.

She quirked the inevitable brow upon hearing his name, but did not comment. "How is Laura?" she repeated Alan Fletcher's question. "We've been so horribly worried."

The senator was looking up at him expectantly. Right in the eye. Trace had always figured any guy who wouldn't maintain eye contact had to be guilty of something.

Of course, he allowed, sometimes it went the other way. The science teacher-serial killer had maintained dynamite eye contact even while insisting he knew nothing about the various body parts soaking in a barrel of hydrochloric acid in his basement.

"I'm afraid I have bad news, Senator." After years of practice, he'd come to the conclusion that there was no easy way to say this. "Your wife is dead."

Alan Fletcher blanched. "Dead?"

"She died at the scene. There was nothing anyone could do."

"Dead?" the senator repeated blankly. Alan looked up at Heather, who'd gone pretty pale herself.

"Oh, my God!" He began to tremble.

"I understand that this is difficult for you," Trace began slowly. Carefully.

"Difficult doesn't begin to describe this outrage. It's horrendous!" The senator took the tissue Heather was offering and blew his nose. "When may I see my wife?"

"Her body's going to be released to the funeral home later this afternoon."

"Her body." He shuddered. "God, that sounds so final."

"I was hoping you might remember something else about the intruders." Trace pulled his notebook from his jacket pocket.

The tanned brow furrowed. "I'm afraid no more than I've already told you. It was all so sudden, and I'd been sleeping."

"No distinguishing marks? Tattoos, moles, warts? Anything like that?"

Alan shook his head. "I don't think so."

"How about what they were wearing?"

The senator shook his head again. "I'm sorry."

So much for the dynamite memory. Too bad the gunmen hadn't offered to contribute to the senator's presidential campaign. Trace bet the senator's memory would have instantly improved.

"Well, if you think of anything, let me know."

"Of course."

"In the meantime, my deputy will bring by some mug books."

"Do you think my wife's killers will be in there?"

"We can always hope. You may see something that strikes a chord."

"I'll try my best."

"I know you will, Senator. In the meantime, are you acquainted with Clint Garvey?"

"Acquainted?" Alan's expression and his tone were calm, although slightly puzzled. "Of course. He's a neighbor."

"Would you call him a friend?"

"Not really. The man's a loner. I doubt if I've run into him more than two or three times."

Trace made a notation. Then paused again. "There's no tactful way I can ask this. Do you happen to know if your wife had been unfaithful?"

"No." Alan's voice regained its earlier strength. His gaze did not waver. "My wife was a saint. Ask anyone who knew her. Why, the work she did arranging medical care for impoverished children of the Third World received U.N. recognition."

"Laura was dedicated to the poor," Heather agreed. Her voice cracked a little. Her whiskey-colored eyes misted.

"Those children were her life," Alan said.

"Speaking of children—" Trace took his time, flipping through the pages of the notebook "—did you know your wife was pregnant, Senator?"

"Pregnant?" Surprise flashed across Alan Fletcher's handsome face. "No."

He lowered his gaze. His hands clutched at the starched white sheets. When he lifted his eyes again, Trace could read doubts in those deep blue depths. "Are you sure?"

"We found a home pregnancy test in the bathroom wastebasket. The autopsy revealed your wife was approximately eight weeks pregnant."

"Eight weeks," Fletcher echoed.

"Approximately."

The senator leaned his head back against the pillow and closed his eyes. Heather Martin walked over to the window and studied the parking lot with unwavering interest.

Silence settled over the hospital room.

Trace let it linger.

Watching Heather he said, "According to my notes—" he was reading from the notebook again "—you arrived in Whiskey River around midnight."

The senator coughed, then grimaced, as if in pain. "Did I say that?"

"Yes, sir. When the paramedics were working on you at the house."

"Ah." The reassuring smile returned, looking as out of place as it had earlier. "That probably explains it. I'd been shot, I was in terrible pain, I was frantic about Laura. I guess I wasn't thinking straight.

"The fact of the matter is, after driving up from Phoenix, I reached Whiskey River sometime between ten and eleven. I returned home to the house around midnight."

"I see." Trace jotted the correction down. "Mind telling me what you were doing between ten and midnight?"

"The senator was with me," Heather offered quickly. A bit too quickly, Trace thought. "We were working on his speech."

"I'm giving a speech on law and order at the Fourth

of July rally,'' the senator explained. ''Heather was helping me fine-tune it. We're announcing my run for the presidency here in Whiskey River before making a fund-raising swing through the southwest.'' He glanced up at his chief of staff. ''I suppose we'll have to make some changes to include this horrible thing that has happened to Laura.''

''Don't worry,'' she assured him. ''I'll take care of it.''

Alan Fletcher was looking off into some middle distance. ''I'll also need to come up with something appropriate for the funeral.'' His gaze cleared as he met Trace's inscrutable one. ''My wife was a wonderful woman. She deserves a proper eulogy.''

Once again he turned to his aide. ''You'll take care of the rough draft, won't you, Heather?''

''Of course.''

''You know,'' he mused, ''though Whiskey River was Laura's home, I was, after all, elected by people from all over the state. The funeral should be held in Phoenix.'' He nodded, apparently pleased with his decision. ''The central location would make it a great deal easier for out-of-town visitors. What with the airport and all.''

''I'll start making the calls right away.''

''You should also call the office and have them fax you a list of Breakfast Club members.'' Trace vaguely recalled that the wealthy group of financial contributors the senator wanted to invite to his wife's funeral had been publicly disbanded after allegations of influence buying had appeared in the *Washington Post.*

''Of course.'' As if realizing the inappropriateness of that particular suggestion, the chief of staff studiously ignored Trace's steady gaze. But embarrassed color darkened her cheeks. ''I know this has been a terrible shock to you, Senator.''

It wasn't a bad save, Trace allowed. At least she was

trying. Heather Martin was obviously efficient and loyal. There was also a good chance she was sleeping with the victim's husband. But that didn't make her a murderer.

Any more than Senator Alan Fletcher's apparent self-serving shallowness made him a killer.

"So," Trace confirmed, "you arrived at the ranch house around midnight."

"Yes."

Trace referred to the notebook again. "And I believe you told me that you didn't go upstairs."

"That's right. I didn't want to wake Laura." His voice cracked the slightest bit on his wife's name.

"That's what you said," Trace agreed. "My deputy was told by witnesses that your wife arrived in town two days ago."

"That's right."

"Is it usual for you to travel to Arizona separately?"

"It's not unusual." Alan Fletcher's blue eyes narrowed, as if seeking the trap. "A vote was scheduled for yesterday that kept me in Washington. Laura came home early to prepare for the barbecue we're hosting for friends at the ranch.

"Oh, Lord, that's another thing," he groaned.

"I'll call the guests," Heather said, right on cue.

The handsome face relaxed. "Is there anything else?"

"There is one more thing." Trace frowned thoughtfully as he flipped through the notebook pages. "Am I to understand that you hadn't seen your wife since the day before yesterday?"

"Laura's flight left National at 8:45 in the morning. I dropped her off at the terminal myself on the way to the Hill."

"I see." Trace nodded. "So, since you didn't want to wake her last night, you're also telling me that it's been at least two days since you and your wife had relations."

"Relations?" Alan repeated blankly. "You mean sex?"

"Yes."

"Really, Sheriff, that's a rather personal question."

"I'm afraid your wife's murder has made it a matter of public interest, Senator," Trace corrected politely.

What he didn't divulge was that the autopsy had revealed the presence of semen. He couldn't discount the possibility that whoever had been with Laura Fletcher last night could have been the last person to see her alive.

"I don't keep track of my wife's and my lovemaking in a little black book." Fletcher's voice turned decidedly cool.

"Could you venture a guess?"

"We've both been quite busy lately. But, if I were forced to pinpoint a day, I'd say sometime last week. Tuesday, perhaps. Or Wednesday."

Trace noted the answer on a clean page. "Thank you, senator. You've been a big help."

The alarm on his watch sounded. Trace closed the notebook. "I have a press conference scheduled, but I'll be back this evening."

"A press conference?" It was the first sign of acute interest Trace had witnessed.

"You're a famous man, Senator," Trace reminded him needlessly. "This time tomorrow, the media's going to be crawling all over this place."

"They will, won't they?" Fletcher rubbed his square jaw. He turned again to his aide. "I'll need my razor. And a change of clothes."

"The house is still taped off," Trace informed him. "But I'll arrange for Ms. Martin to have access."

"Thank you. And please, Sheriff Callahan—" his handsome face turned campaign poster sincere "—find the men who killed my wife."

"Don't worry." Trace returned the notebook to his pocket. "I have every intention of doing just that."

Trace left the room, stopping on the other side of the door to check a note and to hear Heather Martin's angry voice. "Laura was pregnant?" Her palm connected with the senator's firm jaw, sounding like a gunshot.

The two cops on the other side of the hospital room door exchanged a look.

Ben Loftin belched, took a bite of the Snickers bar that had replaced the apple, and returned to his magazine.

As he drove back to Whiskey River, Trace damned whoever the hell it was who'd killed Laura Fletcher.

He'd thought he was beyond caring. He'd honestly believed that his ability to care had been burned out of him by the corrosive, acidic quality of experience. Which was why he'd come to Arizona. He'd been foolish enough to believe that he could sit in a rocker on the jailhouse porch and spend his days whittling toothpicks, waiting for his monthly paycheck to arrive.

Trace's fingers tapped a thoughtful tattoo on the steering wheel. He'd chosen what he thought would be a solitary existence. But he'd been wrong. Other lives had drifted down Whiskey River's currents and collided with his.

A woman was dead.

So now, like it or not, he was going to have to get back in the saddle again and track down her killer.

He owed it to Laura Fletcher.

He owed it to her husband—so long as the guy turned out to be innocent—Trace amended as an afterthought.

He owed it to Mariah Swann, to the residents of Mogollon County whose taxes paid his salary, and to society in general.

Surprisingly, Trace realized he also owed it to himself.

Chapter Six

Just as Trace had feared, the crime quickly gained Roman circus appeal. By noon, Main Street was jammed with television vans. Thick cables ran across the pavement; the satellite dishes atop the vans were capable of transmitting the press conference live to a vast national audience.

Uniformly attractive reporters who had taken over the courthouse steps were recording their stand-ups in front of videocams. Trace saw one brunette he recognized as being a morning anchor from a Phoenix station doing some last minute repairs to her hair with a portable butane curling iron.

The sidewalks, unsurprisingly, were packed with looky-loos. An enterprising hot dog vendor had set up an umbrella-topped stand across the street in the park. Nearby another entrepreneur was doing a brisk business in Italian ices and espresso. Rather than try to drive through the uncharacteristic crush of traffic, The Good Humor man had brazenly parked his truck in a fire tow-away zone. The line for Popsicles, ice cream bars and soft drinks extended around the block.

"Apparently murder is good for business," Trace said as he entered his office ten minutes late and found Jessica waiting. Her white suit looked as crisp and tidy as it had hours earlier, making Trace wonder if she'd had the material coated with Teflon.

"I recall reading that back in the sixties, when Reno was declared Murder Capitol of the country, tourism hit an all-time high," she said.

He poured himself a cup of coffee. "Perhaps someone ought to suggest a new ad campaign to the chamber of commerce."

"Visit Whiskey River—the west's most Western town. Where the shoot-outs aren't faked," she suggested as she made another pass at the coffeepot herself, then sat back down.

When she crossed her legs, the enticing sound of silk on silk drew his attention. Trace wondered if he'd ever outgrow checking out a woman's legs and sincerely hoped not.

"Have I ever told you that you've got dynamite legs, Jess?"

"I believe the term was 'wraparound,'" she corrected as she adjusted her skirt over her knees. "But that was in another time." She took a sip of coffee. "In those carefree, halcyon days of yore before we landed ass-deep in reporters."

"I've always liked your ass, too."

"Thank you. I like yours as well." She smiled at him over the rim of the chipped mug. "And as much as I'd love to spend the rest of the afternoon strolling down memory lane with you, Callahan, I suppose you'd better tell me what you've got so far."

He did. What little he had.

"It's not a lot to go on," she mused, skimming over the notes she'd taken.

''No. It's not.''

''But you'll get more.''

''Yes. I will.''

She sighed. ''We're going to have to give that mob out there something to sink their teeth into.''

''How about the 911 tape?''

She considered that. ''Not bad. It's definitely dramatic enough to keep them occupied while you do whatever it is you intend to do.''

''As a matter of fact, I intend to detect.''

She lifted a brow. ''Detect?''

''That's what we detectives do,'' he reminded her.

''Ah, but you're not a detective anymore,'' she reminded him back.

Trace shrugged. ''That's what I keep trying to tell myself.'' He stood up. ''Ready?''

She rose and brushed at the nonexistent wrinkles in her skirt. ''As ready as I'll ever be.''

Folding chairs had been set up in a conference room. Television lights were pointed at the podium. Although Trace and Jessica entered the room together, she stood aside, inviting him to open the proceedings.

''Good afternoon, ladies and gentlemen,'' he said into the bank of microphones. ''My name is Trace Callahan. I'm sheriff of Mogollon County and I'm in charge of the investigation into the shooting death of Mrs. Laura Swann Fletcher.''

An interested murmur rippled through the room. The audience leaned forward. Several of the faces could not contain their excitement. After all, a murder in Whiskey River was news in itself. Having the victim turn out to be the daughter of the most influential man in town and the wife of a U.S. senator rumored to be on the fast track to the White House cranked up the interest level considerably.

"Mrs. Fletcher was mortally wounded at her ranch house early this morning. The senator was also wounded, but he was taken to Louis R. Pyle Memorial Hospital where he is resting comfortably and is expected to make a full recovery.

"The County Attorney—" he tilted his head in Jessica's direction "—Ms. Ingersoll, wants me to assure you that every resource of Mogollon County has been placed at my disposal until the killer or killers are apprehended. Are there any questions?"

"How, exactly, did Laura Fletcher die?" a twenty-something blond television reporter from the city asked.

"The autopsy revealed that Mrs. Fletcher received two wounds from a .38 caliber revolver, one in the left temple, the other in her chest. The bullet that penetrated her head killed her."

Another reporter called out, "Is it true Middle East terrorists tried to assassinate the senator for his stand on the peace talks?" A buzz ran through the crowd. Terrorists were about on a level with space aliens in the high country. Neither were likely to be seen on Main Street.

"Not that we know." Trace pointed toward a young print reporter clad in khaki who looked like a walking advertisement for an Eddie Bauer catalog.

"There's been a report that it was an Earth First eco-terrorist group, protesting the senator's prodevelopment policies," the reporter, who worked for Flagstaff's *Coconino Sun* said.

Development was as hot a topic as grazing fees and water rights in Whiskey River. Old-timers and environmentalists liked the town just the way it was; yuppies fleeing crime and other problems found in urban areas were pushing for something called "managed growth." Growth was growth, the natives mumbled over morning coffee at The Branding Iron Café. And they didn't like it. Not even a little bit.

"Again, that remains unsubstantiated."

"How about rumors that it was a pro-choice feminist coalition angry about his campaign to outlaw abortion?" another television reporter questioned.

"We intend to check out all rumors, but at this time, there is no indication that was the case."

"What steps do you intend to use to apprehend Laura Fletcher's killer?" This from Rudy Chavez.

Trace's face hardened. "All."

"Do you have any suspects?" Chavez's pugnacious attitude and challenging tone revealed he was still pissed about being forced away from the crime scene.

"Not at this time."

"When can we talk to the senator?"

"Whenever he and his attending physician say you can. That's not my decision to make."

"If the senator and Mrs. Fletcher were both shot, who called the crime in?" a reporter Trace vaguely remembered being from the Camp Verde *Bugle Call,* asked.

"The senator placed the call himself after having been wounded. The 911 tape will be available to the press after this press conference is concluded.

"Now, since that's all I have to say at this time, I'm going to turn the microphones over to Ms. Ingersoll."

As he passed Jessica, Trace murmured, "Have fun, Counselor."

"What kept you?" Mariah said ten minutes later when she opened the door of the suite to Trace.

"Couldn't find a parking space. Every damn space in town is filled up with rental cars."

She folded her arms across her chest. "Seems to me a

sheriff could park anywhere he wanted. Even in a red zone.''

Trace shrugged and did his best not to notice that she smelled like Eden in springtime. ''Wouldn't want to set a bad example. And didn't your mother ever warn you to ask who it is before you opened your hotel room door?''

''I knew it was you.'' She stepped aside. ''How about a beer? You look as if you could use one.''

Trace thought about assuring her he never drank on duty. Then he remembered the beer he'd left on the counter. Had it only been nine hours ago? It seemed a lifetime. ''A beer sounds great.''

''Sit down.'' She gestured toward the couch which was covered in some material designed to resemble a Navaho blanket, then retrieved a beer from the compact refrigerator beside the bar and took out a bottle of designer water for herself. The television was on with the sound turned down.

''There are some nuts. And crackers, if you're hungry. Or I can order us lunch from room service.''

''Beer's fine.'' Trace watched a buffed up soap opera guy and a gorgeous young thing who didn't look old enough to be legal swap spit.

''Whatever.'' She handed him the beer, then sat down in the tub chair opposite the couch and put her bare feet up on the coffee table. She'd changed into a red-and-white striped T-shirt and white shorts. Her toenails had been painted the soft coral color of the underwater reefs where he and Ellen had gone scuba diving during their Hawaiian honeymoon. ''Thank you for coming.''

''I had the feeling that if I didn't you'd just track me down.''

''You're right. I would have.''

The hunk on the screen began to undress the girl. Trace

tilted the beer back and swallowed. It was cold and went down real fine. "This hits the spot."

"I'm so pleased." He'd obviously showered and changed since she'd seen him last, which made him a bit more presentable.

Up close, the man appeared even larger than he had earlier. Overpowering. The breadth of his shoulders seemed almost too wide for the tweed sport coat.

Having learned that he'd spent much of last year in the hospital, she was surprised that his build was so muscular, his stomach so taut. When Mariah caught herself wondering if the male body sitting across from her was as hard as it looked, she immediately dragged her gaze back to his face.

His eyes were intent. And unnervingly watchful.

"Did you get hold of your mother?"

Mariah frowned. "Yes. She's flying into Phoenix later this afternoon."

"You going to meet her plane?"

"I offered. But she insisted on hiring a car." Trace heard her soft sigh and decided that the Swanns weren't exactly the Cleavers. Then again, what family was?

His attention drifted toward the TV where things were progressing nicely. The girl was down to a silky red thing Trace now knew was a teddy. The guy's shirt was gone. The jeans followed. Trace took another longer swallow of beer as the couple fell onto the bed.

"You handled that press conference very well," she said.

"I've had a lot of practice."

"So I was told." She followed his glance. "I wonder if Jimmy still eats those sausage sandwiches for lunch before all his love scenes."

"Jimmy?"

"Jimmy Masters." She gestured toward the man whose

lips were currently working their way down the woman's throat. "I lured him away from his pregnant wife years and years ago. When I first moved out to Hollywood."

"I suppose that's what earned you the title of the Vixen of Whiskey River," he said easily.

She frowned over the rim of the green bottle. "Doesn't anything shock you?"

Trace shrugged. "Not much."

"Not even murder?"

"Murder doesn't shock me," he corrected. "It disappoints me."

"Is that why you quit the force?"

"No." Trace tipped the beer again. He'd made some progress since the shooting, but thinking about those days still made him thirsty. "And by the way, J.D. filled me in on your early acting career. He says you were a very convincing daytime villainess."

"I should have known better than to try and put something over on a cop." Amusement touched her eyes, which reminded him once again of her mother's. They were the type of wide, liquid eyes a man could fall into and drown, if he wasn't careful.

Trace had always considered himself a careful man.

"You should have known," he agreed.

He sneaked a quick glimpse at the television again. The amorous pair had moved under the sheets. The scarlet teddy was on the floor.

"You know, you're a lot better-looking than her."

She glanced up at him, clearly surprised. Not as surprised, Trace considered, as he was to have said it.

"Thank you."

"It's the truth."

Mariah felt a little jolt inside, but managed to smooth it over.

Silence settled over the room.

"Why did you come here?"

"Because you've left a zillion messages. Because I've got some more questions to ask you." He ticked them off on his fingers. "Because I wondered how you were holding up. And because I thought I'd fill you in on the investigation. So far."

"Gracious. Why on earth would you want to do that? Since I'm not technically Laura's next of kin?"

Despite the gravity of the situation, the way she had of jutting her chin forward as she tossed his own words back in his face amused him.

"Are you always such a hard-ass, Ms. Swann?"

"It's Mariah. And yes, I'm usually assertive." She put the bottle down on the table, took a cigarette from the pack beside it and lit it with a haughty-as-hell gesture reminiscent of Maggie McKenna in her prime. "As a woman working in Hollywood, I've had to be."

"Yeah, it must be difficult to be taken seriously when those same producers you're trying to sell your scripts to have seen you cavorting around on the tube in your underwear."

His smile, meant to annoy, was deliberately insolent. It also, she admitted reluctantly, added a wicked charm to his face.

Mariah absolutely refused to be baited. "Don't knock those subliminal powers of persuasion until you've seen me in my underwear," she suggested sweetly. "May I ask a question?"

He leaned back and put his feet up on the table beside hers. "Shoot."

She was truly tempted to. "Are *you* always such a smart-ass, Sheriff?"

"Some people consider me witty."

"Some people have no taste."

"Got me there," Trace said agreeably.

"The people I talked with in Dallas said police brass found you a bit strong-willed."

"Actually, if memory serves, the word used most often to describe me was *intractable*."

She crossed her legs at the ankles. Her thighs were smooth and tan and although he knew better than to allow his mind to go off in that direction, Trace decided Mariah Swann would look terrific in a teddy.

"They also told me that you were a wave maker."

"I've been known to rock a few boats."

As Trace remembered a time when he'd routinely created tidal waves without worrying about the consequences, the walkie-talkie he wore on his belt crackled to life.

"Dispatch to sheriff," the disembodied female voice Mariah had spoken with so many times today called out to him. "Come in, Sheriff."

"What is it, Jill?" There was no immediate answer. Just a sputter of white noise.

"Just a minute, Sheriff." Her frustration could be heard over the interference. "I'm looking up the proper code."

"Why don't you just tell me straight out."

"Cora Mae said I should always use police codes when I'm talking on the radio."

"Cora Mae's not the sheriff."

"Well, of course she isn't." There was another little sputtering silence. "Are you saying I don't have to learn the codes?"

Jill Winters would never get a job designing fuel systems for space shuttles. But she was enthusiastic and willing to learn. However, it was the fact that she and J.D. were planning an August wedding which had made her such an attractive applicant for the job of day dispatcher. Once she and the deputy were married, the county would save on group insurance coverage. Apparently, when it came to health insurance, two really could live more cheaply than one.

"I'm saying give it time," Trace suggested.

"Oh." Her relief was palpable. "You've no idea how happy I am to hear that, Sheriff. I really have been trying, and J.D. has been coaching me at night, but there are so many and—"

"Jill," Trace interrupted patiently, "why don't you just tell me why you called."

"Oh. The senator wants to talk to you. In person. Right away. He says it's urgent. And confidential."

When Trace felt the familiar prickle at the back of his neck, he knew he was hooked. You can run, he reminded himself. But you cannot hide. He pushed himself off the sofa. "Call the senator back and tell him I'm on my way."

"Ten-four," she said proudly.

Galvanized, Mariah stood up as well and stabbed her cigarette out in a ceramic ashtray shaped like a cowboy boot. "It'll only take me a second to change."

"Change?" His gaze skimmed over her shorts and snug T-shirt.

"I'm coming with you."

Twice before he'd been assigned to baby-sit some Hollywood type who was doing research for a role. Neither experience had made Trace want to repeat it.

"This is a murder investigation. Not some phony Hollywood made-for-television docudrama," he said. "I can't allow you to muck around in it."

"Can't? Or won't?"

"Won't." He'd pulled out the same calmly authoritative voice he'd used on more than one occasion to convince a perp to put down a loaded gun.

Trace had no way of knowing that Mariah hated his tone. It was the same one her father had always used whenever he'd unsuccessfully attempted to control her.

She decided, in order to avoid precious time arguing, to ignore the sheriff's uncomplimentary reference to her work and concentrate on his refusal.

"I'm painfully aware that it's a murder investigation, Sheriff. Since it's my sister who was murdered. And in case it hasn't sunk in, I take Laura's death very personally." She lifted her chin in that pugnacious gesture he was beginning to both hate and admire. "So much so that I have every intention of mucking around in your precious damn investigation all I want."

When he plowed his hands through his hair, Mariah had the impression he'd love to put them around her neck.

"Christ, it must be exhausting," he said instead.

"What must be exhausting?"

"Working so hard at being so unrelentingly tough."

"I don't have to work at it," she shot back with a furious toss of her head. "It's a gift. Did it ever cross your chauvinistic cop mind that I *am* tough?"

At least she hadn't called him a chauvinistic pig. Trace decided that was something.

His answering look was long. And deep. It took every ounce of self-control she possessed, but Mariah refused to look away.

"No," Trace said finally. "You're not." His intense gaze slid down to her mouth, lingering there before returning to her guarded eyes. "Not really."

Mariah's emotions, already frazzled because of her sister's murder, began to unravel.

Deciding that if there was ever a time for caution, this was it, she backed up and let out a slow, quiet breath.

"You can't stop me from visiting my brother-in-law in the hospital," she muttered mutinously.

Since she'd already revealed her animosity toward the senator, Trace knew damn well that her desire to visit

Fletcher wasn't due to any sudden need to offer condolences or comfort.

"Wrong again, sweetheart. I can, if necessary, put the senator under police protection, effectively cutting off access to all visitors. Including you."

"I'd love to watch you try explaining that bit of police procedure to the esteemed members of the press clamoring for interviews." She flashed him a challenging smile. "And call me sweetheart again, Sheriff, and I'll break your kneecaps."

"Surely a hotshot award-winning crime writer like you must know that assaulting a police officer is against the law."

"So is police harassment," Mariah countered without missing a beat. She glanced significantly at an old-fashioned clock on a nearby table. "And far be it from me to tell you how to do your job, but we're wasting time here."

Once again frustration moved across his face. "You're not going to let up, are you?"

"No." She met his hostile gaze without flinching. "I'm not."

As another silence settled over the room, Mariah realized that silence wasn't silent at all. It was, instead, an absence of big sounds, which allowed smaller ones to be heard.

The *tick tick tick* of the antique clock seemed as loud as Poe's *The Tell-Tale Heart.* A dove on the balcony outside the window cooed softly to its mate. The soft *ding* of the elevator reaching the third floor echoed down the hallway.

Trace was the first to shatter the suspended silence. "Hell." In that short, fierce curse, she heard frustration, anger and, most importantly, reluctant surrender.

Having won this round, Mariah had the good sense not

to gloat. "It won't take me more than a couple of minutes to change into a skirt."

His eyes glittered with a deadly light. "Try for one."

She practically ran into the adjoining bedroom, shutting the door behind her. Trace heard a drawer open. Seconds later his unruly mind imagined her pulling those brief white shorts down her long tanned legs.

Trace scowled at the errant thought. He'd always prided himself on the ability to remain ice-cool under pressure. Trace Callahan's reputation, both professionally and personally, had always been one of unwavering logic and deliberate action.

But now, against all reason, against his not inconsiderable will, he found himself drawn to a woman who elicited pure emotion.

"Ready." She came rushing out of the bedroom. Although it only increased temptation, he was grateful to see she'd kept the T-shirt on. The shorts had been exchanged for a skirt created of some gauzy white fabric that swirled gypsylike around her calves. The sun streaming through the balcony's French doors rendered the fabric nearly transparent, allowing an enticing view of her long firm legs.

Once again Trace felt the unmistakable pull of desire.

Once again he forced it down.

"Okay. Here's the deal." He crossed his arms over his chest and gave her a dark warning look. "You are only along for the ride. And, more importantly, so I can keep my eye on you and prevent you from screwing up my homicide case."

"I'm not about to—"

"Shut up."

Although Mariah would throw herself off the rocky Mogollon Rim escarpment before admitting it, his low soft voice proved more intimidating than the loudest shout.

Trace nodded in terse satisfaction when she pressed her lips together. "You should probably know, right off the bat, that I don't give a rat's ass how many crime shows you've written. I don't care if you have a house filled with Emmys or Oscars, or whatever the hell other gold statues you prima donna Hollywood types hand out to pat yourselves on the back."

Mariah visibly bristled at his uncomplimentary description, but kept her mouth shut.

"Solving your sister's murder is my department. So, listen very carefully, Ms. Swann, because I'm only going to say this once.

"If you interfere in any way in my investigation, if you second guess my motives, or dare question my integrity, I'll toss you in jail for obstructing justice so fast your head will swim.

"And then I will personally throw the cell door key into Whiskey River."

He put one hand against the wall, effectively cutting off her escape and leaned closer. Their noses were almost touching. His warm breath fanned her lips. "Is that clear?"

Trace Callahan's sheer size overwhelmed Mariah. He was literally radiating a steely, implacable strength she found both appealing and frightening. Even so, she refused to give him the pleasure of knowing he'd intimidated her.

"As glass." Ducking under his arm, Mariah scooped up her quilted red purse from the desk. "Let's go." She was out the door before Trace could respond.

He cursed, then followed her to the elevator.

As the ancient cage creaked its way downward toward the lobby, they stood side by side, looking straight ahead, neither saying a word. Her scent, which reminded him of wildflowers swaying in a sun-filled meadow, bloomed in the confined space.

Trace realized that her stated intention to "muck around in his precious damn investigation" was not an idle threat. Like it or not, it appeared that he was stuck with Mariah Swann for the duration.

With a fatalism that was partly inborn, partly acquired, Trace decided that there were probably worse situations to be in.

Chapter Seven

Ben Loftin had moved on to *Penthouse* when Trace and Mariah arrived at Alan Fletcher's hospital room.

"Any changes in the senator's condition?" Trace asked.

"He was watching television last time I checked." Although the deputy's words were directed at his superior, his attention had focused on Mariah's chest. "His assistant left a while ago."

Trace did not miss either his deputy's unprofessional behavior or Mariah's repulsed shudder. "Before or after the senator called the station?" Irritation caused his tone to be more brusque than usual.

Loftin shrugged. "Beats me. If you wanted me to monitor the guy's phone calls you should have said so. Boss," he added after a brief, deliberate pause.

Every police department in the country—from NYPD in the east, to LAPD on the Pacific Coast, along with even the smallest two-man force in outer boondocks USA—operated along a military type chain of command. The actual titles might differ, the uniforms varied, they might uphold different laws written by different legislatures, but the single thing they all had in common was the unquestionable pyramid of power.

As sheriff, Trace sat alone atop his particular tower of authority. And he was getting damned tired of Loftin's insubordination. For not the first time in the past six months, Trace debated firing Ben Loftin on the spot.

It would, he considered, give him a vast amount of pleasure.

It would also get him in hot water with the mayor, the county commissioners and the civil service board.

Under normal conditions, Trace wouldn't mind the fight.

But these were far from normal circumstances and with a high-profile murder to solve, the simple truth was that he needed every man he could get.

Later, he vowed. As soon as he wrapped up this case. Trace did not allow himself to consider that Laura Fletcher's murder would remain unsolved.

Although his expression remained John Wayne taciturn, Mariah observed the fleeting change of emotions in the sheriff's eyes and wondered if Ben Loftin—who she remembered being a bully—realized how lucky he was not to have been yanked off his chair and thrown bodily through the plate glass window at the end of the hallway.

As their gazes briefly touched, Mariah watched the shutters closing off Trace's thoughts. The lines bracketing his mouth deepened.

"Fletcher asked for confidentiality," he reminded Mariah.

She'd been waiting for him to bring that up. "So?"

"So, you'll have to wait out here."

"Why don't I come in with you? Then, if Alan asks me to leave, I will."

"I won't have you compromising my case."

"Believe me, Sheriff, if there's one thing I definitely don't want to do it's compromise your case."

Trace gave her another long look. Then he shook his head. "Lucky for you, cops tend to have a high aggravation tolerance."

She'd just won another round. The idea, as satisfying as it was, gave Mariah no urge to gloat. Because she knew if Sheriff Callahan truly wanted to keep her out of the hospital room, she'd be forced to cool her heels out in the hallway, subjected to Loftin's licentious leers.

They entered the room together.

The cheating son of a bitch was watching television! Mariah felt the cold fury surge through her like icy needles stinging at her emotions. His wife was lying cut into little pieces on a cold morgue table and senator Alan Fletcher had the unmitigated gall to be watching C-Span? She had an urge to yank the portable TV from its wall bracket and jam it down the man's murderous throat.

"Mariah?" He pressed a button on the remote, muting a rerun of a recent debate on military funding. "This is a surprise." His expression, and his tone, suggested the surprise was not a pleasant one.

"Not as much a surprise as I had this morning," she countered. Frost coated each word, but a flame burned hotly in her eyes. "Arriving at the house and finding Laura dead."

"The incident is unfortunate."

"In my book, murder is a helluva lot more than unfortunate!"

When her fingers unconsciously curled around the plastic water pitcher, Trace decided the time had come to interrupt their less than cordial reunion.

"You told my dispatcher you wanted to talk to me?"

"Yes." He slanted a pointed look at his fuming sister-in-law. "I also informed her it was confidential."

Trace turned to Mariah. "Ms. Swann—"

"All right." The quiet command in his voice was unmistakable. Mariah sighed, knowing she was licked. "I'll be in the snack bar."

She shot her brother-in-law one last glance. "I'll be back." With a theatrical huff worthy of her early soap opera days, Mariah left the room on a swirl of white gauze skirts.

Both men watched her dramatic exit.

"Christ, that woman always has been a handful," Alan muttered.

"I hadn't realized you were that well acquainted."

"Fortunately, my wife and her sister were not close, so I wasn't forced into much contact with Mariah," he allowed. "But I've heard stories. None of them exactly flattering, if you know what I mean."

Trace did. But not having been any Boy Scout himself in his younger years, he preferred to make his own character judgements. He turned his attention to the matters at hand.

"I assume you asked me here because you recalled something about last night?"

"No. I'm afraid nothing's changed in that regard." Alan lay his head back on the starched pillow and closed his eyes, as if garnering strength.

Trace wondered if he should Mirandize the senator.

"You mentioned my wife was pregnant." Fletcher's eyes remained closed. There was a white ring of tension around his mouth.

"Uh-huh," Trace agreed.

"Two months."

"Uh-huh." Trace thought of the letters and figured he knew where this conversation might be headed. "You didn't know." It was not a question.

"No." Alan opened his pain-fogged blue eyes and met Trace's inscrutable gaze. "I didn't know."

With a deep sigh, he turned his head toward the window and stared out at the asphalt parking lot. "Laura and I tried unsuccessfully for years to have a family."

Trace nodded again. "Uh-huh," he said, employing a routine, but highly successful interrogation procedure. *Uh-huh* a suspect to death, keep him talking to fill in the silences—civilians inevitably felt the need to fill in silences—and pretty soon there was no need to call for the hangman. Because if the interrogating cop could just keep his mouth shut long enough, the guilty party would eventually end up putting the noose around his own neck.

Another sigh. "To discover, after Laura's death, that she was carrying a child, is proving extremely painful."

"I can imagine." Trace waited.

"The baby wasn't mine."

"Oh?"

Alan turned back to Trace. "I'm afraid I wasn't entirely honest with you earlier," he admitted reluctantly. "When you asked me about the last time Laura and I had, uh, relations."

"Uh-huh," Trace prompted encouragingly.

He was not surprised. The senator's confession only proved a longtime law enforcement axiom: *Everyone lies.*

"Actually, the last time my wife and I made love was in December. We'd been to a Christmas party in Alexandria, and we'd both had a little too much champagne, and after we got home, one thing led to another. It was the holidays, after all, and well, you know how it goes."

"So that would have been six months ago." Which, if true, definitely took the senator out of the paternal picture.

"Yes."

"Were you and your wife having marital troubles?"

"No more than anyone else." The lie—and Trace

knew, with every fiber of his being that it *was* a lie—hovered between them, like a cloud of noxious smog.

"Uh-huh."

Another, longer, thicker silence settled.

"Shit. All right." Fletcher dragged his slender fingers through his blond hair. "That's not exactly true.... There *were* problems."

Trace waited for him to mention Heather Martin.

"You have to understand my motivation. I was only trying to protect Laura," he said instead.

"Protect her?" Trace thought it was a little late for that.

"Her reputation. But as we watched your press conference, we realized that you may suspect me of my wife's murder, which would keep you from pursuing the real killers."

When Trace didn't respond, Alan cleared his throat, then said, "That's when Heather advised me to tell you the entire truth."

"The truth?" Trace wondered what else the senator's lissome young chief of staff had been advising him on. How to murder his wife, perhaps? Trace also figured he was not the only one who knew about the love letters.

He figured right. "Although it pains me to admit it, even to myself, Laura was having an affair." Another thrust of those long fingers ruffled what Trace estimated to be at least a fifty-dollar haircut. "You have to understand, such behavior was so unlike her, so absolutely uncharacteristic of the sweet, intensely moral woman I married, that I thought, if I merely waited it out, the entire unsavory affair would run its course."

He looked up at Trace for confirmation that he'd made the correct choice.

"I've heard that's often the case," Trace agreed obligingly.

He felt no need to mention that in his own situation,

Ellen had gone on to marry the municipal court judge she'd been sleeping with while still married to him, but in truth, Trace had never blamed his former wife. Just as it took two to make a marriage, it took two to break it.

Hell, in his business, which wasn't exactly geared to domestic tranquility, divorce was not only unsurprising, it was almost expected.

The senator cursed and dragged his hands down his face in a weary, defeated gesture. If it was an act, it was a good one.

"And now you tell me she was pregnant." Alan closed his eyes again, as if the thought were too painful to consider. "With his child."

She's also dead, Trace thought but did not say.

"Do you happen to know who the other man was?"

"Yes." The senator's expression hardened. His eyes turned to chips of blue ice. "Clint Garvey."

His words confirmed what Jessica had already suggested. If the local rancher had been sleeping with Laura Fletcher, he was probably the man who'd gotten her pregnant.

Was he also, Trace wondered, the man who'd killed her?

Mariah was sitting alone at a chipped red Formica table in a corner of the snack bar, a foam cup in front of her. A cigarette burned in the plastic ashtray where an earlier one had been stubbed out. She was staring off into space and from her murderous frown, Trace suspected she was thinking about her brother-in-law. She was so deep in thought, she didn't hear him approach until he was standing in front of her.

"How's the coffee?"

She started at his sudden appearance, then quickly recovered, looking at her half empty cup. "I don't know."

"Couldn't be any worse than the stuff from the courthouse machine."

She shrugged disinterestedly as she drew in on the cigarette. When she exhaled, a wispy cloud of blue smoke rose between them.

Trace turned around an industrial plastic chair and sat down, straddling it, his arms folded along the top. "You know, you should probably eat something."

She flashed him a grim, humorless smile. "Now you sound like someone's mother."

"But not yours," Trace guessed.

"No." She shook her head, sending her hair fanning out in a gilt arc. The scent of flowers wafted on air heavy with the aroma of disinfectant. Her face closed up, like a wildflower sensing an impending storm and she ground out the cigarette with more force than was necessary. "Definitely not mine."

Her slender shoulders slumped, making her appear smaller and more vulnerable. Rather than meet his steady gaze, she began chipping away at the cup, her scarlet fingernails tearing off pieces of white foam. Her lips had left a scarlet crescent on the edge of the cup. Trace frowned as he found himself wondering if Mariah's lips were as soft and succulent as they looked.

Abandoning her destruction of the coffee cup, she put her elbows on the table, rested her chin on her linked fingers and looked straight at him. "Have you ever killed anyone, Sheriff?"

A dark cloud moved over his face. "If you checked me out, you probably know the answer to that question."

"I know that your department jacket listed a provoked and justifiable shooting. But I don't know how you felt about it."

"Too bad you couldn't get anyone to lift the department's shrink's files for you."

His eyes were flint. His granite jaw could have been carved on the side of Mount Rushmore. Mariah knew she was pushing. But although her professional contacts had assured her that Trace Callahan was a good, albeit unorthodox cop, it was important to her to know what kind of man the sheriff was.

"I'd rather hear it from you," she said quietly. Firmly. When he didn't answer, she studied him for a long time. "You didn't like it." While researching her television scripts, Mariah had discovered there were too many cops who got off on the Dirty Harry bravado bandied around local cop bars.

"No." Trace thought back on the nightmares, the nausea, the discomfort of having to accept the back slaps and congratulations of his fellow cops for successfully taking one of the bad guys off the street. "I didn't."

Mariah nodded, satisfied again that this was a good man. An honest man. A cop who took his responsibility to society seriously.

They exchanged a long look. Unbidden and unwanted, tension suddenly sizzled, like a downed hot electric wire snaking across a rain-slick street. Mariah was momentarily rattled by the rising heat in Trace's slate eyes. For his part, Trace viewed the answering flames and silently cursed himself for inviting a complication he definitely did not need.

Something was happening, Mariah realized as she felt every atom in her body responding to Trace in a distracting, dangerous and highly disturbing way. She could have wept with relief when the strident blare of a hospital code from the speaker overhead shattered the suspended moment.

An instant later, Trace's walkie-talkie began stuttering. Grateful for the interruption, he plucked it off his belt. "Yeah?"

His short, harsh tone caused a moment's hesitation on the other end. ''Sheriff?''

Trace softened his tone and prayed for patience. ''Yes, Jill?''

''Oh.'' Another little pause. ''You didn't sound like yourself.'' When he didn't answer, she said, ''You have to come back to the office, right away. We have a three-eleven in progress.''

''An indecent exposure?''

''Oh. No, that's not right.'' The young voice wavered with stress. ''Let me look it up—''

Trace exchanged a what-can-you-do look with Mariah, who smiled faintly in return. ''Jill—''

''Here it is. I meant a *four-fifteen F.* A family disturbance,'' she added unnecessarily. Outside the hospital, an ambulance was pulling up to the emergency room doors. The vehicle's radio caused interference, but through the static Trace and Mariah heard ''*crackle* Matthew Swann *crackle crackle* and his wife *crackle crackle* yelling at each other something awful. *Crackle.* You'd better get back *crackle* right away.''

Mariah cursed. World War III had obviously broken out in Whiskey River. ''She's probably not exaggerating.''

''I'm on my way, Jill.''

''Thank you, Sheriff.'' Even over the annoying static, the relief in the young dispatcher's tone was easily heard.

Trace stood up. ''Do you want to go fight with your brother-in-law, or would you rather come along and play referee?'' Trace asked.

''Actually, given my druthers, I'd rather be lying back on the beach, while some tanned and ridiculously sexy Hollywood hunk from 'Baywatch' rubs sun block on my back,'' Mariah answered. ''But, as I have to continually remind myself, life isn't television.''

She stood up as well, swallowed the remainder of the

now-cool coffee and tossed the cup and the shredded pieces into a nearby trash bin.

"The senator's not going anywhere," she decided. "I'd better come with you. Because if my parents are in top form, you're definitely going to need backup on this call, Sheriff."

Minutes later, as he pulled up in front of the courthouse, Trace viewed the white stretch limo parked along the curb in a space clearly marked with a red-and-white No Parking sign.

After an absence of more than a quarter of a century, Maggie McKenna had returned to Whiskey River.

"Better fasten your seat belt, Sheriff," Mariah warned. "Because it's going to be a bumpy night."

They could hear the argument raging all the way down the hallway. A man's voice, deep and angry, bellowing like a bull, countered by a woman's higher, no less angry tone. Whenever the two combatants would pause for breath, Jill's voice chimed in like a triangle in a preschoolers' rhythm band, ineffectually trying to be heard.

Trace and Mariah paused outside the office door. Through the frosted window they could see the outline of a woman pacing. The minute Trace and Mariah entered, Jill took advantage of her boss's appearance and escaped. "I'm behind on my filing," she said as she dashed past.

Watching her race down the hallway, Mariah experienced an urge to join the young dispatcher. Then she embraced her mother.

Watching them, Trace considered that while Margaret McKenna had been unable to stop the march of time, she'd definitely managed to slow aging to a crawl. Although he knew she had to be in her fifties, she could have passed for a decade younger.

Her hair, pulled back into a chic French roll—all the better to display still striking cheekbones that looked as if they'd been sculpted with a chisel—gleamed the hue of burnished copper. Remarkably, her thickly lashed eyes were every bit as dramatically green as they'd appeared to be on movie screens. The faint lines fanning out from their kohl accentuated corners added character rather than age.

Trace wondered how she managed to keep that milk-maid pale complexion living in southern California, land of endless sunshine. Her wine-hued lips were full and lush, almost as lush as the female body currently clad in a black silk pantsuit that he suspected cost as much as his last truck. As his quick gaze skimmed over the voluptuous breasts draped in that jet silk, reckless memories of lustful teenage fantasies flooded back.

"Ms. McKenna," he greeted her, trying not to appear like the bumbling sex-crazed schoolboy who'd secretly kept the photo of the actress that had come with his wallet. Trace didn't want to repeat J.D.'s earlier starstruck performance toward Mariah. "I'm Sheriff Callahan." He held out his hand. "I'm sorry about your daughter."

Maggie had never been anything if not direct. "Sorry isn't going to catch Laura's murderer." She shook his extended hand with her right, while jabbing the burning cigarette in her left at him like a weapon. "I want to know everything you're doing to solve this crime, Sheriff. Chapter and verse."

She might physically resemble Laura Swann Fletcher, but the energy radiating from her, like a shimmering scarlet aura, along with the crackling impatience, reminded Trace of Mariah. Like mother, like daughter, he figured.

"We've got roadblocks out all over the county." He took off his hat and tossed it in the direction of an oak hook on the wall. For a suspended moment, every pair of eyes in the room—every pair but Trace's—followed the black Stetson's flight.

Mariah was not all that surprised when it landed precisely on target. Neither apparently was Trace, who had already pulled out his notebook. "The medical examiner spent the morning compiling evidence, and—"

"I want to know why I wasn't notified immediately," Matthew Swann broke into Trace's explanation.

Mariah's father was a large man, with a thick shock of silver hair and a hard, solid body like one of his Brahma bulls. His face was tanned to the same hue as the hand-tooled leather belt he was wearing with his jeans.

"My dispatcher attempted to notify you in Santa Fe, Mr. Swann." Trace took the ashtray back out of the drawer and put it on the corner of his desk for Maggie to use. "But you'd checked out of your hotel."

"Probably off screwing some little blond barrel racer half his age," Maggie said, her voice dripping with venom. "While his daughter was being murdered in her bed."

Matthew turned on her. "I was alone, dammit!" His bushy pewter brows plunged downward toward a nose that had obviously been broken on more than one occasion. "And you're a fine one to talk. After all those years of getting smashed at Denim and Diamonds, then spreading your legs for half the cowboys in Whiskey River."

Maggie's eyes were shooting emerald sparks. "That's a lie!" She sucked in a huge breath and tossed her head in that same furiously haughty gesture Trace had witnessed in Mariah.

"Although no one could have blamed me if I did indulge in an occasional afternoon delight," she jeered at her former husband through a cloud of exhaled smoke. "Since the only useful stud around the Swann ranch was the four-legged one you kept out in the barn to service your precious mares."

The argument Trace and Mariah had interrupted resumed, hot and heavy. Mariah turned away, walked over to the window, gazed out at the park and wished she was anywhere else but here. Hearing her parents tearing away at each other reminded her of those long-ago nights when, frightened by their battles, she'd crawl into bed with Laura, who'd held her tight, distracted her with fairy tales and promised to always take care of her.

But who was taking care of you, Laurie? Mariah wondered now. As the familiar guilt clenched her heart, she leaned her forehead against the glass and closed her eyes.

"Ms. McKenna," Trace said, in a low voice that somehow managed to be heard above the increasingly bitter accusations flying back and forth across his office. "Mr. Swann. In case it's slipped your minds, I have a murder to solve. I don't have time to waste listening to the two of you act out a rerun of 'Divorce Court.'"

A stunned silence fell over the office. Mariah opened her eyes and slowly turned around. She doubted anyone had ever dared to speak to either of her parents that way.

"You can't talk to me that way, Callahan," Matthew Swann blustered. Anger flushed his darkly tanned cheeks a deep scarlet. "Do I need to remind you that I happen to be on the board of supervisors of this county? The very same board that hired you can also fire you."

He shot Trace the intimidating glare that had served him well for nearly seventy years. The Swann name was synonymous with power in Mogollon County. A man accustomed to getting results on demand from those who served him, Matthew Swann expected nothing less from Whiskey River's sheriff.

"I can have your badge for insubordination."

"Oh, shut up, Matthew," Maggie snapped at her former husband. "The sheriff's right."

She sat down in one of the brown visitor's chairs, put the cigarette out in the ashtray, then clasped her hands neatly in her lap, as repentant as a Catholic schoolgirl called to the Mother Superior's office.

"I'm truly sorry that you've had to witness such an unattractive display, Sheriff Callahan. All I can say in my defense is that this man has always brought out the worst in me."

When Matthew opened his mouth, obviously intending to respond to the dig, Trace raised his hand and cut him off. "Why don't you have a seat, Mr. Swann." He claimed his own leather chair behind the desk.

Mariah's father folded his arms across his massive chest. "I'd rather stand."

"Obstinate old goat," Maggie muttered under her breath.

"Bitch," Matthew muttered back.

Mariah couldn't stand it another minute. "Would you two just shut up!" Her voice and her legs were trembling. "Laura's dead, dammit!"

She dragged both her hands through her hair in a gesture of absolute frustration. Trace watched as she battled angry tears and won. "Your daughter's dead and all you two can do is behave like a pair of bratty five-year-olds insulting each other in the kindergarten sandbox."

"Don't you dare talk to your father that way, girl," Matthew threatened.

"Or what?" Mariah challenged, caught up in old family feuds herself. "You'll lock me in my room? Send me to bed without my supper? Whip me?"

"Perhaps if you'd had a few more trips to the woodshed when you were younger, you'd have a little respect for your elders."

"Respect has to be earned, Matthew," Maggie broke in. "Although I'll reluctantly admit you've managed to buy it on more than one occasion."

Fed up, Trace pushed himself out of his chair, took his

hat from the hook on the wall and began to walk out of his office.

"Where the hell do you think you're going, Callahan?" Matthew bellowed.

Trace glanced back over his shoulder. "I told you, Mr. Swann, I don't have time for this."

Maggie rose with a lithe grace and went over to where Trace was standing in the doorway, half in and half out of the office.

"Please, Sheriff." She placed a beringed hand on his arm. Her nails had been lacquered a deep rose. "If we promise to be on our best behavior, will you tell us what you know?" She was looking up at him through her thick fringe of black lashes, her green eyes coaxing compliance.

"Hell, Callahan," Matthew grumbled, "don't be so damned thin-skinned."

Trace exchanged a quick glance with Mariah, whose own expression revealed they were thinking the same thing. That this was probably as close as he was ever going to get to an apology from the headstrong rancher.

"It's simply a matter of priorities," he explained with a patience he was a very long way from feeling.

"We'll be good." Maggie's hand was now stroking his arm in a distinctly feminine fashion. "We promise." Her melted emerald eyes hardened as they flicked over to her former husband. "Don't we Matthew?" Her voice turned as flinty as her eyes.

"I just want to know what you're doing to catch the son-of-a-bitch who murdered my daughter."

"And we want to see her," Maggie said.

"Your daughter's body was taken to Peterson's Funeral Home," he divulged. "I can take you over there—"

"No," Mariah broke in. "I'll do it."

Trace gave her a grateful look. "All right. Why don't

we all sit down. And I'll fill you in on what we have so far."

All three Swanns did as instructed.

Trace told them as much as he could, including the fact that Laura had been pregnant. He did not tell the victim's parents that it was not her husband's child. Not because of any moral judgment call on his part, but he didn't want the news to get out until he'd tracked down Clint Garvey. According to J.D., whom he'd sent out to the Garvey spread, the cowboy, who still hadn't returned, appeared to have conveniently disappeared.

Which didn't make Garvey guilty, Trace had reminded his deputy. But he had to admit Garvey's vanishing act looked suspicious.

"What do you know about your daughter's relationship with Clint Garvey?" Trace asked Matthew.

The rancher's face darkened. "There was no relationship."

"That's not true," Mariah said.

Her father shot her a murderous look that she ignored as she turned to Trace. "Laura and Clint were in love."

"She was too young to know the meaning of the word," Matthew interrupted. "That was a long time ago," he informed Trace. "When she was still in high school."

"She loved him," Mariah repeated firmly. "Enough to marry him." She didn't need a crystal ball to figure out where Trace was going with this. Thinking back over Laura's veiled comments these past months, Mariah realized that she'd been trying to find some way to tell her sister that Clint was back in her life.

"They were married?"

"For less than a day," Matthew said.

"Our dear father crashed the honeymoon and succeeded in putting asunder what God had joined that morning in some tacky Las Vegas chapel," Mariah divulged, shooting the rancher a look every bit as lethal as the one he'd pointed in her direction.

Knowing Matthew Swann, Trace was not surprised. Although from what he'd been able to tell, Clint Garvey was a loner who tended to mind both his cattle and his own business, he was a very long way from a presidential candidate. Which would have made him a less than ideal son-in-law in Swann's eyes.

"I heard something else today," he said to Matthew. "About your daughter and Garvey having resumed their relationship."

"That's a goddamn lie." His massive hands—strong enough to wrestle a steer into submission—curled into fists. "Some people don't have anything else better to do than spread filthy rumors."

"I suppose you talked with your daughter about this?"

"There wasn't any need." Matthew's steely gaze met Trace's implacable one, daring the younger man to call him a liar. "Like I said, it was a lie."

Once again Trace thought about the message on Laura Fletcher's answering machine. And about that period of time Matthew Swann hadn't been able to be found. What if he'd returned home from Santa Fe to confront his daughter? What if he'd lost his infamous temper?

Trace dismissed that scenario. The rancher might have lost control enough to hit his daughter. But to shoot her, not once, but twice? Trace didn't think so.

Once again they were back to Garvey. The cowboy undoubtedly harbored resentment about Swann having broken them up once before. What if Matthew had returned to Whiskey River after that phone call and convinced Laura to give up her lover once again?

Several possible scenarios occurred to him. As he mulled over a few of the more likely, Trace found himself wishing for the good old days of the Wild West, when he could have rounded up a posse and ridden out into the hills to track Garvey down.

The intercom on his desk buzzed, interrupting his thoughts. When he didn't immediately pick up, it buzzed again. Longer, more insistently.

Trace punched the Lucite button. "What is it, Jill?"

"The governor is holding on line one, Sheriff." Jill's young voice was filled with awe.

Trace glared down at the blinking orange light, then out the window at the street crowded with news vans. He knew what was coming.

The governor had an election coming up. With his negative opinion rating climbing into the stratosphere, the one thing the politician didn't need was the murder of the wife of a U.S. senator during his watch. The only thing that would be worse for the man's reelection chances would be an unsolved murder.

Something Trace did not intend to happen.

But neither did he intend to take orders from a civilian. Even if that civilian happened to be the chief of state.

"Tell the governor I'm busy with a homicide investigation."

"But, Sheriff—"

"I'll have to call him back." His calm, no-nonsense tone brooked no argument.

"Yessir," Jill obediently answered. But everyone in the room could hear the worry in her tone.

That little matter taken care of to his satisfaction, Trace leaned back in the chair, braced his elbows on the wooden arms and eyed what remained of the battling Swann family over the tent of his fingers.

"Now. Where were we?"

Chapter Eight

The governor was not a happy politician. The murder had been picked up by the national press; having run as a law-and-order candidate, he was insistent that Trace wrap the case up quickly.

Assuring the chief of state that was his intention, Trace hung up, only to be informed by Jill that a coalition consisting of the mayor, the county commissioners and various members of the Whiskey River Chamber of Commerce was waiting in his outer office. Although the desert cities tended to get most of their tourist dollars during the winter months, when snowbirds were fleeing midwestern blizzards, summer was high season in the rim country. That being the case, Laura Fletcher's murder was publicity they didn't need. They wanted Trace to solve the crime. And they wanted him to solve it now.

Trace was not surprised to discover that dealing with politicians was no different in Whiskey River than it had been in Dallas. And just as in Dallas, it left a bad taste in his mouth.

He left the courthouse by the back way and drove the

few blocks to The Shear Delight, which appeared to be a throwback to another time. Like the 1950s, Trace considered as he entered, setting the small brass bell on the inside door handle jingling.

The walls had been painted bubblegum pink. The shampoo sinks and miniblinds on the windows echoed the color scheme. In a futile attempt to modernize the look, someone had hung glossy black-and-white posters on the wall depicting trendy hairstyles that might look great in the big city or on Paris runway models, but weren't much in demand in small-town America.

The chair behind the reception counter was empty. An elderly woman, cloaked in a pink smock sat in a pink chair in front of a mirror. Beside the mirror was a framed beautician's license and a pair of K mart portraits of two grinning, freckle-faced kids. The woman looked at Trace with an avid curiosity she didn't bother to conceal.

"Hi," Trace said.

She didn't answer.

"I'll be right out," a woman's voice called from a back room.

Trace smiled at the customer, who was watching him carefully in the mirror as if he might be an escaped serial killer or rapist, and studied a gold trophy that was taking up a corner of the woman's station while he waited.

The bell behind him sounded. Trace glanced back as Mariah entered the salon. "I thought you'd be with your mother over at Peterson's."

"She decided she wasn't up to it." Mariah shoved her hands into the pockets of her skirt and frowned. "I took her to the lodge and volunteered to stay, but she wanted to take a nap.

"So, I called your office. When Jill told me you were on your way over here, I thought I'd see what you were up to."

Trace decided he'd have to have a little chat with Jill. "I don't suppose you'd believe I was getting a haircut."

"In this place?" Her gaze circled the salon. "Not a chance. Lord, it hasn't changed since Nadine Jones caused all my hair to fall out by leaving the perming solution on too long. Nadine was the hairdresser from hell. You've heard the term, a bad hair day? Well, she invented it."

"That's why I fired her," that same voice called out from the back room.

The woman who belonged to the voice appeared a moment later. Patti Greene was in her late twenties. Her short curly hair was the hue of a new penny and just as shiny. She was wearing a long black skirt and black halter top that gave her a city look and proved an attractive foil for her hair, even as it appeared a bit startling in the midst of all the bright pink. She was pushing a pink plastic cart loaded with perming rods.

"I thought that sounded like you, Mariah." Neither her expression nor her tone were welcoming. She glanced over at Trace. "What kept you?"

Trace wasn't surprised she'd been expecting him. News traveled fast in a small town. "I've been busy. Investigating a murder."

"Yeah." She gathered up a stack of white tissue squares and handed them to the elderly woman who was avidly watching the exchange in the mirror. "I heard your news conference on the radio."

She used the tail of the black comb to separate a few strands of snowy hair, then held out her hand to the client, who handed over one of the papers. "I suppose I should say I'm sorry, Mariah."

There was an underlying tension in the salon Trace didn't quite understand. "Only if you mean it."

Patti shrugged. "I guess I do. But you know, in a way,

she had it coming. Stealing another woman's man obviously runs in the Swann family.''

A little stung by the accusation, Mariah decided that The Shear Delight wasn't the only thing that hadn't changed since she'd left Whiskey River. Patti had hated her then. And apparently, time had done little to change things.

''I didn't steal Jerry from you, Patti. You'd already given him back his ring when he asked me to the Spring Fling.''

''We had a fight. We would have made up.'' She rolled the paper and the hair up tightly onto a purple curler. ''If you hadn't come between us.''

Mariah wasn't about to rehash old grievances. But she had to know. ''Whatever happened to old octopus-hands Jerry, anyway?'' The school dance had been their first and last date after the high school quarterback had tried to wrestle her clothes off her on the seat of his father's pickup truck.

''I married him.'' Patti's and Mariah's eyes met in the mirror. ''You were right to dump him. He was a creep.'' She separated another bunch of hair, pulling a bit too tightly, which caused the woman to let out a little squeak of protest. ''Left me with two kids, a maxed-out Visa card, and a trailer whose roof leaks.''

Trace, who'd met innumerable women just like Patti during his days as a patrolman answering domestic violence calls, suspected she'd been counting on her relationship with Garvey to solve her financial problems.

''I'd like to talk with you about Clint Garvey,'' he said. ''And Laura Fletcher.'' He glanced toward the back room. ''Privately.''

''I'm busy.'' She took another paper and folded it around the white hair. ''But whatever you have to ask, you can ask out here. In case you haven't noticed, Sheriff, this isn't the city. We don't have any secrets in Whiskey River."

"All right." Trace gave her a long hard look in the mirror. "I hear you've been making threats."

"About cutting Clint's balls off with my scissors?" Patti shrugged. "Sure. I also threatened to shoot him through his cheating black heart." This time the curler was pink. "Laura's too."

"I guess you're a pretty good shot."

Patti followed his gaze to the Annie Oakley trophy she'd won for marksmanship at last fall's county fair. "Best in the county," she agreed. "One of these days the chauvinist pigs who run that fair are going to open the men's competition up to women, and I'll prove it."

She was picking up speed. Trace watched her fingers fly as she rolled up the perm. "Doesn't take a lot of talent to shoot a person at close range," he said.

"Sure as hell doesn't," she confirmed. "And for the record, Sheriff, I didn't kill Laura."

"You threatened to," he reminded her.

"Hell, yes." She shot a glance at Mariah in the mirror. "I threatened to kill you, too, remember? Over Jerry."

"I remember." Mariah nodded. "He wasn't worth it."

"You're telling me," Patti muttered. "And as good as Clint is, he isn't worth leaving my kids to do hard time for. No man is."

The hard look she sent Trace's way seemed to include him in that less than admirable group.

"Look," she said, when he didn't answer, "I have a habit of shooting off my big mouth. Things have been hard these past years, what with two kids to feed and Jerry leaving me with all the bills just when I bought this place." She wrapped some cotton around the woman's neck and secured it with a clip. "When Clint started coming around, I thought he was Prince Charming. You know, the answer to all my prayers.''

Trace and Mariah both nodded.

''Then one day Laura comes back to town without her husband, and suddenly Clint tells me that he just wants to be friends.''

She shook her head as she took a bottle of solution and began applying the foul-smelling lotion to the rolled up hair. ''Friends. When a man tells you that, you know it's over. I also knew why.''

''Because of Laura?'' Mariah asked, earning a sharp look from Trace.

''She already had one husband, dammit,'' Patti complained. ''Why couldn't she just have stayed in Washington? Where she belonged?''

Neither Trace nor Mariah answered. Trace pulled a card from his pocket and put in on the station beside the gilded trophy. ''If you hear anything—''

''Yeah, I'll let you know.'' She glanced over at Mariah. ''How long you going to be staying around?''

''As long as it takes.''

''Well, if you need someplace to invest all that Hollywood money, give me a call. I've got a good clientele, but that son of a bitch Jerry ran off with my redecoration fund. After working in Phoenix, it's embarrassing—not to mention depressing—owning a place that looks like a *Steel Magnolias* set.''

''I'll give it some thought,'' Mariah said.

Patti shrugged. ''Sure you will.'' She didn't sound like she was going to hold her breath.

''Tough lady,'' Trace said as they left the salon together.

It was Mariah's turn to shrug. ''She's had a tough life.'' They'd reached her Jeep. Mariah took her keys from her purse, then stopped, looking up at him. "You said Laura was pregnant."

"Two months."

Mariah reached into her purse for the cigarettes, crumpling the pack with shaking fingers when she found it empty. "You know, it's goddamn true."

"What's true?"

"That timing is everything." Her remarkable eyes—replicas of her mother's, albeit turquoise rather than emerald—glistened. For a brief moment Trace thought she was going to cry, but she resolutely blinked the moisture away. "Is Alan the father?"

"He says he's not."

"I assume you're planning to have him tested."

"Yes. I am." He paused again. "How much do you know about Garvey's relationship with your sister?"

"Only what I've already told you."

"He undoubtedly harbored resentment over the breakup."

"I'm sure he did," Mariah agreed. "Wouldn't you?"

"Probably." Several possible scenarios occurred to him. He mulled over a few of the more likely. "If he and your sister—"

"Laura," Mariah interrupted. "She has a name, dammit. But you haven't once used it."

There was a reason for that. When a homicide cop started thinking of murder victims by their names, it made them too real. Real enough that they tended to start haunting nightmares.

"I didn't mean—"

"Yes, you did." She sighed. "And I know why you do it. But I'm asking you, just this once, to acknowledge that Laura was a living, breathing, warmhearted person."

"If Garvey and *Laura*—" he watched her brief, satisfied nod "—had recently gotten back together, the pregnancy would probably cause her to confront the problems in her marriage."

"High time, too," Mariah muttered.

"Being a senator's wife is no small deal. Being First Lady is even a bigger prize. If she'd decided to get an abortion—"

"She wouldn't."

"You're not exactly an unbiased observer," Trace reminded her. "You didn't believe she'd take a lover, either."

"I'm glad she did," Mariah said on a burst of heartfelt emotion. "I'm glad she experienced joy before she died."

Trace thought about the semen in the M.E.'s report and figured that it might have not been exactly joy, but Laura Fletcher's last hours had not been without some pleasure.

"What I'm trying to say is that if she was considering an abortion, there's always a chance that Garvey would have viewed that act as murdering his unborn child."

"So he murdered her?"

"It's been known to happen."

"You don't have to convince me, Sheriff. Since I wrote a similar story for an episode of 'Law and Order.' But the flaw in that reasoning is that if Clint killed Laura, he'd end up murdering his child as well."

"Murder isn't always logical."

"Tell me about it," Mariah muttered as she unlocked the Jeep. She did not protest when Trace put his hand on her elbow to give her a lift up into the high seat. "So, what are you going to do now?"

"Try to sort out some loose ends. Arrange for the senator to be tested, and find Garvey. Among other things."

"Are you going to talk with Heather?"

He was, but decided he didn't have to tell Mariah everything. "Who's running this investigation, anyway?" he asked mildly.

She flashed him a quick, false smile. "You are, of course." She turned the key in the ignition. "I've got to get back to the lodge. Maggie should be awake." Mariah didn't want to admit to this man who already knew too many of the Swann family secrets exactly how afraid she was to leave her mother alone for very long. "But I'll keep in touch."

Trace had no doubt of that. He shut the driver's door, then watched her drive away.

He had people to see. Things to do, he reminded himself as he returned to the office. He couldn't—wouldn't—allow himself to become distracted. Even as he reminded himself of that, Trace couldn't quite shake the memory of her scent which had sneaked under his skin and was lingering in his mind.

The courthouse square looked like a satellite tracking station. The streets on all four sides of the redbrick building were blocked with television vans, the call letters painted on the sides revealing that media from all the bordering states were now on the scene. White saucers, like giant woks perched on top of the vans, tilted skyward, as if trying to pick up signals from outer space. Black, orange and yellow cables twined across the lawn like fat, colorful snakes. Reporters were still camped all over the steps.

Trace decided to send J.D. out to ticket them all.

After telling Jill to hold his calls, Trace poured a mug of coffee, sat down behind the desk and made a chart. At the top of the chart, he put Laura Swann Fletcher's name and underlined it. Beneath that, he wrote *Possible Suspects.* Then, with lines going down at ninety degree angles from the first, he listed the two alleged strangers who'd broken into the house. Two men who appeared to have vanished into thin air.

Next he wrote in the names of Laura's husband, her

lover, her lover's scorned girlfriend and her husband's possible mistress. Then, although he still didn't think it possible, he added Matthew Swann's name.

Fletcher's political campaign would not be helped by a divorce and it would undoubtedly be fatally destroyed if it was discovered that he'd been having an affair with his chief of staff. As a widower, however, he'd gain the sympathy vote.

As for Heather, perhaps she'd simply gotten tired of promises that didn't look as if they'd come true and decided to take matters into her own hands and solve the problem of her boss's marriage once and for all. Since it was obvious she enjoyed her power as the senator's chief of staff, he could easily envision her imagining herself by Fletcher's side in the Oval office—working as a team, like Bill and Hillary.

Garvey, who to some might seem the logical choice to have murdered Laura Fletcher, appeared to have nothing to gain by killing the woman he professed to love. And everything to lose.

And if he'd murdered Laura in a fit of passionate rage—perhaps she'd told him that she wasn't going to get a divorce, after all—wouldn't he have more likely done it earlier, while they'd been alone in the house after making love? Why would he risk leaving, then returning, when he knew her husband was expected?

There was another thing that didn't quite fit about Garvey, Trace concluded as he took a long drink of the bitter coffee that had been sitting on the burner too long. If he had shot the senator, Trace had the feeling that the cowboy—who was known to be an expert marksman—would have made certain the wounds were fatal.

The same, Trace felt, was true for Patti Greene. Although he wasn't going to write her off, his instincts told him that she'd been telling the truth. Of course, he considered, with Laura out of the picture, Garvey was suddenly eligible again. And for a young woman struggling to make it on her own, murder could seem to be the answer. He'd certainly seen people killed for a lot less.

As for Swann, Trace didn't believe the rancher capable of murdering his daughter, no matter how angry he was about her affair. But he could have returned home from Santa Fe and inadvertently set things into motion.

The problem with each of these scenarios, Trace considered, was that they involved a second party. If the senator had killed his wife, then wounded himself to deflect suspicion, he still would've needed someone to remove the guns from the house. Heather Martin seemed willing to do just about anything for her boss. Would she agree to being an accomplice in murder? How about if it meant eventually becoming First Lady?

On the other hand, if Fletcher's story was true about two armed intruders, then the other suspects would have had to find a killer for hire. From what he'd seen of Patti and Garvey, he doubted that was their style. Besides, Patti Greene didn't have the money to pay for a hit. And Garvey didn't appear all that flush, either.

Trace stared at the chart, as if the answer to his dilemma would suddenly magically appear on the yellow lined paper. When it didn't, he flipped the page and divided the paper into two columns entitled *Sex* and *Money.*

Beneath the column headed *Sex,* he listed Laura, Fletcher, Garvey, Patti and Heather, linking the various couples together.

Under *Money,* he wrote a single question: *Who would profit from Laura Swann Fletcher's death?* Again he listed Fletcher. And Garvey. Clint Garvey's ranch didn't begin to equal the land Laura had inherited from her maternal grandmother. There were also rumors of Garvey having a bit of bad luck playing the cattle futures market.

He needed to find Garvey, Trace told himself yet again. And, he decided, it wouldn't hurt to get a look at Laura Fletcher's will. She was a wealthy woman, far wealthier than her husband. It would be interesting to learn who stood to inherit her family fortune.

Maggie answered the knock on her suite door. Instead of the room service waiter she'd been expecting, she found a woman whose face she probably would have recognized even it it didn't routinely appear on the glossy pages of *Town and Country.*

"Freddi." She managed a smile for her elder daughter's best friend. "It's good to see you."

"Oh, Maggie." Fredericka took both Maggie's hands in hers. "I only wish it was under different circumstances." Tears welled up in her eyes. "I've been trying to get hold of Mariah ever since I heard, but she's never in."

"She's determined to help the sheriff track down Laura's murderer." Maggie glanced down the hallway, as if looking for someone, sighed and said, "Come in, dear. I'm so glad you dropped by. You knew Laura better than anyone. I need someone to tell me what kind of woman my daughter grew up to be."

"A wonderful woman," Freddi said firmly as she claimed a corner of the sofa. "She was sweet and loving, and never had a bad word to say about anyone. I have to tell you," she admitted with a rueful smile, "sometimes her unwavering perfection could wear a bit thin on the rest of us poor mortals."

Maggie remembered the joyful, fun-loving little girl with the contagious laugh she left behind and frowned. "I suppose that came from trying to please her father."

Freddi's dark head bobbed. "I suspect so. Matthew was

always a strict father. But after you left, he turned positively tyrannical."

"No doubt determined to stamp out whatever amoral proclivities his daughters may have inherited from me," Maggie murmured. Although Mariah had always stubbornly refused to discuss her father, what she hadn't said had spoken volumes. So many, many things to be guilty for, Maggie mused miserably.

Fredericka had the grace to blush. "Oh, I didn't mean that."

"Never apologize for telling the truth, Freddi." Maggie lifted her chin and garnered renewed strength. "Tell me about my daughter."

During the next twenty minutes Maggie learned how hard Laura had tried to meet Matthew's sterling standard. She'd always been the model daughter, earning straight *A*'s in school, being appointed editor of the Rim Rock High School yearbook, winning valedictorian of her class and going on to graduate from Scripps College—one of the only two women's colleges on the West Coast—magna cum laude.

"I didn't know she was at Scripps." For four years her daughter had been going to school only thirty-five miles east of L.A. Thirty-five miles, and she'd never once broken down and called her mother. "My God, how she must have hated me."

"It wasn't in Laura to hate anyone," Freddi quickly assured Maggie. "But you have to understand, Matthew had declared you dead to the family and threatened to cut both Laura and Mariah completely out of his life if they ever attempted to contact you. I suppose Laura was afraid to take the risk."

He would have done it, too, Maggie knew. The coldhearted son of a bitch! She never should have left her babies under that man's evil roof. But then again, she asked herself sadly, after what had happened on that long-ago fateful night, what choice had she had?

None, Maggie reminded herself sadly. None at all.

"Tell me about Clint." She couldn't remember the man, but she did recall his father. All too well. Ancient pain—and additional guilt—caused dual fists to twist her heart in two.

Freddi frowned. "I have to admire Clint for pulling himself up by the bootstraps, but I never thought he was a proper match for Laura."

"Did you know if she was having an affair with him?"

"If she was, she never said anything to me. I also doubt if it was serious. Her marriage with Alan seemed to be a good one. Of course it had its ups and downs, but what marriage doesn't?"

Having seen the same photos Mariah had, Maggie wondered if the Fletchers had been the idyllic match they'd tried so hard to portray. "Mariah thinks Alan killed Laura."

Freddi frowned at what she obviously considered an amazing idea. "I doubt if Alan's ever touched a gun in his life. In fact, I remember when I was trying to talk him into joining the Whiskey River Rifle club—to help expand his local political base—and he told me he wouldn't even know how to load a rifle, let alone shoot it."

She shook her head. "Although I hate to accuse Mariah of ulterior motives, I think her real problem with Alan is that Matthew treated him like a son, while pretending she didn't exist. The day she left town, she was dead to him."

Just like his wife. Knowing firsthand exactly how rigid Matthew Swann could be, Maggie sighed. And although she was grateful for Freddi's concern, she found herself wishing her daughter's longtime friend would leave.

Because she needed a drink. And she needed it now.

Chapter Nine

After a great deal of arguing, and not a few out-and-out shouting matches between Matthew and Maggie, it was finally decided that Laura's funeral would be held in Whiskey River.

"The problem with that," Alan pointed out during a meeting in his hospital room, "is that the church only holds one hundred people."

"You've got a point there, son," Matthew agreed in the low, rumbling voice that had once been capable of frightening Mariah.

"So have a private service," Maggie snapped. "Limit it to family and a selected few close friends."

"Not that you'd know any of your daughter's friends," Matthew countered. "You haven't bothered to come back to town since you deserted your family twenty-six years ago."

"For your information, it's been twenty-seven. And every morning of every one of those years, I thanked God I didn't have to look at you across the breakfast table any longer."

"Hell, you never got up before lunch."

"Excuse me." Heather Martin bravely stepped into the breach. "Could we please try to stay on the subject?"

The senatorial aide had ended up playing peacemaker during each of these sessions. Her people management skills were flawless, Mariah admitted reluctantly. And her sorrow regarding Laura's death seemed genuine enough. Under any other circumstances, Mariah decided she might have even ended up liking her.

The former husband and wife exchanged a blistering look.

A suspended silence settled over the hospital room.

"A private service at that ranch isn't such a bad idea," Matthew said finally. "We could keep the press away."

"Whatever you think, Matt," Alan agreed quickly.

Despite the painful gravity of the subject, Mariah almost enjoyed watching Alan's bid for nationwide publicity squelched.

"Perhaps," Heather suggested, "we could have a memorial service later in Washington."

"For Laura's many D.C. friends," Alan chimed in. "Did I mention that the majority leader offered to pay his respects?"

Maggie lifted her green eyes toward the ceiling.

"It's amazing," Mariah ground out, "how you can put aside your grief in order to plot how to use your wife's death to boost your political career."

Alan gave her a cold stare. "You have no idea what I'm feeling, Mariah. As for my career, Laura was proud of my contribution to our country. She would have wanted me to continue my work in the White House."

"Spare me the political bullshit, senator."

Heather deftly jumped into the conversation again, determined to keep the peace. "Of course we'd wait until the press coverage has died down. We wouldn't want anyone to think we were capitalizing on this horrible tragedy."

"Who could possibly think that?" Mariah said acidly.

"A Washington memorial service is an excellent idea, young lady," Matthew immediately agreed.

From the way he'd been fawning over his wounded son-in-law, Mariah had the feeling Alan could have suggested holding the service on the Capitol steps and having it broadcast over CNN and her father would have enthusiastically approved of the plan. In Matthew's eyes, Alan could do no wrong.

So what else was new?

By the second day after the murder, even more press hounds had come to town, joining those already camped out in front of the courthouse. Each of the networks' news departments had been calling for exclusive, one-on-one interviews. Trace repeatedly refused, which didn't stop them from trying.

One woman booker from "Nightline" was proving stubbornly persistent and both Diane Sawyer and Barbara Walters had placed their own calls, throwing Jill into an absolute tizzy and even impressing a reluctant Cora Mae. From the way Mariah was also burning up the telephone lines, probing into his every move, Trace came to the frustrated conclusion that females were definitely the more determined sex.

As if the weather had conspired to make things more miserable, a high pressure front had settled over the state, bringing monsoon humidity up from the Gulf of California. The stifling heat had everyone testy; J.D., Loftin and Trace had refereed a half dozen domestic disputes and innumerable bar fights in the past eight hours and if it didn't rain soon, Trace worried that Whiskey River would experience its second homicide in a week.

A lesser, but still aggravating problem was the escalating increase in petty juvenile crimes. With a lack of employment opportunities in this rural county, there were too many teenagers in town this vacation season with too much time on their hands.

They'd called in false 911 calls, infiltrated their way onto the police band radio, and had set off cherry bombs that started spot fires all over the town.

Annoyed at the way the investigation had stalled, Trace found himself facing the seventy-two hour rule—an unwritten rule of thumb stating the killer needed to be arrested in the first three days after committing the crime.

Determined not to let Laura Fletcher's murderer or murderers get away, he was rereading the DPS report, comparing it to his notes yet again, trying to unearth something that could solve this damn crime before things got entirely out of hand, when he heard a renewed flurry of activity on the street outside.

He glanced out the window and viewed a tall man in jeans, a snap-front plaid shirt and a worn fawn Stetson climbing out of a forest green Bronco. Clint Garvey had returned to Whiskey River.

Trace watched the man run the gauntlet of reporters, his head down, his stride unbroken, as if he were pushing against a gale force wind. Trace knew the feeling well. He buzzed Jill. "When Garvey arrives, show him right in."

"Clint's back?"

"Seems to be."

"Will you want coffee?"

"Couldn't hurt."

"I'll put a fresh pot on right away."

"Thanks."

"No problem. Ten-four, Sheriff."

Clint Garvey had the weather-hewn face of a man who'd spent his life outdoors, fighting the elements. His eyes, as blue as a mountain lake, were a startling contrast to his dark complexion.

"Hello, Clint." Trace stood up from behind his desk. "We've been looking for you."

"I've been up riding the rim."

"Looking for strays?"

"Actually, I was looking for peace." Clint gave him a long direct look. "I read about Laura's—" he swallowed "—I read about it in the paper."

He obviously could not say the word *murder*. Or *death*. Not in regard to this woman he'd loved for so long. The woman, Trace reminded himself, who'd once been his wife.

"I'm sorry about that, Clint." He gestured toward a chair and sat down behind his desk again.

"It happened Wednesday night?"

"Actually, early Thursday morning."

"Hell." Clint dragged a broad dark hand down his face, slumped down into the chair, stretched his long legs out in front of him and crossed his booted feet at the ankle. He was quiet for a long time.

Trace waited with the customary patience that had initially been so hard for him to learn. In his misguided youth, he'd been famous for his flash-fire temper.

When Garvey finally looked up at him, Trace viewed the lowest circles of hell in their blue depths.

"The paper said you're looking for burglars."

"That's one avenue of investigation."

"And I'm another." It was not a question.

"At this point I'm not ruling out anyone."

Clint Garvey's mouth drew into a tight horizontal line bracketed by deeply slashed vertical lines. "Including that son of a bitch she was married to?"

"I told you—"

"Yeah, yeah." Clint cut him off with a brusque wave

of his callused hand. "You're not ruling anyone out." He cursed, took off his hat and ran his left hand frustratedly through his chestnut hair. "Well, I've got some questions of my own. So how about you ask yours? Then I'll ask mine."

Back in Dallas, Trace would have been inclined to point out that he was the only individual in the room with the right to ask any questions. But he'd quickly discovered that things were different out here in the sticks. Not only did they move at a slower pace, what worked in the big city wasn't always the right tactic for Whiskey River.

When he'd first become a detective, a seasoned veteran of twenty-five years on the force had taken him aside and told him that sometimes, in the heat and pressure of an investigation, a cop could get so wrapped up in following procedure, he might lose track of his main objective.

"Just always keep in mind what you want to achieve, son," the grizzled, cigar-chomping detective had advised. "And you'll do just fine."

The advice had proven invaluable more times than Trace cared to count. Keeping it in mind now, he reminded himself that while his ultimate goal was to solve Laura Fletcher's murder, his objective at the moment was to get Garvey talking. If that took allowing the suspect a few questions of his own, so be it.

Besides, he reminded himself, no one said he'd have to answer.

"Sounds fair enough," he agreed.

Jill arrived with two mugs of black coffee. Trace thanked her, Clint turned down her offer of sugar or cream and accepted his with a muttered "Thanks." He also refused her offer of the apple bear claws that Iris down at The Branding Iron Café had baked fresh that morning.

"Mind if I tape our conversation?" Trace asked, reaching into the drawer of the desk for the portable recorder.

"Suit yourself." Clint took a long drink of the steaming black coffee and looked as if he wished it were something stronger.

Along with the tape recorder, Trace pulled out a small card. If Garvey *was* Laura Fletcher's murderer, Trace had no intention of blowing the case on a technicality.

"Planning on reading me my rights, Sheriff?" Clint asked as his gaze skimmed over the small white piece of pasteboard.

"I think it might be a good idea." When Clint didn't respond, Trace pushed the black Record button, then read the short Miranda warning aloud.

"Do you understand your rights as I've read them?"

Clint continued to drink his coffee. If he was a murderer, he was one of the least nervous ones Trace had ever seen. "They seem clear enough," he said in the same laconic tone favored by cowboys everywhere.

"Would you like to contact your attorney?"

"I don't think that'll be necessary."

"After hearing these rights, and being so advised, are you still willing to talk with me?"

Clint looked at Trace over the chipped rim of the mug. His eyes were chips of ice, his face could have been carved from granite. "Hell, why do you think I came here as soon as I heard? I *want* to talk to you."

After years of working homicide, there was still a part of Trace that was always amazed and mystified by the way people were so willing to concede their constitutional right to silence. It was the professional murderers who knew how to keep their mouths shut. Two decades after the Miranda ruling, amateurs, thank God, were still willing to put themselves at risk.

"Okay." Trace leaned back in his chair, adopting a relaxed pose designed to encourage his subject to relax as well. Interrogation was nothing more than deceptive role playing. Those cops who earned the highest confession rates were, most often, the most seasoned actors.

"Are you familiar with Laura Fletcher?"

"Hell," Clint growled, showing his first sign of emotion, "if we're going to do this one question at a time, it'll take all night. So why don't I just fill you in on the background stuff, then if you've any questions, you can go ahead and ask them?"

Trace was definitely not accustomed to ceding control in an interrogation. With effort, he reminded himself of his objective. *Keep Garvey talking.*

"Go ahead," he said with a nod.

"Laura and I were just kids when we met," Clint began slowly. "Of course, growing up around here, I knew who she was, but we didn't exactly move in the same circles, if you know what I mean."

He looked at Trace, who nodded back, remembering all too well how it was to be on the outside looking in.

"Then I got hired on for the spring roundup. I was nineteen. Laura was seventeen."

Clint's harsh expression softened. Trace guessed he was thinking about those lost days of young love.

"To make a long story short, we fell in love. When her father caught us, he fired me and grounded her."

"So you eloped."

"We eloped," Clint said flatly. "But when old man Swann caught up with us, Laura caved in and went back home with him."

"That must have made you angry."

Clint barked a harsh laugh devoid of humor. "Nice subtle try, Sheriff. I was madder than hell. I tried to hate her for years afterward. But it wasn't any good. Because I couldn't stop loving her."

"How long was it before you saw each other again?"

"We'd run into each other at the market, pass in the

street whenever she was home from Washington, that sort of thing. Then, after her grandmother left me part of the Prescott spread, we were neighbors, so to speak, so sometimes I'd catch a glimpse of her while I was out riding. But we never spoke."

"Why do you think Ida Prescott left you that land?" Cora Mae had filled him in on the will that had apparently sent more than a few shock waves rumbling through the community, but apparently no one in Whiskey River had been able to understand the old woman's motives.

"Hell if I know. I'd done some work for her from time to time, repairing fences, rounding up strays, that sort of thing, and we always got along.

"After Swann fired me, the old lady told me that he was an ass. She also said that Laura was a damn fool to let her father run her life the way she did. I guess she figured that I got a raw deal and was trying to make it up to me. Or, perhaps she figured if she threw Laura and I together, chemistry might prove more powerful than political ambition."

"Did it?"

Clint shrugged and looked down into his coffee as if seeking the answer in the dark brown depths. "Eventually. But not the way Ida might have thought. It was years later when Laura came to me. I was in Washington testifying on grazing rights and she showed up for the hearing. We went back to my hotel. That's when I finally learned the real reason she went home with Swann that morning.

"The son of a bitch threatened to have me arrested for statutory rape if she didn't get an annulment and promise to never speak to me again."

Pain flooded into his eyes, turning them the color of a storm-tossed sea. "All those damn years wasted," he muttered.

"You don't think Swann would have followed through on his threat?"

Clint stared out the window, but Trace had the feeling it was not the reporters crowding into the courthouse square he was looking at, but the life he'd been cheated out of.

"Hell, of course he would have. Swann isn't the kind of man to make idle threats. And I might have ended up serving some time. But I would have gotten out. And Laura and I still would have been married. And we could have been together."

He looked straight at Trace, his gaze unflinching. "When she came to me, when we made love in my hotel that weekend and it was just the same as it always was, except better, I was fool enough to think we could recapture all we'd lost."

"How long had the affair been going on?"

Clint grimaced at Trace's choice of words. "Six months. And it wasn't any sleazy, backstreet affair. I wanted to marry her."

"The lady was already married," Trace said pointedly.

"She was going to get a divorce." When Trace didn't immediately respond, Clint downed the rest of his coffee and slammed the empty mug down onto the desk. "She was, dammit. She was going to tell the senator this weekend."

Trace was not above a little suspect baiting. "Before or after his Fourth of July presidential announcement?"

"Good try, Sheriff." Clint forced a grin. "But it won't work. Laura wasn't the slightest bit eager to be First Lady, and even if she had been, I certainly wouldn't have killed her."

"Even if she'd refused to leave her husband?"

He looked Trace straight in the eye. "Even then."

"When was the last time you saw her?"

"The night she died," Clint admitted. "The senator was late. I talked to her on the phone, and I could tell she was upset, so I drove over to calm her down."

"Did you have sexual relations with her?"

"We made love." Clint gave him a long hard look that suggested there was a big difference.

"Point taken," Trace agreed amiably.

That was another interrogation tactic. Become a suspect's best friend—his mirror image. You strangled your mother-in-law because she wouldn't stop bitching about you drinking a few six-packs every night after work? Well, hell, pardner, who doesn't fantasize about doing the old battle-ax in from time to time?

Shoot your boss over an overtime dispute? Fuck, the son of a bitch probably deserved to get his balls blown off. Beat your wife to death with your fists? What did she expect, slapping you first, just because you blew the baby food money at the dog track? Become a man's friend and he was more likely to share masculine confidences.

"What did you do after you and Laura Fletcher made love?"

"I went home and waited for her to call and tell me she'd told Fletcher she was filing for divorce. The next morning, when I was still waiting, I figured she'd lost her nerve. Again."

"So this wasn't the first time she'd promised to tell Fletcher she wanted out of the marriage?" Trace watched Garvey carefully.

"No. We'd argued about it."

"Anyone hear you?"

"I don't think so. For obvious reasons, we never went out in public together."

It crossed Trace's mind that Garvey should have requested a lawyer. Because there wasn't a criminal attorney in America who would have allowed his client to reveal such a damning piece of incriminating information.

"So, when she didn't show up, you went out riding."

"Yeah. I'll admit it. I was steamed. But I always believed eventually, she'd get a divorce."

"And marry you."

"Yes." His unwavering stare did not invite an argument.

Trace picked up a pen and began casually toying with it. "What about children? Did you plan a family?"

"Laura couldn't have kids."

"How did you feel about that?"

"Christ, you sound like some radio talk-show shrink, Sheriff," Clint said. "For the record, it was Laura I wanted. I wasn't looking for a brood mare. If she'd been able to have kids, that would've been a bonus. But she couldn't. So I didn't care."

"Sounds reasonable," Trace agreed easily. He didn't think Garvey knew. He was also not looking forward to being the one who broke the news to him. "Do you own a gun?"

"Sure. A shotgun and a rifle."

Along with about ninety-nine percent of the county's population, Trace considered. "No handgun?"

"A handgun's for shooting people. The shotgun's for quail and the rifle is for elk and deer. No, I don't own a handgun, Sheriff, because I don't have anything valuable enough to shoot anyone over. And it isn't in me to kill a man. Or a woman," he tacked on pointedly.

"Would you mind giving us permission to search your premises?"

"Go ahead." He shrugged. "I don't have anything to hide."

Trace had heard that one before. "And I'll want to take your boot and tire prints."

"To match them up to those found at the scene of the crime?"

"That's right."

"Hot damn," Clint said derisively, "you're just a regular Columbo, aren't you Sheriff?"

Trace ignored the sarcasm. "I'm also going to ask a judge to request a blood test."

"A blood test?" Frown lines etched canyons into the dark forehead. "Oh." He dragged his hands through his hair again as he contemplated the reason for the request. "Is that really necessary? I've already told you I was with her that night."

"The blood test is also to establish paternity."

"Paternity?" Comprehension came crashing down. Trace watched it move in waves across the dark face. "Laura was pregnant?" Garvey asked in a rough, broken voice.

"The autopsy put her at two months." Trace weighed revealing more and decided, what the hell. "Senator Fletcher claims the baby couldn't have been his."

"A baby." The cowboy appeared absolutely shell shocked. The color faded from his face, leaving his complexion the hue of cold ashes. "Laura was going to have my baby?"

"That's one of the things I need to find out."

A suspicious moisture glistened in Clint's eyes, but his expression hardened. "I guess I lied, Sheriff."

"About what?"

"About being able to kill a man. If I find the bastard who did this—"

"That's not your job, Garvey." For the first time since the interrogation began, Trace's short, harsh tone was that of the tough, no-nonsense city homicide detective he'd once been. "It's mine."

"Then do it."

Trace met his challenging look straight on. "I intend to."

Soon after Clint left the office, with instructions not to leave the county, Trace's intercom buzzed.

"What is it now, Jill?" Trace snapped, expecting yet another call from some network news producer wanting to put him on the air. Or one of the nuisance calls regarding the kids who'd been driving him up a wall.

His office door opened. "Jill was about to announce me," Mariah informed him. She was wearing a snug white top made from some stretchy material that hugged her curves like a second skin and a short flowered skirt that reminded him of a summer garden in full bloom. She smelled like one, too.

"No point in that," Trace drawled. He was uncomfortable with the way he was inexplicably pleased to see her. "When you do it so well yourself."

Her response, issued through gritted teeth, was satisfyingly obscene. She tossed her hair over her shoulder, sat down in the visitor's chair without waiting for an invitation and glowered across the desk at him.

"Don't push me, Sheriff. I've had an absolutely rotten afternoon and I'm in the mood to start throwing things."

"Don't feel like the Lone Ranger."

Their eyes met in a blaze of shared frustration. And something else. Mariah's stomach tightened in a knot of sexual awareness. Not the first she'd suffered since meeting this man.

She told herself that she should be grateful she could still feel such intense sexual desire, despite the painful battering her emotions had taken when she'd arrived home after so long to find her sister murdered.

And she had to admit that last night's dream—a hot, sexual, strikingly graphic fantasy of Trace Callahan handcuffing her to a lacy, old-fashioned brass bed, then making achingly slow love to her until she was literally begging him to end her torment—was a vast improvement over the nightmares about Laura's murder she'd suffered the night before.

Her eyes were ablaze with emotion. Her lips, tinted the hue of a wild poppy, looked soft and sweet and utterly delectable. Although he knew it to be risky, Trace vowed to taste those lips before Mariah Swann returned to her glamorous life in Hollywood.

Secretly excited by the way his eyes had turned to polished pewter as they drifted over her mouth, Mariah dragged her gaze past Trace, out the window. "Was that Clint Garvey I saw driving away in the Bronco?"

"Yeah."

"So he's back in town." She frowned and rubbed at her temple. "Did he know about the pregnancy?"

"He does now."

"Shit." She shook her head, dug around in her purse for her cigarettes, belatedly remembering she'd chosen this morning to stop smoking. Again. "I sure wish I believed in reincarnation," she muttered, opting instead for a Life Saver. "Because those two definitely deserved a second chance."

Although he didn't respond, Trace silently agreed. So long as Garvey hadn't murdered his lover.

"So what did Clint say?"

"You know that's confidential." Seeing the storm brewing on her smooth brow, and taking seriously her threat about throwing things, Trace added, "he didn't confess, if that's what you're wondering."

"Of course I'm not. Clint didn't kill Laura. I've told you, Sheriff—"

"I know. You still believe the senator killed her."

"And shot himself to deflect suspicion," Mariah

agreed. When she crossed her legs, he was treated to a glimpse of smooth tanned thigh. "I've written it—"

"I know. Scads of times." His mind was still on that flash of honey-hued flesh. As desire pooled hotly in his groin, Trace frowned.

He hadn't been all that surprised when he'd found Mariah infiltrating her way into his thoughts at times he should have been concentrating on his investigation. She was, after all, a remarkably attractive woman. The fact that she was bright and quick and somewhat amusing only added to her appeal.

It was one thing to find Mariah Swann sexually appealing. It was quite another to feel such an intense, uncontrollable pull.

Determined to regain control, he dragged his mind back their conversation. "So, if you were writing this as a teleplay, you want to explain how you'd deal with the little detail of no weapon being found in the house?"

He steepled his fingers. "What did the guy do? Shoot his wife with the .38, carefully wound himself in a nonfatal location with the .25, drive two miles down to the river—which would involve going around a police barricade, don't forget—throw the guns into the water, drive back to the house, call 911, then pass out before the paramedics arrived?"

"It's more likely he had an accomplice who took the guns away after the shootings."

"I assume you're talking about Heather Martin."

"It's obvious that she and Alan are lovers."

"The last time I checked Arizona legal statutes, adultery didn't make a couple coconspirators in a murder."

"Clint couldn't do it."

"Well, the two of you agree on that." Trace's tone suggested his own mind was still open.

"I watched him have to put down a horse years ago. I

could tell it tore him up.'' Mariah shook her head decisively. ''He couldn't have shot Laura.''

''Spoken like a true and loyal friend.''

She shot him a quick, suspicious look. ''How did you know we were friends?''

''It seems to be common knowledge.''

J.D. had told him a little; Cora Mae had been more than willing to fill in the gaps. The elderly woman's mother lode of gossip—and the eagerness with which she shared that personal information—made her a combination of town crier, old-time party line and local tabloid newspaper.

Conveniently ignoring the fact that she'd checked Trace out with the Dallas P.D., Mariah decided that she didn't like the idea of him asking around town about her. Especially when she could guess what people's responses would be.

''Oh, that Swann girl,'' Mrs. Kendall, down at Annie's Antiques would sniff, ''she was always wild. Sashaying down Main Street in those tight shorts that left absolutely nothing to the imagination. I always thought it was a miracle she didn't get raped, the way she dressed.''

''Mariah Swann?'' Mariah could practically see Jeb Young, owner of The Saddlery Tack and Feed pause and spit into the old-fashioned milk can he'd been using for a spittoon since before Mariah was born. ''The gal was a spitfire, that's for sure. Had more boys buzzin' around her than bees around a honeycomb.''

Another wet plug of tobacco would hit its mark. ''Whatever trouble she'd get into, the kid sure as hell could sit a horse,'' Jeb would probably concede. Hadn't he always told her she was a natural born horsewoman? And in the former rodeo champion's eyes, those words were the highest praise of all.

''I would think, with a murderer running loose in Whiskey River, that you'd have better things to do than to investigate me,'' she complained.

''Actually, I was looking for information about Garvey when your name came up. I take it the two of you were close.''

''I never slept with Clint, if that's what you're implying. He was always in love with Laura.''

Her prickliness reminded Trace of other gossip he'd heard over the past two days. Old stories about Mariah Swann's supposed teenage promiscuity. A story Jeb Young had disputed.

''Them boys all trailed after Mariah like lovesick pups,'' the elderly bronc buster had alleged. ''But since the kids knew Matthew would shoot anyone who knocked up either one of his daughters, I always figgered there was a lot less goin' on in all those pickup trucks parked out along the river than the girl wanted people to believe.''

''I only heard you and Garvey were friends,'' he said truthfully. ''Nothing more.'' Everyone he'd spoken with had confirmed what Mariah had just told him. That Clint had only ever had eyes for the eldest Swann daughter.

The tense line around Mariah's mouth softened. Her turquoise eyes warmed in reminiscence. ''Once, when I was twelve, I ran away from home. Clint found me outside of town, trying to hitch a ride on the interstate.''

''Lucky for you he did.''

''I know that now. At the time, I was furious at him.'' The smile that touched her eyes had her lips curving. ''He actually dragged me into his truck, kicking and screaming and threatened to hog-tie me and drag me back to the ranch behind his horse if I didn't shut up and behave.''

''So the guy has a temper?''

''Of course not.'' Mariah tossed her head. ''It was just a threat. And to tell the truth, he only brought up the part about dragging me behind the horse after I kicked him in the balls."

Trace hadn't realized that it was possible to grimace and grin at the same time. "Dragging sounds too kind."

"That's what Clint said at the time."

"So he took you home?"

"Eventually. First we went to see *Jaws* at the theater in Payson and after that we stopped by the DQ for a chili burger, fries and chocolate shake. And then he took me home."

It didn't sound like the behavior of a killer. But Trace knew even the most seemingly mild-mannered people could, under the right circumstances, commit heinous crimes of passion.

"I imagine your father was relieved."

She shrugged and as he watched the light go out in her eyes, like a candle flame extinguished by a cold gasp of wind, Trace regretted mentioning Matthew Swann.

"He never even noticed I'd left." She abruptly stood up. "Well, as much as I've enjoyed our little chat, Sheriff, I've got to go referee another battle."

"It's been rough, huh?"

She could detect honest sympathy in his tone. "It hasn't exactly been a picnic. Which, in a way, is the topic of this afternoon's argument. My father wants to barbecue Swann beef for the funeral supper tomorrow. Maggie, unsurprisingly, insists she'd rather eat sawdust and is pushing to have her caterer fly in *appropriate* dishes from Beverly Hills."

She sighed and shook her head. "At this point, I'm ready to vote for potato chips, supermarket onion dip and a keg of Coors. A huge one. Perhaps I ought to just book a bunk in your drunk tank and buy the keg for myself."

"That's probably not the answer."

"I know." Another sigh. "But there are times..." Her voice drifted off. "Would you do me a favor?"

"If I can."

"Don't let those vultures out there put so much pressure on you that you zero in on the wrong man."

"I'm not in the habit of arresting innocent people."

"That's what they say in Dallas." She gave him a long, judicial look. "Clint didn't do it," she stressed one more time. "I'd bet my life on it."

"I don't intend to let it come to that."

She managed a faint, reluctant smile. "You're a fraud, Callahan."

He lifted a dark brow. "Oh?"

"You pretend to be some jaded, burned out, raggedy-edged cop who just wants to glide quietly through life until you can collect your pension. But you can't quite put away the suit of armor. Even if it is a little tarnished these days."

"Don't look now, Ms. Swann, but your writer's imagination is getting the better of you again."

"Is it?" Mariah smiled. "I don't think so." This time the smile was real. As it reached her eyes, warming them to a jeweled sheen, the power of that smile hit Trace directly in the gut. And lower. "See you around, Sheriff. As they say on the tube—I'll stay in touch, so you stay in touch."

With that she was gone, leaving the evocative scent of wildflowers behind.

Trace stood at the window, watching her deftly answer the questions shot at her as she made her way through the throng of noisy press to the red Jeep brazenly parked in the tow-away zone.

As the sharp claws of desire dug a little deeper, Trace

decided that it was probably time he paid a visit to Jessica Ingersoll. To fill her in on his investigation so far.

And if you buy that half-baked excuse, pal, Trace told himself as he gathered up his files and left the office, *I've got a bridge you might be interested in.*

Chapter Ten

Desperately in need of comfort and not ashamed to admit it, later that afternoon, Mariah drove up the winding road to Clint Garvey's ranch. She found him in the barn, brushing down a lathered gray stallion.

"Hi, Clint."

He turned, saw her standing in the doorway and smiled. A weary smile that nevertheless reached his eyes. "Well, if it isn't the Vixen of Whiskey River." He dropped the currycomb and held out his arms. "Welcome home, sweetheart."

She ran toward the comfort he was offering, wrapped her arms around his waist and breathed in the rich male scents of horse and sweat and leather. "Oh, Clint." She sighed against his shirt. "I'm so sorry."

He didn't answer. There was, they both knew, nothing he could say. For a long, silent time they stood there, arms around each other.

"I loved her," he said against the top of her head.

She tilted her head back and saw the truth, laced with pain in his eyes. She found herself wondering if the baby would have had Laura's emerald eyes, or Clint's startlingly pale blue ones. "I know. Me, too." When she felt herself about to cry, Mariah bit her lip. "I need a favor."

"Anything."

It was, she thought with a rush of emotion, the truth. "I need to borrow a horse. Just for a little while."

"You got it."

She'd come dressed for riding, in jeans, plain brown nubuck boots with a slanted heel, a cotton shirt printed with arrowheads and a straw hat with a classic cattleman's crease and brim. Having spent the past hour galloping over the high country meadows, trying to expunge the pain that was twisting his gut and his heart in two, Clint knew all too well why Mariah was experiencing a sudden need to go riding. He also knew it wouldn't work. But he wasn't going to keep her from trying.

He chose a twelve-year-old cutting horse. He and the mare had won a lot of buckles together; she was as smart as a whip and the most responsive horse he'd ever owned. She'd be careful even if her rider wasn't. Which he didn't expect Mariah to be. Especially given the circumstances.

Laura had always been the cautious sister. For Mariah every morning had been a new challenge. He remembered her tearing through each day, all burners firing, with verve and energy and no looking back.

As he watched her gallop away over the pasture, Clint realized that Mariah was discovering the hard way that the past had a nasty way of catching up with you just when you least expected it.

The mare was truly a wonder. Fast as the wind and as surefooted as a mountain goat. Wildflowers were crushed beneath the flying hoofs as horse and rider raced through the spruce, aspen and fir trees, deftly dodging rocks and those insidiously spreading growths of prickly pear cactus that had worked their way up from the lower deserts. The sky was a vast blue bowl overhead; the noise of civilization had been replaced by the whisper of the wind in the trees, and the sound of hoofs hammering the hard red earth. It was cool here. Peaceful. And seemingly as untouched as it had been during the days when Apaches had sought sanctuary deep in the silent canyons.

Clint's ranch was wedge-shaped, sandwiched between Laura's and Matthew's. As she maneuvered the horse closer to the treacherous, rocky edge of the rim, Mariah wondered how he'd felt spending all those years so close to Laura. Yet so far away.

And, of course it couldn't be easy living in such proximity to the individual who'd broken up his marriage. Not that either man acknowledged the other. From what Mariah had managed to worm out of the evening shift desk clerk at the lodge—whose mother had worked as the Swann housekeeper the past decade—the two ranchers hadn't spoken to one another in years.

Dammit, she didn't want to think about her father, or Clint and Laura. That's what this ride was all about. She needed to rid both her mind and her body of the excess nervous energy simmering inside her. To expunge the pain. And the guilt.

Unfortunately, it wasn't that easy. As she found herself riding toward the boundary line separating Clint's ranch from Laura's, her thoughts trapped in the past, Mariah failed to notice the tassel-eared squirrels playing tag amidst the fallen tree branches, the red-tailed hawk circling overhead, or the bees gathering pollen from the fields of blue and yellow wildflowers.

Nor did she notice the glint of the sun on the lenses of the binoculars focused her way from an outcropping of rocks.

''Well, well. That was certainly a pleasant surprise.''

Trace and Jessica were lying on their backs beside one

another in the antique bed she'd had shipped from her parents' home in Philadelphia. The mahogany gleamed with generations of lemon oil rubbed painstakingly into the wood surface; in the flickering glow of the beeswax candle on the bedside table, their cooling flesh gleamed with a sheen of perspiration.

She rolled over, draped one long leg languorously across his hips and smiled into his eyes. "I didn't think you cared any longer, Callahan."

"I'll always care about you." It was the truth.

He stroked her hair, then ran his palm down her back as she snuggled against him with an easy familiarity very much different from the fiery passion that had resulted in the hastily discarded trail of clothes leading from her front door to the bed.

"And I for you." She brushed his damp hair back from his forehead. She bent her head and touched her lips to his, a slow, soft kiss they hadn't taken time for earlier. "Do you know what I was doing this afternoon?"

"Working the Fletcher case?"

"Well, that too." Her fingernails trailed lightly down his cheek and around his lips. "But along with reading autopsy reports, I was fantasizing about you. It's been too long since I screwed the only man who ever made me scream."

Her caressing hand moved down his chest, following the harsh red line that bisected his torso, over his flat stomach. "She's getting to you, isn't she?"

"Who?"

"The Swann woman." Her long slender fingers curved around him, stroking him with a smooth, practiced touch.

"All murder victims get to me," Trace said as his penis stirred against her hand. "Hazards of the profession."

''I wasn't speaking of Laura Fletcher. I was referring to her Hollywood sister.''

He thought about lying then decided after all they'd shared that he owed her the truth. ''There's no future there.''

''Ah, always the romantic.'' The warmth of her smile took the sting out of the accusation.

''You think I'm a romantic?'' That came as a surprise. Trace had never considered himself a hearts-and-flowers kind of guy. Neither had any of the women he'd known. Including his ex-wife.

''What else would you call a man who lives in a world of heroes and villains?''

She lowered her head, her lips following the seductive trail her fingers had blazed. ''You were definitely born in the wrong time, Callahan. I can see you sitting at the Round Table with all the other knights—although your armor is admittedly a bit rustier than most,'' she allowed. ''Jousting for the honor of fair lady, going off to battle the bad guys for God and country.''

Her hair was splayed across his bare stomach. Her lips and tongue were making him hard again. It was becoming difficult to concentrate.

''Oh, yes, Trace. You are most definitely a romantic.''

Mariah had told him much the same thing earlier. Deciding that both women were wrong, Trace dove his hands into her hair.

''You keep that up and my dick is going to explode.'' He arched his hips up. ''You want to talk? Or fuck?''

Jessica's answering laugh was throaty and just as sexy as the rest of her as she shifted positions and sat astride him, knees on either side of his hips.

Trace's last coherent thought, as Jess lowered herself onto him, was to wonder how Mariah was surviving amidst the battling Swanns.

* * *

They'd come to the edge of the sheer cliff. Mariah sat astride the horse, staring out over the vast hundreds of miles of seemingly endless green landscape, drinking in the sight of blue hills covered in pine and juniper and manzanita, realizing for the first time how much she'd missed it.

When the mare first snorted and sidestepped skittishly, Mariah's first thought was that the horse had sensed something. A rattlesnake, perhaps. She leaned forward, patting the sleek chestnut neck and murmuring soothing words as she scanned the ground around them.

But before Mariah could identify the source of the mare's nervousness, the horse suddenly reared, sending Mariah flying.

Utilizing his political pull, Matthew had the road to the Swann ranch blocked off for the funeral. When Trace refused to take J.D. off the murder investigation to stand guard at the gate, the rancher hired private security guards from Flagstaff, instructing them to shoot at the first reporter who attempted to cross the barricade onto the property.

When Trace got wind of those instructions, he immediately let the guards know that if they so much as raised their rifles to one of the admittedly obnoxious reporters, he'd run them in for assault with a deadly weapon.

Three days after her murder, Laura was buried on Swann property not far from the ranch house where she had lived. And died.

It was raining. A steady, slanting rain that was unusually cold for the first week in July, even here in the mountains. Since the cooling relief was welcome after days of stultifying heat, no one in Whiskey River complained.

As she sat beside her mother beneath the big black awning provided by Peterson's Funeral Home, Mariah ignored the protest of her aching body—the result of that stupid and embarrassing fall off Clint's mare yesterday—and remembered Maggie, before she'd returned to Hollywood, telling her a bedtime story about how rain was really angels weeping.

Mariah watched the white flower-draped casket being slowly lowered into the wet ground and decided that in Laura's case, the story was all wrong. Any angels lucky enough to have Laura joining their heavenly ranks would undoubtedly be singing hosannas.

Alan, who'd been released from the hospital that morning, rose from the folding chair, braced on one side by Heather, the other by a tall, silver-haired man Mariah didn't recognize. From his Saville Row suit, she suspected he was not from Whiskey River.

Although he'd left the hospital in a wheelchair, Alan was managing, with obvious effort, to walk with a cane.

"Now we know who the real actor in the family is," Maggie murmured in Mariah's ear. Her voice was faintly slurred. With grief? Mariah wondered. Or—dear Lord, please not now—something else?

Putting aside that looming problem for now, Mariah steeled herself for the sound of dirt hitting atop her sister's coffin and was relieved when instead the minister handed Alan a small silver scoop.

Alan handed the scoop to Heather, who bent down to fill it with earth, then returned the scoop to Alan. Mariah's temper flared. His mistress had no right taking part in Laura's burial!

As if reading her mind, Maggie reached out and placed a black-gloved hand on her daughter's knee, giving it an encouraging squeeze.

Drawing in a deep, calming breath, Mariah covered her mother's hand with her own. When she felt the moisture on the back of her hand, at first she thought the awning had sprung a leak. Then she realized that behind the black veil Maggie was wearing—for dramatic effect, Mariah had thought when she'd first seen it this morning—her mother was silently weeping.

Alan tipped the silver scoop, sending a spray of earth downward.

"Good night, sweet wife," he said, paraphrasing Hamlet's farewell soliloquy to Horatio. As she watched the tears stream down his tanned face and heard the choked sob in his deep voice, Mariah decided that Maggie was right. The man was one hell of an actor. "May flights of angels sing thee to thy rest."

And then it was over.

Well, almost over, Mariah thought as they made their way back to the black limousine waiting on the other side of the wrought iron fence. There was still the supper to get through.

On a nearby hilltop, Clint Garvey sat astride his gray stallion, the rain dripping off the brim of his hat as he watched the funeral. As the casket disappeared into the ground, he tried to think about the good times he and Laura had shared, as few as they were.

But instead all he could think about was that last fatal argument. After Matthew Swann, back unexpectedly from Santa Fe, had shown up at his ranch, loaded for bear.

He heard the steady *clip clop* of another rider approaching. Turning in the saddle, Clint felt yet another sting of guilt when he viewed Patti Greene riding the Morgan he continued to board at his place for free because he figured he owed her.

"I figured I'd find you up here," she said. Her expression revealed honest concern, but he knew her well enough to detect a faint victorious glint in her green eyes.

He didn't answer. As if she hadn't really expected one, Patti reined the Morgan gelding in beside his stallion. Both silently watched the mourners walking away from the gravesite.

Leaving Laura alone, Clint thought, as he experienced another stab of pain, sharper than all the others so far. Alone in that cold dark ground. Cursing beneath his breath at the fucking futility of life, he slumped lower in the saddle, guilt riding heavily on his shoulders.

The funeral party returned to the Swann ranch house, where Maggie had once lived with Matthew, where Mariah had grown up, and where ten-year-old Laura had done her best to provide a stabilizing influence after Maggie's defection.

Mariah was standing in a corner of the enormous living room, nursing a glass of wine, worriedly watching Maggie like a hawk, when, out of the corner of her eye, she saw Heather slip through the French doors at the far end of the room and go out onto the wide porch that surrounded the house. She was unsurprised when Alan followed moments later.

Glancing around, Mariah decided she was the only one who'd seen the pair leave. Putting her glass down onto a marble topped table beside an original Frederic Remington bronze of a bucking bronc, Mariah followed.

Having expected to catch them in a heated, surreptitious embrace, Mariah was surprised to find the senator and his aide engaged in what appeared to be a heated argument. Although she didn't dare open the doors, which precluded her from overhearing their conversation, it was obvious from Alan's rigid stance that he was furious.

For her part, Heather had thrown off her cheerfully efficient attitude and was openly crying. She kept dashing at the moisture on her cheeks with the back of her hands even as she refused to back down from her boss's obvious attempt at intimidation.

Mariah was just considering risking slipping out onto the porch when she heard a familiar voice behind her.

"Mariah, dear."

Biting back a curse, she turned around. As Freddi Palmer touched cheeks, Mariah was smothered in a thick cloud of Obsession. "I am so, so terribly sorry. What a tragedy. What will we all ever do without our darling Laura?"

Tears misted Freddi's doe brown eyes. The Realtor was wearing a black slubby silk Albert Nippon suit that as recently as last week had been on sale at Neiman Marcus for slightly under a thousand dollars. Mariah knew exactly how much the suit cost because she'd gone shopping with Maggie, who'd tried to talk her into trying it on. At the time, Mariah had refused, quipping that she wasn't planning to attend any funerals anytime soon.

The memory of how mistaken her flippant response had turned out to be sent a stiletto right through Mariah's heart.

"I don't know, Freddi." Mariah inwardly swore as she watched a grim-faced Alan slip back into the room. Her opportunity was lost.

"I still can't believe it." Freddi clucked her tongue. "A murder in Whiskey River. I mean, maybe I could accept it if it'd been a couple of cowboys or a jealous husband or boyfriend, the kind of people who hang out at Denims and Diamonds. But Laura? Who on earth would have anything against such a sweet, warmhearted person?"

"That's what the sheriff's going to find out."

"Do you honestly believe he can?" A slim, perfectly arched black brow arched. "I mean, Mariah dear, rumor has it that our sheriff is little more than a burnout victim, come to our fair town to avoid crime, not to solve it. Why, if he wasn't servicing our county attorney, if you know what I mean, I doubt if he would have even been hired."

"He's sleeping with Jessica Ingersoll?" It shouldn't bother her, Mariah told herself. But dammit, it did.

"Of course. Ask anyone in town. It wouldn't be anyone's business, I suppose, except for the fact that a horrible crime has been committed and there's no evidence the sheriff is capable of tracking down the perpetrators. Especially since it's obvious that Laura was killed by outsiders—"

"Why is that obvious?"

"What?" Frown lines etched their way across Freddi's smooth brow.

"I said, why do you think my sister was killed by strangers?"

For what Mariah suspected to be the first time in Fredericka Palmer's life, the woman appeared to be at a total loss for words. "Well, that's what everyone's saying. That she was killed when a burglary went awry, which is more than a little upsetting when you realize how complacent we've all become, believing that crime is reserved for cities like Phoenix or Los Angeles. But Whiskey River?"

"Maybe it was outsiders." Mariah shrugged. "Maybe not."

Freddi gave Mariah a curious look. "Are you telling me you know something different?"

"It just seems like an awfully pat answer."

"Maggie told me that you think Alan killed Laura. And I can certainly see how your vivid imagination would want to embellish what is unfortunately a horribly mundane crime, but I can't believe you're right about this, Mariah."

Mundane? Her sister, Freddi's best friend, was dead and that was the best adjective she could come up with? Mariah was trying to decide exactly how to respond when a stir at the other end of the room captured both women's attention.

''Speak of the devil,'' Freddi murmured as Trace entered the room.

He was not wearing his hat. Rain sparkled in his black hair. ''I'm sorry to disturb your mourning,'' he said on what Mariah had learned to recognize as his official police voice.

''I presume you've come to tell us that you've put that son of a bitch Garvey behind bars,'' Matthew said.

Trace had not been able to keep the fact of Laura and Garvey's affair a secret, which hadn't much surprised Trace. Past experience had proven that police departments—no matter how small—tended to leak like a sieve. But it had irritated the hell out of him.

''I haven't completed my investigation yet,'' he answered. ''At this point I'm not prepared to put anyone behind bars.''

''So while you're intruding on our grief, my daughter's murderer is running around free?''

In his black western cut suit and lizard skin boots Matthew looked even larger and more formidable than usual. He was wearing a black string bolo tie with a silver and turquoise slide. When she'd first seen him, it had crossed Mariah's mind that her father could have been ordered directly up from a central casting call for nineteenth century rancher barons.

''Why don't we just give Sheriff Callahan an opportunity to tell his story his own way?'' Mariah suggested.

''Why don't you just shut your goddamn mouth.'' Matthew turned on his remaining daughter. ''You lost the right to be part of this family ten years ago when you stole your sister's car and went off to live like some two-bit slut in Hollywood.''

Trace watched the color drain from Mariah's already

too pale complexion. Her shadowed eyes were deep pools of hurt as she stiffened, like a soldier on parade, trying to deflect the pain her father's disapproval could still cause.

It was not the first time Trace had witnessed such behavior from Matthew Swann toward his daughter.

"Mr. Swann," he said. "I am truly sorry for your loss."

"If that's the case—" Matthew began to cut in.

Trace cut him off with a quick swipe of the hand. "I said, I'm sorry," he repeated on a quiet, yet forceful voice. "However, in the event it's slipped your mind, let me point out that my contract with the county supervisors is to keep the peace in Whiskey River. And as it happens, I'm inclined to take my job very literally."

Matthew Swann rose to his full height. "Are you threatening me, Callahan?"

"I'm simply saying that if you continue these attacks on your daughter—" his words were directed at her father, but he was looking straight at Mariah "—I'll be tempted to bring out the rubber hoses."

Struck dumb for one of the few times in his life, Matthew's mouth opened and closed like a grounded trout. It took a good thirty seconds for the rancher to find his voice. "I don't like your attitude, Callahan."

"You're not the first person to say that," Trace said agreeably. "I keep promising to take one of those Dale Carnegie courses, but things keep getting in the way. Like murder investigations," he said pointedly.

Maggie did not miss the brief glance exchanged by Trace and her daughter. *Interesting,* she thought as she gave the lawman a second, longer study.

"Thank you for coming by, Sheriff," she said, entering into the conversation. Her eyes were slightly glazed and as shadowed as her daughter's. She looked glamorously fragile, like a porcelain statue draped in black. "Would you care for something to drink?"

"Actually, Ms. McKenna, I've come to talk with the senator."

"With me?" Alan arched a patrician brow.

Despite the cane and the faint hospital pallor underlying his tennis court tan, the senator was looking remarkably hale and hearty for a gunshot victim who'd just been widowed, Trace thought. Seeing him like this, in his conservative navy suit, starched white pinstripe shirt and Republican red tie, a stranger would never realize that anything was amiss in Senator Alan Fletcher's privileged world.

"Yes, sir. I have a few more questions."

The senator's helpful, open face closed up. "I'm sorry, Sheriff, but I've already told you everything I know about that horrible night."

Which hadn't been much, Trace considered, thinking back on the stacks of mug books he and the senator had looked through together yesterday. None of the faces had looked remotely familiar and Trace had left the hospital room more frustrated than ever. The damn case had bogged down. Over breakfast with Jessica this morning, she'd agreed that it was time to lean on the senator.

The man in the British suit appeared at Alan's right shoulder. "Is my client a suspect, Sheriff?"

"Your client?"

"I'm Peter Worthington." When he extended his hand, Trace noted irrelevantly that the lawyer's nails had been buffed. "Senator Fletcher's attorney." The two men shook hands and studied each other. "Is the senator a suspect?"

"Not at this time," Trace said, not quite truthfully.

There were inconsistencies in Fletcher's story large enough to drive the Suburban through. Beginning with that first lie about his terrific relationship with his wife.

Of course, Trace had allowed, when discussing the case with Jess, anyone who had the unhappy luck to end up in the middle of a homicide investigation couldn't be expected to be open about all the flaws in his seemingly perfect personal life.

Still, the fact that Alan Fletcher spent the hours prior to his wife's murder with his mistress didn't look good.

"Do you have a warrant for my client's arrest?" Worthington asked.

"Not at this time," Trace repeated. The implication that a warrant could be forthcoming lingered in the air between them.

"Then I'm afraid I'm going to have to advise my client not to answer any further questions," the attorney said. "At last count, Senator Fletcher has been interviewed by you on four separate occasions.

"He's given you descriptions—as well as he could—of the intruders, he's given you a timetable of the events of that night, he's not complained when your people literally camped out in his family home, sealing it off as they removed God knows what personal belongings they might consider physical evidence."

Trace heard a speech coming on. The attorney had a deep not unpleasing baritone that probably delivered a crackerjack summation. Having been on the other side of guys like Worthington in a courtroom, forced to watch as dry, boring investigative details were pitted against slick persuasion, superbly honed acting skills and a lot of razzmatazz, Trace was not a fan of defense attorneys. They ranked below politicians, reporters, and used-car salesmen in his personal professions hierarchy.

"It's the senator's wife's murder we're trying to solve, counselor," Trace reminded the attorney.

"Believe me, Sheriff," Worthington countered, "no one is more aware of that unpalatable fact than my client.

The past days have been extremely trying for him, both physically—due to his own near critical wound—and emotionally.

"Senator Fletcher has told you everything he knows. He's cooperated enough. I don't believe he should have to keep answering the same questions, over and over again."

He reached into his pocket, pulled out a gold case and extracted an embossed ivory business card and handed it to Trace.

"From now on, if you have anything to discuss with my client, I must ask you to speak with me, first."

Fat lot of good that'll do me, Trace thought blackly. "Fine," he agreed.

All during the brief conversation, Alan Fletcher had remained steadfastly, obediently, silent.

Frustrated and determined not to show it, Trace put his hat back on and left the ranch house, headed back to the office to read through the growing pile of paperwork on the case. It wasn't that he hadn't expected the senator to distance himself from the crime, but he had been hoping that like most politicians, Fletcher would find the glare of the spotlight irresistible and continue to cooperate.

Every instinct Trace possessed, honed from years of police work, told him that the senator was holding something back. Unfortunately, unless he was prepared to arrest Fletcher, which he wasn't, there wasn't any law that could make him answer questions against his will.

Three damn days. And he wasn't any closer to solving the case than he'd been when he'd first arrived on the scene.

Somewhere it was written that it was good for a detective to be smart. Somewhere it was also written that it was better to be lucky.

Trace decided that his luck was long overdue.

"Gotta get better," he told himself. Because things sure as hell couldn't get much worse.

Chapter Eleven

The rain had stopped, leaving the pine-scented air smelling fresh and clean. Trace was halfway to the Suburban when Mariah caught up with him.

"I told you," she said.

"Told me what?"

"That Alan was guilty."

"I didn't realize that had been proved yet." Her hair had been pulled back on the sides by two gold combs and allowed to fall in a long cascade down her back. Trace slipped his hands into his pockets to keep them from diving into those shimmering gilt waves.

"Why else would he need a lawyer?"

"You're the liberal Hollywood screenwriter," he reminded her. "How many times have you written the line about even the good guys needing lawyers to protect their righteous asses against us constitution-hating cops?"

"Only about a million. And one." He thought he saw her lips quirk. "And I believed it every time I wrote it, just as much I believe it now. As much as I believe Alan killed Laura.

"And I also know I'm sounding like a broken record, but I'm going to keep saying it until you listen."

"I'm listening."

She looked up at him. Hard and deep. In her eyes he viewed both skepticism and hope. "Really?"

"Really."

She closed her eyes, briefly, as if issuing up a prayer. "Thank you." Since he didn't know if she was talking to God or to him, Trace didn't respond.

"Nice dress," he said instead. It was silk and clingy and sinfully red. With her bright blond hair she reminded him of a defiant scarlet flame.

Mariah glanced down with a total lack of interest. "It seemed like a good idea at the time. Laura always categorically refused to wear black. She said it was too predictable with her red hair." She sighed. "I was thinking about it this morning and decided it was her one private act of rebellion."

"Everyone's entitled to at least one."

"At least." Mariah had given up counting her own rebellious episodes years ago. She'd thought she'd finally grown up. Until she returned home and found herself falling into old destructive behavioral patterns.

"Anyway, knowing how she felt, and just in case she was somewhere watching, I decided to wear this. Unfortunately, even Maggie disapproved." She ran her hands down the front of the skirt. "And Lord knows she's never been the slightest bit conventional. Dad, of course, hit the roof."

Indeed, for a moment, she'd thought he was going to have a stroke. Mariah's bitter, vulnerable laugh tugged at numerous dangerous chords inside Trace. "Old habits die hard," she said.

Like yanking her father's chain. Having watched how

Swann treated his only surviving daughter, Trace couldn't exactly blame her for wanting to get a few hits in herself.

"By the way," Mariah said, "Thanks for sticking up for me in there."

"Sticking up for people is my job."

"To protect and to serve."

"Absolutely."

Mariah had been taking care of herself for so long, it had seemed strange having Trace defend her that way. Strange, but nice, she decided. If she wasn't careful, she could get used to it.

Sighing, she pulled her gaze away from his steady, unreadable eyes and looked westward, in the direction of Clint Garvey's small spread. A brilliant rainbow appeared in the mists, shimmering in a colorful arc over the wildflower dotted meadows.

"Laura and I learned how to ride in those hills," she murmured. She could almost see them, galloping through the pine trees, racing and laughing. And loving. "When I was young, we used to go out there to get away from our parents' fighting. Later, I just went to get away."

"From your father." From what he'd seen of Swann over the past six months, Trace had come to the conclusion that the man was cold and ruthless, totally without compassion. He was not surprised Maggie McKenna had run away. But to leave her daughters…

"And sometimes from Laura," she admitted.

"It must have been tough," Trace said. "Growing up in the shadow of the favored older sister."

"It wasn't Laura's fault that Dad liked her best. To tell the truth, I didn't help make it any easier. For either of us."

Trace understood how Mariah found causing trouble an attractive way to deal with her private pain and frustrations. He guessed he could probably write a book on such self-destructive behavior, based on his own youthful experiences.

"I was going to make it up to her, dammit," Mariah insisted, more to herself, Trace suspected, than to him. "That was what this trip home was all about." She shook her head. "Thomas Wolfe was right. You can't go home again."

She was tense. Too tense. Trace watched her spine stiffen beneath the scarlet silk and realized she was once again struggling to remain strong.

Not considering that such behavior might be deemed inappropriate under the circumstances, he began massaging her shoulders. "We'll get him. Whoever he is."

There were knots the size of baseballs alongside her neck. He began easing them loose with his fingers.

"Lord, that feels good," she murmured, rolling her head to give him greater access to her tensed up muscles. "I didn't realize they taught massage at the police academy."

"Nursing school." His fingers kneaded the rock hard trapezius muscle. "My ex-wife was an RN. She used to try to work the knots out for me after a killer shift."

"Lucky you."

"Yeah." He didn't mention that in the end, his marriage was responsible for more tensed muscles than his work.

"So what happened? With you and your wife?"

He removed her gold earring and began working on the sternocleidomastoid behind her lobe. Her skin was as soft as silk. Trace wondered if it would be so soft all over. He also knew he was asking for trouble allowing his mind to even consider the state of Mariah Swann's naked body.

"Typical cop marriage story. It didn't work out."

He frowned as he remembered the day he'd met Ellen. She'd been working in the ER and he'd been investigating a hit on a minor league drug pusher. At first they'd seemed the perfect couple. After all, who else but an emergency room nurse could understand the shit he spent his waking hours wading through? Who else but a trauma nurse could possibly share a cop's warped perspective about life and death?

They would have a psychologically symbiotic marriage, they'd both thought in those heady days of early romance. Unfortunately, neither had envisioned the consequences of having death as a constant companion. At the dinner table, on holidays, not to mention in bed.

"Ah, yes." Mariah pulled off her other earring, inviting him to change sides. "I've written a few of those episodes."

"Hard not to," he agreed. "Considering divorce is a professional police hazard." A Kevlar vest could protect the heart from bullets. But nothing shielded against the pain of a failed marriage.

"Were you in love with her?"

"I wanted to be." He rolled his knuckles across her shoulders and felt the tautness ease. "So, what about you?"

"Me?" Mariah was thinking that it would be nice if she could just take off her dress, lie facedown on that nearby bale of hay and let his strong fingers do their magic all the way down her spine. She hadn't realized exactly how tense she'd been until he'd started to relax her.

"You ever been married?"

"Once. To an up-and-coming director of teenage horror films. It didn't work out, either."

"Why not?"

She shrugged and brooded out over the pasture. "We were married for eighteen months. For seventeen of those months, we had an ongoing disagreement."

"You divorced a guy over a disagreement?" He

wouldn't have thought her willing to toss in the towel so easily.

"It wasn't exactly your standard, run-of-the-mill disagreement," she corrected, somewhat relieved to discover that what had, at the time, seemed a humiliating personal failure, no longer possessed the power to cause pain. "Steven couldn't see any reason why he couldn't continue dating after we got married. I thought it might be a nice idea to give monogamy a try."

Trace wondered what kind of idiot would want any other woman when he had Mariah Swann all to himself. "The guy's obviously nuts."

She laughed at that, a rich, bubbling sound Trace found himself liking too much for comfort. She turned around again, placed her hands on his shoulders and smiled up at him.

"You know, Callahan, I just may have to reassess my original opinion of you."

"Oh?"

"Actually, when you put aside your Dirty Harry impression, you're not so bad. And I definitely like the way you think."

Her eyes were gleaming with that warm light he'd only caught a glimpse of a few times before. Her wide rosy lips were tilted up at the corners and parted just a whisper. They were standing close enough that it would take only the slightest lowering of his head...

"Thank you," she said softly.

"For what?"

"For making me laugh." From the moment she'd learned of Laura's death, Mariah hadn't believed she'd ever be able to smile—let alone laugh—again.

Deciding the man must be some kind of miracle worker, she drew back ever so slightly to look up at him, to search his face as he was searching hers. She kept her eyes steady and level with his. They were filled with the same doubts he was feeling. And the same needs.

His fingers moved from her neck to play with the tips of her hair. The palm of his other hand cupped her chin; his fingers spread so that her lips were framed between them and his thumb.

"I suppose you've written this scenario more times than you care to count, too."

His voice was deep and rough and did wonderful, frightening things to each and every one of her nerve endings. "What scenario is that?"

Her voice had thickened to a lush and sultry ribbon that wrapped around him in a sensual way that made him ache. He imagined how that voice would sound when she was lying beneath him, warm and naked and oh, so willing.

"A cop falling for a gorgeous, wealthy woman who's worlds beyond him."

She felt a tug—deep and physical. Mariah had never been one to dance around an issue. "Is that what's happening here?" The lingering laughter left her eyes. Her soft, siren's mouth sobered. "Are you falling for me, Callahan?"

The tension Trace had massaged away from her returned to settle at the base of his neck.

He could have been glib. He could have evaded. Trace had used both tactics successfully with women before. "I don't know," he said, opting for honesty.

Yesterday, he'd tried to assure himself that this unruly desire he'd been feeling for Mariah Swann was nothing more than a result of his recent celibacy. It wasn't really her he was lusting after, he'd told himself as he'd driven to Jessica's house. His malady was purely physical; any woman would suffice.

But dammit, as good as things had been with Jess, their lovemaking still hadn't managed to drive away his desire for this woman. And now, as his eyes drifted to her mouth, Trace tried telling himself that perhaps if he could just taste those lips once, his curiosity would be satisfied.

Like hell it would, he blasted himself. One taste and he'd be wanting more. And more. Still grasping at straws, Trace almost managed to convince himself that perhaps it might be easier to quit fighting it and let things progress to their natural conclusion.

If he could only have her, this nagging need would pass. And he'd be free to get on with his investigation. And more importantly, his life.

Even as he told himself that to continue touching her was playing with fire, Trace's fingers left off playing with her hair and stroked her throat. "I do know I'm not immune to you."

"You don't sound exactly thrilled."

It was difficult to hear over the sound of her heart pounding in her ears. His callused thumb was resting at the base of her throat. Mariah resisted swallowing and wondered if Trace could feel the increased beat of her pulse.

A pregnant silence settled over them. Mariah had to ask. "Does part of your reluctance have anything to do with Ms. Ingersoll?"

"Jess?"

Mariah could not miss the intimacy in the way he'd said the prosecutor's name. "Are the two of you still sleeping together?"

"What?" The question had come out of left field, both surprising and embarrassing him.

"I watched you during your press conference. You're comfortable in each other's space. That suggests more intimacy than you'd get merely working together."

"Is that so?" His frown suggested he was not at all pleased by her observation.

"There's also the fact that the town gossip line says you're an item."

"My relationship with Jessica Ingersoll has nothing to do with my feelings for you," he said. It was the truth. So far as it went.

"I'm in the middle of a homicide investigation," he reminded them both needlessly. "And unfortunately, at this point, I don't exactly have a plethora of hard evidence. I can't afford distractions." Even ones that smelled like a spring garden and had legs that went all the way up to her neck.

His gritty tone and his description of her as little more than a pesky hindrance to his work stung, but Mariah had spent too many years on the performing end of a television camera not to be able to act, when called upon. She also noticed he hadn't exactly answered her question about the current state of his affair with the sexy blond attorney.

"With compliments like that, Callahan, I'm amazed you don't have to beat away the hordes of women with a stick."

The sensual mood eased. For now.

"Why do you think we cops carry a nightstick?"

She smiled at that. "You know, Callahan, sometimes I think I really like you."

"And other times?"

"I don't know. I'll have to think about it."

"Fine. You can think while we drive over to Garvey's place. I need to talk to the guy some more and having you there might ease the process."

Her smile faded. "I'm not going to help build a case against Clint."

Knowing how eager she was to be in on the investigation, Trace once again admired her loyalty. "I just want to talk to the guy, that's all. Besides, if you're friends, it seems as if you wouldn't want him to be alone on the day the woman he loves is buried."

"You're sneaky," she accused. "But right. Let's get going. I've had about all the strolls down memory lane I can handle for one afternoon."

"Why don't you wait in the truck," Trace suggested, handing her the keys to the Suburban. "I'll go tell everyone you're coming with me."

"Fine." He'd turned and was headed back toward the house when she called out to him.

He looked back over his shoulder. "Yeah?"

"Would you do me a favor and check on Maggie?" Trace could see Mariah's frown all the way across the crushed gravel parking area. "I'm worried about her."

Trace discovered the reason for Mariah's concern when he entered the library in search of Maggie and found her filling a sterling silver flask from a crystal decanter.

"Oh!" She spun around at the sound of the door opening and sloshed the clear liquor onto the Navaho rug underfoot. "You startled me, Sheriff."

Her voice was slurred and her remarkable eyes even brighter than usual. Trace was not surprised that Maggie was on her way to getting drunk. Hell, if he was burying his kid, he'd probably tie one on, too. What saddened him was that she was drinking alone. And in secret.

"I'm sorry."

"Don't worry 'bout it." She returned the decanter to the desk with exaggerated care and managed to replace the top on the second try. "I do hope you're not planning to give me a breathalyzer test, Sheriff. Because I'm afraid I might fail."

With several percentage points to spare, Trace agreed silently as she made her way unsteadily toward him. "You're not driving back to the lodge, are you?"

"Of course not. I'm a star, darling." Frown lines momentarily furrowed her brow. ''Or I once was.'' The frown faded, chased away by a soft smile he suspected was directed inward. ''Surely you know that we stars always travel in limos.''

''That's what I've heard.''

''Well, as we speak, mine is waiting for me outside.'' She waved a slow, graceful hand. ''I never—ever—drive drunk. Not since...well—'' she shook her head distractedly ''—that's not important.''

''Mariah wanted me to tell you that she's leaving with me.''

''I don't blame you both for wanting a little time alone.'' She sighed. ''I certainly remember when I was young.''

''Actually, your daughter's assisting me on the investigation.''

''What a good idea.'' She nodded enthusiastically, causing a few more hairs to escape the French roll. ''Mariah's a very bright girl. And she writes crime dramas all the time, so she'll be a grand help in solving your crime.''

She was literally swaying, like a graceful willow in the breeze. Trace worried that she was on the verge of passing out.

''Would you like me to help you out to your car, Ms. McKenna?''

''That would be charming.'' She gave him her full, thousand-watt Technicolor smile. ''But please, darling, you must call me Maggie. Ms. McKenna makes me feel so horridly old.''

She placed a beringed hand on his arm. Several excellent quality diamonds glittered like ice beneath the diffused light of the overhead brass and copper chandelier. ''It's so nice to know chivalry still exists.'' Only her remarkable acting talent kept her words understandable. Her breath was warm and tinged with the scent of juniper berries. Trace felt his stomach lurch at the all too familiar aroma. Although never known to be overly choosy—about her men or her liquor—his mother had favored gin.

"May I ask you one more favor, Sheriff?"

"Of course."

"Please don't tell Mariah I've fallen off the wagon. The poor darling does worry so."

From her concerned expression when she'd asked him to check on Maggie, Trace had a feeling Mariah knew exactly what was going on with her mother. "Don't worry." He put his hand over hers and wrapped his other arm around her wasp-slender waist, to hold her up. "Your secret's safe with me."

"You're such a nice man. My knight in shining armor." She went up on her toes and kissed him. Smack on the lips. A wet, friendly kiss that Trace was relieved carried no sexual undertones.

Unwilling to submit her to her ex-husband's contempt, Trace slipped Maggie out the back way, through the kitchen door.

"Aren't you clever." Relief at avoiding Matthew vibrated in Maggie's husky voice. "Do you know, if I were only a few years younger, and Mariah wasn't my daughter, I believe I might be tempted give her a run for her money where you're concerned, Sheriff."

"I don't think you understand my relationship with your daughter."

In a sudden move that took him by surprise, she straightened and gave him that riveting gaze that had transfixed two generations of moviegoers. "I may be tipsy, Sheriff. But I'm not stupid. Nor am I blind. You're attracted to Mariah. As she is to you."

Her high heels were not made for walking in gravel. When she stumbled, Trace was there to catch her and keep her on her feet. "I think it's wonderful Mariah has finally found someone good enough for her,'' the older woman declared. ''If only poor dear Laura had stayed with Clint.'' A single tear slipped out of the corner of her eye and trailed forlornly down her cheek, sparkling like a loose diamond on her porcelain skin. ''She'd still be alive today.''

Her eyes chilled with an icy anger that reminded Trace of stilettos of ice. ''Damn Matthew for breaking them up,'' she spat out. ''If only Laura had held her ground.... If only she'd trusted in love....''

The Phoenix limo driver—his crisp navy uniform incongruous in this rural western setting—saw them coming. He tossed down his magazine and scrambled out of the car to open the back door with a flourish.

''Thank you, darling.'' Maggie patted the driver's tanned cheek.

''Do you believe your son-in-law killed your daughter?'' Trace asked.

Maggie's eyes momentarily cleared again. Her direct, no-holds-barred gaze reminded him of Mariah.

''Of course Alan killed Laura. Who else is there?''

Who else, indeed? Trace wondered as he returned to the Suburban.

''She's drunk, isn't she?'' Mariah asked in a flat tone.

''Look,'' he began to defend Maggie, ''she's had a rough couple of days, and—''

''You don't have to make up excuses. I know them all.'' Mariah slumped down in the seat, folded her arms across her breasts and shot a baleful look after the departing limousine. ''Damn. She's been dry for nearly a year.''

He twisted the key. The motor came to life with a roar. ''Dry isn't sober.''

She glanced over at him. ''True.''

He appreciated her not asking. Enough so that he decided yet again to tell her the truth. "My mother was a drunk."

"Oh." She digested that. "So, I guess you and I have something in common after all, Callahan." Besides a dangerous desire to jump each other's bones, she tacked on silently.

If anyone had ever suggested that he and Mariah Swann might have anything in common, he would have compared the surface of their individual lives and insisted the idea was crazy. But now, thinking back on that all too familiar glaze in Maggie McKenna's movie-star emerald eyes, Trace decided there was some truth in Mariah's softly issued statement.

There were seemingly no similarities between Maggie McKenna and Reba Callahan. One had been a movie star, the other a prostitute. One spent her days in a mansion in Beverly Hills that had once belonged to a famous silent film star, the other, while she'd been alive, had moved from trailer to trailer, jail to jail. One lived in a world of privilege, the other struggled in an endless cycle of abuse and pain.

But the single common, undeniable denominator shared by both women was an overwhelming weakness for gin.

And that being the case, Trace realized that Mariah might actually know something about his own days spent in hell.

"You might just have something there," he conceded.

Chapter Twelve

The interview with Clint Garvey was short and would have been mostly uneventful if it hadn't been for the unwanted surge of emotion—a feeling dangerously like jealousy—that coursed through Trace as he watched Mariah being enfolded into the rancher's strong arms.

"Poor Clint," she murmured later, as she and Trace drove back to town. "He looked even worse than I feel."

Trace silently concurred. Garvey's weather-hewn face had been the unhealthy color of ashes and his eyes had been home to a thousand-yard stare Trace had witnessed in cops who'd seen one too many grisly homicides. The slightly glazed look in those distant eyes suggested Maggie hadn't been the only one hitting the bottle that afternoon.

He'd considered telling Garvey that booze wouldn't help, then decided against it. Hell, he was a cop, not a social worker. And besides, Trace knew all too well that the way out of hell was long and hard.

"I hope you're not using Clint's financial problems as a motive," Mariah said. "Most of the ranchers play the futures market. And they all take a bath from time to time."

"Maybe some can afford it more than others."

She shrugged. "The greater the risk, the greater the reward."

To herself Mariah vowed to figure out some way to talk Clint into letting her lend him some money. The problem was, the man was a typical rancher—frustratingly independent.

"By the way, what was it you wanted to talk to Alan about?"

"Nothing in particular. I'm just trying to reconcile some discrepancies in his story."

"Any you care to share with me?"

"Not particularly." If Fletcher had murdered his wife, Trace wanted to be able to hand a prosecutable case over to Jess. He had the feeling that Mariah would be willing to stomp all over the senator's constitutional rights to put him behind bars.

Her next words confirmed his suspicions. "I should shoot him myself."

"I wouldn't advise it," Trace replied blandly. "Accommodations at Whiskey River's jail are not up to the standards you're undoubtedly used to at the Beverly Hills Hotel."

"There you go again, stereotyping me as some Hollywood rich bitch," she complained. "Besides, ridding the world of Alan Fletcher would probably be worth doing hard time."

He thought about his long-ago days on the other side of the criminal justice system. When he'd spent eighteen months as a guest of the Texas State Correctional System.

"That's easy to say. More difficult to do."

They both fell silent, lost in their own thoughts.

Mariah was looking out the passenger window. The

view of the valley below was spectacular, but from the dejected slump of her shoulders, he suspected she wasn't enjoying the scenery.

The guilt had crept back, like a thief in the night.

"You know, you're not to blame," he said.

She looked toward him, clearly surprised that he'd divined her thoughts so accurately. "Our fight ten years ago was all my fault." She felt a painful hitch in her heart. "If we'd stayed closer, I would have known what was happening in her life."

Despite her vow not to cry, a lump rose in her throat. Mariah swallowed to force the words past it. "I could have helped her, dammit." Her voice was frail and fractured, her eyes forlorn.

Although he knew little about comforting a woman, Trace was struck by an urge to pull over at the upcoming turnout, put his arm around Mariah's slumped shoulders, draw her close and kiss those full, trembling lips. An urge he resisted.

"Maybe. Maybe not. It's still not your fault that Laura's dead."

He was a fine one to talk, Mariah considered. She gave him a long, serious look. "The same way it's not your fault that Daniel Murphy died?"

Even after all this time, his partner's name struck a painful chord. The sick frustration he always felt whenever he thought of that day twisted at his gut. Uncomfortable with both the subject and her examination, he shifted. "That's different."

"Is it?" She looked at him for another full moment, her own pained eyes turning soft and thoughtful. "I don't think so."

Silence settled over them again. Realizing that she'd gotten all she was going to get out of Trace for now, Mariah sighed and returned her gaze out the window.

Neither spoke until he pulled up in front of the lodge. As he pulled beneath the porte cochere, she went for her door handle. "Thanks for the lift."

"I'll walk up with you."

Although she opened her mouth to tell him that it wasn't necessary, Trace had pocketed the key and was out of the truck before she could get a word out.

She stopped at the desk and retrieved a stack of pink message slips. "Condolences, condolences, sorry for your loss," she read as they rode the elevator up to the third floor. She shook her head. "Your loss. As if Laura were some keys I misplaced. Or a ring that was stolen."

"People have a hard time with death."

"I know." Another faint, rippling sigh. As they walked down the hallway, her hips swayed, causing her red silk skirt to rustle softly, like the wind in the top of the pine trees outside. "And I suppose murder makes everyone even more uncomfortable."

"Death is natural. Murder isn't."

"Ain't that the truth," she muttered. As she went to unlock the door, Mariah was appalled to discover that she was not as calm and collected as she'd been trying so hard to appear.

Without a word, Trace took the coded card from her trembling hand and slipped it into the lock. The door opened onto a room filled with flowers. Arrangements covered every flat surface; larger bouquets had been placed on the floor. Trace thought it looked as if someone had thrown a grenade into the middle of the Rose Parade.

"You must have a lot of friends."

"Mostly acquaintances. Hollywood's not exactly the type of place geared to deep and lasting relationships."

He stopped in front of an enormous spray of orchids and tiger lilies. "'Keep your chin up, kiddo,'" he read aloud as Mariah crossed the room to the bar. "'Sly.'" He shot her a quick look. "As in Stallone?"

She shrugged. "I did a little fix-up work on one of his scripts a few years ago. Actually, he might be one of the few people who qualifies as a friend. He taught me some martial arts and I taught him that putting a little romance into his stories wouldn't drive away his core audience of teenage boys."

Even as he told himself that it was absolutely none of his business, Trace wondered if she'd added a little romance to the actor's personal life. That was when he realized that if the sight of her in Garvey's arms had caused a prick of jealousy, the thought of her in a clinch with some overly macho movie star was even worse.

Cursing himself for allowing Mariah to get under his skin this way, Trace reminded himself that these flowers were proof positive that the lady was definitely out of his league.

She was looking into the bar refrigerator. "Want a beer? Or I seem to have quite a selection of hard stuff."

Annoyed by his reaction at the innocuous card, Trace said, "No time. I've got to go."

She glanced up, surprised by the sudden gruffness in his tone. "Fine." She refrained from pointing out that if he was in such a damn hurry, he shouldn't have bothered coming upstairs with her in the first place. "Thanks for the lift."

"No problem."

He was already headed toward the door. Weaving her way through the baskets of flowers, Mariah caught up with him.

"I've got another cheery Swann family meeting in the lawyer's office tomorrow morning at nine." The reading of Laura's will. "I'll drop by your office afterward and fill you in on the details."

"Fine." He'd already tried to get a copy of the victim's will prior to today's funeral, but her attorney—a stubborn old cowboy lawyer from the old school—had refused to let him see it until after the reading, citing attorney-client privilege. Trace had considered getting a court order, but decided that since none of the suspects were going anywhere, he could wait a few hours.

He was standing in the open doorway, looking down at Mariah in a way that made her feel as if she were not being looked at, but into. His eyes were like warm, sensual fingers, touching her everywhere. She felt the sudden charge in the air and couldn't quite decide whether to fight it or go with the flow.

"Is there something else?" she asked.

"Yeah." Driven by a recklessness he could not quite understand, nor control, he did what he'd been wanting to do since she'd climbed down from her Jeep at the Fletcher ranch and came stomping toward him in her pointy-toed boots, her long legs eating up the ground, breasts bouncing in that scarlet silk blouse, eyes hidden by wide wraparound glasses, radiating a fuck-you, rebellious attitude that was palpable. She'd reminded him of a female James Dean in skintight designer jeans. The kind of woman who could give any red-blooded male a fever.

His head swooped down, like an eagle diving for prey, and then his mouth was pressed hard against hers. The suddenness of the kiss, and the way it literally stole her breath away, made Mariah's head swim. Sensation after sensation streamed into her system like a fast-flowing river, crashing into hot rising tides of desire.

His hands fisted in her hair, holding her hostage to the mind-blinding kiss, preventing her from breaking away. As if she could, even if she'd wanted to. Which she didn't.

Through her wildly spinning senses, as she plunged

greedily into the kiss, Mariah realized that for the first time in her life, she had neither mind nor reason. Nor will. Swept along on that raging torrent, she was totally in this man's power. And what was even more of a surprise was that instead of finding such surrender frightening or demeaning, Mariah found it thrilling.

Emotions she'd kept locked up inside her since identifying Laura's body broke free, like from behind a broken dam. With a shudder and a half sob, she wrapped her arms around his neck and clung. A low, throaty moan escaped her when he changed the angle of the kiss and separated her lips with his tongue, filling her mouth with his taste.

Control disintegrated as she met the probing thrust of his tongue eagerly, desperately. Never had she been so helpless. Never had she been so needy. And never had she felt so aroused.

She would have done anything. Given him anything. Sensing that, Trace reluctantly decided that things had already gone far enough. If she kept moving her hips against his groin that way, he'd end up taking her here and now, surrounded by all those flowers. And while it might do something for the ache, it would be an unneeded complication to his case.

As quickly as the heated kiss began, it was over. Trace abruptly severed the wonderfully devastating contact, leaving Mariah stunned. She blinked up at him, uncomprehendingly.

"I'm sorry." His tone was more gruff than planned.

"Sorry?" She was stunned, confused and resentful about the way he'd made her lose control, then had the nerve to look at her as if it had been all her doing. "About what?"

"That shouldn't have happ[illegible]"

She refused to let him see [illegible]s words stung. "You didn't do it alone." She cross[illegible] [illegible]er arms over her chest and willed herself to some semblance of calm. Which was difficult since every nerve ending in her body was still tingling from that devastating kiss.

"No." Both his expression and his tone were grim. The consequences of his impulsive behavior had been as uncalculated as the kiss had been unplanned. Trace was furious at himself for wanting her so badly and irritated at her for making him want her. "But it could be a problem."

"Only if we let it." She could still taste him on her lips. Unconsciously Mariah gathered in the lingering flavors of rich, dark coffee, cinnamon chewing gum and aroused male.

The sight of her tongue circling those rosy lips he could still taste caused a surge of unbridled lust. Cursing under his breath, Trace took off his hat and dragged his hand through his hair. As she watched the thrust of his fingers, Mariah was struck by a needle sharp desire to feel those strong dark hands on her body.

From the expertise in his heated kiss, she had no doubt that the sheriff had bedded more than his share of women. And, she had no doubt, satisfied them all. So why should the act of two adults sharing a simple kiss make him so angry?

All right, she admitted reluctantly, it was more than a simple kiss. It was a world-class humdinger of a kiss that had left her feeling hot as sin and tingling all over. But the attraction, and their heated response to it had been entirely mutual. So what was his problem?

As she continued to look up at him, Trace, who was a pro at keeping his mouth shut during interrogations, felt an uncharacteristic need to fill in the lingering silence.

"Damn." He jammed the black Stetson back atop his head. "The thing is, you've had a rough day. I had no right taking advantage of you that way."

"Ah." He was, she considered with grim humor, definitely one of the good guys. In fact, from what she'd seen of him thus far, if she'd been working in Hollywood during those days of the old western melodramas, she couldn't imagine a man more suited to wearing a white hat.

"Let me see if I understand this correctly." She leaned against the doorjamb, feeling a sense of humor she'd thought had died with Laura beginning to return. "You're feeling guilty because you're afraid that in my weakened emotional condition, I wasn't able to say no. Is that it?"

He frowned, sensing where she was going and knew there was a trap at the end of the road. "In a way, I suppose, that's what I was thinking."

"You were supposed to be a hotshot detective in your past life, Callahan. So tell me, did you happen to notice any signs of resistance?"

"No, but—"

"You didn't because there weren't any. I wanted that to happen. Actually, I was hoping you'd kiss me earlier, back at the ranch. And for the record, that kiss was the first time I've felt alive in days."

Trace felt foolish and relieved at the same time. "In that case, I'm glad to have been of service. Any time you need a booster, just let me know."

Her laughter was quick and appreciative. "I'll dial 911."

"I'll see you at my office tomorrow morning, then," he said, even as he reminded himself that back in Dallas, he never would have permitted civilians this much access to a case.

"Before noon," she agreed. After all, how long could it take to legally inform Alan what everyone already knew—that he was now the proud owner of a century-old ranch?

Promising to latch the door behind him, she stood in the open doorway and watched Trace walk back down the hall to the elevator.

For a moment, just before the elevator door shut, Mariah was tempted to call him back. But having nothing left to say, she resisted the impulse.

Trace returned to his office and was studying the crime scene photos when his intercom buzzed.

"It's Fredericka Palmer," Jill announced.

He slipped the photos into his top desk drawer. "Send her in."

The Realtor entered the room surrounded by a cloud of perfume designed to hit a man straight in the groin. Her black silk suit revealed an enticing shadowing of breast and her stiletto high heels were more suited to a city hooker than a rural real-estate agent. Then again, he reminded himself, Fredericka Palmer was no typical rural real-estate agent.

"Hello, Sheriff." Somehow, her tone and her smile managed to make the usual greeting sound like a sexual invitation.

From the day he'd met her, the woman had made it obvious that she wouldn't be adverse to a more intimate relationship. Although he'd yet to take her up on her not-so-veiled offers, that hadn't kept her from continuing to try.

He stood up. "Afternoon, Ms. Palmer."

"Please." A soft sigh escaped pouting lips. "I keep telling you, Trace, it's Freddi."

She sat down in the visitor's chair and crossed her legs, displaying a flash of lacy black garter. Above the tops of the jet nylons, her thighs were porcelain pale. The contrast, Trace admitted in spite of his best efforts to remain unmoved, was more than a little appealing.

Trace sat down as well.

"I was sorry we didn't have a chance to speak at the funeral supper," she said.

"I wasn't exactly there in a social capacity," he reminded her.

"Actually, what I need to discuss with you is business. I'm afraid I might have bad news." She paused. For effect, Trace thought. "The Worths are considering putting their house up for sale." Trace was currently renting the house in question.

"I see." Trace figured it was a good thing he'd never gotten around to unpacking everything.

"I warned you about the possibility when you agreed to that month-to-month lease," she reminded him. "Instead of buying something of your own."

Trace shrugged. "That you did," he agreed easily.

He'd resisted the agent's attempt to sell him a home when he'd first arrived in town because he hadn't known if he'd find Whiskey River to his liking. And although lately he'd begun to feel as if he were settling in, finding someplace new to live was the least of his worries right now.

She tapped a scarlet finger thoughtfully against a white front tooth, drawing attention to her wide mouth. "You know, Sheriff, my development company is about to break ground on a new golf course community. We expect it to be quite popular. This is a golden opportunity to get in before the prices escalate."

"I'll think about it."

"Do you play golf?"

"Never had the time to learn." Nor the bucks to join one of Dallas's exclusive country clubs.

"You should." She crossed her legs again. "I've always believed that we should play as hard as we work."

"That's not a bad philosophy," he agreed mildly, having a very good idea of what game Fredericka was playing right now. "So, when do I have to move out?"

"Oh, no time soon." She waved away the potential problem with a crimson-tipped hand. "I just thought I should keep you apprised as to the possibility." Her smiling face turned worried. "There is another thing."

"What's that?"

"There's some concern, what with this terrible thing that's happened to Laura, along with the attempt on the senator's life, that there might not be sufficient security for the Fourth of July rally. The Cow Belles are hosting our annual barbecue and I'd hate for anything to happen."

"I've assigned all my deputies to the rally and I plan to be there as well. In addition, DPS is loaning us what officers they can spare from highway patrol."

"I'm so glad to hear that." Her deep sigh of relief drew his gaze once again to her lush breasts, just as she'd planned.

As she leaned toward him, giving him an unrestricted view of her cleavage, it crossed Trace's mind that Fredericka had all the tenacity—both professionally and personally—of an aluminum-siding salesman.

"You've no idea what a relief it is to be able to assure the girls that you'll have things well in hand." She stood up.

"We do our best."

She smiled. "So I hear." She was almost out the door when another thought occurred to her. "By the way, that was quite impressive, the way you rescued Mariah today. You reminded me of Lochinvar. Or Sir Galahad."

Trace was getting a little tired of the shining armor comparisons.

"Did Mariah tell you that she may be staying on in Whiskey River?" Freddi asked conversationally.

"I don't believe it came up." It sure as hell hadn't.

"She called me last week from L.A. to set up a meeting. She was behaving rather strangely, even for her."

"Strangely?"

"Secretive. She asked me not to tell anyone about her call. Or the meeting. Even Laura. Naturally, that piqued my curiosity."

"Uh-huh."

"Then, a few days later, when I first saw her in the lodge, she told me she had to cancel, which was a surprise, of course, but when I heard about what happened to Laura, I understood. Obviously, Mariah isn't in any shape to even think about negotiating a realty contract. Especially since she must be feeling so horribly guilty."

"Guilty?"

Fredericka flushed, as if realizing she'd gone too far. "It's nothing. Really." She managed a weak laugh. "Sometimes I really do talk too much."

He gave her his hard cop stare. "What would Mariah have to feel guilty about?" His tone was mild, even friendly. But his eyes had turned to flint.

"Well, you have to understand that Laura and I were best friends forever." She was obviously flustered. A sheen of perspiration glistened on the creamy flesh framed by the jet collar of her funeral suit. "And although I've tried to understand Mariah, I never approved of the way she treated her sister. Who'd always tried to make up for their mother's desertion," she said with a flash of hot loyalty.

"I was under the impression they'd reconciled their differences."

"So Mariah says."

"It isn't true?"

"Well, of course, Laura was never one to hold a grudge. Laura," she assured him, repeating what he'd al-

ready heard innumerable times over the past three days, "was a saint.

"Mariah, unfortunately, was the opposite side of the coin. She always resented Laura for being their father's favorite, never minding that Mariah's own rebellion kept her in constant trouble with Matthew. As for her feelings about her sister's marriage..."

She bit her lip and looked away. "I'm sorry, I've already said too much."

"Your best friend is lying dead six feet under," Trace pointed out, his unpleasant description designed to keep her talking. "I'd think you'd want to do whatever you could to make certain justice is done."

"Well, of course I do, but..." Her voice dropped off and her kohl-lined eyes widened. "Surely you don't suspect Mariah—"

"Tell me what you were going to say," he suggested.

Fredericka was chewing nervously on a fingernail. Her expressive eyes were darting around the room like frightened birds. "It's just that I've been thinking lately, about Laura and Clint?"

"Uh-huh."

"Well, what if the rumors were true? What if Laura really was going to leave Alan and marry her high school sweetheart?" The Realtor shook her head and sighed. "Laura and Alan had their problems," she admitted reluctantly. "But what marriage doesn't? And especially such a high-powered, high-profile one.

"Anyway, I was thinking about Mariah, and how, if Laura had told her about their problems, it would have given Mariah the upper hand in their relationship."

She gave Trace a long, knowing look. "The term sibling rivalry could have been coined about Mariah's feelings toward her older sister," she said. "Ask anyone. Anyway—" she shrugged her silk clad shoulders "—if

Mariah found out that not only was Laura going to finally find happiness with Clint, but was going to have his baby too, the balance would have shifted."

Her thoughtful frown slowly metamorphosed into a faint, embarrassed smile. "Listen to me," she said. "I sound as silly as Mariah. Perhaps I should try my hand at writing TV scripts."

"You don't sound silly," Trace assured her. "Although I get the feeling Mariah Swann isn't one of your favorite people."

"It's not that I dislike her. Not really. But, hell, Trace, you have to understand. I loved Laura from the time we were children. We were like sisters. Mariah forced a lot of people to take sides a long time ago. And it's not that easy to suddenly switch loyalties."

"I can understand that."

Freddi sighed again. "Oh, well, if Mariah is intending to stay in Whiskey River, one thing's for certain."

"What's that?"

"She'll definitely bring some excitement to this dusty old burg."

With that she was gone, leaving a cloud of perfume behind.

Trace sat back down behind his desk and pulled out the legal pad. In his business, he couldn't allow himself to ignore any possible lead. Even if it was one he didn't want to consider.

That being the case, he reluctantly added Mariah to his suspect list.

Even as his pen formed the letters, he found himself recalling with vivid clarity the power and passion of their shared kiss.

The kiss had been a mistake. But worth it.

Some inner instinct warned him that nothing about Mariah Swann was simple. She was the kind of woman who could strip away a man's hard-won self-control, layer by layer, until nothing was left but raw, unprotected emotion.

Always mindful that as sheriff, jumping to conclusions could make for some very embarrassing public landings, Trace reminded himself that there were any number of reasons Mariah could have wanted to talk with the Realtor. And only one of those reasons would point to her guilt.

Still, the thought that Mariah could be a murderer was definitely not a pleasant one. But even worse was the thought that he might be willing to compromise his case because he was hot for her.

Back when he'd been a rookie cop, patrolling Dallas streets, he'd been offered bribes to overlook speeding tickets. Later, while working Vice, a sleazebag cocaine dealer he'd arrested—and who ultimately walked when the evidence mysteriously disappeared from the police property room—had offered him a quarter of a million dollars for tipping him off the next time the cops planned to make a bust.

Over the years, Trace had had innumerable offers to look the other way.

In none of those instances had his integrity ever been put to the test as it was right now.

Trace cursed and closed his eyes in a mute prayer for strength. He wasn't used to wanting anything or anyone so badly. Mariah's heated, unrestrained response to his kiss had told him he could have her.

But at what cost?

Chapter Thirteen

The reading of the will was conducted in Thatcher Reardon's office. There had been a Reardon serving as Swann legal counsel since the two families had first arrived in Whiskey River over a century ago. Having never been one to buck tradition—with the exception of her love for Clint Garvey—no one was surprised that Laura had chosen Thatcher to draft her will.

Mariah could not keep her attention on the reading. So many thoughts were tumbling around in her mind that she was having trouble concentrating on any one of them.

Foremost, of course, was her reason for being here today. Although it was beginning to sink in that Laura was really, truly dead, there were fleeting instances when she'd open her mouth to say something to her sister, then belatedly realize that the image that had flickered in front of her mind's eye was no more substantial than the mirage that shimmered just out of reach on the bubbling-hot black asphalt of the interstate every summer.

Her second concern was for Maggie, who hadn't returned to the lodge until nearly midnight. When Mariah, exhausted and sick with worry, had angrily confronted the limo driver for not driving her mother directly home from the ranch after the funeral supper, a drunken Maggie had lost her temper and slapped her daughter hard. Right on her cheek.

It was the first time her mother had ever struck her and during those suspended seconds afterward, when the three of them—Mariah, Maggie and the driver—seemed frozen in place, Mariah had felt like a wounded seven-year-old.

The feeling, not pleasant, lingered this morning, along with continuing concern and not a little resentment. Maggie's life was her own, Mariah had told herself during the sleepless predawn hours. What her mother did was her own business; Mariah wasn't responsible for her behavior.

Which worked real nifty in theory. Unfortunately, although Maggie McKenna would never win the Mother Of The Year award, she was the only real family Mariah had left. And, despite Maggie's flaws, which were as bold and dramatic as the woman herself, Mariah loved her mother. Dearly.

The third problem that had kept sleep at bay and continued to nudge at her concentration this morning was Trace Callahan. Mariah had spent the past ten years in California, where people tended to tell everything about their intimate lives at the drop of a cocktail napkin. In contrast, the sheriff was an intensely private person.

Which was, Mariah mused as the lawyer droned through the usual preliminary bequeathals—two thousand dollars to the man who shoed Laura's horses, five thousand to her housekeeper, fifteen hundred to someone named Marty, who kept her driveway clear of snow in the winter—something else they had in common. If she'd been keeping track. Which she most definitely wasn't.

A buzz of excited conversation drew her attention back to the attorney and Mariah belatedly realized that everyone in the room, with the exception of Thatcher, was staring at her.

Her father's face was the color of a sun-ripened beefsteak tomato. A furious fire burned in his gaze and an angry blue vein pounded at his temple.

In contrast, although Maggie's eyes were still hidden by the sunglasses she had not taken off when they'd entered the suite of offices, Mariah thought she detected a ghost of a smile hovering at the corner of her mother's full lips.

Alan's expression was schooled to one of polite surprise, but there was some hidden emotion lurking deep in his eyes that sent a frisson up her spine.

"Congratulations, darling," Maggie drawled. There was no mistaking the smile now; she looked like a very satisfied feline who'd just brunched on a very fat canary and had a bowl of freshly churned cream waiting in the wings. "It appears you're in the ranching business."

She shot her former husband a satisfied look that was obvious even through the darkened lens of her glasses. "Imagine, all that land. Not to mention all those cows. And they're all yours."

"Mine?" Mariah asked uncomprehendingly. Obviously somewhere after the five-hundred-dollar bequest to the paperboy, she'd missed something significant.

"It appears Laura believed her grandmother's ranch should remain in the Swann family," Alan revealed. His tone and his expression were mild. His eyes, as they locked on hers, were not.

Mariah shook her head, stunned by this unexpected development. Laura had always been the most sensible, logical person Mariah had ever known. So why on earth would she have done the one thing that made absolutely no sense?

"I don't understand."

"That makes two of us." Matthew was on his feet, his broad hands braced on the polished mahogany desk as he glared down at the attorney. "What the hell were you thinking of, Thatcher?" he demanded. "Letting my daughter write a goddamn will like that?"

"It was Laura's ranch," Thatcher Reardon pointed out calmly. In land, money and political influence, he could claim equality with the man hovering over him, which kept him from being intimidated by Matthew Swann's power. "Just as it was her right to give it to anyone she chose."

"This is a community-property state, dammit!" Matthew pounded the desk with enough force to shake the green-shaded banker's lamp. "Anything Laura owned belonged to her husband."

The lawyer straightened the lamp. "Personal inheritances are excluded from community property in Arizona, Matthew. As you no doubt know, considering the way you successfully blocked your wife from making claims on your own holdings."

"Former wife," Maggie corrected. In contrast to her ex-husband, she appeared quite at ease with the unexpected events. "And for the record, Mr. Reardon, Matthew didn't block any claim from me in the divorce. Because I never made one in the first place."

Matthew dragged his attention from the attorney to glower at Maggie. "Only because you knew you couldn't win."

She lifted her chin. "Because I didn't want anything of yours," she corrected.

"Not even your own daughters," he snapped.

Didn't they ever stop? Mariah opened her mouth to beg them to please be quiet, but her brother-in-law beat her to it.

"It's all right, Matthew," Alan Fletcher assured the

older man. "Whatever Laura wanted is fine with me. I loved my wife, and if it would make her happy to know her sister is living in our home, that's all I need to know."

His tone was too slick, too polished. Too phony. Mariah was tempted to call him on his obvious lie, then decided she just didn't have the strength to do battle today.

"Thank you, Alan," she murmured, matching his saccharine tone. "That's very generous of you."

He nodded and gave her a sad, brave smile. "I hope you'll be as happy as we were in the house, Mariah." He stood up and held out his hand in a gesture of peacemaking. "I also hope you'll give me a few days to get my personal belongings out."

"Of course. Take all the time you need."

"Thank you." His fingers curled around hers with a bit more strength than necessary, giving Mariah the impression he'd love to put them around her neck. "Heather will inventory my things right after this afternoon's rally," he promised.

Radiating shock and disapproval, Mariah stiffened and jerked her hand away. "You're actually going through with the rally?"

"All the plans have been made," he said quietly. "The governor has come up from Phoenix, the national press has been notified, my speech is prepared. But mostly," he said with absolute certainty, "it's what Laura would have wanted."

"I'll bet."

"You haven't been close enough to your sister these past years to realize that she had a dream for America. A dream we hoped to achieve together."

Mariah heard the speech coming on. He and his mistress were already incorporating his dead wife into his campaign. Mariah was not surprised. But she did feel sick to her stomach.

"If you'll all excuse me," she said, pushing herself out of the leather chair, "I have to go."

"Of course," the lawyer agreed, looking relieved to get the family out of his office before Matthew and Maggie started throwing his priceless collection of Hopi kachina figures at one another. He cleared his throat. "I do have some papers for you to sign—"

"Perhaps tomorrow." The room was closing in on her. The air was growing thick and heavy. "I'm sorry, but I really am late for an appointment."

Her head was spinning and her hands had turned clammy. Mariah turned and escaped the suddenly stultifying office on a near run.

Trace was driving to his office when he saw Mariah sitting on the concrete steps of the brownstone legal building. Making a U-turn, he pulled up at the curb, parked behind her Cherokee, climbed the steps and sat down beside her.

"Meeting over?"

Her elbows were braced on her bent knees, her chin rested in her fists. "Over enough."

"Feel like talking about it?"

"No." She sighed. "But you'll find out anyway." Another sigh. "Laura left the ranch to me."

He'd been hoping like hell she wouldn't say that. "That must have come as a surprise."

Immersed in her own turmoiled emotions, Mariah didn't notice how intently Trace was studying her. "That's the understatement of the millennium."

Knowing the others would be coming out at any time, she looked over him and said, "Could we continue this in your office? I really could use a cup of coffee."

"Sure." He stood up, extended his hand, which she

took without hesitation, and helped her to her feet. "Want to drive? Or walk?"

"The walk might clear my head," she considered. "But I'm not up to running that damn press gauntlet."

He wasn't all that wild about the idea himself. "How about following me to my place?"

"That depends. Are you inviting me up to see your Wanted Posters?"

He put his arm around her shoulders and began walking toward their trucks. "You bet."

Trace's Victorian house, which Mariah recognized as being marvelously restored, had all the personality of an anonymous interstate motel room. Were it not for the packing boxes stacked up in the foyer, she would have thought it uninhabited. "We can talk in my office," Trace said.

The office was an improvement over the rest of what Mariah could see from the front hall. Although definitely lacking any decorative touches, at least it appeared lived in. The floor-to-ceiling shelves were filled with books.

In front of a window was an old rolltop desk and although her Malibu home had been furnished in what her Beverly Hills decorator had called California contemporary, Mariah recognized it as an authentic antique. The top of the desk was distractingly neat. A few pens in a walnut holder, a week-at-a-glance calendar and a yellow legal pad. He'd drawn some type of chart, she saw, trying to read it upside down.

"Is that something to do with Laura's case?"

"Yeah."

"Can I see it?"

"Sorry." He closed the desk and locked it. "There are still some aspects of this case that are off-limits to civilians."

She felt a prick of irritation as she watched him slip the

key into his pocket. He was not a man who trusted easily. Then again, she considered, thinking of all he'd seen, all he'd been through, why should he?

"Afraid I'll rifle your desk, Sheriff?"

"Would you?"

"Probably," she admitted. "Given the chance. But only because I get the feeling you're holding something back."

How about the fact that even before she'd inherited twenty thousand acres of prime Arizona real estate plus grazing rights for another hundred, he'd had reason to put her on his suspect list?

"Police prerogative," he said mildly.

Mariah tried telling herself that she was lucky to have the access to the investigation that she did. Call her greedy, but she wanted more. "I never would have figured you for a by-the-book kind of guy, Callahan."

"I have my moments."

Giving up for now, she crossed the room and began examining his bookshelves. The selection was eclectic, ranging from nonfiction to classics to current bestsellers. She pulled a celebrity autobiography from the shelf. The back cover photograph was a twenty-five-year-old publicity still, showing Maggie in a body-clinging flesh-colored beaded gown that made her look as if she were wearing nothing but perfumed and powdered female flesh and a few strategically placed crystal beads.

Her thick hair had been teased into a wild auburn mane; her glossy red lips were erotically parted, showing just a hint of gleaming white teeth and the invitation in her kohl-lined emerald eyes so blatantly sexual it was nearly impossible to look away. She radiated passion the way a branding iron radiated heat.

"You've got Maggie's book." Although she'd already decided this man was impossible to pigeonhole, there was no way Mariah would have suspected him of reading ghostwritten Hollywood tell-all autobiographies.

''I bought it in a moment of weakness. Maggie McKenna was my first crush.'' Although he'd thought the admission—which he'd never confessed to another living soul—would make her smile, Trace watched Mariah's lips draw into a tight line. Parentheses bracketed either side of her mouth.

''Yours and every other male's in the country, seemingly.''

Her voice was thick with disapproval. Could she actually be jealous? Of her own mother?

''Your mother was the last of the larger-than-life Technicolor stars.''

''So why don't you tell me something I don't know?'' She abruptly shoved the book back onto the shelf.

He arched a brow at her sharp tone. Remembering what Fredericka had said about Mariah's strong feelings of rivalry, he hoped like hell that something else was going on here. ''Did I hit a nerve?''

''Not at all. And even if you did, my relationship with my mother is none of your business.''

''Isn't it?''

''No.'' She lifted her chin. ''Whatever problems I have with Maggie or my father, or once had with Laura, are not for public scrutiny. This is my private life we're talking about, Callahan.''

''Wrong.'' He caught her aggressive chin between his fingers and held her gaze to his. ''Because as far as I'm concerned, no one who knew your sister has a private life.''

She tried to toss her head and only succeeding in causing his fingers to tighten. He was towering over her in a way that secretly made her mouth go dry. But refusing to let him see that she was the least bit intimidated, she glared right back at him.

"You're as disgusting as all those reporters. Always mucking around in our lives, delving under rocks, trying to unearth ugly family secrets."

What ugly family secrets was she hiding? Trace wondered. "The only thing I'm trying to find is Laura's killer. If you didn't pull that trigger, then you don't have anything to worry about."

Mariah's first thought was that for a supposedly hotshot detective, Trace Callahan didn't know what the hell he was talking about. Because thanks to Maggie's headlong tumble off the wagon, she had a lot to worry about.

Mariah's second thought, and the one that sent shock waves reverberating through her, was that he may actually believe her capable of having murdered her own sister.

"Are you saying I'm a suspect?"

His expression gave nothing away. "I told you, everyone's a suspect."

"Well, I certainly didn't do it. As *I* told *you,* I was stuck in Camp Verde. Because of your damn barricades," she reminded him archly. If she'd only gone around them…

"The clerk at the Pinewood Motel agrees with you about the time you checked in. Unfortunately, since you didn't come by the office when you checked out, he has no idea what time you left."

She couldn't believe this! "You actually checked me out?"

"Of course."

"Of course," Mariah echoed flatly. Deciding that she'd made a mistake coming here, she turned back toward the door. "I think it's time I left."

"You haven't told me how things went at the lawyer's," he reminded her.

"Just nifty. My sister died and left me the ranch, which allows me the pleasure of evicting her rat of a husband, who, as we speak, is preparing to announce his candidacy for the presidency on a platform built on top of his dead wife.

"My father, unsurprisingly, nearly had apoplexy, my mother used the opportunity to slash away at him and you've practically accused me of murder." Her feelings were still stung by his accusation. "So far, it's been a dandy day. I can't wait for tonight's fireworks."

"I'm sorry." Trace couldn't stop the sudden surge of tenderness. To make sure he behaved, he shoved his hands deep into his pockets. "You needed a friend and I acted like a cop."

"You *are* a cop."

"Yes. I am." The message hovered in the air between them, in huge capital letters, too bold and too clear to ignore. She hadn't needed to kiss Trace to know that he was attracted to her. As she was to him. But as much as he wanted her, as many official rules as he'd reluctantly bend for her, he couldn't be anything other than what he was.

"You and Sam Spade," she murmured.

"Spade was a private detective."

"True. But he still turned in Brigit O'Shaughnessy. Even though—" When she realized what she'd been about to say, Mariah shut her mouth so quickly and so hard her teeth slammed together.

"Even though he loved her," Trace said, finishing her thought, his eyes on hers.

He saw embarrassment in those deep turquoise depths. But it was the lambent hunger he also viewed there that was making his blood run a little warmer and his heart beat faster. With the rigid self-determination that had pulled him back from the edge of the grave after the shooting, he cooled the first and leveled the second.

It might not be love he was feeling for Mariah Swann. But whatever it was, it was dangerous enough to make a careless or foolhardy man forget his priorities. Fortunately, Trace had never considered himself either careless or foolhardy.

"Spade had no choice," he said. "Brigit O'Shaughnessy was a murderer."

Mariah knew they were no longer talking about Dashiell Hammett's famous *Maltese Falcon.* She also understood all too well that if he truly believed her guilty of murder, Trace would put aside any personal feelings and arrest her. "Well, I'm not," she said firmly.

He nodded. "I'm glad to hear that."

An expectant silence settled over them.

"I should be getting back to the hotel," she said reluctantly.

"I have to go over to the fairground to boost security for the senator," Trace said at the same time.

"Too bad you can't call in sick," she muttered. "With any luck, there really is a crazed assassin out there who'd love the opportunity to get a second shot at the bastard."

"Not in my county."

Mariah would have expected him to say nothing less.

They were about to leave the house when the phone rang at the same time his radio sputtered to life. Trace scooped up the phone.

"Callahan."

As he listened to the caller, Mariah watched the anger move across his face like a thunderhead.

"I'll be right there." He hung up as abruptly as he'd answered. Then he cursed.

"What's the matter?" Mariah's first worried thought was for Maggie.

"It's Heather Martin," Trace said, his voice as grim as his expression. "She's dead."

Chapter Fourteen

It looked like an accident.

The paramedics had already thrown in the towel when Trace arrived at the lodge. Although they'd pulled Heather Martin's lifeless body from the antique, lion-footed tub, they'd left the rest of the evidence where they'd found it. A lacy bra and panties had been laid out on the lid of the closed commode; a fluffy white towel lay atop a wrinkled terry bath mat on the moss green tile floor. Beside the towel was an antique brass rack. There was approximately a foot of scented water cooling in the tub.

Appearances suggested the aide had stood up, reached for the towel and slipped on the slick oil at the bottom of the tub, which had caused her to pull the rack off the wall before hitting her head on the side of the porcelain tub.

Experience had taught Trace not to trust first impressions. It had also taught him to suspect easy answers.

Like a historical biographer, whose job it is to reconstruct a person's life from boxes of moldy old letters and diaries, in the basement of the Whiskey River courthouse, Dr. Stanley Potter attempted to image the last moments of Heather Martin's life.

"Rigor mortis is present in the extremities," the physician observed, his flat business-as-usual voice echoing around the cold cavernous autopsy room.

"It's only been a little over two hours," Trace noted.

"She was taking a bath. You should know as well as I do, Sheriff, that hot water speeds up the process."

"So does a violent struggle before death."

The doctor gave him a sideways look. "You're jumping the gun."

Trace's answering gaze was steady. "Someone's killing people in my town."

"Someone sure as hell killed Laura Fletcher," Potter agreed as he returned to studying the body. "But the jury's still out on this one....

"Subject has a tattoo measuring—" he pulled out a clear plastic ruler "—one centimeter in diameter on her left breast."

From what he'd been able to tell the few times they'd met, Heather Martin had favored a classic, traditional look that suggested private schools, stone houses with rolling green lawns and summers abroad. The gaudy blue-and-red butterfly was definitely a contrast to the congressional aide's professional outward appearance. But then so was having an affair with your married, very high-profile boss.

Still waters, Trace thought. "There's also some bruising." He leaned forward to better see the discolorations marring the smooth white flesh of the aide's chest. "But they're whitish, so they're obviously postmortem. From the resuscitation attempt?"

Potter nodded. "That'd be my guess."

He continued methodically measuring, dictating and cutting.

"Two cracked ribs, which are also consistent with a resuscitation attempt."

Two hours later, he was finishing up his autopsy. "No

fractures,'' he said after examining the skull. ''Nothing that would suggest she was knocked unconscious, which goes along with the water in her lungs.''

''Are you saying she drowned? In a foot of bathwater?'' Trace's voice was thick with disbelief.

''I'm not saying anything. Yet. But it's not impossible. Hell, 350 people drown every year in bathtubs,'' the doctor informed him.

''I know the statistics, Doc,'' Trace muttered. He also knew enough to trust his instincts. Heather Martin was no drowning victim.

''Well, well, would you look at this.'' Potter had pulled the skin at the back of the victim's head down, revealing two faint bruises at the base of her skull, one on either side of her neck.

It was a handprint, Trace realized. A thumb on the left side, fingers on the right.

''Gotcha,'' he murmured.

After holding a brief press conference to state that Heather Martin had died of ''undetermined causes,'' and to also assure the gathered reporters that his department was not focusing on any one person or motive to the exclusion of others, Trace returned to the lodge, where, after this morning's surprising revelation in the lawyer's office, Alan Fletcher had checked into a room on the second floor.

Only days ago, the senator had been a man sitting on top of the world. He was rich and powerful, had a beautiful, intelligent wife and from what Trace had surmised, an equally beautiful and intelligent mistress. And if that wasn't enough, the presidency of the most powerful country in the world looked within reach.

This evening he looked like a man who'd just discovered the hard way that he'd been living on an earthquake fault and had awakened to find his entire privileged life turned to rubble.

"I'm sorry to intrude, Senator," Trace began, "but—"

"You have some more questions."

"Yes."

Peter Worthington appeared behind the senator. "I've already told you, Sheriff—"

"No." Alan shook his head. His handsome face was vacant; Trace could read not an iota of emotion. "It's all right, Peter. I want to talk to the sheriff."

He moved aside, inviting Trace into the suite. "Can I get you anything?" he asked, gesturing toward the bar. "A drink, or some coffee, or—"

"Nothing, thanks."

Trace took the small card from his pocket. He'd decided on the drive from the courthouse that it was time to Mirandize the senator. There were now two dead women who'd been involved with the guy. If Fletcher was guilty, or in any way involved, Trace wasn't going to risk blowing his case on a technicality.

After reading the warnings, Trace asked Alan if he was still willing to speak with him.

"I told you, Sheriff, I *want* to speak with you."

"As your attorney, I must warn you against this, Alan," Worthington stressed.

"I've nothing to hide, Peter." Alan sat down in a tub chair and gestured Trace toward the couch facing it.

Trace studied Alan for a moment, looking for some subtle sign, something to tell him that his instincts were more than a cop's justifiable suspicion along with a dislike of politicians in general.

In Trace's world, politicians were the guys who tended either to fuck up investigations in order to protect some high-flying contributor, or who muscled in and took credit once a case turned out well.

He didn't like them. And he didn't trust them. Which was pretty much the way he was feeling about Alan Fletcher. His internal gyroscope was telling him that the senator knew a helluva lot more than he was telling.

During his days in Dallas, Trace had followed a cardinal code: if it looked like a skunk and walked like a skunk it was probably a skunk. And although in Fletcher's case, the putrid scent of skunk lingered over both women's deaths, Trace knew that Jess Ingersoll needed to walk into that Mogollon County courtroom armed with a helluva lot more than a bad smell.

"I know we discussed this earlier, Senator," he said, "but I'd appreciate it if you could tell me again about how you found Ms. Martin's body."

"Of course." Alan looked thoughtful. "We were planning to leave for the rally together. Heather was a stickler about punctuality, so when she didn't answer my knock, I was immediately worried that something might have happened to her."

His voice cracked ever so slightly. "I was afraid someone shot her. Like Laura."

"Why would you think that?"

He shook his head. "I don't know. I was just worried about her. With good reason, as it turns out."

"Uh-huh." Trace took out his notebook, paused and wrote something down. "How did you get into Ms. Martin's room?"

Fletcher's expression gave nothing away. "I had a key. We worked closely together," he said quickly. A bit too quickly, Trace thought. "There were times when I needed to be able to retrieve things from her briefcase or her desk."

"I see." Trace made another notation. "The thing is, Senator," he said, flipping back through the pages, "we've got a problem."

"A problem?"

"You haven't been entirely honest with me from the beginning." He found the page he was looking for. "For instance, at first you told me that your marriage was a happy one. And that you and your wife had engaged in sexual relations only days before she arrived in Whiskey River to prepare for the barbecue you were hosting for friends.

"Then, later, you admitted that your marriage wasn't exactly idyllic, after all. You also admitted you'd hadn't had sex with your wife for six months."

"I explained about those misstatements—"

"Yes." Trace nodded, and resumed turning the pages. "You stated that the reason for your *misstatements*—" he laced the pretty word for lies with a slickly sarcastic tone "—was that you were trying to protect your dead wife's reputation."

Ignoring the bait, Fletcher agreeably nodded. "That's precisely what I was doing."

"Okay. So whose reputation were you trying to protect when you failed to tell me that you and your aide were having an affair?"

"That's not true."

Trace resisted rolling his eyes and put on his most sympathetic face. "You have a law degree, don't you, Senator?"

Alan's eyes narrowed, as if seeking the trap. "From Harvard," he agreed.

"And, if I remember correctly, before being elected to the senate, you were a district attorney in Phoenix."

"That's right. In Maricopa County."

"So you know that in the eyes of the law, there's a helluva big difference between first degree murder and manslaughter."

"Of course, but if you're implying—"

"I'm not implying anything. All I'm doing is suggesting that the two scenarios are not the same. Nor are the penalties," he commented pointedly, practically inviting Fletcher to choose the lesser now, while the options were still open.

Trace wasn't particularly surprised when the senator managed to keep his mouth shut.

"Perhaps you promised Ms. Martin, during one of your little political jaunts together away from the capitol, that you'd marry her," he continued to press. "Perhaps, after your wife was no longer in the picture, she reminded you of that promise."

"That's not—"

"Perhaps—" Trace stood up now, towering over Fletcher, using his superior size to intimidate "—she even threatened to tell things about your wife's murder that would implicate you."

"That's impossible! I had nothing to do with Laura's death."

"So you keep saying. But, let's put that aside for now. Let's suppose that you're telling the truth about that night. That your wife's death was just one of those convenient coincidences. Two masked men broke into your home and killed her, leaving you a free man."

"I was shot, too."

Trace was rapidly losing patience. He'd also decided that diplomacy was for diplomats. "Give me a break," he all but growled. "Want to know what I think, Senator?"

The sweat beading on Fletcher's brow was the only sign of his discomfort. "What?"

"I think you got sick and tired of being trapped in a bad marriage, but even though you knew your wife was sleeping with her ex, you were afraid to divorce her because of the political fallout. So, you worked out this plan to get rid of her.

"And Ms. Martin knew about it and decided it was time you made an honest woman of her, which you weren't prepared to do. At first you tried to reason with her, but like most women in love, reason wasn't what she wanted to hear."

Trace was leaning down, face-to-face with Fletcher. "The lady wanted marriage and she pushed and pushed and threatened to go public and pushed and pushed some more until you were so mad, so frustrated, that you lost control of your senses and to shut her the fuck up, you shoved her head under that bathwater and you held her there. And when she began struggling, you kept her head beneath the water until finally she wasn't struggling anymore.

"Because she was dead. Like your wife. Like Laura."

Trace saw anger flash across the senator's face before he quickly controlled it. "I didn't kill Laura. Nor did I kill Heather."

"I suppose next you'll be telling me it was the one-armed man."

"You're skating on very thin ice, Sheriff," Worthington interjected quickly. "Any more insinuations like that and I'll be forced to report your cowboy behavior to the governor."

"Is that a threat, Counselor?" Trace asked in a dangerously soft voice.

"Merely a warning," the attorney corrected. "Need I remind you that my client is a very important man?"

"Laura Swann Fletcher was important too," Trace retorted. A memory of Mariah Swann brushing her dead sister's auburn hair from her forehead flashed in his mind's eye again. "And it's my job to find her killer."

Trace turned his attention back to Fletcher. "Come on, Senator. Let's close this thing up so we can all get on with our lives. Tell me about Heather. Tell me what happened."

Alan lifted a brow. "The truth will set you free?"

The guy was damn good. Trace would give him that. He'd never witnessed anyone who could remain so cool under pressure. "Not necessarily. But lying sure as hell won't help, either."

"Am I a suspect?"

"You tell me."

The senator exchanged a long look with his attorney. As Fletcher folded his arms over his chest, Trace waited for the inevitable. He didn't have to wait long.

"I believe I've said all I intend to say, Sheriff."

It figured, Trace thought.

Although it was early evening, the room was dark, the silvery twilight shut out by thick wooden window shutters. Clint Garvey was sprawled on his back on the leather sofa in his office, where he'd passed out after polishing off a bottle of Southern Comfort. He was dreaming of Laura. Of the life they'd planned together. The life her father had vowed to prevent.

He was dreaming of their baby, a green-eyed little girl with her mother's soft auburn hair, who'd be able to charm her way around his little finger.

She felt so warm. So soft. Clint wrapped his arms around her and drew her close. He pressed his lips against her throat, feeling her blood beat.

The dream lingered.

Murmuring her name, he ran his hand down her body, vaguely surprised to find that she was naked. Laura's weakness, he'd been delighted to discover, was frothy silk, satin and lace lingerie, which he loved to take his time stripping away.

An unfamiliar, but erotic scent surrounded her like a

seductive cloud, making Clint wonder, through the mists clouding his mind, when she had changed her perfume. But then her nimble fingers unbuckled his belt and she began massaging him and the puzzle was immediately forgotten.

He touched her in all the intimate places he'd learned she liked. On cue, she moaned and arched against him, her nails raking down his back, her thighs trembling as he brought her to climax with only his clever, stroking touch.

He held her, waiting for the shudders to subside.

"My turn," she whispered. Slipping her fingers beneath the elastic waistband of his briefs, she caressed him with a feathery soft touch that made him ache.

"God, I've missed you, Laurie," he murmured groggily, steeped in the dream, in the fantasy.

"I've missed you too, baby," she murmured silkily, freeing his erection. She ran a fingernail up its length, circling the tip in a teasingly seductive way that sent thrills of pleasure humming through his body. "And I've missed this."

When her mouth slid over him, Clint thrust his hands into her hair and surrendered to the moment.

He came quickly, calling out Laura's name at the moment of release.

His body was still throbbing when she ran her lips up his chest. "That was nice, wasn't it?"

Clint murmured a sleepy agreement.

"Nicer than with your married mistress?"

Reality returned swiftly, bringing with it a killer headache and the unwilling knowledge that he'd just made one of the biggest mistakes of his life. Cursing, Clint forced open his eyes and turned on the lamp. The woman lying on top of him was definitely not the woman of his dreams.

"Fredericka."

''In the flesh,'' she agreed, pressing her breasts against his chest.

''Dammit, Freddi—'' He pushed her off and sat up. Lightning bolts shot through his skull. ''Oh, Christ.''

''Poor baby.'' Her voice was languid and husky, her eyes vaguely amused. Appearing unperturbed by his rejection, she reached out and stroked her fingers over his forehead. ''I'll get you an aspirin.''

''I don't want any damn aspirin.'' Clint brushed her away and stumbled out of the room and down the hall into the kitchen, where he took a beer out of the refrigerator and chugged it down. His stomach rebelled for a long, dangerous moment, but then the alcohol began to numb the pain. His legs were a little steadier as he returned to his office.

''All right, Freddi.'' He jerked his briefs back on, not bothering to turn them right side out. Then he pulled up a straight chair, turned it around and straddled it. ''What's the game?''

She was stark naked save for the diamond studs that glittered coldly at her earlobes. Appearing totally unperturbed by her nudity, she perched on the end of the couch and crossed her long legs. ''I thought you could probably use a little feminine comfort. After the terrible thing that happened to Laura.''

''I thought Laura was your best friend,'' he mumbled.

''She is. Was,'' Freddi corrected with a frown. ''But she's dead, Clint. As you undoubtedly know all too well.''

His head was still throbbing and his mind was still muddled by the copious amount of alcohol he'd ingested, which was why it took a little while for her implication to sink in.

''Are you saying you think I killed her?''

She shrugged her shoulders. ''Well, you are the obvious choice, sweetheart. Considering the fact that we both know she never would have gone through with that divorce.''

''I don't know that.''

''Matthew wouldn't have let her. And he would have seen you dead before letting you screw up all his plans for Alan.''

Clint wondered if her accusation was merely a lucky shot in the dark, or if Freddi somehow knew about the fight between he and Matthew the night of Laura's murder. The night Swann had threatened not only to burn down his barn and all his horses, but kill him as well.

''I don't get it.'' He dragged his hand through his hair. ''If you honestly think I killed your best friend, why would you want anything to do with me?''

''I told you,'' Freddi said patiently. ''I've missed you. Perhaps Laura's death has made me uncharacteristically introspective, but lately I've been thinking about old times and decided perhaps I was a bit hasty giving you up for that silly old commodities broker. Even if he was richer than God.''

Clint decided not to mention that he'd never been hers to give up. Sure, he and Freddi had rolled around in the hay from time to time. But what man in the county hadn't slept with Fredericka Palmer? There had even been, for a time, rumors about her and Matthew Swann.

Her attitude, and her words, reminded Clint he'd never really liked the forthright Realtor. ''Let me give you a little word of advice, sweetheart,'' he muttered. ''Sneaking into bed with me after I've passed out sure as hell isn't the way to start things up again.''

''You liked it.''

There was no way he could deny that. ''I didn't know it was you.''

''So?''

"So, doesn't that bother you? That I thought you were Laura?"

"Not really." When she shrugged her shoulders, her breasts jiggled. "Everyone's entitled to a fantasy life. Why, to tell you the truth, there was a moment there, just before I came, when I pretended you were our manly new sheriff."

She flashed him the smile that was one of her best tools. A sensual glint highlighted her eyes as she reached up and lazily combed her hands through her tousled jet hair. The gesture showed her surgically enhanced breasts to their best advantage.

Coming over to stand in front of him, her rose-tipped breasts a breath away from his mouth, she gave him a sly smile Clint didn't quite trust.

"Why don't you go take a shower," she suggested. "No offense, darling, but you do smell a bit like a saloon."

She ruffled his hair. "And while you freshen up, I'll make us some coffee."

Clint could resist the temptation of those smooth round breasts. Just as he could resist the pink tongue that came out to wetly circle her pouty lips.

But coffee was another matter.

"You've got a deal. On one condition."

"What's that?"

"You get dressed first."

Keeping her eyes on his, Freddi touched a hand to his face. "You sure that's what you want?"

He eased away an instant before her lips touched his. "Positive."

"If you insist." She bent over and began picking up the clothing she'd folded over the back of his recliner. "And later, after you're cleaned up and have had your coffee, you and I have a little unfinished business to discuss."

As he stood in the shower, the hot water sluicing over his mutinous body, Clint leaned against the tile, closed his eyes and wondered how the hell he was going to extricate himself from the unholy mess he'd gotten himself into.

From a secluded spot outside the ranch house, Patti Greene witnessed Fredericka's arrival. Not long after that, she saw Clint through the kitchen window. That he was naked told her all she needed to know.

Fury flowed hotly through her veins. It was bad enough that Laura Swann's sister was already moving in on him—Patti had nearly gagged at that tender scene in the barn the other day, when Clint had given the Hollywood bitch his favorite mare to ride—but now Freddi was trying to stake her claim on him, too.

Which wasn't fair, since everyone knew that Fredericka had dumped him to marry that rich old guy in Chicago. The same man who conveniently died shortly after their honeymoon, leaving his bride a very rich widow. As if the Realtor needed any more money! As Patti thought about all those bills piling up on her kitchen counter, the ones with all those fluorescent red past-due stickers, her blood ran even hotter.

Going back to her ten-year-old truck, which needed a valve job she couldn't afford, Patti pulled her former husband's black steel commando boot knife from the glove compartment. It was one of the few things the son of a bitch had forgotten to take with him when he took off.

After the way she'd shown up to support him while his married mistress was being buried, Clint had no right fucking any other woman! Just as Freddi had no right to move in on another woman's man.

Fed up with being a victim, Patti decided to teach the

pair a lesson. Clint and Freddi were going to pay, she decided, tightening her fingers around the black handle. Both of them. The same way Mariah Swann had.

Everyone in town knew Mariah had always resented her older sister's favored status in the Swann family. Which didn't make it all that surprising, Patti supposed, that she'd subsequently staked her claim on her dead sister's lover, as a way of proclaiming victory, even after Laura was in the grave.

But it still wasn't fair, dammit! Mariah Swann had everything—looks, money, fame. But obviously, all that wasn't enough for the greedy, rich bitch.

Patti frowned, thinking that it was too bad Mariah hadn't fallen all the way over that cliff yesterday.

Chapter Fifteen

After leaving Fletcher's room, Trace took the stairs to the third floor.

Mariah opened the door seconds after his knock. "Well?" she demanded.

"Hello, to you, too." She was wearing her floaty gauze skirt again, topped with a lacy white, off-the-shoulder peasant blouse that made her resemble a sexy shepherdess. Delicate pastel seashell earrings, like miniature wind chimes, dangled nearly to those smooth, tanned bare shoulders.

"If that's a dig about my manners, don't bother. We don't have time to be subtle, Callahan."

"We? I hadn't realized the commissioners had appointed you my deputy."

"Don't get up on your high horse." She was still irritated by his refusal to let her accompany him to this latest crime scene. "I've learned over the years that being ladylike and submissive doesn't cut it in a man's world."

Night was settling its dark cloak over Whiskey River. Outside the window, Mariah heard the unmistakable sound of John Philip Sousa rising from the nearby town square. A thought occurred to her. "Why aren't you providing extra security at the rally?"

"Fletcher called off his speech in light of this latest incident. J.D. was eager to strut his uniform in front of his entire hometown, so I put him in charge of crowd control." What little need there was for such things in Whiskey River.

"I'm truly sorry Heather's dead. How did she die?"

"Ms. Martin's death is officially being ruled due to 'undetermined causes.'"

"I saw you say that during your television press conference." She didn't mention how downright sexy he'd looked, standing on the courthouse steps in front of that bank of microphones in his warrior pose. "But you and I both know that's a cop-out."

"Not really." He put his hat on the coffee table and sat down on the couch. "*You* should know that calling a cause of death isn't always cut-and-dried. Ms. Martin was found unconscious, lying facedown in the bathtub, which ruled out natural causes, which tend to be from disease.

"Since she was nude and there were no notes or anything else to suggest she'd taken her own life, suicide was also dismissed as cause."

The crime writer in Mariah was momentarily distracted. "What does her being nude have to do with anything?" She sat down beside him, her usual bright wildflower scent seeming hotter tonight. Sexier. Resisting the temptation to see how much of her silky skin carried that provocative scent, he pulled back. "Most suicide victims found in bathtubs are fully clothed."

"Oh." Trace watched her mulling his explanation over. He could see the wheels turning in that gorgeous blond head and figured she was filing the information away for a future plotline.

"That makes sense, I guess. Kind of like a woman putting on her best nightgown before taking a handful of Seconal."

"Exactly. Anyway, to get back to the point, there *were* things that made the medical examiner uncomfortable calling the death accidental."

"What things?" She was back on track.

Trace shook his head. "Sorry. Although I've done my best to accommodate you, like I told you when you wanted to come to Ms. Martin's room with me, I have to set some limits on this investigation."

"Whatever those things were," she probed, "I take it they weren't enough to call the death a homicide?"

"No. They weren't." Not officially. But those bruises on the base of Heather Martin's skull were enough to convince him that the woman's death had not been any bathroom accident.

"Damn."

She was on her feet again in a furious swirl of skirts, pacing the floor. Trace had already determined that Mariah's slender body contained too much pent-up energy to allow her to sit still for very long.

He wondered, not for the first time, how such vitality would translate in bed. Her long legs were clearly visible through the gauze and as he imagined them wrapped around his hips, fire spread through his blood, deep into his bones.

She paused long enough to light a cigarette from the half-empty pack on the bar, then resumed pacing. "So that's it? Alan gets away with another murder?"

"No one's going to get away with anything," Trace corrected mildly.

It was time, he decided.

"I need to ask you a question."

The reluctance in his tone caught her immediate attention, causing her to stop in her tracks.

"Why did you call Fredericka Palmer last week?"

"What?" It was not what she'd been expecting. "How did you know about that?"

"She mentioned, in passing, that you'd called from L.A. to set up an appointment. And that you'd were quite secretive. She suggested you didn't want your sister to find out about the meeting."

"Secretive. Christ." Mariah frowned, gave her cigarette a sharp look of annoyance and crushed it out. "Fredericka always had a flair for the overdramatic. Perhaps she should be the one writing for television instead of me."

"So it's not the truth? You didn't ask her to keep your appointment to herself?"

She could have written this script herself. Mariah sighed and found herself wishing for a commercial break to ease the tension that had suddenly stretched between them.

"That's an overstatement. I did ask her not to mention our appointment. But not because I was trying to hide anything."

"Uh-huh." Trace fell silent.

She recognized the technique even as she felt it working. "Don't pull out the Joe Friday act with me, Callahan. It's the truth, dammit."

"I didn't say it wasn't."

Another silence.

Irritation that he could suspect her of killing anyone, let alone her sister, warred with Mariah's relief that he was not about to let any stone go unturned in the search for Laura's murderer.

"I called Freddi because I was interested in looking into buying property."

"Here? In Whiskey River?"

She could hear the disbelief in his tone and understood

the reason. ''I know. I never made any secret of the fact that I couldn't wait to get out of town. But I was just an angry, mixed-up kid when I left, and although I know it sounds like a cliché, lately I've been missing any sense of roots.'' She'd also been missing her sister. *Too late,* Mariah reminded herself yet again. She'd come home too damn late.

Trace watched the cloud of sorrow move across her turquoise eyes. ''So you were intending to leave L.A.?''

''Not entirely. I've been thinking of moving into feature films for a long time. I love my work, but lately I've been feeling boxed in by television's restraints.

''Unlike TV programs, feature films aren't dependent on commercial sponsors. You don't have to worry about some CEO getting spooked by any trumped-up letter-writing campaigns from conservative watchdog groups.

''Plus, the longer length allows more depth of characterization and story. So, when I was offered an opportunity to write screenplays, I jumped at the chance.''

''I thought you had to live in Los Angeles to write screenplays.''

''It doesn't hurt,'' Mariah agreed. ''Especially in the beginning. But I've been in the business a long time, I've paid my dues and my credentials are strong. So, although I'm not giving up my beach house, at this point in my career, I've earned the luxury of doing the work I love, while living away from the hype and artifice of Hollywood.''

Although Trace wanted to believe Mariah, the professional in him could not entirely count her out.

''All that sounds reasonable,'' Trace allowed. ''So why did you ask Fredericka to keep your meeting confidential?''

She angled her chin, daring him to call her a liar. ''Because I wanted to test the waters. I knew there was a chance that I was romanticizing the move. And since I'd already supplied Whiskey River with more than my share of gossip, I didn't want to be perceived as a failure if this trip didn't work out."

Trace had to ask. "I've got another question."

The man who'd massaged away her tension after her sister's funeral was gone. In his place was a stiff-jawed, no-nonsense cop who would stop at nothing to close his case.

"Ask away."

Her smile was a lie. He hoped her answer would be the truth. "Did you know your sister was going to leave you her ranch?"

Even expecting the question, it hurt. "No, Sheriff. I did not somehow discover that Laura was going to rewrite her will and no, I did not find out that she was leaving me the ranch, and even if I had, there was no way in hell I would have killed her for it."

Temper flared. "Dammit, despite our problems, despite all those years we weren't speaking to one another, I loved my sister, Callahan. And she was the only person who ever truly loved me back.

"She didn't care that I was a famous television writer. And although she sent me flowers when I won my last Emmy, I knew she'd feel the same way about me if I was a waitress down at The Branding Iron Café. All she ever wanted was for people she cared for to be happy."

Mariah took a deep, shuddering breath. "Laura was the gentlest person I ever knew. Will ever know. I gave her hell over the years, but when most people would have written me off as hopeless, she continued to love me, for myself, with all my flaws. She was the only person ever in my life who loved me openly and honestly and without strings."

Despite her vow not to cry, a single tear escaped, trailing wetly down her cheek. She brushed it away with a furious, unsteady swipe of her hand. "Which is why I'm going to make damn sure her killer is arrested and put behind bars if it's the last thing I do."

He watched her valiant attempt to remain brave and felt something inside his heart clench. Despite her bold words, Mariah appeared younger than her years. Defenseless. And distractingly desirable. "I believe that's my job."

She looked at him and her lips curved into a faint smile. Unlike the earlier feigned one, this smile was honest and trembled slightly with lingering emotion from her passionate outburst.

"Of course it is. But don't forget, Sheriff, even the Lone Ranger needed Tonto's help from time to time."

Trace returned her smile, taking her words as an offering of a truce.

"May I ask a question?" Her voice was soft, but not the least bit hesitant.

He knew what was coming, knew he should stop it, but found himself powerless to resist. "Go ahead."

She sat back down on the couch, tucked her legs beneath her, and turned toward him. "Is this interrogation over?"

Her beguiling scent surrounded him, drawing him in. "It wasn't an interrogation."

She leaned forward, until their faces were scant inches apart and looked deep into his eyes. "All right." Her breath fanned his lips like a soft summer breeze. "Let me put it another way." Needs too long denied stirred painfully in his gut. And lower still. "Are you through asking me questions, Sheriff?"

Unable to resist her sultry siren's lure, he ran the back of his hand down the side of her face. Trace wasn't exactly thrilled by the way such hard-fought control seemed to disintegrate whenever he allowed himself to get close to this woman.

To lose his edge was dangerous. It was insane. But knowing the risk didn't change a thing.

He wanted her. Needed her. With an intensity that bordered on desperation. Although he'd done his best to resist temptation, what he wanted to do, needed to do, was make love to Mariah. Now, while he was only thinking of her, and not all the reasons why he shouldn't.

What he was on the verge of doing was against every police policy he'd ever been taught. Trace knew he was standing on the banks of his own personal Rubicon. Cross this and there'd be no turning back.

Reminding himself he'd never been known for playing by the book, Trace said, "I do have one more question."

Mariah turned her head, brushing her lips against his knuckles. "Yes." Her turquoise eyes, lustrous with sensual feminine invitation, smiled up into his from beneath her lush fringe of lashes. "The answer is yes."

As he lowered his head, Trace watched Mariah's ripe lush lips part in anticipation. His desire to take warred with his desire to give. And although some primal inner urge had him wanting to drag her to the floor and take her fast and hard, another, even more elemental part of him vowed to use whatever patience he'd honed over the years, whatever skill he'd acquired, to bring her pleasure.

Mariah expected passion. Braced herself for it. But in contrast to the heated kiss that had rocked them both the evening of Laura's funeral, this time Trace's lips did little more than nibble at hers, testing. Teasing. Tempting.

Their breaths mingled, became one.

With a soft moan, she wrapped her arms around his neck. Her breath caught, then shuddered out. Her lips clung to his, parting like the silken petals of a rose, offering more, inviting everything.

Her taste, as fresh as a spring morning, as sweet as summer sunshine, was drugging him, making him weak. *Too soon.* Not having realized the edge of desire could be sharp and so jagged, he dragged his mouth away and began lingeringly kissing her silky cheek. Her temple. The tender skin at the nape of her neck.

"You've changed your perfume." Passion radiated from every fragrant pore. He was hypnotizing her, drawing her into the mists without so much as touching her. Her mind clouded, her blood sang. It was both enervating and exciting at the same time.

"Yes," she managed to say on a soft, shimmering sigh as he nibbled lazily on her earlobe. Her head fell back, allowing his clever, wicked lips access to her throat.

Outside a band was playing patriotic marches in the town square, families were feasting on the Cow Belles' annual barbecue, children were playing tag and hide-and-seek among the oak and cottonwood trees as they had for generations, since Whiskey River's earliest days.

Inside, the world had narrowed. There was nothing but Mariah for Trace. Nothing but him for her.

"It's more sultry than your usual scent. It reminds me of heat-soaked scarlet flowers warmed by a tropical sun."

Every nerve ending in her body had begun to tingle, anticipating his intimate touch. As his lips grazed her lids, her eyes drifted closed. "I wore it for you," she murmured, her voice little more than a whisper.

Hungry for another taste of those rigidly cut lips, she drew his mouth back to hers. He tasted dark and dangerous and so very, very male. "To seduce you."

"I thought that might be the case." She tasted like honeyed temptation. A temptation Trace had given up trying to resist.

Mariah circled his mouth with the tip of her tongue, rewarded by his deep shudder. "Is it working?"

It was not in her nature to be coy. But there was something about Trace Callahan that brought out instinctive feminine responses she'd never known were lurking inside her.

He captured one of her hands and pressed it against his throbbing groin. "You tell me."

His stony sex stirred violently against her palm, sending fiery sparks shooting through her. "Gracious, Sheriff," she said on a low, lush laugh that vibrated all the way through him, "is that your gun? Or are you just glad to see me?"

"I'm always glad to see you." He ran his hands over the silk of her shoulders, down her arms. "Even when I don't want to be."

She was not offended by his obvious reluctance. Even through the mists clouding her mind, Mariah understood that this was difficult for Trace. He might not always follow all the rules, but she knew he was an intensely honorable man. To find himself attracted to a woman involved in his murder investigation undoubtedly presented an ethical dilemma.

Not wanting to discuss it, not now, Mariah pressed a palm against his dark cheek. "I'm always happy to see you, too," she admitted softly. "Sometimes so much it terrifies me."

"Join the club."

Even now she could hear the lingering reluctance in his voice. "I know you didn't want this to happen," she murmured as she rubbed her cheek against his. The roughness of his evening beard was a stimulating contrast to the softness of his lips. *Please,* she prayed to whatever fates had brought them together like this, *don't let him change his mind.* "But you still have a choice."

He fisted his hands in her hair and tilted her head back

to meet his gaze. "No." His eyes filled her vision, gravely dark, steely gray. "I don't."

Before she could respond, he lowered his mouth to hers again. The soft kisses grew longer. Deeper. Darker.

Her lips were warm and moist and so very generous. She welcomed his tongue with a breathless moan that burned through him like wildfire. When his teeth scraped at her bottom lip, his name tumbled from her lips and she clung to him, pulling him down on the sofa cushions.

"Oh, more," she gasped as he buried his mouth in the hollow of her throat where her pulse was hammering hot and fast.

"Much, much more," he promised.

Her body was moving desperately beneath his, kindling smoldering fires he'd struggled valiantly to bank. Erotic images that had been torturing what little sleep he'd gotten since Laura Fletcher's murder flashed through his mind, arousing him like no other woman.

With hands that were not nearly as steady as he would have liked, he slid the gathered sleeves of her peasant blouse down her arms, freeing fragrant breasts that spilled enticingly over the top of a strapless ivory silk camisole.

Her sun-kissed California flesh gleamed in the lamplight like molten gold. Just looking at her, lying beneath him, so beautiful, so willing, caused a silken fist to squeeze his heart.

When he trailed a fingertip over that luminous skin, he was suddenly all too aware of the calluses first earned that long-ago year when the Texas correctional system had decided to crack down on youthful offenders. The program, which had been touted to the politicians and the press as a stonemason class, had, in truth, been nothing but good old-fashioned convict rock busting.

When she shivered, he said, "I'm sorry. My hands are too rough."

His strong hands were bringing her a pleasure she'd never known existed. His fingers felt like the finest grade of sandpaper against her flesh, stimulating nerve endings.

When he went to take those masculine hands away, she grasped his wrists, kissing each roughened fingertip in turn. "Don't stop." Her eyes, lush and luminous with anticipated desire, locked on to his. "I like it." With her gaze still on his, she pressed her lips against his right palm. Then his left. Smiling softly, she returned them to her breasts which were aching for his continued touch.

Following her lead, he continued to caress her, skimming his palms with tautly controlled patience over those silken slopes, brushing his thumbs over rosy nipples that hardened and ached in response. When she would have rushed, he slowed the pace, continuing to seduce her with slow hands and tender lips.

Mariah had no idea how long he treated her to such torment. It could have been minutes. It could have been an eternity. She only knew that flames were rising deep in some secret center, spiraling outward to her fingertips and if she couldn't feel him there—where the heat was most intense—she'd go crazy.

"Trace." She was moving beneath him, arching up against his hard male body. She heard the plea in her voice but felt no shame. Only hot, desperate need. "Please." His mouth had claimed a taut nipple, his tongue and teeth creating a dazzling, pulsating tension between her legs. Framing his face with her hands, she pulled his mouth back to hers. "I need you. All of you."

Groaning his own need, Trace complied, leaving the couch and lifting her in his arms in one gloriously strong movement to carry her into the adjoining bedroom.

The mattress sighed as he laid her on the bed with uncommon tenderness. It whispered again when he sat down beside her.

"You are so incredibly lovely." He caressed her from shoulder to thigh. "You take my breath away."

Men had called her lovely before. But no man had ever possessed the power to make her blood burn. Men had wanted her before. But never had she wanted a man with an intensity that bordered on madness.

Anticipation had risen to a fever pitch. Mariah managed a shaky smile. "You're pretty magnificent yourself, Sheriff."

He winced at that. No woman had ever called him magnificent before. But then again, he considered, no woman had ever looked at him the way Mariah was looking at him now.

The room was draped in long purple shadows. A tree, sighing in the soft summer night breeze, brushed its leaves against the window. Outside, music drifted on the air; inside there were only soft sighs and low moans as Mariah and Trace undressed one another, reveling in the wonders of fingertips brushing over naked skin, of flesh pressing against warm flesh.

When she saw the ugly scar bisecting his chest, Mariah could not quite hold back her gasp. "Oh, Trace."

Her voice was thick with dull horror. She'd known about the shooting, of course. Known of the open-heart surgery that had managed, just barely, to save his life. But to see such a vivid reminder…

"It'll fade." His own voice was gruff. He didn't want to talk about the shooting. Or think about it. Not tonight. Not when heaven was within reach. "They all do."

Understanding why he'd declared the subject off-limits, but needing to somehow show her feelings, to let him know how glad she was that he'd survived, she pressed her lips against the angry red line, trailing kisses down his chest, over his stomach, lower, then lower still.

The touch of her lips on his throbbing penis was like a

fiery brand. Trace's mind emptied of everything but Mariah. Mariah of the golden hair, the turquoise eyes, the soft, perfumed flesh. Mariah whose clever, circling tongue was enough to make a grown man weep.

When she took him fully, deeply into her warm, wet generous mouth, he buried his hands in her tumble of silken hair and closed his eyes, allowing her to take him closer and closer to the edge. Just when he was hovering on that steep precipice of release, he caught hold of her bare shoulders and pulled her up beside him.

"Not yet." He kissed her and tasted himself on her lips. "We've plenty of time."

And then, gloriously, his hands, his lips were everywhere. Relentlessly caressing her flesh, probing, biting, licking, bending her to his will. When she would have rushed, he ruthlessly slowed the pace. Never, in a million years, could she have suspected that such a large man could be so tender. Or that such strong hands could be so gentle.

Helpless to resist, Mariah felt herself melting, like a candle left too long in a hot tropical sun. She could hear her own breathing in the hushed stillness of the darkened room. Feel her heart pounding in her chest, her throat, her ears. Never had she been so aware of her body. Never had she known such mindless pleasure.

When his tongue cut a hot swath down her spine, she moaned and shifted anxiously beneath him. When his teeth nipped at the tender cord at the back of her knee, she choked back a sob.

And when his breath—as hot and erotic as a desert sirocco—feathered the soft curls between her legs, she drew in a ragged breath and waited, every nerve ending poised, for the inevitable.

She was hot and burning. And remarkably, she was his. Her sensitive pink lips, framed by those blond curls, were glistening like dewy rose petals. Drawn to their silky softness, Trace caressed them first with a fingertip, then his lips.

When her legs began to tremble, his wide rough hands cupped her hips, holding her against his mouth. His tongue plunged into her heat, sending shock waves of pleasure and pain surging though her that had Mariah crying out. She reached blindly for him. Her body was rapidly building toward its flash point; she was desperate for him to be inside her when it happened.

Helpless, stripped of control, gasping for air, she begged for him to end her torment even as she wanted it never to stop. As she was racked with a sharp, shuddering climax, Mariah told herself that there couldn't possibly be more. That pleasure could not be any sharper, nor passion any richer than this.

She was soon to discover how wrong she was. His lips, warmed by her skin, returned to hers at the same time as he plunged into her, like a hot steel sword all the way to the hilt, filling her still tingling flesh, pounding so hard, so deep, that everything that had gone before paled in comparison.

She locked her legs around him, her hips meeting his, thrust for thrust. Her hands fitfully roamed his back, exulting in the feel of each glistening muscle bunching and straining.

Release exploded, hot and hard, first hers—again!—then Trace's close behind. They were still engulfed in the blinding fireball when a thunderous boom rattled the windowpane and the night sky was filled with the dazzling red, white and blue brightness of Fourth of July fireworks.

"I don't believe it!" Mariah said on a breathless laugh when she could finally speak again. "I'd never get away with writing a clichéd scene like this."

Feeling more satisfied than he'd ever been in his life,

Trace grinned down at her and brushed a few strands of moist hair away from her face. "It may be clichéd. But you gotta admit, it works."

For the first time since she'd met him, Trace actually looked relaxed. He'd been ruggedly handsome before, but the boyish grin made him downright devastating.

"I'll admit to being impressed, Sheriff. Not many women get fireworks. So how are you at making the earth move?"

He pressed a kiss against her smiling lips. "Next time."

Mariah was disappointed, but not all that surprised when Trace's walkie-talkie began to crackle from the other room.

He cursed as he pushed himself out of the cozy warmth of her bed. He wasn't ready to return to the real world. And he definitely was not eager to get back to work.

Mariah remained where she was, frustrated that she could not make out his murmured words. She was debating following him into the living room of the suite when he returned and began to scoop up his clothing from the floor.

"I'm sorry." He pulled on his briefs. His jeans followed.

She managed a smile she didn't quite feel. "I understand."

"I really hate rushing off like this." *Smooth move, Callahan,* Trace blasted himself. Take the lady to bed then get the hell out before things get too sticky. Standing beside the rumpled bed, he shrugged into his shirt.

"Don't worry about it." She went up on her knees and twined her arms around his neck. "I realize you have a job to do." She trailed her fingers through the light arrowing of hair bisecting his rugged chest and tried not to think about how he'd received that hateful scar. "I'm not going to feel abandoned."

"You're not?" If that was true, she would be the first. With the exception of Jess, of course. But as County Attorney, Jessica knew all too well that criminals weren't obliging enough to work bankers' hours.

"Of course not." She ignored the little twinge of guilt at the white lie and tried to assure herself, and him, that it was mostly true. "Tonight was wonderful, Callahan. Better than wonderful. But it was only sex."

He wondered if she actually believed that. Then he wondered why, if she did, he wasn't relieved. Deciding to think about that later, when he wasn't being tempted by her fragrant, love-slick flesh and tantalizing lips, he began to button his shirt.

"It's these kids," he explained, trying not to look at her breasts which were still tantalizingly within kissing distance. "They've been driving me crazy all summer.... Damn." He glared down at the front of his misbuttoned shirt.

Mariah bit back a smile, pleased that he was still not entirely immune to her. Although she wasn't prepared to admit it, their lovemaking, as wonderful as it had been, had left her wanting more. She'd given Trace Callahan her body and, whatever happened, would never regret it. What worried her was the fact that although she'd never planned for it to happen, she'd also given him her heart. "Let me." She unbuttoned the shirt and began again, this time from the bottom. "What kids?"

He watched her deft, slender fingers and remembered, with vivid and painful clarity, how they'd felt on his heated flesh.

"A bunch of local teenagers. They've been setting cherry bombs off all over town."

"It's the Fourth of July." She finished with the shirt, but unable to resist touching him again, smoothed her palms down the front of it. "And kids will always be kids."

"True." Her casual touch was almost enough to lure him back to bed. "But if I don't stop them at this stage, the next thing I know they'll be stealing cars. Then it's not that big a leap to knocking off convenience stores."

Thinking back on some of her own juvenile stunts, Mariah frowned. "Don't you think you're exaggerating? Just a bit?"

"Someone has to make the rules." As Mariah watched, she saw a distant shadow darken his gray eyes. "If their parents don't care enough to set boundaries, it's my job."

His expression, so loving only minutes earlier, had turned grim. The shadow lifted from his gaze, revealing swirling emotions too painful to look at.

Curious about what drove this man who was so unlike any other man she'd ever met, but knowing this was no time to push, she said, "I knew you were one of the good guys, Callahan."

He saw the questions in her eyes and was grateful she'd chosen not to ask them. Would she still admire him, he wondered, if she knew the truth about his rocky past? "You've been watching too many cop shows," he grumbled, uncomfortable with compliments.

There were hidden depths there. Secret sorrows. Mariah wished she knew what they were. "Guilty," she said with a quick grin designed to lighten the mood.

Leaving the bed, she went over to the closet. Watching her cross the room, Trace decided that as great as Mariah's ass had looked in those skintight jeans, the true test, which she passed with flying colors, was to look that good naked.

"If you catch your firecracker criminals, perhaps you can come back for a late supper," she suggested. She pulled out a short, red silk robe that barely covered the essentials. "Room service shuts down at midnight, but..."

He'd tried telling himself that once he'd made love to Mariah Swann, his desire would pass. But he'd been wrong. Because even as he knew he was playing with fire, Trace found himself unable to resist.

"I'll try." Succumbing to his need to taste her once more before he left, he bent his head and kissed her, a long deep kiss that made his blood hum and her knees go weak.

When the devastating kiss finally ended, Trace exhaled a rough, frustrated breath and said, "God, I want you again. But I can't promise to make it back tonight."

"Don't worry, Sheriff." Still slightly dazed, Mariah pressed a finger against her lips and felt the heat he'd left behind. "I'm not asking for any promises."

They both knew they were not talking about any late suppers.

Chapter Sixteen

He didn't come back. Mariah wasn't terribly surprised. But she was disappointed.

When the antique clock chimed seven o'clock in the morning, and Trace had still not so much as called to offer an excuse, she decided she'd spent enough time sitting by the phone.

She'd always been a woman who allowed herself to be led by her emotions. Although there were times when such behavior resulted in her being hurt—such as that long-ago fight with her sister which had resulted in years of estrangement—in the long run, Mariah could not imagine living her life any other way.

Last night, with Trace, was the same. In making love with him, she'd blithely followed her heart. And if this morning, in the bright light of day, she was realizing that she may have made a misstep, the pleasure and the passion they'd brought one another was worth it.

So why did she feel so let down?

''What you need,'' she decided as she blew her hair dry after her shower, dragging her brush through the long strands with more force than necessary, "is one of Iris's gooey cinnamon rolls."

Mariah had never met a funk that a sugar fix couldn't cure. And the one thing she'd missed about Whiskey River over all those intervening years was the café owner's oversize, homemade sweet rolls.

Trace was feeling frustrated and exhausted and guilty. As the hours had passed, he couldn't stop thinking about Mariah waiting for him back at the lodge. But, there were times when, like it or not, work had to come first.

Which is what he was telling himself as he sat across the table from Jessica, waiting for her to finish reading the papers found in Heather Martin's room at the lodge.

"Well?" he said, when she laid them down.

"You're right, of course. Southwest Development, Incorporated is a mob-fronted construction company."

"Whose CEO just happened to have contributed to the senator's campaign," Trace added.

He'd admittedly been surprised when Ben Loftin, while searching the room with J.D., had unearthed the list of contributors tucked away in the congressional aide's Filofax. It was, Trace considered, the first piece of investigative work he'd witnessed from the deputy during his six months in Whiskey River.

"Do you think Fletcher knows who he's taking money from?" Jessica asked.

"I wouldn't doubt it. The guy's a lot of things, but he isn't dumb. The thing is, when I first ran across Southwest in Dallas, they were paying off state legislators, trying to get gambling introduced into the state."

"That's pretty much what they've been doing here," Jessica revealed. "What with the lottery and the casino gambling on the reservations, and with Nevada right across the Colorado River, there's been a push to bring a casino to Lake Havasu City."

"Which would spread throughout the state."

"Like measles," Jessica agreed.

"But Fletcher wouldn't be involved in any state votes," Trace mused out loud.

"No. But his opinion pulls a lot of weight. Let's face it, barring indictment for murder, the guy's on the fast track to the White House. Every state politician from the governor on down to the county dogcatcher wants to be on his list of political appointees. That being the case, he can pretty much call any tune he wants."

"What do you think would happen if he took the money, then for some reason changed his mind, and decided not to back legalized gambling?"

"Double-crossing the mob is not exactly a smart career move," Jessica responded.

"Laura's murder could have been a hit."

The county attorney chewed thoughtfully on her bottom lip. "It makes sense," she decided reluctantly. "It also explains why the senator wasn't killed."

"After being taught a lesson, he'd be more likely to fall back into line."

"Most people would."

Trace followed the thought to its logical course, trying to figure out why Heather would have been killed. "It's also possible that the Martin woman, who undoubtedly also knew where her boss's money was coming from, realized exactly how dirty that money really was when Laura got killed," he concluded.

Jessica nodded. "And threatened to spill the beans."

"Shit." Trace scowled into his coffee. With this latest piece of information, the outlandish story about two masked gunmen no longer seemed all that improbable. And if they had been professional hit men, it certainly explained how they'd been able to pull such a good disappearing act.

"I hate mysteries," he muttered darkly.

When she saw Trace's Suburban parked on the street in front of The Branding Iron Café, a burst of involuntary pleasure left Mariah feeling giddy. Light-headed. And lighthearted.

A joyful anticipation was bubbling in her veins. A bubble that burst when she walked through the front door and saw Trace sharing one of the red vinyl booths at the back of the cafe with Mogollon County's Grace Kelly lookalike attorney, Jessica Ingersoll.

Mariah's first instinct was to turn and run. Now, before they saw her. Then she reminded herself that she certainly had nothing to be ashamed of. Neither, she admitted reluctantly, did Trace. He'd warned her that he was offering her no promises, just as she'd assured him she wasn't looking for any.

But that had been last night. This morning, in the clear mountain light of a new day, Mariah secretly admitted that by following her heart, she'd been led down a path that could ultimately end up hurting her.

Even as she recognized her own vulnerability, Mariah pulled up all her acting skills, pasted a bright smile on her face and headed toward the booth at the back of the restaurant.

"Don't look now," Jessica murmured, as she noticed Mariah's approach. "But we've got company."

He sensed her first. The energy that surrounded her like a vibrating aura crept under his skin, seeped into his bloodstream. Her scent followed, reminding him of warm feminine flesh, hot rumpled sheets and fireworks.

He slowly lowered his chipped mug to the Formica tabletop and braced himself.

"Good morning," Mariah greeted them. There was no sign her smile or her cheerful tone were forced. "I woke up this morning with the strongest craving for Iris's cinnamon rolls. Can you imagine? After ten years?" Another smile flashed, even brighter than the first. "Better watch out, Sheriff," she warned with a glance at the fresh cheese Danish in front of him, "Iris's sweet rolls are addictive."

Yesterday he would have fallen for her Little Mary Sunshine routine. But that was before they'd been as intimate as two people could be. This morning, understanding that she was more complex, more vulnerable than she liked to appear, Trace could see the faint hurt in her smiling turquoise eyes, hear the faint tremor in her voice.

"I'll keep that in mind."

Uncomfortable, he introduced the two women, watching as they checked one another out. Thinking that small-town life was definitely turning out to be more complicated than he'd expected, he slid closer to the window, making room for Mariah on the seat beside him.

"Why don't you join us?"

Jessica, watching Trace's discomfort with suppressed amusement, smiled up at Mariah over the rim of her white mug. "Please do. It's not often I have a chance to meet someone famous."

"Actually, if the sheriff does his job," Mariah said, a bit too sharply, she realized too late, "you'll have the opportunity to try someone a lot more famous than me."

It was Jessica's turn to lower her mug to the table. "I assume you're talking about your brother-in-law."

"Of course. He's guilty as sin. You know it, I know it, and the sheriff here knows it. The thing I can't understand is why the hell Alan hasn't been arrested yet."

Although he hated the accusation lacing her tone, Trace was relieved that at least Mariah was back to revealing honest emotion.

"I don't have enough evidence to cinch a conviction. And although once in a blue moon the defense gets an opportunity to retry a conviction on appeal, an acquittal is forever.

"What do you want me to do? Pick Fletcher up without cause, have him go to trial and get off because I hadn't done my job?"

She was tempted to suggest that eating a cozy breakfast with his lover wasn't exactly doing his job. Instead Mariah said, "Alan Fletcher murdered my sister. If you two can't put him away, I'll just have to get my father's shotgun and take care of matters myself."

"Christ, I wish you'd quit saying that," Trace complained. "Did you ever think that perhaps your own feelings about the guy have colored your judgment? That if we did arrest him and get a conviction and he isn't guilty, that Laura's murderer would still be on the streets, free to kill some other woman's sister?"

"Are you saying you honestly don't think Alan killed Laura? And Heather?"

It was a thought that had occurred to him on more than one occasion lately. Even before Loftin had presented him with the list of campaign contributors. Alan Fletcher was obviously a highly intelligent man. Could he actually be stupid enough—desperate enough—to risk murdering not one, but two women close to him?

"I told you, at this point—"

"Everyone's a suspect." Her frustrated huff ruffled her bangs.

"Ms. Swann," Jessica interjected soothingly as peacemaker, "please, why don't you sit down and have some breakfast with us?"

"I don't want to interrupt anything important." Damn, she couldn't believe how petulant she sounded.

"Actually, Trace and I have just about concluded our

business. And there's something I think you should know. Before the press learns of it.''

The bait was impossible to resist. Unballing her hands, Mariah sat down beside Trace. When their thighs brushed, she felt her pulse rate soar.

''Why do I have the feeling I'm not going to like this?''

Before Jessica or Trace could answer, the waitress—a buxom young thing in a denim miniskirt, tight red banana print cotton blouse and fringed vest—arrived at the table.

''Hi, Mariah.'' Her frown was a contrast to the perky Dale Evans outfit. ''It's good to have you back. But I'm so sorry about what happened to poor Laura.''

The smooth young face was vaguely familiar. ''I'm sorry, but—''

''Oh, of course you don't recognize me.'' There was a trill of laughter. ''I'm Jennifer Trent.''

For not the first time since returning home, Mariah felt as if she'd aged a century during her time away from Whiskey River. The sexy young thing with too much makeup and waist-length palomino platinum hair was another one of the kids she used to baby-sit while in high school.

She managed a smile. ''How are you doing, Jennifer?''

''Pretty good.'' She poured Mariah a cup of coffee. ''I graduated from NAU this year,'' she revealed. ''In theater.'' As she leaned across the table to refill Jessica's cup, her bouncy breasts brushed against Trace's arm, something Mariah didn't believe to be an accident. ''I'm only working at The Branding Iron to make money to go to Hollywood.'' She refilled Trace's cup, pausing at his murmured thank-you to give him a smile brimming over with feminine invitation. ''My professors say I have a lot of talent,'' she revealed.

''Well, I wish you luck,'' Mariah said.

''Thanks. I'll need all I can get.'' She pulled her pad

out of the pocket of the tight denim skirt. ''Maybe when I get to town I can look you up.'' Her voice went up a little on the end, turning it into a question.

''Of course,'' Mariah murmured. Then, before she found herself promising to write the girl a starring script, she ordered a pecan cinnamon roll, her tone sharper than planned.

Planning to overtip to make up for her lack of manners, Mariah turned back to Jessica. ''You were saying?''

''Trace tells me that you know about a particular letter found during the search of Clint Garvey's house.''

He'd told her about it on the drive to Clint's ranch after the funeral. ''The letter from Laura, suggesting that after they're married, he'll be in charge of running the ranch. Sure. But Clint explained all about that.'' She turned, reminding Trace of his conversation with the rancher. ''Laura loved the land, and the horses, but she was never much into the day-to-day business end of ranching.''

''It's been suggested,'' Jessica continued, ''that if Laura changed her mind about leaving her husband, Clint would have lost a very lucrative situation.''

''I doubt my sister was going to change her mind, Ms. Ingersoll. She loved Clint and she was going to have his child. There's no way she would have called the wedding off.''

''Since I have a feeling we're going to be seeing a lot of each other, why don't you call me Jessica?'' the attorney suggested.

''Fine.'' Mariah nodded. ''And I'm Mariah. And you're right about us seeing a lot of each other. Because I'm not going away until my sister's murderer is behind bars. And that man is not Clint.''

''Although I hate to delve into family rifts, you really aren't in a position to know how your sister felt about marrying Clint,'' Jessica said gently.

"She was married to him once before."

"That was a very long time ago. For a day. When they were both very young," Jessica said.

Mariah frowned, thinking how close Clint and Laura had come to having a second chance. The belief that life was not a dress rehearsal, and fear of lost opportunities—such as those suffered by Clint and Laura—was the reason she'd always believed in living every minute to the fullest. It also explained why she'd risked making love to Trace last night.

She shook her head, to clear it of the vaguely distressing thought. "Besides, in any event, even if Laura had called the marriage off, Clint would never kill anyone for money."

"That's your opinion."

Mariah met the attorney's eyes with a level look of her own. "Everyone who knows Clint Garvey will tell you the same thing."

"Everyone but your father."

"My father has his own agenda where both Clint and Alan are concerned." Suddenly the reason for this conversation sank in. Mariah turned toward Trace. "You're not planning to arrest Clint, are you? Because of that letter?"

Trace took a long drink of coffee, willing his own temper to cool. "There's more."

The would-be starlet returned with Mariah's order. Conversation was suspended as she placed the plate with the oversize roll on the table, along with a handful of paper napkins. The cinnamon roll had been heated; white frosting melted down the sides, a fragrance wafting from it under normal conditions would have been enough to make Mariah's mouth water.

Unfortunately, nothing had been normal about her life

since her return to Whiskey River and she suddenly found she'd lost her appetite.

"It seems," Trace continued after Jennifer returned to her place behind the counter, "that there was a dispute over title to a section of land."

"A dispute?" Needing a cigarette, Mariah began digging around in her bag, belatedly remembering that she'd smoked her last one sometime before dawn.

"Want me to buy a pack from the machine?" Trace asked, watching her futile search and knowing it revealed exactly how much strain she was feeling.

"No, thanks." She dragged her hands through her hair in another nervous gesture he'd come to recognize. "I'm okay."

She didn't look okay. "You sure?"

"Of course I'm sure. I was planning on quitting. This is as good a time as any." Her voice rose, surprising and embarrassing her.

Trace studied her for another long moment. Then shrugged inwardly. "A surveyor Garvey hired says Laura had encroached on his property."

"So?"

"So," Jessica interjected, "although I personally don't believe it's all that crucial, your father believes it provides Clint Garvey with a motive."

Frustrated, Mariah turned toward Trace. "I thought you said motive wasn't important."

"It's not necessarily all that important when figuring out who committed a crime," he agreed. "But going to court without a strong motive is dangerous."

"Juries feel the need for motive," Jessica explained. "They want to know *why* people do things, which I suppose is only natural curiosity, but I've never tried a case that I haven't gotten the impression the jury is secretly waiting until the last day of the trial, when the guilty suspect breaks down on the witness stand and confesses.

"Personally," she mused, "I've always thought it comes from watching too many Perry Mason episodes."

"Ouch," Mariah complained. "Once again television gets blamed for society's ills. But if you're looking for a motive, how about Alan wanting to get out of his marriage so he could marry his lover?"

She shot a look at Trace. "You're from Texas. Surely you've heard of the fine old western tradition of a Smith & Wesson divorce?"

"Divorced politicians are becoming a dime a dozen," Trace retorted. "Look at Reagan, Rockefeller, McCain, Kennedy, Warner—"

"Warner doesn't count," Mariah said testily. "He was married to Elizabeth Taylor, which made divorce a given."

"The problem is," Jessica said, returning the conversation to its original track, "I received a call from the governor late last night."

"Pressuring you to arrest Clint," Mariah said flatly.

"I wouldn't exactly use the word *pressure*," Jessica said. "But he did suggest that I take the evidence against Clint Garvey to a grand jury."

"Hell. This has my father's fingerprints all over it."

Jessica paused, carefully choosing her next words. "I received the impression that the governor and your father are friends." Her upward inflection turned it into a question.

"They went to college together. The governor was Laura's godfather," Mariah answered flatly. She could also see how, as a political officer of the court being pressured by the state's chief executive and party leader, Jessica Ingersoll was finding herself caught in one very sticky career dilemma.

"Ah." Jessica nodded. Then sighed, looking into her mug as if searching for answers in the light brown depths.

"So, are you going to indict him?" Mariah asked.

"Grand jury proceedings are conducted in secret," Jessica reminded her.

"I'm well aware of that. And you didn't answer my question."

Jessica's silence was all the answer Mariah needed.

"This is ridiculous! You don't have any proof that Clint is guilty."

"The burden of proof is different for a grand jury," Jessica reminded Mariah. "I don't need to prove the State's case beyond a reasonable doubt. I just need to show probable cause that a crime was committed."

"Probable cause being based solely on police testimony," Mariah muttered. She knew that prosecuting attorneys could successfully indict anyone at any time of anything before any grand jury. Indeed, she'd heard more than one lawyer allege that a grand jury would indict a ham sandwich.

"The physical evidence at the scene—footprints, tire tracks, along with a DNA match on the semen—point to Clint Garvey. The man has motive, opportunity and if a grand jury does subsequently indict him, it's my job to prosecute."

"Wouldn't want to risk your job."

Trace inwardly cringed at Mariah's unflattering accusation. Knowing Jessica as he did, he was not surprised when she temporarily abandoned her cool professionalism and displayed a passion usually reserved for behind closed doors.

"Do you think we indict people for the hell of it?" she snapped. "Do you think I prosecute innocent citizens because I like to see my name in the paper?"

She tossed a few bills on the table, then stood up.

"Trace told me how you feel about Clint, Mariah. I'm truly sorry about this. But I have no choice." She turned her attention to Trace. "Keep in touch. I may need you to go out and pick him up."

That said, she left the café.

Mariah didn't want to believe this could happen. But knowing her father as she did, she wasn't all that surprised. "What about Alan?"

Trace polished off the rest of his coffee. "We keep digging."

Mariah wanted to believe him. But her father's control was nothing to scoff at. If he wanted Clint convicted for his daughter's murder, how much freedom would Whiskey River's sheriff have to keep investigating other suspects?

None, she thought flatly. None at all.

"Hey," Trace said.

Unwilling to look at him when she knew he could so easily read her unflattering thoughts, she pretended sudden interest in a poster advertising Whiskey River's upcoming Frontier Days.

"Look at me, dammit," he insisted in a quiet, deep voice. He took her chin in his hand, his fingers strong and stubborn as they turned her face toward his. "I told you, I'm going to bring in Laura's killer. And no one—not even your father—is going to stop me. Is that clear?"

She wanted to believe him. Was desperate to believe him. She curled her fingers around the handle of her mug as if it could anchor her. "You could lose your job."

He shrugged. "Jobs are easy to come by. A good night's sleep is a lot more important."

A good man, she told herself—and her sister—yet again. Her gaze moved over his rugged face, taking in the deep indigo shadows beneath his steely eyes, the dark growth of beard that appeared even rougher than it had been last night.

"Speaking of sleeping, when was the last time you actually got a good night's sleep?"

"I'm still working on that. Things keep coming up." An intimate smile creased his face. "Not that I'm complaining, you understand."

His eyes darkened to slate with shared memories. The outside world began to narrow, the kitchen sounds of cutlery crashing, the hiss of bacon on a grill, the pop of the toaster, the murmur of conversation from the other café customers, all receded until Mariah was only aware of Trace.

"I waited for you to come back." The words were out of her mouth before she could censor them.

He'd worried about that. Worried first that she had and worse yet, worried that she might not care enough to wait.

"I tried. But the kids had a busy night. Not only did they slash some tires, they were letting loose with those damn firecrackers again."

He frowned as he thought about the possible reasons Freddi Palmer might have had for visiting the Garvey place. Unlike his behavior in the office, last night Garvey had looked guiltier than hell, leaving Trace to consider that relationships in Whiskey River were a helluva lot stickier and complex than they appeared at first glance.

"Anyway, by the time I rounded up those hellions and took them into the station, then tracked down their parents to come and retrieve them, it was already morning. I was on my way back to the inn when Jess paged me and—"

The ache came. She pushed it down. "You don't have to explain."

"It feels like I do." Strange, but he didn't feel nearly as foolish saying it as he had thinking it.

"Really, Trace, it was no big deal."

He felt his emotions heat up, then tangle, as they always

seemed to do with her. She was fascinating, stubborn, tempestuous and infinitely desirable. But she wasn't safe.

He'd known the danger even before he'd touched her. And having once touched, he knew that he'd be driven to touching her again and again.

"If it isn't important, then would you like to explain why I'm suddenly feeling as if I'm back in high school?"

His expression was so grave, so inordinately serious, she found herself smiling in response. "I think we're a little old to go steady."

"Just as well. I never got around to getting a class ring." He decided not to mention that he'd spent his senior year of high school behind bars and had managed to earn his degree by studying evenings after a backbreaking day of hammering away at rocks. "I don't suppose you'd be interested in wearing my badge?"

The mood lightened, as he'd intended. "Only if I can use it to arrest a certain murderous senator."

"Ah." He loved her terrierlike tenacity even as it was driving him crazy. "We're back to that."

"Always. Until it's ended."

"Until it's ended," he agreed, wondering if they were still talking about his investigation. Or something else.

Chapter Seventeen

Knowing Clint and Laura's history, no one in Whiskey River, Clint included, was surprised when the Grand Jury indicted him for murder.

"I've been expecting you," the rancher drawled when Trace showed up to arrest him. If he was a murderer, he was the least concerned one Trace had ever seen.

"I don't suppose you feel like confessing," Trace suggested as he handcuffed his prisoner.

"The only thing I'm guilty of is loving another man's wife. As for rumors of the land dispute, the boundary question was uncovered during a routine road survey done by the county. Laura and I were both surprised to learn she'd inadvertently encroached on my property."

"You didn't argue over it?"

"Hell, no. We laughed about it. Then, since we were going to be married, neither of us gave it another thought."

Although there was no proof to back up Garvey's assertion, Trace believed him. Unsurprisingly, Matthew Swann did not.

''You did a bang-up job, Sheriff,'' he told Trace after the hearing where Clint was denied bail. ''The town can rest easy, knowing that killer's behind bars.''

''Garvey hasn't been convicted of anything yet,'' Trace reminded the rancher. ''Which technically makes him innocent until proven guilty.''

Having spent his entire adult life trying to put the bad guys behind bars, Trace was uncomfortable defending a suspect. On the other hand, he knew he'd feel a helluva lot worse if an innocent man was convicted, allowing a killer to escape.

''Technicality is for the courts to wrestle over.'' Matthew's satisfied manner suggested he was confident that the legal system would uphold his own ideas of guilt and innocence. ''Everyone knows Garvey killed my Laura. And now he's going to pay.''

''Not everyone,'' Maggie interjected.

She'd arrived at the courthouse, clad in another of her seemingly endless supply of silk designer suits, dripping in diamonds, looking every inch the glamorous movie star she'd once been. The TV crews had crawled all over themselves to get a shot of the former actress and Trace had no doubt that pictures of Maggie McKenna, emerging from that white stretch limo, would appear on nightly news broadcasts all over the country.

She'd paused for a moment, as if surprised by the throng of fans lining the sidewalk. She managed a sad, brave smile—the same one, Trace noted with a detective's eye for detail, she'd used for her Oscar-nominated role of Jackie Kennedy—and waved. The fans, naturally, cheered. When she blew them a kiss, they went wild.

Strobes flashed, cameras whirred, people crowded forward, straining against the blue police sawhorses Trace had instructed J.D. and Ben Loftin to put up that morning.

Once again he was reminded that Hollywood was a land

of images and illusion. The Maggie McKenna who was going to top the evening newscasts appeared to be a glamorous, grieving superstar. What viewers would not see was the unnaturally bright sheen in those emerald eyes hidden behind the dark lenses of her Ferrari sunglasses. Nor would they know that underlying the scent of Chanel No. 5 was the unmistakable aroma of juniper berries or notice her stumble on the top step of the courthouse, when only the steady hand of her chauffeur kept her from falling.

Now, alone in Trace's office, Maggie whipped off the dark glasses and gave her former husband a hard look. "I like Clint. And it's obvious that he truly loved Laura. If she'd been allowed to stay married to the man, instead of being married off to this self-serving, egocentric politician—" she tossed her bright head in Alan's direction "—like some sultan's daughter being traded for a herd of camels, her life would have been far different."

Alan did not bother to rise to the bait and defend himself. Instead, he turned away, walked over to the window and looked down on the courtyard square.

Anger moved across Matthew's sun-weathered face in dark, dangerous waves. "You don't have any right criticizing my parenting," he roared. "Not after abandoning your family. Maybe if you'd been a decent mother, Laura would still be alive today."

"That's not fair," Mariah insisted. Like Alan, she too, knew the futility of entering into one of her parents' battles. Unlike her former brother-in-law, she could not permit her mother to go undefended. "If you hadn't been such a harsh, unbending man, Maggie wouldn't have had to leave in the first place."

"Thank you, dear," Maggie said on a wet, wobbly smile that had Trace fearing they were on the verge of a crying jag.

Matthew straightened to his full height and glared down

at Mariah. "For your information, young lady," he said, his deep booming voice reverberating around the office, loud enough for Jill to hear on the other side of the door, "your mother, whom you've always been so damn quick to defend, left Whiskey River to avoid prosecution on a drunk driving charge."

"Matthew—" Maggie's face had gone as white as a wraith. She held out a hand in a silent, trembling plea.

But her former husband was not to be silenced. "Ask her about the man she was with that day." His dark eyes shot fatal daggers at his wife. "Ask her how it feels to be responsible for another person's death."

Although Maggie had begun to weep, there was not an ounce of sympathy on Matthew's stony face. "Of course she can empathize with Clint Garvey," Matthew ground out. "Because they're both murderers."

"Damn you, Matthew Swann!" Maggie was sobbing openly now, tears streaming down her face, melting her carefully applied makeup. "You promised when I signed that paper—"

"You should never have come back to Whiskey River, Margaret." With that he turned on his heel and left the office, slamming the door behind him so hard the frosted glass rattled.

As if realizing his presence would be unwelcome, Alan followed.

A thick hush settled over the room. Trace was the first to break it. "I'll tell Jill to have the chauffeur bring the car around to the back entrance."

"Thank you." Mariah could feel herself trembling. "Come on, Mama." Mariah was too distressed to notice that for the first time in her life, she hadn't called her mother by her given name. "Let's go home."

"He promised," Maggie repeated, her eyes glazed, her once exquisite face slack. "So many years."

Trace watched them go. Closing his eyes, he pinched the bridge of his nose with his thumb and forefinger. Then he cursed.

Then, having no time to indulge in personal feelings, he turned his attention back to the one thing he could do to help Mariah. Solving her sister's murder.

The monsoon air was thick with humidity. Pink-and-gray thunderheads, usual for this time of year, were gathering overhead. Lightning flashed on the horizon, the thunder still too far away to be heard.

As he worked alone in the office in his rented home, poring over the expanding files on Laura Swann Fletcher's and Heather Martin's deaths, Trace found himself hoping that the building storm would hit with a vengeance soon. With any luck, a heavy rain might short out the remaining satellite rigs still parked outside the courthouse.

He read the reports again and again, frustrated when he found his mind drifting back to the lodge. To Mariah. He needed a clear head to solve these murders; unfortunately, his head hadn't been clear since he'd met the lissome Hollywood writer.

The room grew dark. Trace turned on the lights and decided to heat up the remains of some take-out Chinese for dinner. He'd tried calling Mariah, to see how she was doing and to ask if she was in the mood for company, but each time the operator had rung her room, there'd been no answer. Nor had anyone answered when he'd had the operator try Maggie's room.

Outside, the storm that had been threatening all day arrived with a fury. A thunderhead stalled overhead, spitting out chains of bright lightning across the darkened sky. Rain streamed down the windowpane.

Trace had just put the white cartons onto the tile counter when the doorbell rang.

Mariah Swann was standing on his front porch. ''I really hate to bother you at home,'' she said, in a small frail voice that was almost lost in a clap of thunder. ''But you told me once, that if I needed a booster...''

Her voice quavered. A mutinous sheen appeared in her eyes. She pressed her fist tight against her mouth, as if trying to hold back a sob. ''Ah, shit, Callahan...''

Compassion stirred as he looked down at her. Her hair was wet from the rain, clinging in damp strands to her forehead, cheeks and neck. Having neglected to put on a raincoat, her jeans and cotton sweater had gotten soaked on her dash from her red Cherokee parked on the street, to his front door. She looked small and frail and distressingly vulnerable.

Trace opened the door wider, inviting her into his house. And his heart.

''What's wrong?'' he asked as he closed the door behind her. *And you call yourself a detective, Callahan,* he blasted himself, remembering how she'd looked the last time he'd seen her. ''Hell, I'm sorry, that was a stupid question.''

''Try asking what's right,'' she suggested grimly. ''The answer will be shorter.''

''But there's no emergency?'' His first thought, considering how she'd looked when leaving his office, was that something had happened to Maggie. His second, and more unpalatable thought was of Mariah taking justice into her own hands.

''No.'' She cursed and shook her head. ''Things just piled up on me tonight.'' She drew in a deep shuddering breath. ''I just wanted to shoot someone.''

''Which you didn't do.''

Her eyes cleared and she gave him a wry look. ''No, Sheriff. I did not put a .44 caliber bullet through my brother-in-law's cheating heart.''

Trace hadn't realized how worried he'd been about just that until he felt the cooling relief flood over him. "I'm glad to hear that. The jailhouse roof leaks and you're already wet enough."

When, on cue, she began shivering from the cold, he said, "We'd better get you out of those wet clothes."

"Nice line, Callahan." He watched the defensive parapets going up again and realized Mariah was at her most flippant whenever she felt the most vulnerable. "You wouldn't stand a chance with it at any singles bar in L.A., but I guess women are easier out here in the boondocks."

"I wouldn't know," he said mildly. "Actually, I was merely trying to keep you from coming down with pneumonia."

"Ah, yes. To protect and to serve, right?"

"Got it on the first try."

She'd been right to come here, Mariah thought as his slow, easy smile managed to warm her all the way to the bone. Things had been rough for Trace Callahan. Even if she hadn't had access to his departmental jacket, she would have not been able to miss the ghostly shadows in his dark eyes.

But somehow he'd found the strength to keep on living. Mariah wondered if he could pass his secret on to her.

"It takes time," he said, surprising her once again with the uncanny ability to read her mind. His tone and his gaze were gentle and reassuring.

She knew he wasn't talking about the investigation. "How long?"

He shrugged, deciding for discretion's sake, not to tell her that until her sister's murder had given him a reason to get up in the morning, he'd been brooding, feeling sorry for himself.

Neither did he reveal that he'd been getting sick and tired of all the self-pity that had kept him in the grips of what he'd come to think of as his own personal depression monster.

"I suspect it's an individual thing. But I do know you can't rush things. And that it does get better. Day by day."

She gave him a long considering look. "I guess I'll have to take your word for that."

"Do that." His gaze skimmed over her again. "Now we'd better get you out of those clothes."

"If you want me to take off my clothes, Sheriff, all you have to do is ask."

"That's reassuring," he managed to say in a dry tone. "But the fact is that you're dripping all over the oak floor and if it ends up with water stains, Fredericka Palmer won't give me back my security deposit."

"I wouldn't worry about that, Sheriff. Since I have a feeling that Freddi would probably give you just about anything you wanted. Of course you'd have to move pretty fast afterward."

"Oh?"

"She's always reminded me of a black widow. And you know what they do to their mates."

Trace decided Mariah had the Realtor pegged pretty closely. He also decided that there wasn't exactly any love lost between the two women. "I'll keep that in mind."

She nodded. "You do that." She shivered again. "Did you say something about dry clothes?"

"I've got a sweat suit you can put on," he said, heading toward the stairs. "Feel free to take a hot shower, if you'd like to warm up."

Mariah followed. "A shower sounds heavenly."

"Fine." He moved aside, allowing her to go in front of him. As they climbed to the bedrooms on the second floor, Trace couldn't help noticing, once again, that Mariah Swann had a very nice ass.

"The bath is right through there," he said, gesturing

toward the master bedroom. "I'll leave the sweat suit on the bed. When you're done, bring your wet clothes downstairs and we'll stick them in the dryer. I was planning to heat up some Chinese leftovers for dinner, if that's okay with you."

"I love Chinese."

"Good." His eyes met hers again and held. "Then we can talk."

Mariah had never been one to share her thoughts or emotions. All those private feelings she saved for her writing, exorcising ancient demons by bringing them to life in her scripts. But for some reason she would think about later, when her head didn't feel surrounded by cotton batting and her heart wasn't breaking, she found herself drawn to share confidences with this man.

Trace heard the sound of water running in the ancient pipes and envisioned Mariah standing beneath the shower, her nude body slippery with soap. Remembering the soft sweet taste of her mouth and the way she had clung so invitingly against him, remembering how her eyes had widened when he took her over the edge, his mutinous mind spun up a picture of himself stepping into the glassed-in stall, taking that green bar from her hands and running it over her body, across her shoulders, down the crests of her breasts, her stomach, spreading a billowy cloud of lather that would be washed away by the hot water streaming over them.

He imagined his lips following that slick, fragrant trail; he could hear the soft, ragged moans escape from between her ravished lips when he dipped his tongue into her moist, feminine heat. With no difficulty at all, Trace could picture her hot and hungry, her long legs wrapped around his waist as he pressed her back against the tile and...

Dangerous thinking, Callahan, he warned himself even as he felt his body responding to the erotic fantasy. The part of him that wanted to do the right thing tried to remember that the lady was in an emotionally vulnerable state.

But hell, it wasn't as if they hadn't been good together. And although he was not the kind of rogue alley cat his mother was always dragging home, neither would Trace ever profess to be a candidate for sainthood.

From her soft knowing smile, when he opened the sliding glass shower door, Trace knew Mariah had been expecting him. He took her in his arms, she lifted her face to his and they held each other so tight the cascading water couldn't come between them.

Lips clung. Greedy hands roamed over hot wet flesh. They became lost in a fragrant cloud of steam. Time faded. Yesterday spun away. Tomorrow was far away, out of sight, out of mind. There were no questions to be asked, no answers to be sought. There was only this suspended moment of sweet, sensual pleasure as they took each other into the mists.

Much, much later, they went downstairs and warmed up the Kung Pao shrimp, pork fried rice and Sesame chicken in the microwave, which they ate at the card table he was using as a kitchen table.

Since his sweatshirt had fallen to her thighs, Mariah had foregone putting on the oversize pants. Though she'd rolled up the sleeves, her slender body was engulfed. With her still damp hair hanging loose over her shoulders and a pair of fuzzy, too large ski socks on her feet, Trace thought she appeared guileless and unsophisticated.

Mariah found Trace's surroundings more than a little dreary. "Doesn't it depress you?" she asked, glancing around the barren room, mentally adding a few copper pans hanging from the wrought iron ceiling rack, a hutch filled with colorful earthenware pottery against the far wall, and some undyed muslin curtains at the window.

"What?" He followed her gaze to the window. "The rain?"

"This house."

"I haven't given it a lot of thought." He shrugged and took a pull on his beer bottle. "It's cheap. Which is all I care about."

He frowned and glanced around again in a way that made Mariah think it was the first time he'd actually looked at the room. "What's wrong with it?"

"Actually, it's a lovely house. It's just that it looks as if it's inhabited by hoboes."

A frustrated Jessica had told him much the same thing when he'd turned down her invitation to go shopping for furniture. "I've been busy since coming to town."

"I can certainly understand that. Whiskey River is infamous for its crime sprees."

"Surely you didn't drive all the way over here in the rain to insult my housekeeping skills."

"No." She sighed. "I came over here because I needed company tonight. And you're the only person in town I know anymore." That wasn't exactly true. There was her father. And Alan. And Freddi Palmer.

"What about your mother?" Trace asked carefully.

The last time he'd seen Maggie, she'd looked dangerously shell-shocked. Given what he knew about alcoholics, he'd have guessed that she'd been on the verge of a bender. He'd have also thought that Mariah would have wanted to stand guard to try to prevent that from happening.

Not that she could. Trace knew all too well the futility of keeping a drunk away from a bottle.

"Interested in comforting your first crush, Sheriff?"

He arched a brow at her sharp tone. What was it? Jealousy? Anger? ''Would it bother you if I were?''

''Not at all. It would also be none of my business.'' She angled her chin.

''As appealing as your mother still is, I'm more attracted to her daughter,'' Trace said mildly. ''I was only suggesting that given how she looked when she left my office, she probably shouldn't be alone tonight, either.''

''Maggie's not alone.'' Remembering, she closed her eyes and turned away.

Wondering if the anger that had simmered between Mariah's parents could have actually flared into something else, Trace said, ''Everyone has to deal with pain in his or her own way.''

''I know that!'' Her head spun back toward him, her eyes hot and hurt. ''But that doesn't make it any easier. Seeing your mother in bed with some hunk nearly a quarter of a century younger than her.''

His mind spun through a mental Rolodex. ''Your mother was in bed with the chauffeur?''

''Not yet. But she was drunk and her blouse was unbuttoned, and the guy—who just happens, coincidentally, to be a would-be actor—was hanging all over her, so it doesn't take a Hollywood writer to create a final scene to that particular script.''

From what Matthew Swann had implied about his wife's behavior while she'd lived in Whiskey River, along with the mention of her picking up cowboys at Denim and Diamonds, Trace concluded that the scene was undoubtedly one both Laura and Mariah had witnessed before.

''I'm sorry,'' he said, meaning it. Trace remembered all too well the first time he'd understood what his mother was doing with all those men behind the curtain in their rented room. At least Maggie was giving it away, he considered.

Mariah sighed. Then cursed. Then managed a wobbly smile. "I should be used to it," she said quietly, confirming his earlier suspicions. "It's just that she's been doing so well lately..."

She didn't finish. There was no need. Proof again, Trace considered, that wealth couldn't buy freedom from pain.

Mariah braced her elbows on the table and rested her chin on her linked fingers. "At least I finally found out why she never returned to Whiskey River for the custody hearing." Another sigh. "Maggie's version, anyway."

Trace waited.

Mariah realized that her need to share the story with someone was one of the reasons she'd come running over here in the rain. She could count on one hand the people she trusted unconditionally. Trace Callahan was, she'd realized on the drive from the lodge, at the top of that very short list.

"She was out drinking one night with the ranch's very married foreman. They were driving home from Denim and Diamonds when the car hit a patch of ice and spun out of control. My mother was driving the car. The man died. My father used his influence to keep her from being arrested in exchange for her agreeing to give him sole custody of Laura and me. And never returning to Whiskey River again."

Mariah closed her eyes and drew in a deep shuddering breath, remembering how her mother's story—told haltingly between bouts of copious weeping—had made her feel so conflicted. On the one hand, it had been a relief to learn that Maggie hadn't abandoned her daughters because of any lack of maternal love.

On the other hand—and there was *always* another hand, Mariah thought sadly—the thought of her mother's drinking being responsible for a man's death was horribly depressing.

"There's more. The foreman's name was Cole Garvey."

"Clint's father."

Immersed in her own pain, Mariah didn't notice that Trace failed to sound surprised. "One and the same." She dragged her hands through her hair. "I knew Clint's father died when he was twelve. I just never knew how."

They both fell silent, lost in their own thoughts. Trace finally understood why Matthew Swann's animosity toward Clint ran so deep.

"So," Mariah said on a soft, rippling sigh, "it seems Maggie and Laura had more in common than either one of them ever would have believed." Her eyes filled. "Maggie told me that she'd been planning to leave my father for Cole. And take Laura and me with her."

How their lives would have been different, Mariah mused sadly. Perhaps not better. But for Laura, anyway, she doubt if things could have been any worse.

"Anyway, I had to be alone," she told Trace. "Just for a little while, so I could try to sort things out."

"That's understandable."

When she opened her eyes and looked at him again, he viewed pain in the turquoise depths. "When I went back to Maggie's suite, to tell her that it was okay, that I understood the pressure she'd been under, I found her with her driver."

Frustration. Anger. Loss. She'd felt them all in that single blinding moment. Her shoulders, engulfed in Trace's gray Dallas Police Department sweatshirt, slumped.

"So I came here."

He ran his palm down her damp hair. "I'm glad you did." And not just for the great shower sex.

When he took her hand, she let her fingers curl into his and felt warm and safe. "So am I."

"There's something you should know. About Maggie."

She shook her head. She couldn't think about her mother anymore tonight. Or, for that matter, Laura. For this one stolen night, she wanted to be selfish. She wanted to let Trace comfort her, she wanted him to help her forget all the painful problems she'd be forced to face along with the morning sun.

"I don't want to hear—"

"She wasn't driving."

"Please, Trace, I really don't... What?" Her eyes widened as his words belatedly sunk in. "What did you say?"

"Maggie wasn't driving her car that night."

Chapter Eighteen

Mariah stared at Trace.

"How can you possibly know that? Maggie told me the records were sealed. It was part of the deal my father cut with the prosecutor." A man who later, after a hefty campaign contribution from the Swann ranch, had been elected to the state legislature.

"The records *were* sealed. But I happen to have friends in high places." He lifted their joined hands, brushed his lips against her knuckles and said, "They're in the other room."

She walked with him, hand in hand, into his office, settling in a corner of the couch while he crossed to the desk and retrieved the manila file, which he handed to her.

"You got this from Jessica Ingersoll, didn't you?"

"I can't tell you that. But it does make interesting reading. Would you like an after-dinner drink?"

She stared down at the folder on her lap as if it were a diamondback rattler, poised to strike. "With the risk of sounding like Maggie, I have a feeling I might need one."

She watched him pour the liquor into the glasses, observing the way the crystal appeared even more delicate when held in his large hands.

He sat down beside her, shoulders and thighs touching. Mariah did not move away. Neither did he.

Stalling while she worked up her nerve to read the accident report, Mariah took a sip. The amber liquor flowed through her veins, warming her blood.

"This is good." And expensive, she knew.

"It was a housewarming gift."

"Ah." That made sense, she decided. It also explained the Waterford, which she could not imagine Trace buying for himself. Another gift from Ms. Ingersoll. She wondered if they were still lovers, wondered if what she and Trace had shared gave her the right to ask.

Trace could guess what Mariah was thinking, but was unwilling to get into a discussion about his complicated, yet easy relationship with Jess. "Your mother deserves knowing the truth," he said, tipping his head toward the folder. "After all these years."

The accident report was written in curt, unimaginative police legalese. It had been snowing the night of the accident, a week before Christmas. The steep, curving road to the ranch, treacherous in the best of weather, had been icy.

Patrons of Denim and Diamonds, most of them none too sober themselves, disagreed on exactly when Maggie and Cole Garvey had arrived at the honky-tonk. The one thing they all agreed on was that the couple had been drinking for several hours before going out into that snowstorm. Two customers, who'd been arriving as the pair left, had also reported seeing Garvey climb into the driver's seat of Maggie's Mercedes sedan.

An assertion corroborated by the report written up by the DPS officer on the scene, who'd found the foreman's body lying in a snowbank a few feet away from the wreckage. From what the investigating officer could determine the car had hit a patch of ice, the driver had overcorrected, sending it skidding off the road into the ditch, causing it to overturn.

Garvey, who hadn't been wearing his seat belt, had been thrown from the car and had broken his neck when his head had hit the unyielding trunk of a ponderosa pine tree. Death, the coroner had later ruled, had come instantly.

Maggie had been luckier. Even as drunk as she was, she'd managed to fasten her seat belt. The first patrolmen on the scene had found her, unconscious, not from any injuries, but from the alcohol she'd imbibed earlier.

As Mariah read the damning pages, Trace sipped his brandy and watched the color drain from her face.

"He lied," she said flatly when she finally finished. She polished off her barely touched brandy in thirsty gulps, willing the alcohol to jolt her stunned mind back to life.

"Yes." Trace put his glass on the pine coffee table, took her empty snifter and placed it beside his. Then he took hold of her hand. It was ice cold. He felt a need to warm it, and her. "It seems he did."

"That son of a bitch." Her words were angry, but her eyes were flat and drained of emotion. "His lies cost us our mother."

"Perhaps he felt you'd be better off—safer—with him than living in California with Maggie," Trace suggested, playing devil's advocate. He didn't point out that if Laura and Mariah had been in that car, they could have died as well.

"That's not the point, dammit!" Color rose again in her cheeks. Warmth flooded into her eyes, her hands. "He could have fought for custody on the grounds of Maggie's drinking. And won.

"But the underhanded methods he used, the way he

allowed her to think that she'd been the one driving, to believe for all those years that she was directly responsible for a man's death, the way he forced her never to see her daughters ever again and encouraged Laura and me to believe that she'd never wanted us in the first place, all that was horrendously cruel. Even for him."

She'd known her father could be autocratic and controlling. She also knew, all too well, that he was a vindictive man. What Mariah had never realized, until now, was exactly how diabolic Matthew Swann could be. "I hate him." Her tone was flat. Final.

He ran his thumb around her jawline. "In the long run, that'll probably end up hurting you a lot more than him."

Mariah sighed. "I hate it when you're right, Callahan." She looked up at him, all her tumultuous feelings swirling in her sober gaze. "How did you get so smart?"

He framed her face in his hands. "Life, I suppose." He stroked his thumbs soothingly up her cheekbones. "If it was meant to be easy, it'd probably be boring."

It was something he'd once believed, something he'd said on innumerable occasions over the years. Until the shooting. Until he'd watched Danny die. Then, caught up in his own helpless feelings of anger, he'd lost his focus. Now, slowly, surely, Trace realized he was getting back on track.

Something flickered in his dark eyes and made her pulse jump. She felt the chains around her heart loosen ever so slightly.

"Ah, a small-town sheriff philosopher." Mariah's reluctant smile creased the silky skin beneath his hands. "I think we might have an idea for a series here, Callahan."

The mood was changing. The air around them became warm and sultry. "Sounds good to me." He ran his hand down her throat and watched her eyes cloud. "But doesn't a new series concept take a great deal of research?" His hand continued over her breasts, his fingers flicking tantalizingly at the nipples engulfed in folds of fleecy sweatshirt, drawing a soft moan.

"Of course it does." Mariah thrust her hands into his silky dark hair and went willingly, eagerly, as he laid her back on the couch. "But I told you, Sheriff, I've always prided myself on my research."

While Mariah allowed Trace to ease her pain, Alan let himself into the house his wife had left to her sister. With his father-in-law's help, he'd already packed the few personal belongings he intended to take with him back to Washington. They were currently in cardboard boxes down at Waggoner's Lock and Store, awaiting shipment to the Capitol. But there was one more thing. Something he hadn't been able to retrieve with Matthew hovering over him.

He went into the den and made his way directly to the fireplace where he removed a sheaf of papers from behind a loose stone. He dropped it into the metal wastebasket, took a fireplace match down from the mantel, struck it against the front of the fireplace, then touched it to the papers.

He stood there, watching silently as the evidence that could derail his presidential hopes went up in flames.

Two days later, Mariah was back at The Branding Iron, waiting for an order of sticky buns to go.

"So," Iris, whose family had run the café for three generations, said as she refilled Mariah's cup of coffee, "today's the big day."

Mariah was not all that surprised that Iris knew about her plans to move into Laura's house today. "I guess so." She ran her finger around the rim of the cup.

"Kind of a surprise, I'll bet," the sixty-something café owner offered. "Laura leaving you her house that way."

"That's putting it mildly," Mariah agreed grimly.

"You gonna stay?" Iris scooped up the buns with a white waxed paper square and placed them in a pink box the same color as the walls of The Shear Delight salon.

"I don't know." Mariah shrugged. "Right now, I'm just trying to take things day by day."

"Makes sense, I suppose. But I gotta tell you, girl, if it were me, I wouldn't be in any hurry to hightail it back to California. Not if I had a chance to have Trace Callahan's boots under my bed."

Mariah felt the damning color rising in her cheeks and realized that in spite of two deaths having occurred in this peaceful town, she and Trace were still managing to provide entertainment for Whiskey River's residents.

It was not easy, moving into what, during Mariah's childhood in Whiskey River, had been her grandmother Prescott's house. Especially since memories of Laura continued to live on in every room, making the transition painful.

When she first entered the ranch house, although it was a bright sunny July day, Mariah felt chilled all the way to the bone. The investigation had left the house a mess, but Mariah didn't focus on the papers scattered all over the floor, the overturned drawers, the fingerprint powder still dusting the bannister, the doorways, the desk drawers. Instead, at first, she saw only a vague blur.

Then gradually, she began to focus. The furniture was Ethan Allen traditional country, with a comfortable western influence which suited the casual ranching life-style. The knotty pine paneling looked buttery in the slanting sun streaming in through the oversize windows that overlooked the back pasture and beyond that, the woods.

Various personal items—family heirlooms—were scattered about in what Mariah suspected was a vain attempt to make the Fletcher house a home.

She recognized her grandmother's pewter watering can by the living room fireplace. It had been used as a vase, although the fresh daisies and black-eyed susans had died. Their white and yellow petals were scattered carelessly on the red brick hearth. A leather-bound photo album sat on a pine plank coffee table, its pages filled with faded sepia photographs of ancestors and more candid shots of the family from happier times.

Although there were no pictures of Maggie, which made Mariah assume that her father had destroyed any reminder of his wife, there were several shots of herself as a young girl: seated astride Buttermilk, her first pony, standing beside Whiskey River, a toothless grin splitting her face as she held up an eight-inch rainbow trout.

She paused at a picture of herself and Laura, decked out in western wear for some long ago Fourth of July and holding huge slices of watermelon, their joyous smiles offering no proof of the rift that was to come.

Saddened by the image of those two young girls—herself at eight, Laura, at thirteen on the threshold of womanhood—Mariah bit her lip and closed the album, unable to continue toward the time when her presence would no longer appear in the family annals. She had no idea how long she sat there, remembering, regretting. The towering grandfather clock in the corner had not been wound; its pendulum was motionless, its once cheery Westminster chimes silenced by death.

When she finally went into the den and saw her brother-in-law's blood still staining the back of the leather sofa, Mariah's head began to swim. She sank down on a nearby chair and pressed her fingers tightly against her eyes.

It was not that she felt any sympathy for Alan Fletcher. On the contrary, she still believed he was responsible for Laura's death. But viewing the scene of his shooting reminded her all too well what awaited her upstairs. And although she knew it was cowardly, Mariah was not prepared to witness the room where her sister had died.

Her first night in the house, Mariah slept downstairs, in a little room off the kitchen that in her grandmother's day had belonged to the cook employed by the Prescott family. The cot she'd found packed away in the camping equipment was hard and narrow, but since she doubted she would have gotten any sleep anyway, Mariah didn't mind.

Her second night, she managed to move upstairs, to the guest room. But she turned her head away as she passed the master bedroom.

She avoided her sister's bedroom for two additional days. Then, finally, knowing she could no longer put it off, Mariah ventured into the room where Laura died. It was a mess. Clothes and personal belongings had been strewn everywhere. Like downstairs, fingerprint dust had drifted over everything. The faint odor of dried blood lingered, giving testimony to what had occurred here.

She began shortly after dawn and worked all day, scrubbing the floor, the walls, the headboard, picking up Laura's scattered clothing and jewelry.

Since she could not bring herself to rid the house of her sister's presence, as if preparing the room for Laura's return, she returned the lingerie to the bureau, the paperback romance novel to the drawer in the mission-style bedside table, and changed the bedding.

One thing she had no qualms about throwing away was the framed wedding photo of Laura and Alan.

Little by little, as the days went by, and she began to settle into the house, the good memories began to outweigh the bad and gradually, Mariah began to believe that perhaps Laura was, as usual, right.

Perhaps she did belong here, after all.

It was late. Jill had gone home and Cora Mae was settled behind her desk, knitting away at an afghan for her granddaughter. The phone had been blessedly silent, allowing Trace an opportunity to review the information on Southwest Development's alleged business ventures in Arizona. He'd requested, and received, the information by fax from the attorney general's office in Phoenix. The AG assured Trace that he was keeping a close eye on the company, but since the elected official was known for his political ambition, and there were rumors of Alan Fletcher having promised his longtime friend a cabinet post, Trace had wanted to read the paperwork himself.

To someone ignorant of the company's origins, Southwest would have seemed like nothing more than an extremely successful construction company. They'd built a senior citizen condominium project in Tucson, a timeshare resort hotel in Sedona, and a federally funded low-income housing project in Phoenix.

Trace could find no record of any permits requested or issued for any project in Whiskey River. Or Mogollon County.

Wondering if he was wasting time on a wild-goose chase, he'd just filed away the papers when Cora Mae appeared in his doorway.

"You have a visitor, Sheriff."

Trace glanced up at the wall clock. It was nearly midnight. "A little late for visitors," he noted. Unbidden, the thought that Mariah might have driven down from the ranch popped into his mind.

Cora Mae's frown took up her entire fleshy face, from her three chins to her wide forehead. "Not this visitor," she harrumphed. ''The only surprise is she didn't wait until the bars closed.''

His curiosity aroused, Trace said, ''Send her in please, Cora Mae.''

She nodded brusquely, causing her pewter corkscrew curls to bob. ''You're going to need coffee,'' she informed him. ''I'll make some.''

''Thank you,'' Trace said, still as mystified as ever.

Cora Mae marched out, her spine, beneath the tan uniform she insisted on wearing, as stiff as the trunk of a ponderosa pine.

Trace heard two voices, both female. A moment later, a woman he didn't recognize appeared in his doorway.

''May I help you, Ms.—''

''Jones. Nadine Jones.'' The woman, who Trace guessed to be about the same age as Maggie McKenna, looked every day of her fifty-some years. Her hair was a mass of bleached fuzz that reminded him of a yellow Brillo pad. Looking at it, Trace suddenly recalled where he'd heard the name before. Nadine Jones, he remembered, was the infamous hairdresser from hell.

''Won't you come in, Ms. Jones.'' He stood up, went around his desk and held out a chair.

''Thank you.'' She smelled of cigarette smoke, beer and cheap, sweet perfume. ''I want you to know,'' she informed him right off the bat, ''that I've never been in any trouble with the law.'' She lit a cigarette, drawing in the smoke with an ugly rattling of her lungs.

''Uh-huh.'' Trace nodded.

She gave him a stern look. The whites of her eyes were lined with more red than a road atlas. ''You can look it up in your files.'' She waved the cigarette toward the beige metal cabinets. ''You won't find me in there.''

''I'll take your word for that,'' Trace said agreeably. ''What can I do for you, Ms. Jones?''

''Call me Nadine, honey,'' she drawled. He could smell

the beer on her breath from across the desk. "I've never been much for formality."

"Are you here to file a complaint, Nadine?"

"Actually—" she drew in on the cigarette again "—I'm here to tell you who killed Laura Swann." An acrid blue cloud billowed between them on the exhale.

Despite Nadine Jones's beery proclamation, the next day Trace was no closer to solving what he still considered a double homicide.

He did, however, find it mildly interesting to learn that Patti Greene had a habit of slashing tires. According to Nadine, the tires on her Camaro had been slashed after she'd threatened to tell the state cosmetology board that Patti was doing the occasional wash and blow-dry at her house. And off the books. Either act, if proved, could cost the hairdresser her license.

In addition, Nadine had professed, there was a little matter of selling shampoo and hair coloring to customers without a resale tax permit.

When he'd told Nadine he couldn't see how that led to murder, she'd gone on to say, with that slow, drawn out speech pattern peculiar to drunks, that Patti had bragged to her about slashing the tires on Laura Fletcher's Blazer after she found out the senator's wife had spent the night at Clint's ranch.

"Don'tcha see," the former hairdresser from hell had said, "when that didn't stop Laura from seeing Clint, Patti shot her."

It was a quantum leap from slashing tires to shooting a person in the head at close range. But Nadine wasn't finished. "She shot her husband." Another wave at the files. "Look it up."

Trace had, although it took him a while to find the paperwork, which had been misfiled. According to the report written by Ben Loftin, Patti Greene had peppered Jerry Greene's jean-clad behind with birdshot from her Ithaca shotgun after catching him making out in the parking lot of Denim and Diamonds with the girl singer. The singer subsequently left town and after having the doctor at the Payson emergency room pick the buckshot out of his ass, Jerry had spent the next two weeks sitting on a pillow and promising his trigger-happy wife that he'd behave himself. Which, of course, he hadn't.

Although he reminded himself that Nadine obviously had an ulterior motive for declaring Patti to be the killer—she had, after all, been fired by the salon owner—Trace was in no position to overlook any lead. No matter how small.

Which was why he was hanging around the outside of Shear Delight, waiting for Patti Greene to show up. ''Home with my kids,'' she said when he asked where she'd been the night of the murder. ''I told you, I didn't kill Laura.''

''But you did slash her tires?''

She pushed the door open, setting the bell tinkling. ''Who the hell told you that?'' She slammed her purse onto the reception counter and began turning on lights. The salon smelled vaguely of ammonia. ''It was Nadine, wasn't it? Lord, I'd love to wring that old bitch's neck.''

Although she didn't admit to the crime, her anger was confirmation enough. ''How about Clint's and Fredericka's tires? Did you do them, too?''

She pulled some combs and brushes out of the sanitizing solution. ''You going to take me in, Sheriff?'' She held out her hands, dripping the liquid onto the pink-and-black tile floor. ''Why don't you just put the cuffs on me and get it over with?''

Behind the anger flashing in those bright green eyes, Trace could see fear. And exhaustion. Remembering the kids and the trailer with the leaky roof, and looking at this place so badly in need of a paint job, he decided nothing would be solved by taking the woman in for vandalism.

"I'll make you a deal."

"What?" She eyed him suspiciously, giving him the feeling that most of the time when this woman made a deal with a man, she found herself on the losing end.

"You arrange to make restitution on the tires, and I won't write it up."

She tossed her red curls and lifted her chin in a way that reminded him of Mariah. "I'm not a goddamn charity case. Not yet, anyway," she tacked on under her breath.

"I didn't say you were." He put his hat back on. "I figure Clint'll be understanding. If you have any trouble with Fredericka, let me know and I'll see what I can do."

The defiance left her eyes, which filled up, threatening to brim over. "Why?"

Despite the fact that he still couldn't take this woman off his suspect list, Trace smiled. "Didn't anyone tell you? I'm one of the good guys."

Satisfied with the way he'd settled that crime wave, he left the salon. As he pulled away from the curb, he saw her standing in the window, watching him, still, he suspected, not quite understanding his behavior.

"Who was that masked man?" Trace asked himself out loud, feeling for the moment, pretty damn pleased with himself.

Back at his office, Trace couldn't shake the feeling that Laura Fletcher's death had nothing to do with her infidelity, or Clint Garvey's expectations of their marriage, or even Alan Fletcher's desire to be free to marry his congressional aide.

For not the first time since he'd arrived at the Fletcher ranch—now Mariah's ranch—on the morning of the murder, his thoughts came back to the idea that Laura was killed not for sex, but for money. Which, in this case, translated into land.

Which, he told himself glumly, once again, pointed directly at the individual who had inherited all that land. Mariah. Even as he reminded himself that she already had more money than she could spend in several lifetimes, Trace knew from experience that some people never seemed to have enough.

He didn't want to think her capable of committing any crime, let alone cold-blooded murder for profit. His need that she be proved innocent, more than anything, scared the hell out of him. His years in Dallas had taught him not to be surprised by anything, not to trust anyone, and most importantly, never, never to get involved. That had been rule number one. A rule he'd always followed.

Until now. Until Mariah.

If it was just sexual attraction he was feeling, Trace figured he could deal with it. The same way Sam Spade had dealt with the larcenous, murderous Brigit O'Shaughnessy, he mused, thinking back on Mariah's earlier comparison of their situations.

But it was more than sex. More than attraction.

Irritated by the way his mind was always returning to her, Trace pushed away from his desk, poured a cup of coffee and stood at his office window, looking out the window at the grassy square across the street.

These days, at least, his view was no longer blocked by that teeming mass of television news vans. Once Garvey had been arrested, most of the media had declared the case closed and had returned to their home bases. Although he knew they'd be back for the trial, Trace was enjoying the ability to enter the building without having to run the gauntlet of irritating, stupid questions.

These days, only the random Arizona reporter showed

up requesting an interview and even most of them seemed willing to accept his noncommittal answers about no case being fully closed until someone was convicted in a court of law. The exception was Rudy Chavez, who continued to dig around in the case.

The last bit of information the reporter had managed to unearth was the fact that two short months before she'd died, Laura Fletcher had put a hefty mortgage on the ranch. Having discovered that same fact only hours before Rudy, Trace begrudgingly granted the reporter's investigative skills a new respect.

The bank in question was on the other side of the town square and as he stared out the window, Trace viewed Mariah, coming out the bank offices with a young man clad in jeans, a navy blazer, chambray shirt and a string tie. He watched as they hugged, then, irritated by the sight of Mariah in another man's arms, looked away.

Of course there'd be men, he told himself. A woman like Mariah Swann would always have males buzzing after her. Even in a town the size of Whiskey River. *Especially* in a town like Whiskey River, where the only other women who came close to exuding big-city glamour were Jessica Ingersoll—who usually stuck to attorneys and the occasional businessman from Phoenix or Flagstaff—and Fredericka Palmer, who was too falsely sophisticated for Trace's personal taste.

The embrace lasted only a few seconds. But it was too long. With effort, Trace reminded himself that they'd agreed *no promises.*

Despite her having inherited the ranch, despite her having admitted that she'd been thinking of buying land, Trace didn't believe that Mariah would actually remain in the hometown she'd been so desperate to escape. Especially since her sister was no longer alive.

From what he'd seen of Matthew and Mariah's already-rocky relationship, which had been made worse by her discovery of what her father had done to keep his daughters from their mother, Trace sincerely doubted he'd be invited to any family reunion barbecues at the Swann ranch anytime soon.

He figured Mariah would probably last out here in the sticks another month. Two at the most. Then, ultimately, her need for excitement, the lure of trendy Malibu restaurants, glitzy Hollywood premieres and shopping at exclusive, appointment-only Beverly Hills jewelry stores where she could sip champagne or designer water while picking out a new gem-studded bauble would become too strong to resist. They could have this time together. And then they'd go their separate ways. It was, he reminded himself, what they both wanted.

He watched Mariah watching the man walk away. Then she shoved her sunglasses on her face and ran her hand through her thick blond hair in that gesture of stress he'd come to recognize. Her shoulders, clad in a short-sleeved, red silk bolero jacket, rose and fell in a weary shrug.

She turned toward the Jeep, than reconsidering, walked across the newly mown grass to a green bench situated in front of a small fishpond.

The lure to be with her was stronger than ever. The lifelong rule of keeping his professional life separate from his personal one paled in comparison to the sight of her hair gleaming like gold in the summer sun and her long legs, tanned the color of honey and showcased by a short white skirt and white sandals with gilt straps.

He tossed back the coffee, rubbed his nose between his thumb and forefinger and told himself that a strong man could resist the need that arose full-blown whenever he looked at Mariah Swann. Whenever he thought of her.

A smart man would turn away, now. Before he found himself in dangerous waters, over his head.

Knowing he'd regret it, Trace put his empty mug on his desk and left the office.

Chapter Nineteen

Mariah was watching the fish, enjoying the peaceful flash of orange and silver in the bright afternoon sun when she sensed Trace coming toward her. She didn't need to look up; it was as if she'd developed a personal radar that could alert her whenever he was anywhere in the vicinity.

Mariah hadn't thought he could hurt her. She'd thought, having survived the very public humiliation and private pain of a philandering husband, that she was immune to having her heart wounded by any man ever again. She'd been wrong.

"You've been digging into my business," she accused, her gaze still directed toward the swimming carp.

"I've been investigating your sister's murder." He sat down beside her and stretched his legs out. "Looking into her bank records comes with the territory."

"That's what my attorney told me. I wanted to go up to your office and start throwing things, but he advised me against it."

So that's who the guy in the blazer was. Trace wondered if he handled criminal cases. Hoped she wouldn't have to find out.

"Sounds like you've hired yourself a clever counsel." A fly made the mistake of landing on the surface of the water. An orange tail swished. Seconds later, the hapless insect became an entrée.

"Brady came highly recommended. From Jessica."

"I see." Trace wondered what else the two women had talked about and hoped like hell they'd kept the conversation on a professional level.

"Don't worry, Sheriff," Mariah said. "We didn't exchange any female secrets about your bedroom skills."

"I wasn't worried."

She turned toward him, her eyes unreadable through the dark lenses of the glasses. "Weren't you?"

"Maybe just a little," he admitted.

"I've never been one to kiss and tell." Mariah crossed her legs. A sandal dangled from one exquisitely arched foot, capturing his attention.

"I'm glad to hear that." Relieved was a better word.

Without warning, she was on her feet, her hands balled into fists on her hips, glaring at him through the dark glasses.

"Don't worry, Callahan. When I write my X-rated memoirs, I doubt if you'll garner more than a line. Or a footnote. Somewhere, around page 256, I'd imagine. Between my blazing affair with some soap-opera stud and my ménage à trois."

The words exploded out of her from between clenched teeth. Her cheeks were flushed the color of the Perfume Delight blooms gracing the Rose Society's nearby display garden. She was vibrating with barely restrained fury.

Closely, patiently, he examined her. "I don't suppose you'd care to tell me what you're so angry about now?"

"Me? Angry?" She arched a blond brow above the tortoiseshell frames. "Whatever makes you think I'm angry?"

"How about the fact that you look as if you've moved beyond throwing things and would like to take my .38 and shoot me?"

She tossed her head. "Don't tempt me."

They were drawing attention. A family of picnickers at a nearby table had stopped talking and was watching them with undisguised interest and one of the elderly garden society members, who'd dropped by the park to snip off dead blossoms, was openly staring, her eyes wide and interested beneath the brim of her yellow straw hat.

"Do you think you could lower the volume just a bit?" he suggested.

"I hate it when you pull out that calm, sensible cop tone, Callahan." As an act of rebellion, she raised her voice even higher, not giving a damn if the entire town was eavesdropping. Hell, perhaps, with luck, Rudy Chavez might put the exchange in the *Rim Rock Weekly Record,* Mariah thought furiously.

As frustrated as Mariah, and confused by her sudden flash of temper, he stood up as well, towering over her, fully aware that he was using his superior size to intimidate and refusing to apologize for the tactic.

"At least sit down." He curled his fingers around her upper arm.

"If you don't let go of me, I'll have Brady slap you with a police brutality suit."

He clenched his jaw and did his level best not to shake her. Fed up with not being able to see her eyes, with his free hand, he yanked the sunglasses off her face.

"Let the kid do his best. After he bails you out of jail."

"Jail?" Her voice rose high enough to scatter a flock of birds in the tree overhead. "Are you threatening me, Sheriff?"

"It's no threat." Trace was wondering how the hell he'd gotten himself into this situation. This is what happens, he reminded himself grimly, when you forgot Rule Number One. "If you don't put that tight little ass back down on the bench and lower your voice, I'll haul you in for disturbing the peace. *My* peace."

She tossed her head again, angled her chin and shot him a searing glare. "You wouldn't dare."

"Try me." His eyes met the fury in her eyes, then slowly, involuntarily, drifted down to her lips. "Sit down, Mariah. Please. And tell me what I did to upset you."

She ran an agitated hand through her hair. "If you don't know—"

"Dammit, don't do this." Forgetting their avid audience, he ran the back of his hand down her face. "I don't want to play games."

She struggled to maintain her pique even as his stroking touch began to soothe her frayed temper. "Don't you?" Suddenly drained from her emotional outburst, she sank back down to the bench. "You treated me like some Hollywood slut you can take to bed for a one-night stand then forget."

He'd worried about hurting her. Worried that they'd both end up hurt if he'd allowed their affair to continue. *Fucked up again, Callahan,* he thought grimly.

"It was more than one night." He sat down beside her, close enough that their thighs were touching, close enough for their breathing to become synchronized. "And I certainly haven't forgotten you."

"You didn't call." Realizing how pitiful she sounded, Mariah turned away, staring unseeingly across the street toward the bank.

"I wanted to." What he wanted to do right now was to take her into his arms, cover those trembling, pouting lips with his and show her exactly how much he'd missed her.

"I suppose you're going to tell me you were busy with the investigation."

"No." When she turned back toward him, surprise in her eyes, he said, "I have been busy. But I could have called. Should have called."

"Why didn't you?"

"Because I was afraid."

That came as a surprise. Mariah wouldn't have thought there was anything that could frighten this man. "Of me?"

"Of you," he agreed roughly. "Of me. Of us." He took both her hands and sandwiched them between his. "Of where we were going."

"And where is that?" she asked carefully.

"That's the problem." He managed a rough laugh, but his expression remained guarded. "I don't know."

Mariah thought about that. "And you'd need to, wouldn't you?" she asked quietly.

"I'm not real fond of surprises." The last one had almost gotten him killed.

Remembering the ugly scars on his chest, knowing what she did about the shooting that had taken his partner's life, Mariah could understand the reasoning behind Trace's grittily issued statement.

"I thought we'd agreed." Her breath, which seemed trapped in her lungs, came out slowly. "No promises."

"That's what we said. But it isn't working." He laced their fingers together. "Is it?"

"No." She looked down at their joined hands and felt the emotions rise and tangle. "It isn't."

They both fell silent, watching the fish in the cool blue water, listening to the birds in the tree branches, feeling the warmth of the sun on their faces.

It was too nice a day for fighting, Mariah thought. Too lovely an afternoon for dwelling on all her problems—her sister's still-unsolved murder, the new problems she'd discovered concerning the ranch, her confusing, disturbing feelings regarding Whiskey River's sexy, complex sheriff.

"Am I still a suspect?" she asked suddenly, wondering if that was the reason Trace had been keeping his distance.

"No." Even as he said it, Trace knew it to be true. Mariah Swann was ambitious, stubborn, exasperating. She also had a temper, which, if provoked, could probably blow a lesser man off the face of the planet. But she was not a murderer. He'd stake his Suburban, his badge and his job on it.

Which was exactly what he was doing, Trace realized, if he was eventually proven wrong.

They fell silent again.

"So what kind of lawyer is this Brady?" he asked with studied casualness.

"He specializes in corporate and estate law."

"Ah."

He was doing it again. Knowing full well that the monosyllabic response was designed to encourage her to elaborate, Mariah decided that since she didn't have anything to hide, there wasn't any reason not to oblige him.

"I found out why Alan didn't fight me for the ranch. It turns out to be mortgaged down to the last little doggie."

"Is that going to be a problem?"

She shrugged. "It might have been for Laura. But it's not that big a deal for me. Freddi, of course, has already offered to take it off my hands. At a pretty good price, actually."

"You thinking of selling?"

"Not to her. Although I was tempted when Clint suggested he'd be interested. Since I have a feeling that if Laura had known she was going to die when she did, she would have gotten around to changing her will to leave it to him, anyway.''

''I wouldn't think he could afford it,'' Trace offered, thinking of Garvey's recent losses in the futures market.

Another shrug. ''I guess he figured I'd carry the paper. But it's a moot point. Since I've decided to keep the ranch. For now.

''I've already instructed my Malibu banker to wire enough to pay off both the first and second mortgages, so I won't have to worry about making payments.''

''Must be nice to be rich.''

She heard the quiet accusation in his tone and sighed. ''That's the real problem between us, Callahan, isn't it? My money.''

''I don't know what you're talking about.'' It was the first lie he'd told her.

''Don't you?'' She gave him a long, judicial look. ''Let me ask a hypothetical question.'' Before he could respond, she asked, ''How would you feel about marrying a woman who had more money—a lot more money—than you?''

''Is that a proposal?'' Trace inwardly cursed when his flippant attempt at humor fell decidedly flat.

''It's a hypothetical question,'' she reminded him. She folded her arms over the front of the red, white and blue striped silk blouse she'd brought to Whiskey River for the Fourth of July rally and waited.

''Hypothetically speaking,'' he said, stressing the all-important word, ''although I know it's a politically incorrect feeling left over from the Dark Ages, I can't quite shake the belief that the man of the family should be the breadwinner.''

''I suspected as much,'' Mariah said with a faint nod of her head. ''So, if I'm understanding you correctly, you believe that the male of the species is supposed to go out and kill the woolly mammoth to feed his family, drag the meat back to the cave, while fighting off any other lesser males who couldn't make their own kill who are trying to take his away."

"That's an exaggeration. I said it was a feeling. In the real world, I know it doesn't always work that way."

Giving him reluctant points for honesty, she sighed as she crossed her legs on a flash of tawny thigh that had him wanting to skip this conversation, drive her over to his place, and spend the evening rolling around in his bed. Or the shower. Or the floor. Hell, the ceiling, for that matter.

"Let's move this away from the hypothetical," she suggested.

"Do we have to?" He was picturing her body racked in the throes of passion, was thinking about all the things they'd already done, all the things he wanted to do with Mariah Swann before she left town.

"Humor me." She leaned back and focused a deep, somber gaze on his face. "Exactly how much money would I have to give away before you could accept me just for myself?"

"That's ridiculous."

"Is it?" Her smile was soft and sad. Frustrated at discovering such an outdated belief lurking inside an intelligent man like Trace and saddened that he might actually believe her to be so shallow as to judge a man by his bank account, Mariah shook her head. "I don't think so."

He wanted to argue, but in good conscience, couldn't.

What was even worse was that on a deeper level, Trace secretly worried that he was just a new toy for the glamorous Hollywood writer and former soap-opera vixen. What would happen when she got bored with him—and Whiskey River—and returned to Tinseltown?

While his mind was struggling to come up with an answer that would neither insult nor hurt her, or worse yet, make her angry again, his walkie talkie began to sputter. *Saved by the bell.*

"Just a minute, Jill," he barked sharply. Too sharply. Now he'd have to apologize when he returned to the office.

Frustrated and impatient, Trace turned to Mariah. "I'm sorry, but—"

She was on her feet again. "I know. Duty calls." She shoved her sunglasses back on. "Don't worry, Sheriff. As it is, I have a lot to do myself this afternoon."

He didn't want to leave this matter unresolved. "We need to talk," he insisted. "Why don't I come out to the ranch tonight? I can pick up some chicken and ribs at The Branding Iron."

"That sounds lovely," she said with a pronounced lack of enthusiasm. "But as it happens, I have plans for dinner."

"With your lawyer?"

The dark jealousy that moved across his face gave Mariah a faint glimmer of hope. A jealous man was not an indifferent one.

"No, not Brady." She wondered what Trace would say if he could have heard the young man waxing enthusiastic about his new bride and viewed the wedding pictures the attorney carried around in his attaché case.

"Not your father." He was being forced to drag it out of her. For not the first time since meeting Mariah, Trace was painfully aware that this was a woman who could make a man crawl.

"No." Taking pity on him, she said, "Actually, Jessica and I are driving into Payson for Mexican."

"Sounds as if you and Jess are becoming close."

"Don't worry." Mariah's tone was as dry as the red dust that rose up from the logging roads crisscrossing the Rim. "Ms. Ingersoll has assured me that she'd have no problem prosecuting me if it came to that. But,'' she added with a spark of her usual fire, ''she also said that she knows it won't come to that. It seems *she* trusts me.''

She ran a fingernail down the front of his shirt. Tantalizing. Taunting. ''You might give it a try, yourself, Sheriff,'' she advised.

On that note, she turned and walked away, leaving Trace to wonder, yet again, exactly where he'd lost control of the situation.

Fearing the revelation would set off World War III between her parents, Mariah had vacillated telling Maggie the truth of what had happened on the night of Cole Garvey's death. But knowing her mother had the right to know the truth, and realizing she could not keep putting it off forever, she dropped by the lodge before driving to Payson.

To Mariah's surprise, Maggie took the news with remarkable equanimity, going so far as to say that there wasn't any point in confronting Matthew after all these years.

''What's done is done,'' she said, after wiping away her tears. Tears of relief or regret, Mariah could not tell. ''Attacking Matthew for such a vicious lie will not bring back those years. And it won't give me back Laura.'' With a teary smile, she reached out and took Mariah's hand. ''At least I still have my younger daughter.''

Her mother certainly didn't seem drunk. But Mariah didn't quite trust her fatalistic attitude. ''I have to admit, I'm surprised by how calmly you're taking this.''

Maggie looked a little puzzled by that as well. ''Perhaps I'm finally growing up,'' she mused.

She slanted a wobbly, misty-eyed smile toward her driver, who had, at Maggie's insistence, remained in the hotel suite during the intimate conversation between mother and daughter. ''Thanks to Kevin. He's been a wonderful lifeline during these terrible days.''

''Your mother's been on her own for a long time,'' he replied in response to Mariah's sharp look. For someone that she'd thus far only thought of as at best, a male bimbo and at worst, a gigolo, Mariah had to give him credit for holding his ground beneath what people had told her could be an intimidating glare. ''It's time she had someone to care about her and help her over the rough patches.''

Watching the two of them exchange warmly intimate glances, Mariah was tempted to ask what the hell they thought she'd been doing all these years.

Then she realized that it wasn't the same. During her past decade in Los Angeles, she'd come to see her mother as a burden. An exciting, dazzling, larger-than-life problem just waiting to happen. Even during the times when Maggie was not drinking, Mariah had felt about her mother in much the same way she would a lit fuse of dynamite. The question was not *if* Maggie was going to explode, but *when.* Regrettably realizing that her constant support of her mother had been due more to duty than daughterly love, Mariah decided she was in no position to judge anyone.

Trace returned to his office to find Alan Fletcher waiting for him. The senator was obviously on the road to recovery from the deaths of his wife and aide. He looked tanned, fit and ready to run for the presidency.

''Good afternoon, Sheriff.'' Fletcher stood up as Trace entered his office and held out his hand.

''Senator.'' Trace shook the proffered hand, then sat down behind his desk. ''What can I do for you?''

''Actually, I've come by to thank you for all you've already done. Apprehending Laura's killer has eased my mind considerably.''

With a politician's knack for only focusing on the message of the day, he did not mention Trace's earlier accusation that he'd killed his wife and aide.

"I'm glad to hear that." Since Garvey's guilt or innocence was now up to a jury to decide, Trace didn't bring up his doubt that the correct man was behind bars. Nor did he mention the investigation was not yet closed. "I only wish we could have gotten a more conclusive diagnosis on Ms. Martin's death."

"Heather." Trace, who was watching Fletcher carefully, saw a shadow of pain move across the senator's eyes. But he did not see guilt. "I don't know how I'm going to get through this campaign without her."

Having observed Fletcher at close hand these past days, the senator's egocentric view of the situation did not surprise Trace in the least. "I'm sure you'll manage somehow," he replied.

His dry tone flew over Alan's head. "This country is headed down the wrong path. Someone needs to turn it around."

Afraid that he was about to get a preview of the senator's stump speech, Trace braced his elbows on the scarred arms of his chair, folded his hands together and said, "Is there anything else I can do for you, Senator?"

"No." Getting the hint, Alan stood up. "I just wanted to convey my appreciation before leaving."

"You're returning to Washington?" The news did not come as a pleasant surprise. But Trace also knew he had no official reason to prevent the senator from leaving town.

"Eventually. I'll be in Whiskey River a couple more days. Friday I'm beginning my campaign swing though the Southwest."

"I recall Ms. Martin saying something about that," Trace agreed. "I hadn't realized it was still on."

The senator flashed him one of those attractive Redford smiles. ''To tell you the truth, I was considering canceling, but I've received so many cards and letters of support, that I realized that the people really do want me to carry on.''

''Mustn't disappoint the voters.''

This time Fletcher caught the faint innuendo. He frowned, but did not comment on it. ''I work for the people.'' His gaze narrowed in a way that made Trace feel as if he were being viewed in the cross hairs of a gun scope. ''As do you.''

It was a threat. Pure and simple. Trace chose, for now, to ignore it. He wasn't through with Senator Fletcher yet. But he preferred to choose his battles—and the time for confrontation—himself.

''Got a point there,'' he said agreeably. ''By the way, Senator, did you realize your wife had put a mortgage on the ranch?''

Fletcher shrugged. ''No. But it wouldn't have surprised me. That place was always draining money from her trust fund. If it had come out of our joint account, I probably would have paid more attention, but as it was, I merely considered the ranch Laura's little hobby.''

About this, Fletcher sounded sincere. Trace stood up and came around the corner of the desk. ''Have a good trip back to the Capitol, Senator,'' he said. ''I'll keep you informed regarding Garvey's trial date.''

''I'd appreciate that.'' Fletcher stopped in the doorway and asked, as if on an afterthought, ''I don't suppose there's any way you can hurry the case along?''

So any innuendo regarding the senator's guilt, or his affair with his aide would be long forgotten by election time? Trace supposed. ''That's up to the judge and the opposing counsels.''

"Of course." Alan nodded. "Well, I just hope it's soon. So we can all get on with our lives."

Personally Trace thought the senator was already doing a bang-up job of that, but managed to hold his tongue.

Trace stood in his window, watching Fletcher drive away. Then he left his office, headed for the jail to talk to Garvey about what he knew, if anything, about the mortgages Laura Fletcher had put on the ranch shortly before she died.

Chapter Twenty

Mariah was leaving the lodge just as Alan entered.

"What are you doing here?" he asked, not bothering to hide his antipathy.

Deciding that her conversation with her mother was none of his business, Mariah didn't answer. "You're going to have to display a bit more western hospitality than that, Alan," she said instead, "if you intend to be elected president."

She flashed him a smile they both knew was totally feigned. "People aren't very willing to contribute to the campaign of a candidate who all but tells them to go to hell."

He arched a mocking blond brow. "Somehow I doubt you've come here this afternoon to contribute to my campaign."

"I'll say this about you, Senator, when you're right, you're right."

Eyeing him with forced dispassion, noting how casually handsome he looked in his linen slacks and Ralph Lauren polo shirt, Mariah wondered how many women in America would actually vote for a man just because he reminded them of Robert Redford. When Dan Quayle immediately came to mind, she felt more depressed than ever. She wished there was something she could do to ruffle the man's calm. Her sister was dead, and he was still on his way to the White House. It wasn't fair, dammit!

A thought suddenly occurred to her. A reckless, wonderful idea Mariah figured that, while it wouldn't prove his guilt, it might make the bastard squirm a little.

"I wouldn't be in a hurry to order my inauguration suit if I were you, Alan. Because it just so happens I've come across some papers in the house that will prove you killed Laura."

His gaze sharpened. Watching the color drain from his handsome, tanned face, Mariah experienced a surge of satisfaction that her totally unplanned, fictitious statement had hit so close to the mark.

Unwilling to give him time to try to pin her down, she turned on her heel and marched out of the lodge.

Clint Garvey sat on the edge of his narrow jail cell bunk. He seemed, Trace thought, strangely resigned to his situation.

"Sure, I knew the ranch was mortgaged," he said with a shrug. He took a long pull on his cigarette. "So what? Most of the places around here belong to the bank. Mine included."

"Yet you offered to buy the ranch from Mariah at a time when your own finances aren't exactly running in the black."

"I figured we could work something out. It's not as if she needs the money," he said with a casual disregard that hit a vaguely false note with Trace.

"About the mortgage on the Fletcher place—"

"The Prescott place," Clint corrected sharply. It was

the first sign of emotion Trace had seen from the rancher since he'd been arrested. "If Laura had wanted Fletcher's name on her property, she wouldn't have used her own collateral to get the loan."

"So Fletcher didn't know the ranch was mortgaged?"

"Not that I know of." He exhaled a thick cloud of smoke on a disgusted sound. "The guy was only interested in the ranch because it gave him instant status as an Arizonan. Marrying into the Swann family made people forget that he was nothing but a carpetbagger who'd moved to Phoenix after his commercial development business had gone belly-up in Chicago."

He flicked the cigarette onto the floor, crushed it with a booted heel and lit another. "Hell, the guy wouldn't know a steer from a cow."

Trace decided Garvey had hit a bull's-eye with that analysis.

"From what I can tell from the Fletchers' tax returns, the ranch was profitable until this year."

Clint shrugged. "The ranching business has its ups and downs. But Laura got hit pretty damn hard this spring."

"How was that?"

"Her roundup came in way short. We thought, in the beginning, that I might have accidently gotten some of her calves mixed up with mine. But that didn't turn out to be the case."

"Are you saying her calves were stolen?"

"Couldn't prove it. But the numbers were too low to be anything else. And it sure as hell wouldn't be the first time some cowboy started his own spread with borrowed calves."

As he returned to his office, Trace wondered what the guys back in the city would say if they knew he was chasing down cattle rustlers.

* * *

Mariah couldn't help herself. Although she hadn't really wanted to like Jessica Ingersoll—who was, after all, a rival of sorts—she found herself thoroughly enjoying the attorney's company. Over margaritas, nachos and chimichangas, Mariah could also see exactly what had attracted Trace.

Jessica was intelligent, and beneath her cool, icy image, Mariah sensed a very passionate woman. The kind of woman, she considered, who'd make a perfect match for an equally passionate man. Add in the fact that their work would require long hours spent in each other's company and it was no wonder she and Trace had become lovers.

"By the way, Mariah," Jessica said as the two women walked out to their individual cars in the restaurant parking lot, "after spending the evening tiptoeing around the subject, I think you should know that Trace and I are just friends.

"Close friends," she admitted, when Mariah arched a challenging brow, "but there was never anything permanent about our relationship. Nor could there ever be."

"Why not?" Mariah couldn't help asking.

"Trace isn't really my type."

Mariah couldn't help laughing at that; Jessica joined in.

"Really," she insisted. She leaned against her car and folded her arms. "I'm not saying I don't find him enormously sexy. What woman wouldn't?"

What woman indeed, Mariah thought, thinking back to Iris's comment the other morning. Trace Callahan was the type of man that sexual fantasies were built on. "But?"

"But you have to understand, I was brought up in a very strict family. My father ruled the roost with an iron hand."

"I get the picture," Mariah murmured.

"I thought you might," Jessica agreed, having had several long conversations with Matthew Swann lately. "All my life I struggled to be the proper daughter my parents expected me to be.

"Then, as soon as I got my law degree, I packed my books and clothes into the back of my BMW and headed west, where no one knew me. Where there were no expectations."

"Where you could be whoever and whatever you wanted to be."

"Exactly. And I actually believed I'd escaped my father's influence until I realized that with the exception of Trace, the men I become involved with, while intelligent, also allow me full control of the relationship."

"I can't see Trace giving up total control."

"Nor can I. Which is why, although we get along wonderfully, for short periods of time, we'd never last. Because, if—and this is a very big *if,*" she qualified, "I ever *do* decide to get married, it will be to a man who's content to let me wear the pants in the family."

"I see."

"I thought you might," Jessica repeated. Her gaze, reflected in the spreading yellow glow of the parking lot light, turned thoughtful. "But I've watched the way Trace is with you. And although I never would have believed it possible, you actually seem to be teaching him the fine art of compromise." She grinned again. "The only thing I can figure out is the guy must be in love."

Love. The word ricocheted through Mariah, leaving her stunned and momentarily speechless. Need. Want. Desire. Even lust. Those were easy words. Love wasn't. Love required patience, demanded commitment. Love was terrifying.

"I think you misunderstand our relationship."

Jessica gave her a long look. "Perhaps," she murmured. "Then again, perhaps not." She bestowed a generous, sympathetic smile on Mariah. ''I'm afraid I'm about to do something I never do. Something I've always had a rule against, actually.''

''What's that?''

''Offer advice. Give it time. And trust your instincts. You and Trace haven't met under the best of circumstances. But with patience, I have a feeling things will work out fine.''

''Patience has never been my long suit.''

Jessica laughed at that. ''Join the club.''

Mariah was still standing in the parking lot, considering Jessica's surprising words as the taillights disappeared from sight.

''Patience,'' she muttered to herself as she climbed into the Jeep. ''I'm told it's a virtue.''

Actually, the cardinal virtues were justice, prudence, temperance and fortitude, Mariah remembered learning in a college ancient-philosophy class.

''Well, hell,'' she decided as she headed toward Whiskey River, ''two out of four ain't bad.''

She'd driven through the town and had turned onto the steep, winding road leading up to the ranch when it began to rain. Not a typical torrential July monsoon, but enough that she was forced to turn on the wipers. There was a new moon; the overhead sky was low and as black as pitch, the towering pine trees lining the road appeared as dark and ominous shadows.

Decreasing tax revenues from downturns in timber and cattle sales—the economic lifeblood of the county—had cut back on county services so that the narrow road was still filled with potholes from the previous winter, making the ride jarring.

Although Mariah had never been the nervous sort, she found the sea of black beyond the headlights oddly spooky. When her flesh prickled with goose bumps, she cursed and wished she'd given in to temptation and bought a pack of cigarettes from the machine back at the restaurant.

"Sissy," she scolded herself, even as she reached out and tuned the Jeep's radio to a Flagstaff talk station so she wouldn't feel so alone. "Keep this up and you'll have to write horror films. Gruesome slashers about women in jeopardy."

She was gripping the steering wheel so hard her forearms ached. To add to her discomfort, the topic tonight seemed to be romance. Caller after caller phoned in, eager to share increasingly depressing stories of love gone wrong.

"See," she told herself, switching over to a country station, "it's just too risky. And it never lasts."

If she believed in happily-ever-after endings, she told herself, she'd be writing fairy tales.

As she continued maneuvering around the switchbacks, Mariah considered leaving Whiskey River now, before things became too complicated. Too painful.

"That's it." Mariah shook her head in a gesture of self-disgust. "Run away again. After all, that's what you do best."

She'd run away from her father. From Laura. From the family rift that she herself had helped to create.

And although she had never blamed herself for the failure of her marriage, Mariah had, in a very real way, avoided the responsibilities of any further romantic involvements by burying herself in her work.

This time it was going to be different, Mariah vowed. This time she wasn't going to turn tail and run as soon as things got a little tough. This time she was going to stick around long enough to see things through.

Whatever happened.

Feeling upbeat about her decision, Mariah felt her

shoulders relaxing. The ache behind her eyes eased and her fingers relaxed on the steering wheel. Although the rain had increased and the road was no less treacherous, for the first time since arriving back in Whiskey River, she felt almost at ease with herself. And her situation.

She was singing along with Reba McIntyre when she heard a sound like a car engine. And although night sounds in the woods were often hard to pinpoint, she could have sworn the sound was coming from behind her. A glance in the rearview mirror, however, revealed nothing.

Shrugging off the imagined sound, she joined in on the chorus, stopping when she heard the sound again. It was definitely the roar of an engine and it was coming closer. She lifted her eyes to the mirror. Still nothing.

Even as she told herself she was being paranoid, Mariah stepped on the accelerator and felt the Jeep surge around the sharp, S-shaped curve.

The Cherokee hit a pothole, jarring her teeth. But with the instinct of the suddenly hunted, Mariah knew that she was in danger.

Her fingers tightened around the steering wheel again; her teeth clenched so tightly her jaw ached. She struggled to keep her mind on her driving and the Jeep on the serpentine curves while at the same time monitoring the road behind her in the rearview mirror.

The roar grew closer, sounding more like a truck than a car. She looked down at the speedometer. She was already going fifty—a stupidly dangerous speed on this road even if it were a clear day—and still she could hear the engine gaining. And gaining.

She maneuvered around another hairpin corner, the Jeep vibrating under the too-fast speed, but as she came out of the turn, a pair of headlights flashed on behind her, piercing the inky blackness, blinding her with their glare in the rearview mirror.

Before her eyes could adjust to the sudden brightness, those same headlights reared to the right, coming around to the side, cutting her off, pushing her closer and closer to the steep edge of the narrow road.

As big as the four-door Jeep Grand Cherokee was, the murderous truck was even larger.

As Reba gave way to Garth Brooks singing about the damned ole rodeo, Mariah twisted the steering wheel, trying to regain lost ground. She heard the unmistakable, screeching sound of metal against metal; she felt the jarring sensation of the other truck pushing against hers.

And then, as the Jeep careened violently over the side of the cliff, Mariah screamed.

Chapter Twenty-One

His heart pounding in his ears, Trace burst through the double doors of Payson's Louis R. Pyle hospital.

He'd thought he'd experienced fear.

But he'd been wrong.

Dead wrong.

Because even in the suspended moment when he'd entered that warehouse and found himself facing the business end of that murderous Street Sweeper, he'd still not been as frightened as he'd been when J.D. had called in with the news that an unconscious Mariah had been airlifted to the hospital after driving her Jeep over the side of a cliff.

As he'd raced to Payson, for the first time in a very long while, Trace had prayed. Disjointed, incoherent prayers, pleas that she would be all right. Rash, wild promises of what he'd do if only she were.

"Where is she?" he demanded of the night receptionist on duty. He flashed his badge. Although Trace was accustomed to his authoritative manner getting results—and if that didn't do it, the .38 on his hip invariably did—the elderly woman behind the counter did not blink an eye.

"Where is who?"

"Mariah Swann. She was brought in by air evac."

"Ah." She nodded. "Ms. Swann is in examining room A."

"Thanks." He tore off in the direction she was pointing.

"Excuse me." When he didn't pause, the woman raised her voice, jumped up, rushed around her counter and followed on his heels. "I said, excuse me. Sir! You can't go in there. It's restricted to hospital personnel."

Ignoring her protests, Trace found the room that consisted of three curtained cubicles. The curtains on two of the cubicles were open, the examining tables empty.

As he crossed the room, the clerk right behind him, Trace decided that the fact that the curtains were closed on the third cubicle was a good sign. If Mariah was critically injured, a trauma team would be bustling all around her.

Unless…

No! He would not allow himself to think that he might have arrived at the hospital too late. This wasn't going to end up like Danny, he told himself. He wouldn't let it!

He reached the white curtain just as the clerk caught up with him. She grabbed his arm at the same time he jerked the curtain open.

When Trace saw Mariah sitting on the edge of the examining table, he let out a rough, relieved breath he'd been unaware of holding. A white-jacketed man stood beside the examining table. When he turned around, Trace recognized him as the doctor who'd been on duty when Alan Fletcher had been brought in.

"It's all right, Gert," the physician assured the receptionist. "You can go back to your desk."

The woman darted anxious eyes from the doctor to Trace, then back again. "If you're sure."

"Positive." The doctor turned toward Trace. "Hello, Sheriff," he greeted him impassively, as if a wild-eyed man bursting into his emergency room was all in a night's work. Which, Trace considered, remembering that the doctor had previously worked in one of Oakland's roughest neighborhoods, it probably was. "What can I do for you tonight?"

He looked past the doctor, addressing his words to Mariah. "I heard you'd been in an accident."

"I'm okay," she assured him.

She was wearing a blue hospital gown. A white paper sheet had been draped across her legs. Her feet were bare, revealing toenails lacquered the hue and sheen of rubies.

He reached out and took hold of her hand. "Are you sure?"

"Ms. Swann's a very lucky woman," the doctor informed Trace before Mariah could respond. "From what your deputy tells me, her truck is totaled. But thanks to her air bag, she walked away without a scratch."

His heart, which had been pounding like a jackhammer on the drive to Payson from Whiskey River, began to settle down to something resembling a normal beat. "Cora Mae said you were unconscious." With unsteady hands he brushed her hair back from her forehead, as if looking for signs of injury.

"That's the embarrassing part. When they cut me out of the Jeep—"

"They had to cut you out?"

"The doors wouldn't open. I guess hurtling over the edge of the Rim is a bit too off-road. Even for a Jeep."

"Christ." He closed his eyes at the terrifying image.

"But the doctor's right. I'm fine. I just was so relieved, that I got a little light-headed and fainted."

He turned toward the doctor in alarm. "Are you sure she doesn't have any head injuries?"

"None that I can detect. But I want to admit Ms. Swann for observation, just in case."

"You never said anything about me staying here." She tried to get down from the table and was restricted by Trace's broad hand holding her where she was. "I want to go home."

"You're going to follow doctor's orders," Trace said.

"That's ridiculous."

"You'll either stay willingly, or I'll have an orderly take you to a room and handcuff you to the bed."

"You wouldn't!"

"Try me."

Furious turquoise eyes dueled with implacable gray. This time Mariah was the one to back down. "I hate it when you go into your high-handed cop routine, Callahan."

More relieved than he'd ever been in his life, Trace grinned. "I am a cop."

"Yeah. So you keep reminding me." She looked over at the doctor. "This really is a waste of time. And money. Not to mention that I'll be taking up a hospital bed someone else might need."

"Don't worry, Ms. Swann," he said pleasantly. "We're not even at half capacity tonight. Your presence isn't going to cause any other patients to end up sleeping on gurneys in the hallway. If you don't have any complications, Dr. Davis will sign you out of here at noon." He smiled at Trace, his teeth flashing in a broad, man-to-man grin. "I'll leave you two alone to talk. When you're finished, just tell Gert and she'll arrange to have someone escort Ms. Swann to her room."

Mariah swore in frustration as he walked away. "Well, so long as you're here, Sheriff, I need to file a complaint."

"A complaint?"

"Against Alan Fletcher."

"What now?"

"He ran me off the road tonight," Mariah explained with what Trace felt was amazing aplomb, considering the gravity of her accusation.

He wondered if she'd received a head injury the doctor had failed to spot. "Are you saying what happened to you tonight wasn't an accident?"

"Of course it wasn't an accident. I happen to be a very good driver, Trace. And I grew up driving on that road. If it hadn't been for that truck—"

"What truck?"

"That's what I'm trying to tell you."

She went on to explain about the truck that had been following her, about the way the driver had kept his headlights off until he was right behind her, then flashed his brights to blind her.

"Then he pushed me off the road. Which is why I want to press charges against Alan," she finished up.

"It couldn't have been Fletcher."

Trace tamped down the cold fury that coursed through him at the idea of anyone trying to harm Mariah. Although a very strong part of him wanted to rush out and kill the son of a bitch, whoever he was, Trace forced himself to stick to more judicious investigative techniques.

"He was in the lobby of the Lakeside Lodge an hour ago." He refrained from reporting that the senator had been having dinner with Fredericka Palmer.

"Well, of course I don't think he'd have the guts to do it himself. Obviously he hired someone to kill me."

Trace folded his arms and looked down at her in that steady patient way she admired even as it drove her crazy. "Why do you think the senator would want to kill you?"

Mariah was not quite ready to reveal what she'd told Alan just before driving to Payson for her dinner with Jessica. She had a crushing headache and wasn't prepared for the shouting she suspected such a revelation would invite.

''For the ranch, of course.''

''A heavily mortgaged ranch.''

''Not any more,'' she reminded him.

''One very strong problem with your hypothesis,'' Trace said deliberately, ''is that while I'll agree about Fletcher's lack of character, he hasn't shown a lick of interest in the ranch. Besides, I still don't think the guy has the guts to commit cold-blooded murder.''

''I told you,'' Mariah insisted, ''he undoubtedly paid someone.''

''Too risky.'' Trace shook his head. ''The kind of low-lifes who'll take on a murder for hire also have a nasty habit of not keeping their mouths shut. They tend to brag to girlfriends in bed, to drinking buddies in bars, and if they're ever picked up for some other crime, they'll sing like the proverbial canary in order to cop a plea.

''One thing Fletcher isn't is stupid. He'd never take such a potentially destructive career risk.''

''Point taken,'' Mariah agreed reluctantly. ''But I would like to know one thing.''

''What's that?'' He didn't quite trust her seeming acquiescence.

''If you don't believe Alan's guilty, then what are you doing hanging around the lodge, keeping an eye on him?''

''I said it was unlikely. I didn't say it was impossible.''

''What about Clint?''

Mariah's sources in Dallas had told her that the single thing Trace had always cared most about was closing a case. His single-minded devotion to his work had cost him his marriage, and on more than one occasion, nearly cost him his career. But as much as she knew how important his closure rate was to Trace, she couldn't believe he'd be willing to put an innocent man behind bars in order to do it.

Trace frowned, his discomfort obvious. "I trust Jessica's judgment. I also understand the pressure she's under." All too well.

"I imagine you do," Mariah murmured.

Her sources had also told her Trace had never been interested in advancement, recognition, or even praise. When working a case, he was inclined to ignore politics and procedure. It was a trait that garnered results even as it often had him skating perilously close to the razor's edge of suspension. Indeed, his refusal to follow orders he believed to be wrong had been one of the things that tended to land him in hot water on a regular basis.

"The problem is, although he hasn't been completely honest with me, Garvey just doesn't feel right," Trace said.

The so-called intruders had resulted in a dead end as well. The entire case was turning into blank walls and blind alleys. The longer it dragged on, the longer he was afraid of losing it.

"I'm relieved to hear you say that. I was afraid you were going to settle on Clint because you're already behind the seventy-two hour rule."

Trace rolled his eyes and looked up at the acoustical ceiling, as if praying for patience. "Spare me from Hollywood crime writers. This is not an episode of 'Murder She Wrote.'"

"You shouldn't insult me. Not after I've been in what could have been a fatal accident."

"Hell. I'm sorry."

"That's all right. I've certainly been called worse." She was still too pale, but Trace thought he viewed a spark of humor in her eyes. "Besides, I kind of insulted you first.

Suggesting that you went along with arresting Clint because time was running out.''

He folded his arms across his chest. ''I wouldn't do that.'' His voice was low and deadly, reminding Mariah that this was a man who would only allow himself to be pushed so far.

''I know.'' They fell silent, him looking down at her, her looking up at him. Something had changed. They both felt it.

There was a suspended moment of awkwardness as Mariah considered how strange it was that she, who made a living with words, could not think of a single thing to say.

Although she was far from at her best, clad in the ugly wrinkled gown with her feet dangling down and her hair tangled, and those weary circles beneath her eyes, Trace felt as if she could have been a siren, luring him into the warm turquoise lagoon depths of her eyes.

Needing to touch her, he slipped his hands beneath the paper sheet and ran them up the silky skin of her thighs. ''I have to go talk to Loftin.''

In his eyes Mariah read both regret and need, recognizing the emotions easily because she was feeling them herself. ''Oh.'' She was breathless. But that was impossible. The doctor had listened to her lungs while she'd breathed in and out on command and proclaimed her fit as a fiddle. ''I can think of better things to do on a rainy night.''

''You and me both, babe.'' The paper sheet rustled as his touch roved higher, leaving a weakening trail of warmth.

Suddenly remembering that except for a pair of skimpy panties, she was naked beneath the sheet and gown and worrying that the harridan from reception might be hovering on the other side of the curtain, Mariah caught Trace's wicked hand.

"Callahan." It was part protest, part plea. "Someone could come in."

His stroking touch was creating absolute havoc to the flesh of her inner thighs. "I don't suppose they'd buy the excuse that I was searching for clues?"

"I don't think so," she said on a strangled sound as his fingers slipped beneath the elastic leg band of her panties.

"I *am* a professional investigator."

"Try telling that to Gert." Despite her words of protest, she was practically purring. In another minute she'd be begging him to make love to her right on this narrow examining table. Heaven help her, Mariah thought, she had absolutely no shame.

She tugged his hand from beneath the sheet. But she was not yet ready to let go.

"We really do need to talk," she said, lacing their fingers together atop the wrinkled sheet covering her lap. Unreasonably nervous, she licked her suddenly dry lips.

The absently innocent gesture created a surge of heat in Trace's groin. He lifted their joined hands and felt the increased pulse at the inside of her wrist thrumming against his lips. "Not about the case," he guessed.

"No." Her gaze was inordinately serious. A line of tension circled her lips. "Not the case." She swallowed, feeling horribly as if she were fourteen again, asking Johnny Patterson to the Sadie Hawkins dance in the high school gym.

"We'll talk later." Since she was still hanging on to his right hand, he used his left to brush some tangled hair away from her face. "After you've had some sleep."

"Later," she agreed reluctantly, wishing she could ask him to stay with her, then reminding herself that it was more important he find whoever it was that ran her off the road.

Trace took her uncharacteristic acquiescence as a sign

of how emotionally drained she was. Knowing he should leave, but unwilling to go without at least one taste of those silken lips, he lowered his head and kissed her.

His mouth was soft, yet firm. Warm. Tender. As she sank into its gentle heat, Mariah realized on some distant level that this kiss was oddly different from the others they'd shared.

His mouth was as sensual as ever, but careful. Not the slightest bit tentative, but testing. As if his lips were echoing the unreadable question she'd seen in his pewter gray eyes just before their lips had met.

The kiss lingered. Mariah felt herself drifting on slow, easy tides of rising desire. When he finally backed away, she viewed in his eyes again that same serious question she'd felt on his lips.

''Be a good girl,'' he said, running his hand down her tangled hair, ''and do what the doctor ordered.''

Her temper predictably flared. ''I told you—''

''I know. You're not a girl.'' His fingers cupped her chin and he treated her to another short, fiery kiss that affected her even more than the first. ''And even when you were, you were never—ever—good.''

The dancing devils in his eyes assured her she'd been expertly baited. ''You did that on purpose.''

''I wanted to put some color in your cheeks.'' He ran the back of his hand down the side of her face and watched, satisfied as even deeper color bloomed.

''Don't toy with me, Callahan.'' She was smiling when she said it.

Because he was tempted to slip his hand beneath the sheet that was, at this very moment, slipping off her bare legs, he stuck his hands into his pockets. ''As soon as the doc gives you a clean bill of health in the morning, I'm taking you home, where I intend to spend several long and stolen hours toying with you in every way imaginable. And a few unimaginable ones as well."

Smiling her pleasure, she ran her hand down the front of his shirt. Then lower still, feeling a surge of feminine power as she felt him stir against her palm.

"Equal time, Callahan. Don't I get to toy with you?" she asked with a coy seductiveness she'd never used with any other man.

His answering grin caused lines to crinkle around his eyes, making him look almost carefree. "I was counting on it."

He backed away, viewed her clothes on a nearby molded plastic chair and scooped them up.

"What do you think you're doing?" Mariah demanded.

"Keeping you from leaving the hospital until the doc springs you."

Laughing at Mariah's heated string of curses, Trace left the emergency room to track down Ben Loftin.

The deputy, who'd been the first to respond to the DPS call, insisted that Mariah's accident was undoubtedly caused by a cowboy driving under the influence.

It sounded good, Trace allowed. But it was also too easy.

That deep-seated instinct he'd always trusted told him that someone had tried to kill Mariah, or at the very least, scare her back to California.

After instructing J.D. to go to the hospital and remain outside Mariah's room, just in case whoever it was who ran her off the road might try again, Trace got into the Suburban and headed out of town. To where the DPS had discovered the wrecked Jeep.

"Lady was damn lucky," the trooper remarked as he and Trace watched the Cherokee being lifted onto the flatbed trailer of the tow truck. Trace had impounded the Jeep for testing.

"Lucky," Trace murmured. He turned and looked back up at the edge of the cliff, where the Jeep had left the road. Then down into the canyon below. If she hadn't hit that huge red boulder head-on…

The driver's door had been cut away; the passenger door was badly caved in. As the tow-truck driver fastened the moorings, something captured Trace's attention.

He focused his flashlight on the passenger door. "Look at this." The DPS officer turned his own beam on the spot. A streak of forest green paint marred the creased tomato red door.

"Looks like she was telling the truth about having been run off the road."

Trace murmured an agreement and wondered if, just possibly, Mariah could also be right about Alan Fletcher.

Sometimes—hell, most of the time, Trace amended—the guy who looked the most guilty really was the bad guy.

Even if he was a U.S. senator.

Trace was on his way back to the hospital when Jill called to let him know that the DPS crime lab had finished with its analysis of the clothing J.D. had retrieved from Clint's hamper when he'd searched the rancher's house.

At the time, J.D. had tagged the chambray shirt because the stain on the front of it looked like dried blood. A suspicion the state chemist confirmed. He also confirmed that the thread J.D. had found on the carpet could have come from that same shirt. Which should have made Garvey look guilty as hell, Trace considered as he read through the report.

Except for one thing. The blood, which the chemist declared to be human, was not Laura Fletcher's. Nor was it Clint Garvey's.

The cowboy had a lot of explaining to do.

"Shit." Trace scowled down at the report, irritated at

Garvey for interjecting this new twist into an already convoluted case. The fact that he was going to have to interrogate his prisoner again, when he'd rather be with Mariah, did nothing to improve Trace's already-rotten mood.

As soon as Mariah was unwillingly settled into her hospital room, she placed a call to the lodge.

"Maggie," she said, when her mother answered the phone, "I need you to do me a big favor."

"Of course, darling. Anything."

"I'm in Payson at the hospital."

"The hospital? What's wrong?"

"Nothing," Mariah said quickly, hearing the thready note of panic in her mother's voice. "I had a little accident and they were going to keep me until morning, just for observation, but that's not going to be necessary after all.

"Could you have Kevin drive you to the ranch and pick me up something to wear home?"

"Of course. But what happened to your clothes?"

"That's a long story."

"Are you certain you're all right, darling?"

"Positive. And Maggie, there's one more thing I need you to do, if you wouldn't mind."

Mariah knew that Trace would hit the roof if he suspected what she was about to do. Fortunately, Maggie had not a single qualm about such subterfuge.

"If I wouldn't mind?" Maggie asked after Mariah had explained her admittedly impulsive plan. "Sweetheart, I wouldn't miss this performance for the world."

Step one accomplished, Mariah thought with satisfaction as she hung up the phone.

Her next step: getting out of this hospital so she could prove that Alan Fletcher murdered his wife.

Chapter Twenty-Two

Five hours after helping her daughter escape, Maggie McKenna was pacing the floor of her suite. It occurred to her that this just might be the greatest performance of her career.

"Dammit, Maggie," Alan complained. "You have to stop crying long enough to tell me what you called me up here for."

"You don't understand," she wailed. On cue, tears streamed down her face.

"Dammit, Maggie," he said again. Clearly frustrated, Alan thrust impatient fingers through his hair. "Take a deep breath." He nodded as she drew in a ragged gulp of air. "That's a girl. Now another. Fine. Okay, now, why don't you start at the beginning?"

"I j-j-just got a call from the sheriff," she managed. "You won't believe what he's going to do!"

Impatient, he grasped her shoulders. "Calm down." He shook her. Hard. Maggie decided it was a good thing Kevin wasn't here. It was going to be hard enough explaining to the wonderfully protective young man how she'd gotten the bruises Alan's rigid fingers would undoubtedly leave behind.

"He's threatening to d-d-dig her up," Maggie said, her voice going higher and higher, like a soprano practicing her scales.

Alan blanched. "That's unthinkable. And totally unnecessary, since he's already got the murderer behind bars."

"He said he was going to get a court order to exhume her body," Maggie insisted. She splayed her hand across her silk-clad breast and took another deep breath designed to look like a valiant attempt to keep from spinning out of control. "I guess he doesn't believe Clint's guilty."

"Of course Garvey's guilty," Alan snapped. He released her and began to pace. "You need a lawyer to block the order."

His voice was trembling. With anger? Maggie wondered. Or fear?

"I don't know any local attorneys." The tears resumed anew. Hotter. Wetter.

"Call Matthew."

"He's out of town."

"Where?"

"How the hell do I know?" Her answer was half sob, half wail. "In case you haven't noticed, my former husband and I didn't exactly part on the best of terms. He doesn't keep me up to date as to his comings and goings."

"Shit." He raked his hand through his hair again. "All right, don't worry. I'll take care of things. Just try to stop crying, okay?"

He was good. But Maggie wasn't buying his act for a minute. To borrow one of her former husband's more vile expressions, Alan Fletcher was as slick as deer guts on a doorknob.

"But—"

"Callahan's just a small-town hick cop. We'll stop him."

A hick cop? Maggie had to force down the urge to kick the son of a bitch in the knee. She liked Trace. A lot. She liked the idea of Trace and her younger daughter even better. "Why would he want to do this?"

"He's undoubtedly trying to bring the press back on the case. These guys are all the same. They can't resist showing up on the nightly news. It's like a narcotic, they get hooked and they keep needing a fix more and more often."

It took a herculean effort to resist the urge to point out that his description sounded an awful lot like politics.

"The idea of exhuming my little girl's body is absolutely ghoulish." Maggie shuddered.

"Don't worry. I'll get the order blocked." He frowned. "What do you know about that evidence Mariah is claiming to have?"

"Evidence?" Maggie's still-damp emerald eyes were wide and innocent.

"She says she found something out at the house."

"I don't know anything about any evidence."

"We need to find out. It may be all we need to convince the court to refuse the order."

"Mariah's at the hospital. She had an accident last night. She could have been killed."

He actually looked surprised by the news, Maggie considered. Which was puzzling, considering that Mariah believed—and Maggie agreed—that he'd arranged for her "accident."

"How is she?"

"The doctor says she'll be fine. But he wanted to keep her for observation. She's not allowed visitors," she added.

"We'll see about that." His expression was grim. And

determined. "Sit tight," he informed her. "While I take care of things."

"Thank you, Alan." Maggie glanced over at the tall case clock in the corner and realized she needed to stall. She twisted her fingers together. "There's something else."

Alan Fletcher looked as if he were about to implode. "Now what?"

"No matter what Matthew says about me, I'm not so stubborn that I can't admit when I've been wrong. I realize I've been hard on you, Alan." Her eyes turned soft and earnest at the same time. "And I've totally overlooked the possibility that my daughter's murder turned your life upside down."

She held out her hand. "I do hope you'll accept my apologies. And my gratitude for helping me with this horrible problem."

He gave her a long hard look. Neither her expression, nor her hand, wavered. Finally, after what seemed an eternity, he made his decision. "You're welcome.

"Christ," he muttered as he left the suite, headed down the hall. "All the Swann women are just one goddamn problem after another."

While Maggie was keeping Alan occupied in her suite, Mariah was on her way to Alan's room when a white-jacketed room service waiter carrying a tray containing a sterling silver coffeepot, two gilt-edged cups and a damask-covered wicker basket passed her. An aroma of fresh-baked muffins wafted from the basket. He smiled at her, his warm brown eyes revealing his appreciation for the white eyelet bustier and matching petticoat skirt Maggie had retrieved from her closet.

Damn. She'd been hoping not to be noticed.

Offering a vague smile in return, she kept walking past

Alan's door, all too aware of the waiter as he stopped across the hall.

As soon as he'd disappeared into the room, Mariah pulled the coded card from the pocket of her skirt and slipped it into the lock. The light blinked green. She heard the click as the door opened.

Once inside, she went over to the desk and began going through his attaché case.

"There has to be a smoking gun." Literally and figuratively. Actually, if you wanted to get technical, there were *two* guns missing. "So where the hell is it?"

An hour later, Mariah arrived back at the ranch in the Bronco she'd rented in Payson after leaving the hospital. She was frustrated and depressed. Although she'd searched through all of Alan's things, she could find not a single piece of evidence to link her brother-in-law to either her sister's murder or last night's attack on her.

Stunned, but on some level realizing she should have expected this, Mariah stood in the doorway, staring in at the destruction. Someone had trashed the house. And hadn't bothered to conceal the effort. Books had been pulled off shelves, drawers had been turned upside down onto the floor, art had been pulled off the wall.

Through her shock, she was vaguely aware of the sound of a truck approaching the ranch. Afraid it might be last night's assailant, returning to do the job right this time, she spun around. When she viewed the Suburban with the Mogollon County Seal on the side, Mariah almost wished she could take her chances with the would-be assassin.

Trace was out of the truck like a flash and strode furiously toward the house. "What the hell do you think you're doing?" he bellowed.

"About what?"

"Don't play innocent with me, sweetheart. Not after what you tried to pull this morning."

Distracted, it took him a minute to focus on the destruction just inside the door. "Aw, hell." He pulled his service revolver from its holster. "Wait here," he instructed in a voice as grim as his expression. "While I make sure the guy's gone."

More than willing to leave the really dangerous stuff to the experts, Mariah didn't argue.

Moments later he was back. "Whoever it was didn't stick around," he revealed.

"That's a relief."

Mariah entered the living room. This was obviously Alan's work, she thought with a small measure of satisfaction. She and Maggie obviously had the man on the run.

"Are you going to dust the place again?"

"Wouldn't do much good. Since whoever it was wore gloves."

"How can you tell that?"

He picked up a mirror that had been hanging over the sofa by the corner. Amazingly, the beveled glass hadn't broken, although the paper backing had been torn away. "See that smudge?"

She looked closer. "No fingerprint lines."

"Very good. Obviously you're not as dumb as your recent behavior would indicate. I was beginning to wonder."

Deciding that discretion was the better part of valor, and since lambent fury still gleamed in his wolflike eyes, Mariah didn't rise to the unflattering description.

"Would you like some coffee?" she asked. "I can put a pot on—"

"I didn't come here for any goddamn coffee."

"I see. I take it you did come here to yell at me."

"I'm not yelling!" he exploded. His rugged face was

drawn with tumultuous, terrifying emotions. Emotions that surfaced as white-hot anger.

All the way up to the ranch, he'd been trying to decide whether to murder her himself, or drag her kicking and screaming back to Whiskey River, handcuff her to his bed and never let her go. Both tactics, he'd finally decided reluctantly, could be viewed as overkill.

"Sounds like yelling to me."

"And if I *were* yelling, which I'm not, I'd say I have a pretty damn good reason." Trace was overreacting and he knew it. But he couldn't forget how desperate he'd felt when he'd shown up at the hospital to find her missing.

Towering over her, Trace looked hard and dangerous. With his black Stetson and treacherous sidearm back in the leather holster on his hip, he reminded her of a gunslinger, yet Mariah refused to flinch under his blistering gaze. Having seen the gentle side of this man, she trusted him not to physically hurt her.

"Would you care to tell me exactly what I've done to make you this angry?"

"What you've done?" He looked at her with a mixture of fury and disbelief. "What you've done?" he repeated. "Let me count the ways."

Watching the muscle jerk in his jaw, Mariah had a feeling he was not about to quote a verse from the *Sonnets from the Portuguese.*

"First, you left the hospital when the doctor expressly told you he wanted you to remain for observation."

She drew herself up straight. "There wasn't any need. I was fine."

He let out an impatient breath. "Now you're a doctor?"

"No, but—"

"Don't tell me. You've played one on TV."

"You don't have to be so sarcastic."

"You left the hospital," he repeated firmly. "Without even bothering to check out."

"I was afraid Gert would feel duty-bound to notify the doctor."

"How the hell did you get past J.D.?"

"Is that really important?"

"It is to me. And since he was called on the carpet for abandoning his post, it's also damn important to J.D."

That was the only thing that had bothered her about the plan from the beginning. When Maggie had informed her that the deputy had been posted outside her door, Mariah had realized that she had no choice but to finesse the situation. She'd do it again, in a minute. But that didn't mean she didn't feel guilty for having endangered J.D.'s career advancement.

"Maggie helped," she mumbled.

"Maggie? What does Maggie have to do with anything?"

"She brought me some clothes," Mariah explained. "Then, later, after I was dressed, she pretended to get dizzy, so J.D. would go get her some water."

"And that's when you made your escape."

"I wouldn't exactly call it an escape."

"What would you call it?"

He still couldn't deal with the idea that she could have been in danger again. And that he would have been helpless to protect her. He took hold of her arms, his fingers digging into her flesh, but he managed, somehow, not to shake her.

"Do you have any idea how it felt to come back to the hospital, only to discover you missing?" His hands moved roughly down her arms, squeezing hers until they ached. "Do you have even the slightest glimmer of an idea of what I was thinking?"

That, unfortunately, had never crossed her mind.

"When you put it that way, I suppose I have to admit that perhaps I did behave a little impulsively."

Perhaps? That had to be the understatement of the millennium. "That's just for starters. How about your criminal behavior?"

"If you're referring to me skipping out on my hospital bill—"

"I'm referring to you breaking into Alan Fletcher's hotel suite."

How could he possibly know that, Mariah wondered. Deciding it wasn't important *how* he'd discovered her subterfuge, she did the only thing she could think to do. She tried to bluff her way through.

"Gracious, news travels fast."

Trace controlled the wave of fury. "Next time you decide to search a guy's underwear drawer, perhaps you ought to take note of how he folds his socks."

Damn Alan Fletcher anyway! Who would have suspected anyone could be so anal retentive as to notice a stupid thing like that. As it was, it had taken her twice as long as she'd expected to go through his things because he was so ridiculously neat.

Anger at her former brother-in-law created a flare of heat that had her tossing her head. "He called you."

"As soon as he got back upstairs from Maggie's—who, it seems, has had nearly as busy a day as her meddling daughter—and discovered that someone had been rifling through his things.

"Dammit, Mariah, what kind of crime writer are you? Haven't you ever heard of the 'fruit of the poisonous tree' doctrine?"

"Of course I have. It prevents the use of evidence originating from illegal conduct—"

"Like an illegal search," he interjected.

"From illegal conduct," she repeated, ignoring his

pointed interruption, "on the part of an official on the grounds that the evidence is tainted, and therefore can't be trusted."

"Very good. So you want to tell me what you were going to do if you *did* find anything that pointed to Fletcher?"

"I was going to tell you, of course," she answered promptly.

He swore in response.

"Really, I was," she insisted. "Besides, if you want to get really technical, the poisonous tree theory doesn't apply because I'm not an official."

His grim expression told Mariah that Trace was less than impressed with her distinction. "Spare me the legal loopholes from TV Writing 101," he growled. "Fletcher wants to file charges."

"Is that why you're here, Sheriff?" Frost tinged her eyes, where only an instant earlier a flame had burned. "To arrest me?"

"Don't tempt me." Was she deliberately challenging him? Trace was not used to feeling this frustrated. He was a cop. A sheriff, dammit. Ordinary citizens ignored his orders at their peril.

"I came here to let you explain what the hell you thought you were doing, interfering in a homicide investigation."

Her temper flared. "I was only trying to find proof that Alan was guilty. Which someone sure as hell needs to do, since..." Realizing what she was about to say, she clamped her jaw shut. Hard.

"Since I won't?" he asked in that dangerously silky tone Mariah had learned to respect.

She pulled loose, turned away and walked over to the window to stare unseeingly out at the summer day. What she'd been about to imply had been as wrong as it was hateful.

"That wasn't what I was about to say."

"Wasn't it?" The words she'd left unstated twisted painfully inside him. Trace wasn't about to let her get off that easily. "Do you remember, that first day, how I told you that solving your sister's murder was my department?"

He was standing right behind her, having crossed the room in that spooky, quiet way he had. His voice was soft, but an aura of barely restrained anger still surrounded him.

"I seem to recall something about that."

He took hold of her shoulders, not gently, and turned her toward him. "Do you also recall me warning you that if you interfered in any way in my investigation, if you second-guessed my motives, or dared question my integrity, that I would toss you in jail for obstructing justice so fast your head will swim?" His fingers crept into her hair. Tangling, but not painfully. His silky, dangerous tone made her throat dry.

"It rings a bell," Mariah responded on a falsely flippant tone. "Along with threatening to personally throw the cell door key into Whiskey River."

"That idea is sounding better and better." He tugged on her hair, tilting her head back so she had no choice but to meet his blistering glare. "Let's just suppose Fletcher is guilty—"

"He is," she insisted defiantly.

His fingers tightened in her hair. "Shut up." With his free hand he captured her defiant chin. "So, in the event that the senator is a killer," he rasped through gritted teeth, "what would you have done if he'd returned and found you pawing through his underwear?"

"That wouldn't have happened. Maggie was going to call me if he left too soon."

"What if she didn't? Your mother," he said pointedly, "doesn't have a history of reliability."

"I could have handled the situation." At his disbelieving snort, Mariah insisted, "I could have. For your information, Callahan, I've taken self-defense training. He couldn't have hurt me."

He ran his hand slowly, deliberately, over her bare shoulders, over the crest of her breasts, then down the front of the white eyelet bustier. "I don't feel a bulletproof vest." The intimate caress, meant to insult, aroused. "What if he'd pulled a gun?"

As his palm brushed over the taut point of her breast, Mariah felt an involuntary need rise. "I could have handled things," she insisted in a voice she wanted to be strong, but wasn't.

"Show me." His wicked hand moved between them to press against her quivering stomach. "Show me how you would have prevented him from attacking you." Between her thighs. "Show me all the ways that instructor in your Beverly Hills lady-in-distress class taught you to keep a man from taking what he wants from you."

When he pressed his palm against her, creating an enervating heat to pool in her loins, Mariah struggled to remember the various tactics she'd learned.

She could do this, she assured herself. After all, she'd paid 350 dollars and spent an hour every Wednesday evening for six straight weeks learning to hone her self-defense skills.

Since she was wearing sandals, grinding her high heel into his foot was out. So was jabbing her car keys into his eyes. Her pepper spray was in her purse, out of reach.

There was one thing that had worked pretty well when

she'd tried it on her partner—a petite star of a popular prime-time situation comedy.

Her instructor had warned her that such a response to a threat of danger could be risky. But he'd also told the class that desperate situations sometimes called for desperate means.

Taking a deep breath, Mariah shifted her weight, let out an enormous yell, and moved to throw him.

Seconds later, when she landed flat on her back on the Navaho rug, with a very large and glowering Trace on top of her, Mariah considered asking for her money back.

Chapter Twenty-Three

"So much for your self-defense skills."

At any other time, his mocking tone would have ignited Mariah's temper, but right now, as she lay beneath Trace, a different, far more dangerous flame had been kindled.

Their bodies were pressed together, so close that the heat from Trace flowed into her. His face was inches from hers, his breath hot against her lips, his eyes molten pewter in which flames burned.

"Not everyone has your professional training." She'd wanted to sound defiant, but heaven help her, instead every word shimmered with her escalating need.

Lord, she was driving him crazy! An utterly irresistible blend of passion and insolence blazed in her eyes. Her breasts heaved, warm and unbearably pliant against the wall of his chest. Beneath him, her body seemed to be melting into his.

"True enough." Trace slipped his hand between them and tugged on the white ribbon lacing the front of the bustier together.

"But the senator is still a man." As was he. And never

had Trace been more aware of a woman. "Which, like it or not, makes the guy a helluva lot stronger than you." As he continued to unlace the eyelet bustier, his knuckles grazed her awakened flesh. "If he'd wanted to touch you like this—" he flicked a careless thumb against her nipple, drawing a quick, intake of breath "—what would you have done? Or if he'd put his mouth on you like this—"

When he took her breast in his mouth, Mariah heard her own ragged moan. "I wouldn't ever let him do that."

"Dammit, you still don't get it, do you?" He lifted his head; his eyes seared into hers. "You wouldn't have had a choice." He pressed himself against her again, chest-to-chest, thigh-to-thigh, causing her pulse to thud in secret, intimate places. "Just like you don't have any choice now."

"I do." Desperate to hang on to some vestige of control, no matter how slight, she lay limp beneath Trace, vowing not to give him the satisfaction of knowing how she was finding the feel of his strong male body pressing against her secretly thrilling.

Trace was frustrated. By the case he'd yet to solve, and by the feelings that this woman had unearthed in him from the beginning. He was angry. Angry at the situation, angry at her for continually putting herself at risk, angry for reasons he no longer knew but was fed up with trying to control.

Their faces were locked, their eyes close.

"Prove it," he said roughly.

There was no hesitation. No fears. No doubts. Mariah dragged her hands through his hair, straining closer as she pulled his mouth to hers.

Thunder rumbled deafeningly in his head. Lightning sizzled down his spine. Diving into the hot kiss, Trace demanded passion and with a moan, Mariah willingly answered. She was clinging to him, giving back even as she demanded more. Her body sprang to frantic life wherever he touched her, she murmured his name as she buried her lips in the hollow of his throat and sent the blood racing to his loins.

As thrilling as their previous lovemaking had been, Mariah never imagined that she could feel like this. Never had she been so aware of her body—every nerve ending.

In a frenzy, she jerked his shirt from his belt. Her eager hands raced across his damp back, reveling in the powerful roping of male muscle. She was moving beneath him, inviting him to take anything—everything—he wanted. All that he needed.

His breathing was ragged as he tore the bustier away, giving his hungry mouth full access to her aching breasts. Mariah heard the sound of rendered material and welcomed it. Need burst through her like a torrid spirit; her fingers fumbled as she struggled with his shirt, finally following his example, ripping it open.

At the first touch of burning flesh against flesh, Mariah cried out. Wrapping her arms around him, she held him tight, their skin fused, her avid, open mouth on his, devouring as she was being devoured.

His .38 was digging into her hip. Cursing, he managed to unclip the holster and shove it out of the way.

Sweat sheened on her skin. And his. Bruises went unfelt as his strong greedy hands streaked over her, kneading, possessing, tormenting. The air grew steamy hot and heavy. Mariah struggled to drag it into her lungs, only to lose it again on a low, shuddering moan as his ravenous mouth followed the path his fingers blazed, at her throat, over her shoulders, her breasts.

Trace couldn't get enough of her. Every taste intoxicated, her scent inflamed. He could feel the sharp sting of her nails in his back and drew a throaty moan when his teeth, in passionate retaliation, scraped against her stomach.

The rest of her clothes were stripped from her, as if torn away by a screaming sirocco. The pulsating pressure spiraling outward from her most intimate core became unbearable. Little caring that she was begging, Mariah pleaded with him to stop. To never stop.

As she writhed helplessly beneath Trace, with only his mouth and his clever, wicked, wonderful hands, he brought her to a mind-blinding, shattering release. She was still gasping as she began struggling to unfasten his jeans, desperate to touch him, as he'd touched her, but he caught both her wrists in one hand and held them above her head.

"Not yet." He gazed down at her, all flushed and warm and naked and vowed that he would be the only man who ever saw her like this. "Not nearly."

He lowered his head again and drove her back into the darkness, the heat.

After the second climax had shuddered through her, Mariah went limp. She wouldn't have thought it possible to experience such passion and survive.

"That was..." She couldn't think. Couldn't move. Yet unbelievably, even as sensation after sensation shuddered through her, Mariah was aching for more.

"Only the beginning." His own body dangerously close to exploding, Trace half dragged, half carried her to the couch. "I'm going to take you up again, Mariah. Until you understand that I'm the only one who can take you there."

He kissed her with a masculine possessiveness that both thrilled and terrified.

"You're the only one," she breathed against his mouth as her fingers fumbled at the snap at his waist. "The only one I'll ever want."

He left her only long enough to pull off his boots and

socks. Then together they struggled with his jeans, dragging them and his cotton briefs over his hips and down his legs. His tongue plunged into the moist dark recesses of her welcoming mouth, his hands grasped her hips and lifted them off the cushions.

His heart pounding so hard he thought it was going to explode from his chest, Trace plunged into her.

Mariah clutched at his shoulders; her legs wrapped around his waist. They began to move together, harder, faster, higher. He was beyond the capacity for thought. A bloodred haze shimmered in front of Trace's eyes. Heat spiraled outward from the base of his spine.

Mariah's breathless cry, as he poured into her, reverberated through Trace like an echo.

When his breathing had finally returned to normal and his body had cooled, Trace felt something twist inside him when he viewed the dark bruises marring her skin.

"I hurt you."

"Don't be silly." Her lips curved in an unconscious smile at the thought. "You could never hurt me."

At the sight of one particularly dark mark on her hip, Trace cursed.

Finding his grim tone a distinct contrast to her own satiated feelings, Mariah finally opened her eyes. When she saw him studying the bruise with obvious self-disgust, she sighed.

"You didn't hurt me, Trace." Framing his face between her palms she gave him a warm, reassuring smile. "As for any bruises, if you want to know the truth, I found that part rather exciting." She pressed her smiling lips against his harshly set ones in an attempt to coax an answering smile in return. "Thrilling."

Her efforts failed. Miserably. "That's not the point." His voice was rough and raw as he pulled her hands from his face and ran a roughened fingertip over the bluish marks braceleting her wrists.

There was something else going on here, Mariah realized. Something she couldn't quite get a handle on.

Almost, but not quite pushing her away, he stood up. When he viewed the ruined piece of white eyelet, he felt as if someone had shoved a knife into his gut. "I ripped your top."

"So? I ripped your shirt. And I'm not about to apologize."

She just didn't get it. "I hurt you. I left bruises."

"When you get a chance, take a look at your back. You won't be able to go without a shirt for a week."

"That's different, dammit!" His jaw was set, his eyes so dark they appeared almost black. "The purpose of the exercise, at least when it started, was to demonstrate that there's no way you could have held your own against a man who intended to harm you. I've seen what happens to women who get involved with men who hurt them."

"In your work."

Something painful moved across his shadowed eyes. It was here and gone so quickly that if Mariah hadn't been watching Trace so carefully she would have missed it.

"Yeah." His tone was flat. Remote. "In my work."

Once again she sensed there was more to this than what she was seeing on the surface. Reminding herself that Trace was an intensely private man, Mariah decided not to push. For now.

But she couldn't allow his brutal self-accusations to go unchallenged. "Whatever you've seen, Trace, no matter how terrible, has nothing to do with you and me. Because you're not that type of man."

He arched a dark, challenging brow. "You think not?"

The old, controlled cop was back. In spades. Loving him as she did, as deeply as she did, Mariah accepted this admittedly difficult part of him as easily as she accepted his gray eyes and magnificent body.

"I know you, Trace."

"Do you?"

"I know you're a good man. A kind man. And," she insisted, when she felt the argument coming, "a gentle man. As for what happened here, I wanted you as much as you wanted me. It was consensual, Callahan. And it was good. Better than good."

Her own gaze softened and she held out a hand that only trembled slightly. "Now will you please stop beating yourself up and come over here? It's been much too long since I've been kissed."

Until this moment, Trace had believed himself to be in full possession of his heart. Looking down into her exquisite face, reading the uncensored emotion in her remarkably soft eyes, he realized that somehow, when he hadn't been paying attention, he'd given it away to this woman.

He returned to the couch, sat down beside her and lowered his forehead to hers. "I really am sorry."

"Would you stop saying that?" She linked her fingers together behind his neck. "And just kiss me?" She tilted her head back and smiled at him. A seductive, feminine smile that slammed into his gut. "Or do I have to beg?"

"Never." Deciding that his feelings were too strong, too complex to consider now, while he was already wanting to make love to her again, Trace bent his head and brushed his lips lightly against hers. When her lips parted invitingly, the kiss that had begun as a snowflake soft touching of lips lingered.

"Do you think there's room for two in that antique copper tub upstairs?" he asked against her mouth.

He felt her smile. "Absolutely."

* * *

Afterward, Mariah sat at the kitchen table, clad in the gauze skirt he'd come to love and a stretchy spandex top the color of lilacs. Professing that she couldn't send him back to town bare-chested, she was sewing buttons back onto his shirt while Trace cooked them both a western omelet.

A buttery late-morning sun was streaming into the homey kitchen. The song of meadowlarks singing outside the open window added a counterpoint to the country radio station playing softly in the background.

"This is nice," Mariah murmured her thoughts out loud.

They shared a quest—finding Laura's murderer—and they'd shared passion. They'd fought like cats and dogs and made love like tigers. Even during those brief moments of shared understanding—like the day of her sister's funeral when he'd proven so surprisingly kind—Mariah couldn't remember a time when they'd relaxed their guards long enough to be comfortable with one another.

"Very nice. Thanks." Trace took the mended shirt she held out to him. "I didn't realize modern career women still did things like this."

"What's the matter, Callahan," she quipped, "don't I remind you of your mother?"

"Hardly."

The growled response, when they were getting along so well, took her by surprise. *Patience,* Mariah reminded herself.

"Oh, I'm just full of surprises." Her smile reminded him of the Cheshire cat.

"No argument there." Trace divided the omelet onto two plates, took a stack of whole-wheat toast from the warming oven, refilled their coffee mugs and sat down across the pine trestle table from her.

This was dangerous, Trace reminded himself. It would

be too easy to get used to this, sharing breakfast with Mariah in the morning before he drove to the office and she settled down to writing her screenplays.

Then, at night, he'd drive back up the Rim and find her waiting and she'd greet him with a smile and they'd make love because, after all, they would have been waiting an entire day, then they'd have dinner, and after dinner, she'd read him her pages, then they'd go upstairs and make love again, and…

Belatedly, Trace realized she'd asked him a question. "I'm sorry, what did you say?"

"I asked you what you were thinking about." She'd watched, intrigued, at the softening of his usually rigid features, the warmth that had flooded into his eyes. "Not the case," she guessed.

"No." Upstairs, while creating tidal waves that nearly flooded the bathroom, Trace had vowed to put the murder investigation temporarily out of his mind. "Actually, I was wondering if you could cook."

From the lambent flame she'd viewed burning in his faraway gaze, Mariah had the feeling that he hadn't exactly been thinking about her culinary skills, but decided, yet again, not to push.

"As a matter of fact, I'm a dynamite cook."

"Really?"

She took a sip of coffee and eyed him with repressed humor over the rim of the mug. "Really. Although I'm no Julia Child, I've taken lessons in Southern Italian, French, Chinese and Indian."

"I'm impressed."

"You're suppose to be. Did you think I sent out to Spago every night for boiled water?"

He managed a self-conscious grin. "I suppose I was guilty of stereotyping you. Just a little."

"More than a little." Her own grin was quick and more

than a little seductive. ''Lucky for you, I'm not the type of woman who holds a grudge.''

''Lucky.'' His gaze unconsciously shifted from her smiling face to her bruised wrist.

Viewing his frown, Mariah stifled the spark of frustration. ''What is it?''

''I don't know what you're talking about.'' The force with which Trace stabbed his omelet told Mariah differently.

''You know,'' she murmured, ''it's really not fair. You know everything about me. About my relationship with Laura. With my father. With Maggie. You even know about my marriage. But I don't know anything about you other than what I read in your jacket. And what little you've told me about your wife.''

''Not everything is in my file.''

''My point exactly.''

''There are some things I've done that I'm not proud of.''

''Join the club.''

Thinking of what he'd heard of her own tempestuous youth, and knowing that she was assuming his was no worse, Trace laughed at that, but the sound held no humor.

''The reason you didn't find any record of my more colorful exploits was because the court records were sealed.''

''Court records?''

Her surprise, Trace decided, was not feigned. ''It's the old story,'' he said with a brusque casualness he was a very long way from feeling. Sure, she was hot for the law-and-order sheriff, the guy in the white hat. How would she feel about him after she learned that he'd been convicted for armed robbery and assault?

What was even worse was how much Trace cared about her reaction.

"Hell," he said gratingly, "you've probably written it a dozen times yourself—the standard inner-city career choice—whether to grow up to be a criminal or a cop."

"You chose to be a cop."

"That was later." He took a drink of coffee and wished it was something stronger.

No longer hungry, he pushed his plate away, braced his elbows on the table and decided she was right. There was little he hadn't unearthed about Mariah. It was only fair that she know exactly who it was she was sleeping with.

"This could be a long story," he warned.

She leaned back, crossed her legs and said, "I'm not going anywhere."

It was amazing, Mariah thought, as Trace began unraveling his life story. Although they'd been born into totally different environments, they had so very much in common.

Both had been virtually abandoned by their mothers at an early age, although unfortunately for Trace, his kept coming back to reclaim him, whether because of some fleeting maternal need or simply a financial one—in the form of her bimonthly Aid to Dependent Children check—Trace never knew.

And as bad as things had been in so many of his foster homes, they'd been far worse with Reba Callahan. Trace told his tale in a low, flat unemotional monotone, but blessed—or in this case cursed—with a vivid imagination, Mariah could envision all too clearly the drinking, the beatings, the men.

When he described finding his mother horribly beat up on more than one occasion her heart went out to the angry, terrified young boy, who could not protect his mother. From her poor choice in men. Or from herself.

Unable to continue this conversation with the table between them, she stood up and went around the table to sit in his lap.

"It isn't the same at all." She placed her hand against his cheek and felt a muscle clench. "What you and I have."

"I know that. In here." He touched his temple. "But it's still not that easy."

"We'll work on it," she promised. "Together."

The words went straight to his heart. What had he ever done in his life Trace wondered, to deserve this woman? "Together."

"What about your father?" she asked quietly. "Wasn't he ever around?"

"I never knew my father. Hell, I don't think my mother even knew who he was."

Although *her* father had been a mixed blessing at best, at least he'd provided for her physical comforts, Mariah considered. And fortunately, she'd had Laura's stabilizing influence to keep her from getting too far out of hand. While Trace had had no one.

"Cops have a saying when a perp tries to resist arrest. We can do this easy. Or we can do it hard."

Mariah nodded. "I've heard it."

"I was always hard." She listened with an aching heart as he went on to describe his rocky adolescence, when he'd gotten into trouble with almost monotonous regularity. "The juvenile justice system was a joke," he told her with a shake of his head. "Little more than a revolving door. Then one night, I finally got into the kind of mess that landed me in an intense repeat offenders' program."

As surprising as his story had been thus far, Mariah was stunned by the idea of Trace being arrested for armed robbery. And assault.

"I didn't actually pistol whip that 7-Eleven clerk," Trace assured her quickly. "To tell the truth, I didn't even know the robbery was going down. But I was in the car, waiting for Al and Joey to filch those six-packs. We were going to the dump,'' he revealed, ''to shoot rats.''

''Nice combination,'' Mariah couldn't help murmuring. ''Kids and alcohol and guns.''

''Pure TNT.'' Trace's tone was as grim as his expression.

It was then that Mariah understood why he'd been so concerned about the teenagers who'd been driving him crazy with what she'd considered little more than kids' pranks. Trace, more than anyone, could understand what a slippery slope it was from setting off illegal firecrackers to armed robbery.

''The program was like something from every chain gang movie you'd ever seen,'' he revealed. ''*The Defiant Ones, Cool Hand Luke,* you name it.''

Mariah shuddered at the idea. ''That's horrible.''

''Not so horrible.'' Surprised at how painless this was turning out to be, Trace kissed one bare shoulder, then the other. ''I was throwing away my life. I needed a wake-up call.''

His lips were feather soft. Even as she considered his tough self-analysis, Mariah felt herself melting into his lap. ''I've never thought prisons are the answer.''

''Spoken like a true bleeding-heart liberal.''

''That's right.'' He was teasing, but only partly. ''A cop and a liberal,'' she mused, linking her fingers around his neck, ''who would have thunk it?''

''Who indeed?'' He ran a finger along the top of the spandex bodice and kissed her. A brief flare that ended too soon for either of them. ''But in my case, the liberal social workers had all thrown up their hands. It was the detective who made the bust, then stuck around, who helped me see the error of my ways.''

''That's why you became a cop,'' she decided.

"John Gallagher was part of the reason. Along with the discovery that breaking rocks into gravel wasn't exactly an ideal life plan," he agreed. "Six months into the program, I decided that if I was going to spend my life in the criminal justice system, it'd be a helluva lot easier on the other side of the bars."

"I'm so glad you were clever enough to make that choice." She skimmed her lips up his cheek.

"It doesn't bother you?" His fingers curved around her chin, holding her gaze to his. "Where I came from? Who I was?"

"It angers me that you had such a rough childhood. It makes me sad to think of you not knowing love. But whatever you experienced, the good and the bad, is what made you who you are, Trace."

Realizing that she was on the verge of telling him that he was, first and foremost, the man she loved, Mariah took a mental step back. "A good man," she said instead.

"I seem to recall you calling me a hard man."

"Why, now that you mention it, I seem to remember that as well," she agreed. Turning so she straddled his thighs, she pressed against him, soft female breasts to hard male chest. "But you know what they say."

Her skirt was bunched up around the top of her slender golden thighs. Heat pooled. "What's that?"

She laughed. A low throaty laugh that shot straight to the groin. If Eve had laughed like that, Adam never would have gotten around to eating that apple, Trace thought. "That a hard man is good to find."

She touched her smiling mouth to his. Tilted her golden head back and opened to him.

"You're in love."

Mariah did her best not to squirm beneath her mother's judicious gaze. "I hadn't realized it showed."

"Well, it does." Maggie poured them both a cup of tea from the pot room service had just delivered. "And I have to tell you, darling, I wholeheartedly approve of your choice."

She picked up a pair of tongs and dropped two lumps of sugar into Mariah's cup. Ever conscious of her weight, Maggie settled for a slice of lemon.

"Isn't it strange, how fate works," Maggie mused aloud. "You and I were so eager to leave Arizona, yet here we both are, like Dorothy, discovering that the happiness that has eluded us for so long is right here, in our very own backyards."

"I take it you're referring to Kevin?"

Although Mariah truly hated admitting she was wrong, she'd reluctantly come to the conclusion that the Phoenix actor who had originally been hired to drive Maggie's limousine, was proving to be far more important to her mother.

She had also been more than a little embarrassed to learn that she'd misunderstood the situation the day she'd discovered her mother half undressed.

Kevin *had* been putting her to bed. But alone. After which he'd emptied the gin bottles down the bathroom sink. The next morning, Maggie had informed Mariah with a certain wonder, not only had he not taken off running when he saw how haggard and ancient she looked but he'd vowed to stay around as long as it took to help her through this crisis.

For the first time that Mariah could remember, Maggie actually appeared at ease with herself and with her life.

An attractive pink that had nothing to do with the expertly applied blush stained Maggie's cheeks. "I know he's impossibly young and doesn't have a lot of money, hell, he doesn't have any, but he's good for me, Mariah."

Her expression was as earnest as Mariah had ever seen it. "He says he loves me."

A week ago, Mariah wouldn't have believed it for a minute. Then again, a week ago, she never would have believed she could have come back to her hometown and fallen in love with Whiskey River's new sheriff, either.

"Congratulations." She realized she meant it. "How do you feel about him?"

Maggie sighed. "I'm afraid I love him, too."

"Then what's the problem?"

"It doesn't bother you?"

"Your life is your own, Maggie. What I think shouldn't matter. But," Mariah tacked on with a smile, "I am happy for you."

Tears welled up in Maggie's eyes. "I have to go to Phoenix this weekend. To meet his parents. Lord, can you believe it? His father's president of a small liberal arts college. And his mother is a philosophy professor. And a docent at an Indian art museum." She took a drink of tea, seeking calm. "Can you imagine me sitting around a Sunday dinner table with those people?"

If Maggie's expression hadn't been so nervous, Mariah would have laughed at the idea of her mother having to pass muster with her young man's parents. "They'll be thrilled to meet you. Why, I'll bet they're telling all their friends and neighbors right now. When you and Kevin drive up in front of their house, the sidewalk will undoubtedly be jammed with people wanting to get a glimpse of the famous Maggie McKenna."

"Do you really think so?"

It always surprised Mariah how her mother, for having been a worldwide household name, could have such little self-confidence. It also explained how her father had managed to pull off his Machiavellian stunt concerning Maggie's fatal accident. Anyone else would have insisted on seeing the police report firsthand. But Maggie, shattered and insecure, had believed the worst of herself.

"I know so." Mariah gave her an encouraging smile. "You're a movie star, remember?"

"I *was* a movie star. Past tense."

"Tell that to the Gray Line tours that still bring people by your house. Or all the tourists who brave Hollywood just to stand in your footprints outside Grauman's."

Maggie looked only partially reassured. "I could go to Phoenix with you," Mariah suggested. "If you'd like."

"Would you do that? For me?"

"I'd be doing it for my mom," Mariah said simply.

Tears welled up in Maggie's still remarkable eyes. "Thank you." As mother and daughter embraced, Mariah felt as if Laura were watching. And giving her approval.

Mariah was leaving the lodge when a couple entering the lobby caught her attention. Ducking behind a potted palm, Mariah watched Fredericka Palmer and Alan Fletcher approach the elevator.

Fredericka's usually smooth hair was ruffled, as if the wind had been blowing through it, which was impossible, since the summer air today was almost stultifyingly still. Her poppy red lipstick was smeared at the corners. As they entered the elevator, Mariah guessed they weren't going upstairs to discuss real estate prices.

Perhaps, she thought, Freddi had picked the senator to be her new husband. Perhaps Alan thought the Realtor's close ties to the wealthy California financial community could give an important boost to his presidential campaign. Perhaps Heather Martin hadn't been the only other woman in Alan Fletcher's life.

Mariah remembered the comment that Fredericka had made about only being a small-town Realtor. For a woman for whom image meant so much, how lofty would the role of a senator's wife seem?

Mariah knew that Freddi was a member of the Whiskey River Gun Club. She had access to guns and the skills to use them. She could have easily shot Laura and Alan. Then, to get rid of the rest of her competition, she could have killed Heather, making it look like an accident.

A single woman, especially one who lived in a city as dangerous as Washington, D.C., would never allow a strange man into her hotel room. But a woman, that might be different. Especially one who possessed a large checkbook at the same time Heather was trying to orchestrate a campaign fund-raising drive.

Mariah quickly went over to the antique phone booth in the corner and called Trace's office, becoming frustrated when she learned that he wasn't in.

"Do you know where he is?" Mariah asked.

"Not exactly," Jill responded. "He had to go to the jail, then the courthouse, then—"

"Can't you page him?" Mariah broke in.

"His walkie-talkie broke this morning. They're sending some repairman down from Flagstaff, but he's not here yet."

Mariah struggled to keep from biting the young dispatcher's head off. "Could you try to track him down?"

"Oh." A thoughtful pause. "I suppose I could do that."

"Thank you. And when you find him, please ask him to call Maggie McKenna's suite."

"Maggie McKenna," Jill repeated slowly, giving Mariah the impression she was writing it down. "She's at the lodge, right?"

"Right. Look, it's important that he get the message."

"I'll do my best," Jill promised. Which, from what she'd seen of the young woman, didn't give Mariah a lot of hope.

Moving to the beige house phone, Mariah rang Maggie's room, told her about Alan and Freddi, and asked her to pass the message on to Trace.

Then, deciding that the couple were bound to be occupied for some time, Mariah left the lodge, determined to uncover proof of Freddi's involvement in Laura's death.

She stopped by the Kendall's Drug Emporium, where she bought a pair of disposable surgical gloves and impatiently endured snapshots of Lillian Kendall's newest granddaughter. Number eight, the obviously proud grandma had proclaimed.

After escaping the pharmacy, as she drove around the lake to the Realtor's north shore house, Mariah reminded herself that whatever she discovered would never hold up in a court of law.

"All you have to do is find the evidence," she said out loud. "Surely Trace and Jessica will be able to think up probable cause to get a proper search warrant."

Mariah knew that what she was about to do was not only unconscionable, but illegal. At this point, she didn't care.

Fortunately, Whiskey River was still the type of community where people didn't lock their houses, and although Freddi was urbanized enough to secure her front, back and kitchen doors, Mariah found an open French door in the bedroom.

The bed was a revelation. Covered with a black satin spread, it took up most of the room. Mariah pressed a gloved hand down on the oversize water mattress and created a tidal wave that was reflected in the overhead mirror.

There was a control panel built into the bedside table. Mariah pushed a button and blackout drapes closed on the windows and across the French doors. Another button caused the lights to dim. She pressed a third, which caused a satin-padded wall across the room to open, revealing a home theater. A cursory check revealed an extensive library of pornographic videotapes, along with home recordings, undoubtedly, Mariah considered, starring Fredericka herself.

Obviously, Flat-backed Freddi hadn't changed since her cheerleading days when she'd been rumored to have screwed the entire offensive line of the Whiskey River football team beneath the bleachers after a winning playoff game.

Mariah opened a drawer on the bedside table and found a pair of handcuffs, various sex toys and a book of Chinese erotic drawings. Since sex had always been a routine part of Freddi's life, Mariah decided that the contents, while as intriguing as the rest of the room, did not point to murder.

She decided to focus on the other thing that interested the Realtor: money.

She went down the hall into the library, where, on top of the desk was a surveyor's plat map for a new recreational development called Whispering Pines.

''So she's planing another subdivision. Well, well. Would you look at this.''

Mariah was not as surprised as she might once have been to see that the land in question used to belong to her sister. And now belonged to her.

Greed, Mariah reminded herself, was a time-honored motive.

The plat, she considered, was a start. But it would not be enough to prove guilt. Nor would it get Clint out of jail.

Remembering what Trace told her about needing to concentrate on *how* a crime was committed, Mariah dug deeper.

''What you have to do,'' she muttered, staring around the room, ''is find the damn guns.''

She stood in the center of the room and slowly turned around.

Unlike the bedroom, the library was a tribute to traditional values. The furniture was thick, handcrafted and covered with a rich, bloodred leather. Oak-paneled walls had been darkly stained. British hunting prints hung on three of the four walls. The fourth wall was home to floor-to-ceiling bookcases lined with leatherbound classics. The books brought back a script she'd written a few years ago for a made-for-television "Columbo" movie about a wealthy mystery writer who'd murdered his agent. The detective had known the writer did it, but he couldn't find the gun.

Until the writer's penchant for first editions had caught Columbo's attention.

"It's too easy," Mariah murmured as she crossed the room to the bookcase. "It's the first place anyone would look."

Reminding herself that not everyone watched television, she began pulling books off the mahogany shelves.

She went through an entire set of Dickens, Dostoyevsky and Balzac. Moving down one shelf, which brought her into this century, she checked out Hemingway, Faulkner, and Tennessee Williams, dismissing Fitzgerald because the stories, while among her personal favorites, were too short, the spines of the novels too narrow for her purpose.

One by one she examined every book, becoming discouraged when she was down to the bottom shelf. "When are you going to learn," she muttered, as she reached for Gore Vidal's *Lincoln,* "life really isn't like television."

The instant she lifted the book from the shelf, Mariah knew she'd found it. She opened it slowly, not realizing she had been holding her breath until it came shuddering out.

The novel had been hollowed out. A rectangular hole

had been cut in the book's pages. Inside the hollowed-out space were two guns: a .25 caliber pistol and a .38.

As she stared at the larger revolver, Mariah knew, without a shadow of a doubt, that she was looking at the weapon that had killed her sister.

''Looks as if we hit the jackpot.'' Mariah closed the book. ''I sure as hell hope you look good in stripes, Freddi.''

''Oh, I don't think that's going to be a problem,'' an all too familiar voice behind Mariah answered.

Clutching the book tightly to her breast, Mariah turned slowly around.

Fredericka Palmer was standing in the library doorway, not looking at all as if she'd just gotten out of her lover's bed. Her makeup had been repaired and her sleek hair had been brushed to a smooth glossy sheen.

Her skillfully outlined ruby lips were pulled in a tight line and her dark eyes were every bit as unwelcoming as the Beretta she was pointing directly at Mariah.

Chapter Twenty-Four

Trace called Maggie from his truck as soon as he got Mariah's message. When the actress told him about Fredericka and Alan, another important piece of the puzzle slipped into place.

"Where's Mariah now?" he asked.

There was a pause. "I don't know."

"Dammit, Maggie!" Trace's feelings for Mariah had him discarding polite police behavior. "This is serious. If your daughter is out playing cops and robbers again, she could get herself killed."

There was another pause. "Surely you're not saying you think Freddi killed Laura?"

Trace thought about what he'd discovered during his search of the courthouse land records. "Where is she, Maggie?"

"She really didn't tell me." He heard the unmasked stress in the actress's voice and knew she was telling the truth. "But now that you mention it, I wouldn't be surprised if she's gone to Fredericka's.... Oh, no!"

"What's the matter?"

''I was just downstairs in the lobby and I saw Fredericka leave. If she arrives home and finds Mariah there—''

''Don't worry.'' Trace tried to sound encouraging, though he was more worried than Maggie. He'd seen Laura's and Heather's bodies. ''She'll be all right.''

He was about to hang up when something else occurred to him. ''Is Kevin there?'' Mariah was not the only one who'd recognized the calming influence the young driver seemed to have on the former star.

''Yes.''

''Let me talk to him.''

After ensuring that Kevin would stay with Maggie, Trace told the pair to sit tight and promised to keep in touch.

Although he'd refused to let himself get discouraged, he'd been relieved to finally have a break in the case.

It had been Cora Mae who'd brought the recreational land deal to his attention. Her nephew had been hired by the Realtor to survey the properties involved. It was then that Trace belatedly recalled Freddi mentioning the golf-course development. A check of the county court records revealed a plat on file.

Trace thought of the mortgages Laura had put on the ranch. Remembered what Clint had told him of the missing cattle. And although he still had no proof, he knew that Fredericka Palmer was involved in this mess up to her slender neck.

When she found herself facing the business end of the automatic pistol, Mariah's hands turned to ice. Adrenaline rushed to her heart, causing it to hammer wildly. To her brain, driving out coherent thought and leaving it absolutely blank.

''Talk about your quickies.'' Mariah's voice sounded high-pitched and thin, even to her own ears. ''I should have guessed Alan would be one of those 'slam bam thank you ma'am' artists."

Fredericka clicked her tongue. "You always had a smart mouth, Mariah. Didn't anyone ever tell you that might get you into trouble?"

Face-to-face with her sister's killer, Mariah decided she'd rather die than let Freddi know how frightened she was by that deadly-looking pistol. Her second thought was that she didn't want to die at all. Not today, at any rate.

The thing to do, she told herself, was to stall. Until she figured a way out of this fix. She was, after all, a professional crime writer. She'd won Emmys for writing dozens of characters out of similar predicaments. Surely she could do the same for herself.

She cleared her throat. Her mind dutifully kicked into high gear, trying to get ahead of this deadly situation.

"Didn't anyone ever tell you that you shouldn't point a gun at people if you don't intend to use it?" That was better. Her voice, while maintaining a faint nervous edge, was steadier.

"Oh, but I do, darling." Fredericka's smile was cool and deadly. She reminded Mariah of a shark. Or a rattlesnake. "Just not yet. Not until I find out exactly how much you and your hick sheriff lover actually know.

"Put the book on the desk, Mariah, dear." She gestured with the Beretta toward an oxblood leather chair with brass studding. "And sit down."

Having scant choice, Mariah did as instructed, watching as the other woman placed a call to the sheriff's office and requested to speak with Ben Loftin.

"He'll be here momentarily," she revealed after hanging up. "Meanwhile, you and I can pass the time with a nice little girl-to-girl chat."

Mariah folded her arms over her chest. "I've nothing to say to you."

Temper flashed in the other woman's dark eyes and was immediately controlled. ''Fine. We'll just wait until Ben gets here. I'm sure he'll be able to find some way to convince you.''

She gave Mariah another one of those deadly false smiles. ''For a man who looks so unattractively Cro-Magnon, Ben can be surprisingly imaginative. When encouraged.''

Comprehension dawned as quickly and clearly as if two wires had suddenly been connected in Mariah's head, completing a circuit. ''Loftin ran me off the road.''

''Of course.''

''Why?''

''Because you were in the way.'' Fredericka's tone was mild.

''In the way?''

''You'd inherited the ranch, which I have to admit, came as quite a surprise, since the plan had been for Alan to inherit, then sell to me. Then you had your chance to save yourself by letting Clint take it off your hands. But you refused.''

''I refuse to believe Clint had anything to do with Laura's death.''

''Of course not, silly. He had no idea I had anything to do with his lover's death. But he *did* owe me a great deal of money. So, when I threatened to call his loan unless he helped me get that last piece of land I needed so badly, he reluctantly agreed to make you an offer.''

''That land has been in my family for generations.'' Mariah's initial fear was subsiding. In its place was a cold, laser-focused anger.

''Do you know, that's exactly what Laura said. Obviously you two were more alike than anyone thought.''

''So you killed her for the land.'' It was not a question.

Freddi didn't respond. ''If only you hadn't been so stubborn, Mariah,'' she said instead. ''If only you'd agreed to sell.''

''I still can't believe you'd actually kill for some stupid recreational development.''

''It's not a stupid development! Why, Whispering Pines is going to be a world-class resort. A group of Kuwaiti investors has already committed to investing millions of lovely Middle Eastern petrol dollars and Southwest Development has drawn up plans. It will be,'' she confided, ''a wonderful boon for the entire community. At a time when Whiskey River desperately needs an economic boost.''

''Gee, you're just full of civic responsibility, aren't you?'' Mariah drawled. ''Perhaps the Rotary Club will nominate you Citizen of the Year.''

Fredericka's eyes narrowed and to Mariah's amazement, she actually appeared surprised by both the accusation and the deprecating tone. ''Surely you can't think it was personal?''

''Of course not,'' Mariah replied acidly. A thought occurred to her. ''Did you have anything to do with my horse bolting?''

''Horse?'' Freddi looked honestly confused. ''What horse?''

Since she'd been open about everything else she'd done, Mariah decided her accident had been simply that. An accident.

''It doesn't matter,'' she said. ''I was terrified half out of my wits, run off a cliff and left to die. Why the hell should I take that personally?''

The other woman sighed and shook her head. ''It really was such a nice plan. Who would have expected your truck to hit that ridiculous boulder?''

''I've always been lucky.''

''So it seems. But unfortunately, darling, your luck is

about to run out.'' She glanced out the window at the black-and-white cruiser that had just pulled into the red-brick driveway. ''Starting now.''

Trace had just reached for his mike to call the office and have Jill send J.D. out to Freddi's house when the radio buzzed.

''Hey, Sheriff,'' the young deputy's voice came over the police band along with the static, ''the DPS crime guys just called with the paint analysis from the door and right rear side of Ms. Swann's Cherokee.''

''What did they say?''

''It came from a county truck.''

''Are they sure?''

''Positive. Seems the commissioners got a deal on that same dark green paint from a wholesaler who was going bankrupt about the same time all the county vehicles needed repainting. The lab guys also told me that no truck manufacturers use that particular color, which pretty much narrows it down to either one of the two snowplows, or a road maintenance vehicle.'' Coincidentally, Ben Loftin's cousin happened to be supervisor for the county vehicle repair shop, Trace remembered.

''Where are you right now?'' he asked J.D.

''At the office.''

''Call me right back on the car phone.'' The line wasn't as secure as Trace would have liked, but it was a lot more private than the police band.

''Yessir, Sheriff.'' There was a noticeable curiosity in the deputy's voice. ''Ten-four.''

A second later the phone rang. ''It's me, Sheriff.''

''Where's Loftin?''

''Haven't seen him. He got a call a few minutes ago, and took off. Said something about checking out another one of those damn juvenile arson fires out by the Whiskey Spring campground."

"Okay." Trace was glad to hear the deputy was occupied on the other side of the county. "You know the Palmer place?"

"The big house out by the lake? Sure."

"Meet me there. Code Two." Urgent, no lights, no siren.

"Yessir! Want me to call Ben?"

"No. I don't want you to call Loftin. And I don't want you to use the radio. If you need to contact me, stick to the phone. Is that clear?"

"Ten-four, Sheriff." J.D.'s excitement was so palpable, Trace could practically feel it crackling through the cellular phone.

Trace couldn't wait to see his deputy's face when he got to fasten his handcuffs around a bona fide killer.

If it wasn't for his concern about Mariah, the thought would have made Trace smile. Instead, hoping against hope that she hadn't decided to take matters into her own hands again, he headed toward Fredericka Palmer's lakefront home.

Mariah's Jeep was in the driveway. Along with Ben Loftin's patrol car. Knowing firsthand the dangers inherent in rushing into a situation, he was forced to cool his heels on the side of the road, waiting for his deputy's arrival.

Less than five minutes later—five minutes that seemed like a lifetime—J.D. pulled up behind him.

"Where the hell have you been?" Trace greeted him sharply.

"Sorry, sheriff." The deputy flushed the color of the wild strawberries growing along the lake. "But I was passing the park when Jill called in with a ten-eighty at that location."

"It was probably just those damn kids with firecrackers

again,'' Trace ground out. Normally, a report of an explosion would earn the highest priority. But not today. Not when Mariah was in danger.

''That's what it was, all right. The problem was, they were setting them off right by the playground and one of the sparks landed in a baby carriage, setting the blanket on fire. Since I knew you wanted me here right away, I confiscated the evidence and threw the kids in the back of the car for now.''

Trace noticed the two teenagers for the first time. ''Shit.''

''Did I do the wrong thing?''

That was all he needed, civilians at a potential hostage scene. ''We'll discuss it later. For now, I want you to cover me while I check out the situation.''

The deputy unsnapped his holster. ''Yessir!''

Trace crept up to the house, grateful for the stand of pine trees dotting the lakeside lot. He located the trio in what he took to be a den. At the moment, they appeared frozen, like a tableau from a movie poster. Fredericka was armed with a Beretta, while Loftin was pointing his .44 Magnum—the weapon favored by Dirty Harry—at Mariah, who was sitting in a leather club chair. Although her face was as white as new snow, Trace was relieved that she didn't appear terrified. On the other hand, from her rigid spine, jutting jaw and red spots staining those pale cheeks, it was obvious that she was angry.

Unfortunately, caution was not exactly Mariah Swann's style. He could practically feel the heat of her rising anger and worried that she was going to blow the roof off the situation with her flash-fire temper.

That thought led directly to another. Trace glanced up at the sloping cedar shake roof. And the two gray stone chimneys. And he smiled.

* * *

"So, what do you want me to do with the bitch?" Loftin growled.

Fredericka thoughtfully tapped a fingernail against a front tooth. "I really don't think we have a choice," she murmured. "I'm afraid Mariah's going to have to have another accident."

"Surely you're not going to run me off the road again?"

"No." The Realtor shook her head. "I'm afraid that might look a little suspicious."

"Why don't you just shoot her?" the deputy suggested helpfully. "Make it look like she broke in. After what happened to the Fletcher broad and the senator's bimbo, it'd make sense that a woman living alone might be a little jumpy."

"That might have worked at night," Fredericka conceded. "Unfortunately, I doubt many people would believe that I could be so unnerved in the middle of the day. No," she shook her head again, her eyes thoughtful, "we're going to have to come up with something more imaginative than that."

Mariah wondered if Maggie had gotten hold of Trace yet. And if she had, would he think her lead about Alan and Freddi worth following up right away? It would be stupid to die this way, right now, just when she was starting to get her life in order.

But then again, wasn't that exactly what had happened to Laura?

Not wanting to think about that, not now, when her immediate goal was to keep these two miscreants from putting a bullet through her head, Mariah reminded herself that the name of the game, at this point, was to stall.

"When you think of something, badger breath," she

said to Loftin, "let me know. If it's good enough, I might even use it myself someday."

"Shut your fucking mouth." The deputy struck Mariah, the vicious slap sounding like a rifle shot in the stillness of the room.

Her cheek felt as if it were on fire. But Mariah refused to give him the satisfaction of rubbing it. "At least we should probably discuss character motivation."

"Dammit, Ben," Fredericka complained, "if you mark her up, we're going to have a more difficult time setting up a believable scenario."

"Hell, let me just take the bitch out and shoot her."

"What a dandy idea," Fredericka shot back. "Shoot her with a gun everyone in the damn town, including the sheriff, knows is yours. Will you call the state prison and reserve our cells? Or shall I?"

A scarlet flush rose from the khaki collar like a fever. "Hell, I wasn't going to shoot her with the .44. I was thinking more along the lines of a rifle. Make it look as if she were accidently hit by some poacher rushing deer season."

Fredericka appeared to be actually considering that when a series of explosions rocked the room. The sudden noises appeared to be coming from the other side of the house.

"Jesus!" Loftin jumped. "What the hell is that?"

"You're the goddamn cop. Why don't you go see?"

She'd no sooner gotten the words out, when there was another volley of blasts. Then another. It sounded as if the entire National Guard had suddenly begun firing automatic weapons in every room of the house. Every room but this one.

Cursing, Loftin left the library in search of the source of the explosions.

"Sounds a lot like the cavalry," Mariah pointed out

when she and Fredericka were alone. She had no idea what was happening. She only knew that now she was back to facing a single gun. Which, while not an ideal situation, beat the hell out of the earlier scenario.

"Shut up!" It was Fredericka's turn to be unnerved. Her usually modulated voice was as fractured as Mariah's had been earlier. Her eyes were hostile. She was finally scared.

Join the club, sweetheart, Mariah thought.

Yet another explosion, even louder than the others, suddenly rocked the library and shattered the windows. The room began to fill with smoke.

Screaming, Fredericka spun toward the fireplace. Knowing she'd never have a better opportunity, Mariah yelled exactly as she'd been taught in self-defense class and flung herself onto the other woman's back. The pistol dropped from the Realtor's hand and went skidding across the oak floor.

They were rolling over the floor. Locked together in a death grip, legs wrapped around each other, hands reaching desperately for the gun. Time took on an eerie, slow-motion feel, like a violent scene from a Sam Peckinpah movie.

"Dammit, Freddi," Mariah yelled when Fredericka's long nails raked painfully down the side of her face, feeling like needles against her skin. "I'm getting sick and tired of you!"

Forgoing the battle for the gun for a minute, she drew her right fist back and hit Fredericka smack in the middle of the face. There was a satisfying crunch beneath Mariah's curled fingers.

"You bitch!" The Realtor's voice rise to the stratosphere. She released Mariah in order to cover her face in her hands. Blood was spurting from between her fingers. "You broke my nose!"

"Pity," Mariah gasped. She lunged for the Beretta and came up holding it in her hands. "After you paid that plastic surgeon so much." She was on her knees, her breasts heaving, the gun pointed in Fredericka's direction.

"Maybe the prison doctor can set it."

Mariah turned her head in the direction of the wonderfully familiar deep voice. He'd come! Just like in the movies. And beside him, hands cuffed behind his back, was Ben Loftin.

"It's about time you got here, Callahan."

"Better late than never," he drawled with a lazy ease that did not reveal the cold terror he'd experienced when he'd first seen those guns pointed at Mariah. He held out his hand. "How about giving me that?" he suggested quietly.

Mariah looked down at the pistol as if she'd forgotten she was still holding it in her trembling hand. "Good idea." She was shaking so badly, she doubted she could hit the bookcase.

"I found the gun that killed Laura," she revealed.

Trace glanced at the open, hollowed-out novel on the desk. "Clever," he acknowledged, addressing Fredericka for the first time. "But Mariah already wrote that in *Murder by the Book*."

"You actually know about that?" Mariah looked at him with surprise. It was one of her best works, but he'd never said a damn thing.

"I told you I'd seen some of your shows." He glanced at the scowling Realtor, who was sitting on the floor, her hand pressed tight against her nose, which continued to bleed. "My guess is that I'm not your only fan."

Trace Callahan a fan? Would wonders never cease. For one of the few times in her life, Mariah was struck absolutely speechless.

Enjoying her surprise, Trace turned to his deputy. "I

guess this means you're off the force, Loftin.'' The moment he'd been waiting for for six long months was proving every bit as sweet as anticipated.

''Hey,'' the red-faced deputy complained, ''I'm not taking any murder rap. Not when I didn't pull the trigger.''

''Shut up, Ben,'' Fredericka warned. She glared at Trace. ''I have nothing to say to you until I speak to my attorney.''

''That's your right,'' he agreed with a careless shrug. He turned back to Loftin. ''How about you, Ben? You want an attorney? Or do you just want to clear the air?''

''I wanna make it clear that I didn't kill the Fletcher broad. It was all Freddi's idea.''

The woman's look was as sharp and deadly as a stiletto. ''Dammit, Ben—''

''Freddi and Fletcher had this deal, see,'' Loftin continued, ignoring Fredericka's repeated warning. ''They were going to make big bucks subdividing the Fletcher ranch.''

''The Prescott ranch,'' Mariah felt obliged to point out. ''It was my grandmother Prescott's. Then Laura's. And now mine. It has never belonged to any Fletcher.''

Loftin stared at Mariah for a long moment, obviously unable to understand her gritty complaint. ''Whatever,'' he grunted finally. ''Anyway, Fletcher, he had this side deal going. He bought up all the vacant land along what was going to be an access road to the development from the highway and once the project was announced, he was going to turn it over at triple the purchase price.''

It made sense, Mariah thought. For years, Alan Fletcher had been financially dependent on his wife. Now he'd found a way to make his own fortune.

''Goddamn it, Ben.'' Freddi looked as if she were about to have a stroke. ''I'm warning you—''

''Shut up, Freddi,'' he shot back. ''I'm fed up with

taking orders from you. And I'm damned if I'm going to hang for a murder you did.

"The only kink in the plan was that Laura Fletcher turned out to be goddamn stubborn," he continued, obviously eager to spread the blame around. "She kept refusing to sell the damn land. No matter how bad things got."

"You stole the cattle," Mariah guessed, earning a sharp glance from Trace who was obviously not thrilled with her interrupting Loftin's confession. The guy was on a roll; Trace was waiting for him to crap out.

"Figured if we ran her into the red, she'd be willing to sell out. But when she took out that damn mortgage, it looked as if it were going to take longer. Problem was, the ragheads were getting impatient."

"The Kuwaitis," Mariah explained to Trace, and to J.D., who'd joined them in the den after having followed Trace's instructions to throw the confiscated cherry bombs down the chimneys and air vents. The young deputy was practically swaggering as he put a pair of handcuffs on Fredericka Palmer. As she heard the metal click around the woman's wrists, Mariah experienced a rush of satisfaction.

"That's when Freddi decided to take matters into her own hands. She killed the Fletcher broad. Then, to make it look as if the murder had been committed during a burglary, she also shot the senator."

"Using a smaller caliber revolver and placing her shot where it wouldn't do much damage," Mariah said, slanting Trace an I-told-you-so look. "I knew Alan was guilty."

"Not in the beginning," Loftin said, surprising Mariah. "'Course, after he recognized Freddi, the night she murdered his wife and shot him, he had no choice but to keep his mouth shut. 'Cause of the land deal."

"So he was an accessory after the fact." Mariah wondered why Alan hadn't just come forward in the beginning and decided that he hadn't been willing to risk his presidential campaign.

"You called it," Loftin said. "Problem was, the senator's girlfriend wasn't some airhead bimbo. The gal figured things out from some papers she found mixed up with the senator's Fourth of July speech. When she was in danger of becoming a loose cannon, I was brought into the deal."

As Loftin went on to explain how Freddi had promised him wealth and political assistance in winning his long-coveted job of sheriff for killing Heather Martin, Mariah was amazed at the lengths the woman who was already wealthy had been willing to go just to get her hands on even more money.

"You also ran Ms. Swann off the road," Trace said after Loftin had explained, with some pride, Trace thought, how he'd gotten in with a passkey and drowned the aide while she was taking a bath. Once again, the senator had not been apprised of the plan beforehand.

"She inherited the ranch," Loftin said simply, as if that alone were reason enough for taking a human life. "And she was turning out to be as damnedly stubborn as her sister."

"It's a Swann family trait," Mariah muttered. "You know. Kinda like greed is a Palmer trait."

She looked at Freddi. "Did you trash my house?"

"I did." Ben volunteered again. "On Freddi's orders, after you told Fletcher you'd found evidence in the house."

Avoiding Trace's sharp look, Mariah thought about her sister. And her sister's baby. Both dead because Fredericka, Alan and some Kuwaitis wanted to build a fucking golf course in the pines.

"Would you just take these two slugs to jail where they belong," she said to Trace. She could feel her temper snapping. "Before I decide to take that gun back and sentence them both to some good old-fashioned frontier justice."

Trace knew the feeling all too well. He remembered the day he'd had to testify in court about the shooting. He'd remembered looking the scumbag who'd killed Danny, furious that the guy didn't reveal an iota of remorse for having struck down a vital, warmhearted young man in his prime. A man who'd left behind two daughters and a wife pregnant with the son Daniel Patrick Murphy never knew.

Although he'd always believed in the system, even knowing firsthand that it was intrinsically flawed, at that moment, Trace had been sorely tempted to put a slug right through the smirking bastard's cold black heart.

"They're on their way," he said. He turned to his deputy. "J.D., take Ms. Swann home. I'll book these two, then go over to the lodge and pick up the senator."

"I want to go with you," Mariah insisted.

She'd been through a helluva lot today. Trace admired the way she was holding up. He also knew that she'd be wrung out once she came down from the adrenaline rush nearly dying can instill.

"Sorry. But you're going to have to sit this one out."

Trace didn't really expect any trouble from Fletcher, but then again, he and Danny hadn't really expected to get blown away while investigating what had appeared, on the surface, to be just another drive-by homicide.

Mariah was seething with impatience. "Dammit, Callahan—"

"Shut up," he said without heat. In no mood to argue, he took her arm and led her away from the others.

"My rules, remember?"

"This isn't fair!" She was the one who'd been saying all along that Alan was involved. She was the one who'd found the murder weapon. It was only right that she be along for the final scene.

"Life isn't always fair," Trace reminded her. He raked his hands through his dark hair. The need to protect her had stopped being professional a very long time ago. "Look, Mariah, I've never been as frightened as I was when I saw those two holding you at gunpoint. I don't want to go through that again."

"You said it yourself," Mariah argued, her eyes touched with frustration and a lingering anger. "Alan doesn't have the guts to shoot anyone."

"That's my belief. But I'm not willing to put it to the test." He wanted to put his arms around her and crush her to him, to ensure himself that she was, truly, alive and safe. Instead he had to content himself with running the back of his hand down her cheek.

"I know how much you want to be in on Fletcher's arrest, but there is no way that I'll risk your life that way again."

It was then that Mariah realized that Trace was blaming himself. The same way he had when he thought he'd hurt her. The same way he'd overreacted when he'd returned to the hospital, found her missing and mistakenly thought she'd been abducted.

His voice was a lush, low ribbon of sound, wrapping around her, warming her to the core. And even as it soothed, Mariah heard the core of steely strength and knew she was licked.

"Will you come by after you pick Alan up?"

"Absolutely."

It wasn't the answer she wanted. But, Mariah reminded herself, the important thing was that Alan Fletcher would be behind bars, where he belonged.

"You win." Her shoulders slumped, but her chin came up, just as he'd expected. "But you're not going to stop me from being at Alan Fletcher's arraignment."

"Not only will I not try to stop you, I'll reserve front row seats for you and Maggie."

That was, Mariah told herself, something. It wouldn't bring Laura back. But it would bring some closure to those she'd left behind.

"You're on."

Chapter Twenty-Five

After locking Fredericka and Loftin up, Trace stopped by Jessica's office. Together they went to the lodge. The open suitcases on the bed revealed that the senator had been about to leave town.

"You probably won't believe this," Alan Fletcher said, when confronted by Trace, "but I'm actually relieved it's all over. Oh, I realize it will undoubtedly mean the end of my political career, but ever since Heather's death, the guilt has become oppressive."

"But not your wife's?" Trace couldn't help but ask.

"Of course I feel terrible about that," Alan said mildly. "But you have to understand, Sheriff, there was never any real love between Laura and me. It had always been merely a marriage of convenience."

"And when your wife subsequently became inconvenient, you did away with her."

Jessica shot Trace a warning look but remained silent.

"I didn't have anything to do with that," he insisted. "Nor was I involved in Heather's death. You have to understand—" he turned to Jessica as if seeking a woman's viewpoint "—I loved Heather!" His voice broke on a sob.

"If that was the case, why didn't you come forward after Heather's death?" Jessica asked.

"Coming forward would not have brought Heather back," Alan argued. "But it would have ruined my career."

"That's all that matters to you? Your career?"

"I have a plan for this country," Alan insisted. "A plan that will enable America to regain its worldwide superiority. Which is a great deal more important than what happens here in Whiskey River."

"Why don't you try telling it to the judge?" Trace said, thoroughly disgusted with the man's egocentric view of the world.

After reading Alan his rights, Trace booked him into jail with the others, then drove out to the Fletcher—no, he corrected—the Swann ranch.

Maggie let Trace in. This time, after she'd thanked him profusely for solving her daughter's murder, when she kissed him on the cheek in gratitude, there was no aroma of gin clinging to her breath.

"Mariah's upstairs in the bedroom." She tilted her auburn head in the direction of the stairs. "Now that I know she's in good hands, I'll leave you two alone."

He found Mariah curled up on the bed, a picture of sorrow. And exhaustion. When she heard him enter the room, she turned her head.

"Hi." He stood there, hands shoved in his pockets, feeling like a tongue-tied schoolboy.

"Hi, yourself." Her voice was soft. And lacking its usual strength.

He crossed the room and sat down beside her. The mattress sighed, then settled. "How are you doing?"

She grimaced. "About as good as I look."

With their faces close, he studied her, letting his eyes roam her exquisite features. She was too pale. There were shadows like dark bruises beneath her eyes, which had also lost their spark. An angry scratch, left by Freddi's fingernails, had left welts down one side of her face.

"You're beautiful."

"Liar."

"It's the truth." He ran the rough tip of his fingers across the purple mark marring her cheek. The bruise was a perfect imprint of a man's hand. "I should have killed Loftin for this." His voice held that frighteningly calm quiet tone Mariah had heard before.

"There's already been too much killing," she said, telling Trace nothing he didn't know. "Besides, it'll fade."

But the memories wouldn't. Trace knew you never forgot a near-miss meeting with the Grim Reaper.

"Maggie said to tell you that she and Kevin were going back to the lodge, but if you need them—"

"Will you be able to stay?" Her eyes were wet.

His fingers continue around her jaw, down her throat. "For as long as you need me." He put his arms around her, the way he'd wanted to earlier, back at Fredericka's lakeside house.

"Did you arrest Alan?"

Trace related the conversation with the senator.

"So it's over," she murmured.

"All but the shouting."

He thought about the other things he'd learned from Clint. About how Freddi had pressured him to talk Mariah into selling the land by calling the loan he'd taken to cover his margin losses with her former broker husband. About how Matthew Swann had come back from Santa Fe early to confront Clint which had resulted in a brief fistfight, which explained the older man's blood on his shirt.

Clint also had revealed how Patti had tearfully confessed to him that not only had she slashed his and Freddi's tires, while stalking Mariah—to make sure she wasn't moving in on him—she'd accidently caused the mare to bolt when sunlight glancing off the lenses of her binoculars had hit the horse in the eye, which had come as a surprise, since Mariah hadn't mentioned the fall.

Trace decided these details, since they didn't directly have anything to do with her sister's death, could wait.

"From the looks of things, it's my guess that the three of them will try to work out a plea bargain, rather than take their chances with a jury."

"I think I hate that idea." Once again Mariah wished she believed in the death penalty.

"We did our job. Now it's up to the courts."

"I hate it when you turn noble on me, Callahan," Mariah muttered.

He brushed her tousled hair back from her bruised cheek. "It'd be nice if these were the days of the OK Corral," he agreed. "When the sheriff could run the bad guys out of town on a rail. Or better yet, just blow them away on Main Street at high noon. But it's not that easy these days." He tried a smile. "I'm told it's progress."

"Sometimes progress isn't all it's cracked up to be."

He smiled at that because it was a thought he often had himself. "Tell me about it."

He drew her close and they sat that way for a while, each lost in thought. Now that it was finally over, the pain Mariah had successfully held at bay during the investigation came flooding over her in torrents.

And because she'd held the tears in too long, Mariah buried her face against his strong, hard chest and began to cry.

Her sobs were raw and harsh, coming from deep down inside her. She clung to him. Hot tears drenched his shirt. And still she wept. And wept. And wept.

Trace knew that there was nothing he could do. Nothing he could say. But hold her. And love her.

"I'm sorry." She sniffed, between bouts of weeping. Her shadowed eyes, as she looked up at him were red, as was her nose. Streaks of moisture stained her cheeks. Her face was twisted with lingering pain. She was the most beautiful woman Trace had ever known.

"Don't be." He pressed his lips against her temple. "You don't have to be strong, Mariah. Not this time." He ran his hand down her hair, across her back, his touch meant to soothe rather than arouse. "Let it all out, baby."

His tender tone was her undoing. Her eyes filled and spilled over again before she could prevent it. Hugging Trace close, she resumed her weeping.

As the shadows grew long outside the bedroom windows, Trace held her, and rocked her and murmured low, inarticulate words of comfort. Until finally, there were no tears left.

"I'm sorry," she said again. "I never cry. Well, hardly ever." Embarrassed, she swiped at the moisture on her cheeks with the backs of her hands, reminding Trace of a child.

"Your sister died." He reached over, plucked a handful of tissues from the box beside the bed and began drying her cheeks. "I'd say you're entitled to a few tears."

She took in his soaked shirt. "That was more like a flood."

"Whatever it takes," he said mildly. He tossed the sodden tissues into a nearby wicker wastebasket.

"What does it take, I wonder?" she murmured, as much to herself as to him. "To get used to losing someone you love."

"Today's a start. I'm not going to lie to you, sweetheart, some days are a helluva lot worse than others. But you get through them."

"I suppose there's no other choice."

"There are always choices," he reminded her of what

he'd told her before. Trace recalled all too vividly an incident a few days after he'd gotten home from the hospital, when he'd been sitting alone with an empty bottle of Jim Beam and his revolver, which he'd pressed against the roof of his mouth.

He'd managed, just barely, to keep from eating his gun that night. And the others that followed. Until finally, suicide no longer seemed a very attractive option. "Some choices just seem better, in the long run, than others."

As she looked into his solemn gaze, Mariah knew Trace, more than anyone, understood what she was feeling. "Could I please have one of those tissues?" she asked on a sniffle.

He handed her two. She blew her nose and tossed them toward the basket, where they bounced off the rim, then fell in.

"Two points."

"I played on the NAU girls' team my freshman year and sophomore years," she revealed.

"What happened your junior year?"

"I discovered drama." She frowned as she remembered that ill-fated night of her play when her father had unexpectedly shown up at the theater. The night that the growing rift between she and Laura had cracked wide open.

He saw the shadow move across her eyes and suspected he knew the cause. "I love you," he said gruffly.

Smooth move, Callahan, Trace blasted himself. After agonizing for days on how to tell her, after picturing a scenario involving roses and champagne and that copper tub filled to the rim with bubble bath, he'd blurted it out like an overanxious schoolboy.

The smile she bestowed upon him was nothing short of beatific. "I know. I love you, too."

How could the very thing that had been keeping him awake at night turn out to be so easy? "Just like that?"

Mariah nodded. She'd always thought love would be terrifying. But instead, it felt absolutely, wonderfully perfect. "Just like that."

"In that case..." His mouth closed over hers and he lowered her back against the pillows.

Wrapping her arms around his neck, Mariah surrendered to the moment. To Trace.

A long time later, Mariah stirred. She'd fallen asleep and it took her a minute to remember where she was. And why.

Then it all came flooding back. Laura, Heather, Freddi, Loftin, Alan. And Trace.

She looked up and found him looking down at her. Their eyes met in an embrace every bit as loving as the one they'd shared earlier.

Smiling, she snuggled back against him, pressing her lips against his chest. "I forgot to ask. Is Clint going to be released now?"

"Jess was filling out the paperwork when I left the office. He's undoubtedly a free man by now."

"I suppose that's something."

"It's a pretty big something. He wanted to come by and thank you, but I suggested he save it for morning."

"You just wanted me to yourself."

"Guilty." He pressed a kiss against her hair. Her ear. Her jaw.

"There was something else I didn't tell you," Mariah offered.

"What's that?" Trace asked absently, engrossed in arranging her gleaming blond hair over her shoulders. Her breasts.

"My father came by earlier. Before you arrived."

"At the same time Maggie was here? I didn't see any signs of breakage downstairs."

"Actually, they behaved amazingly civilly." Mariah combed her hands through her hair. "My father told me he admired my role in uncovering the murder plot. Maggie filled him in."

"I know. He called the office to verify your mother's story."

Mariah nodded. "He said he'd talked to you. He also said your explanation was quite flattering."

"It was the truth."

"Whatever you said, I really do appreciate it." She tilted her head back to look up at him. "He didn't exactly welcome me back into the diminished Swann family circle with open arms, but it *is* a beginning."

"Absolutely." Because it had been too long since he kissed her, Trace bent his head and covered her mouth with his. "And speaking of beginnings—" his lips plucked at hers "—you are going to marry me, aren't you?"

"That depends." Mariah pretended to be thinking the matter over. "Do I have to give away all my money?"

"Actually, after giving the matter a lot of thought, I've come to the conclusion that I kind of like the idea of having a rich wife."

One hurdle down. Mariah tried another. "Can we live here at the ranch?"

"I've always liked horses. But I draw the line at herding cows."

"You won't have to," Mariah assured him. "How about my work? I still want to write."

"I can't imagine you not," he said with that absolute honesty she'd come to expect from him.

"In that case, I accept."

Trace let out an explosive breath. "I promise to make you happy."

She laughed at that, a rich, bubbling laugh that flowed

through him like hot honey. ''If you make me any happier than I am, right now, Callahan, I'll have to give up scripting crime dramas and start writing smaltzy hearts-and-flowers date movies.''

''Sounds like a pretty good idea to me.'' Deciding that although he'd fallen down on the champagne and red roses, the copper tub still held a host of intriguing possibilities, Trace scooped her up and carried her toward the bathroom.

''Since I've recently discovered that I'm a sucker for stories with happy endings.''